"A work of prodigious symbolism… extraordinary set pieces"
TLS

"Sumptuously lyrical"
We Love This Book

"Each scene has the dexterity and the abundance
of a Vermeer… Mortier distills time… Epic"
Wexford Echo

"Helena is an elderly witness to Europe's turbulent twentieth
century. She describes horrific things she saw in the First
World War's trenches but, a fierce aesthete, is unabashed by
pleasures that she experienced close to the front… The book
is the pearl that results from these shining accretions"
New Yorker

"With tenderness and skill, Mortier crafts assured
novels brimming with quiet optimism"
Shelf Awareness

"Intensely powerful… a meditation on the way that we remember,
how memories are evoked, stored, treasured and released"
Rough Ghosts

"Mortier is superb… a poised consideration of
war's long impact on feeling and faith"
Kirkus Reviews

"Mortier writes so well that you are inclined to see
everything else as of secondary importance"
NRC Handelsblad

"A monumental, phenomenal book"
De Morgen

"An important book… One doesn't 'like' such a
book; one is moved by it, and lives in it"
Dolce Bellezza

"An astonishing book… leads us deep into everyday life
during the First World War, and does this so impressively
that it seems the author has experienced it himself"
Frankfurter Allgemeine Zeitung

"If Marcel Proust had a descendant somewhere in
Flanders, he must have been born in Ghent"
Knack

"Probably the most beautifully written book I have
ever read… absolutely lyrical and delicate, yet, at the
same time, hypnotizing, poignant and powerful"
Inbetween Books

"The author skilfully reconstructs the crepuscular atmosphere
of an era that ends with the shipwreck of a civilisation, but,
paradoxically, also with the sensual awakening of a young girl"
Figaro

"Threads the heavy folds of history with
the needle of poetic sensibility"
Livres hebdo

"Multi-layered' is too bland a word for this subtle,
sophisticated novel, which moves between different times
with such aplomb that the reader never loses the thread"
Buchmarkt

ERWIN MORTIER (1965) made his mark in 1999 with his debut
novel *Marcel*, which was awarded several prizes in Belgium and the
Netherlands, and received acclaim throughout Europe. In the following
years he quickly built up a reputation as of one the leading authors of
his generation. *While the Gods were Sleeping* received the AKO Literature
Prize, one of the most prestigious awards in the Netherlands, and
was shortlisted for the *Independent* Foreign Fiction Prize in the UK.
His latest work, *Stammered Songbook: A Mother's Book of Hours*, a raw yet
tender elegy about illness and loss, was met with unanimous praise.
Mortier's evocative descriptions bring past worlds brilliantly to life.

ERWIN MORTIER

WHILE THE GODS WERE SLEEPING

Translated from the Dutch by
Paul Vincent

PUSHKIN PRESS

LONDON

Pushkin Press
71–75 Shelton Street
London WC2H 9JQ

Original text © Erwin Mortier 2008
Originally published by De Bezige Bij, Amsterdam
English translation © Paul Vincent 2014

While the Gods Were Sleeping first published
in Dutch as *Godenslaap* in 2008

This translation first published by Pushkin Press in 2014

This edition first published in 2015

001

Flemish
Literature
Fund

The translation of this book was funded by the
Flemish Literature Fund (www.flemishliterature.be).

ISBN 978 1 782270 79 9

Set in Monotype Baskerville by Tetragon, London

Printed and bound by CPI Group (UK) Ltd., Croydon CR0 4YY

www.pushkinpress.com

WHILE THE GODS WERE SLEEPING

I

I HAVE ALWAYS SHRUNK from the act of beginning. From the first word, the first touch. The restlessness when the first sentence has to be formed, and after the first the second. The restlessness and the excitement, as if you are pulling away the cloth beneath which a body rests: asleep or dead. There is also the desire, or the fantasy wish, to beat the pen into a ploughshare and plough a freshly written sheet clean again, across the lines, furrow after furrow. Then I would look back at a snow-white field, at the remnants the plough blade has churned up: buckets rusted through, strands of barbed wire, splinters of bone, bed rails, a dud shell, a wedding ring.

I'd give a lot to be able to descend into the subterranean heart of our stories, to be lowered on ropes into their dark shafts and see stratum after stratum glide by in the lamplight. Everything the earth has salvaged: foundations, fence rails, tree roots, soup plates, soldiers' helmets, the skeletons of animals and people in hushed chaos, the maelstrom congealed to a terrestrial crust that has swallowed us up.

I would call it the book of the shards, of the bones and the crumbs, of the lines of trees and the dead in the hole down to the cellar and the drinking bout at the long table. The book of mud, too, of the placenta, the morass and the matrix.

I am grateful to the world for still having window sills, and door frames, skirting boards, lintels and the consolation of tobacco, and black coffee and men's thighs, that's all. One fine day you're too old to carry yourself graveward hour after hour, to mutter the

Dies irae in porches, on street corners or in squares for so many figures who have long since flaked away from you, decayed into a squelchy mess your toes sink into. As you get older you no longer see people around you, only moving ruins. Again and again the dead find back doors or kitchen windows through which to slip inside and haunt younger flesh with their convulsions. People are draughty creatures. We have memories to tame the dead until they hang as still in our neurons as foetuses strangled by the umbilical cord. I fold their fingers and close their eyes, and if they sometimes sit up under their sheets I know it's enzymes or acids strumming their tendons. Their true resurrection is elsewhere.

When I was young such daydreams invariably awakened my mother's irritation, if I was unwise enough to confide them to her. She cherished a sacred awe of limits and barriers. Freeing your imagination from the earth was considered a sign of a frivolous disposition. For her the most unforgivable thing a living person could inflict on the dead was to make them speak; they can't defend themselves against what you put into their mouths. In her eyes the coin that the Ancient Greeks put under the tongue of their dead, as the fare for the ferryman who was to transport them to the far bank of the Styx, had a different purpose: it was hush money. If the dead had started chattering, they would immediately have choked on the coin. They have no right to speak, she said, which is why no one must be their mouthpiece.

I myself have my doubts, still. Everything that lives and breathes is driven by a fundamental inertia, and everything that is dead keeps its vanished opportunities to exist shut up in itself like a hidden shame.

*

She would be over 100 if she were still alive. Not that much older than me, and I do my best not to put anything in her mouth, not even a coin. For that matter I don't often think of death any more. He thinks quite enough of me. Every morning after brushing my teeth I run my tongue over them, proud I still have a full set, and read in Braille the grin of the Death's head in my flesh. That suffices as a memento mori.

There are nights when sleep thrusts me up like a remnant from its depths, until I wake with the cold, pull the covers closer and wonder why an image that can sometimes be decades old imposes itself on me with such clarity that I wake up. It's never anything dramatic. It may be the sight of a room, a landscape, a look from someone I've known or an incident without much significance—such as that Sunday morning, a spring day in the 1940s, when I am standing with my daughter at my living-room window, waiting for lunch. We are looking out at the front garden and the road, which are strewn with white dots. The wind is blowing them out of the tame chestnut trees on the far bank of the river across the water, making them swirl in miniature tornados over the road as if it were snowing. The silence in the streets that morning, the pale light, the Sunday boredom, the smell of soup and roast veal, and my daughter saying: "I thought it would rain any day."

Or I am back on the beach, the broad beach at low tide, near the promenade, in the first chill of autumn, one of those days when you can extract the last warmth from the wind. I took my husband and my brother out, or vice versa, to get some fresh air, rather than to be constantly breathing in that hospital smell. They are standing among the huts, out of the wind, in the sun, scarves round their necks, kepis on their heads, and around them the silver-white sand is sparkling. In a fit of humour they have pinned their medals on their pyjama tops and now they are giving each other a light, because I have brought cigarettes for them. They look pale, and frail, in that merciless light, full-frontal September light. Only their cheeks are flushed, bright red.

The scene would have something closed off about it, be for ever self-contained, except that my husband, my future husband, suddenly looks me straight in the eye, from behind the fingers of my brother, who is shielding the flame of the match with his hand: amused, roguish, sharp—a pleasure in which I immediately recognize the intelligence. Meanwhile my brother is peeping intently at my husband. He is not so much scanning his profile as absorbing it with his look. I suddenly realize that we were married to the same man.

When I turn round I don't see my room, my legs wrapped in blankets, or the board with the pen and paper on my lap, but the beach, the wide beach at low tide: the wind whipping up the water in the tidal pools, the thin white line of the surf, the grey-green water, the underside of the clouds, a friendly emptiness that draws me to it.

"The angel of time carried me off," I say to Rachida, the carer, when she helps me out of bed in the morning. I say it to her to see her laugh. "You know the angel of time, don't you? It could be the angel of vengeance or the angel of victory. But it's also the angel of sleep and Dürer's *Melencolia*."

"Yes, Mrs Helena. Your angels are complicated."

I'm glad she laughs, always laughs. Every morning she comes in just as cheerfully, sits me up in bed and arranges the

12

pillows behind my back. She doesn't cut my bread into fussy little chunks, like the harpy who sometimes replaces her and stays sitting on the edge of the bed while I have breakfast, puffing audibly with impatience, before getting up to run the bath and put out the towels—the telegraphy of her impatience with me and my old age.

I'm also glad that Rachida takes care with my body when she frees me from my nightdress, that with equal quantities of devotion and routine she pulls my bony arms from my sleeves, and subjects my head as gently as possible to its daily birth through the narrow neck of my vest, while the other one, that pillar of salt, always manages to molest me with my own limbs. She hugs me to her like a lay figure and drags me across the floor to the bathroom to put me on the toilet. While I sit there until I've finished dripping she shakes up the sheets, pulls up the blinds and yanks the clothes hangers in the wardrobe as if she's plundering the treasures of Rome. From the scourge of the Norsemen deliver us, O Lord.

"Her name is Christine," says Rachida, and though she looks grave, she laughs.

Most images that visit me when I am half asleep are old, but clear as a mirage. They have never been completely tempered by language, which when we are young has still only flushed very shallow channels through the bed of thought in our minds. They are the purest images, which embody the questions by which I was absorbed in my early years and which now, as if the circle might one day close, preoccupy me again.

I can't really call them memories, as I do nothing, they catch me unawares—unless the nature of remembering changes with the years. Sometimes, as I doze, the echo of my breathing in the room around me seems to awaken past acoustic impulses. Rooms which had been piled wall against wall backstage in the wings of oblivion again enclose me. Roof tiles zip themselves over rafters into a skin of stone scales. Bricks converge into their old order. Beneath my feet floors regain their solidity, each hollow, echoing step makes corridors and passages recognize their vaults and niches. Bewildered, almost baffled, I enter those manoeuvrable crypts, as if lost in a cave full of paintings that come to life by trembling candlelight.

When I was young I wanted to know where time came from, whether it was a substance, like water or ether, which you can collect and keep or filter from deep inside things, just as my mother scooped bunches of currants into a muslin bag in July to squeeze the juice out of the fruit. I also wanted to know why I was myself, and not someone else, in a different place, at a different time or, on the contrary, at this time, and in the same place—someone who lived my life, with my relations and my school friends, but was not me.

"Then you'd be your own brother or sister," said my mother abruptly. For her everything was clear-cut. And yet in her life too time must have become less and less homogeneous as she grew older, with days that stretch out like twigs and double their inner volume; minutes in which scores of stories are concentrated, and the same number of dénouements and open endings. It would take centuries, and several universities, to understand the conversations between my mother and me in my childhood, to expose all the nuances and connotations vibrating in them, the presuppositions underlying the words, what we did not say or took for granted, all those fleeting essences, the unexpressed fear, concern, resentment and even love that travelled like stowaways in the belly of the words that we exchanged during our work.

For a long time I wondered why she is so curt when she visits my dreams, why only her voice is so direct and close. "The scissors, Helena!" she cries from a distance that sounds as long and narrow as an underground passage. While my father, sitting at the breakfast table, the table that I more or less recognize as the one in our summer residence, with the peaceful light of a cloudless morning in the bay window at his back, can be almost tangibly present.

He refills his cup or sits and reads the newspaper by his plate. On the walls the reflection of sunlight on water makes bobbing frescoes flow past.

Without looking up he turns to me. Unlike my mother, he speaks in whole sentences, but talks too fast, or too quietly, or too much under his breath, or has started to use a language that sounds Slavonic, with much passage of air between tongue and palate. I can hear him creating tension curves, pausing, laying down his sentences with such care that I become almost jealous of him for mastering the unsayable so fluently. If he were to be silent or say understandable inanities to me, I might wake up less upset.

I can see him before me fully formed, with all his traits and habits, his idiosyncrasies, his charm, as if the earth were summoning up from its mantles and products the material from which he was constructed and stacking him up in front of me again, at breakfast or knee-high in the surf, one day on holiday at the seaside, long ago. I hear the music of the beach as it was then, the women's voices, screaming children, the calls of the pedlars and the snorting of the horses that pull the bathing carriages down to the waves—and there is the intense cold that splashes onto my shins from that sound landscape, the sharp taste of sea water, and his arm is placed over my belly and scoops me up, into the closeness of his body.

The sea water evaporates from the material of his bathing costume, making it rough with salt and releasing his body odour, at once sharp and sultry. When I press tight against his ribcage, out of the sea breeze, with my head on his shoulder and a hand on his ribs, I can immerse myself completely in his smell, and a miniature, private atmosphere surrounds me. I smell his skin, the sweaty hair in the nape of his neck, his sex, and when I hear him breathing in, his body becomes the sound box in which life resonated like nowhere else—because he is he and I am I.

There are people whose existence embodies a virtually pure note, or rather in whose existence life can be translated into sound with the sonority of a Stradivarius, lives that contain the mystery of what it is to be a human being, and there are others that will never produce much more than the shrill tooting of a tone-deaf child on the cheapest recorder. My father wasn't a Stradivarius, nor was he a recorder. More and more often I think that an as yet unread universe would reveal itself if I could populate the stream of his monologues with my mother's staccato vocabulary, his mumbling stories with the separate pebbles of her language.

In my mother's eyes that would probably have amounted to the ultimate offence. In my teenage years she called me a born poetess because of my questions, and it wasn't a compliment. It was considered normal for children to ask questions, with that slightly incongruous imagery that can easily be seen as poetic. Children still have that ability, I expect, but in my own childhood the grown-ups thought that the answers were set in stone, as firmly as their world. There was not much that needed thinking about. Things were as they were. Children's questions were considered peculiar or at most amusing because the answers seemed so obvious.

I think, though, that I was more like an innocent philosopher or a little theologian—that might also have been possible— rather than a poetess. My mother regularly crowned me as a natural talent in some discipline or other, whenever she found it necessary to make fun of me and set both of my feet on the ground, as good mothers do when their offspring threaten to kick over the traces. She usually saved her deepest sarcasm for poets. She called them pseudo-athletes. In so doing she betrayed herself, without realizing it, as a kindred spirit of Plato, who also disliked poets, but my mother lacked Plato's jealousy. She saw me reading and writing, and thought I should not lose myself in the process. But I did anyway.

Undoubtedly she would raise a sceptical eyebrow if she could now hear me say that the substance of the gods has not yet completely seeped out of a child.

"What grotesque self-glorification, Helena," she would sigh, and I'm not putting words in her mouth. I've heard her repeat it often enough, without looking up from the sewing with which we filled the long winter evenings during the war.

Meanwhile I am older than she was when she died. She now shares with the gods the situation of being outside time—and I still believe that I am right about the godliness of children and the childlike nature of the gods. The existence of each has the character of a dreamlike game since they have no knowledge of death. Their cruelties are light-footed, their tendernesses brutal. Melt the infinity of the dead together with the uninhibitedness of the child and what you get is a gruesome godhead.

At this point—I have seen her do it more than once—she would abruptly lay aside her mending. With both hands she would pull apart the worn-out seam of a garment or accidentally prick herself on one of her pins. Then she would get up and move away from the pool of lamplight in which she always did her work, rinse off her bleeding finger and light the gas under the kettle to make tea. From somewhere near the draining board she would moan that I talk nonsense, but it seems to me most probable that she would not say anything. To some sophistries she found a piqued silence the best retort.

She had no patience with things that transcended the immediately tangible. For her I was a poetess because in her eyes poets floated in the air. "That's true," I said to her later. "But head downward." I believe I meant it, though I may have dreamt it up on the spot so as to deny her the last word. I was gradually entering the school of rebelliousness.

Her sarcasm served a higher purpose. She wanted to thrust me into the everydayness of the word, squeeze my thoughts into sturdy winter clothes. Dreary but hard-wearing, and above all waterproof. For my mother trains of argument and items of clothing were one and the same: they must button up tight, while I liked nothing better than lazing about in the hanging gardens of Babylon in my open nightdress, proud of my blossoming curves, and climbing the ziggurats of books. I surrendered myself to the cadence of silent speech that rose from their spines, the Styx of sentences, in which here and there, like driftwood or drowning people, words and images floated, which I more or less already understood, alongside much else that was not much more than shadowy stains in a dark flood.

I still believe that books, like gods and children, inhabit a limbo in existence, a dimension in which effects can lead to causes and yesterdays crawl forth from tomorrows. It is impossible to make final judgements there: who deserves heaven and who hell. Everything is yet to happen and everything is already over; that is the essence of paradise.

As a child I regarded books as a kind of dead people, and actually I still do. Anyone who writes is organizing his own spirit realm. Books were filled with the same stillness as the stiff limbs of relatives on their deathbeds. True, they had more to say for themselves, but seemed like the dead to be yearning for a living spirit to linger in.

I liked the anonymous, the posthumous quality that every book carries in it. I found their titles and prefatory headings an unforgivable genuflection to vanity, or a kind of extenuation of the energy with which a story can take possession of you. That the writer should put his name on it for the benefit of the reader seemed to me almost as absurd as being assaulted by someone who first politely hands you their visiting card. I should have preferred to scratch the names off the covers and tear the title page from the body of the book. I even wanted to go further and liberate all those books from their static array on the shelves of the home library by giving them a home elsewhere, in other rooms, in the garden, among the beams of the shed, in the cellars, like Easter eggs or Christmas presents, nameless, indescribably vulnerable, their fate in the hands of whoever found them.

I have never been able to free myself from that fantasy, and have come to believe more and more firmly in it. Books should band together like feral dogs on street corners. They should have to sleep in piles in shop doorways under cardboard covers, beggars without much hope of alms. They should get soaked through with rain on park benches, or be scattered on the floor of the tram, in order to beguile or bore whoever picks them up, leave them indifferent or irritate them so much that they want to write a reply, which would then blow through the world just as namelessly. Somewhere that book will disturb an order, calm unrest, freeze happiness, commemorate the future or foretell the past, unidentified, announced at most by the rustling of the sheets—the only angels I more or less believe in.

Perhaps my mother's lack of understanding of my questions issued from a dislike of what she considered unforgivably provisional. She was more Catholic than she felt herself to be. However agnostic she might be, the divine was set in her thinking like a plug in a bathtub. God was the dam that people had thrown up in order to prevent the fatal encounter with their own bottomless longing. Pull out the plug or breach the dam, and everything runs out. It's far too late to ask her for clarification, but I know that she didn't like giving up. "We can't hang about hanging about," was her favourite pronouncement. "We must get to work. If the chicken doesn't lay, in the pot with it!" She liked exclamation marks and pronounced them audibly. They stood at the end of her sentences like gatekeepers with flaming swords: thus far and no farther.

I heed her battle cry, albeit reluctantly. A person will never be more than a rough version of themselves, a crude sketch on a sheet of paper that can be screwed up at any minute. Why should I get worked up about full stops at the end of a line, the place of a comma or exclamation marks—and why demarcate spaces, rooms, dwellings, bullet holes, craters? Sooner or later I pick gold coins out of the cold mouths of the dead, the mineral of time without time, and their voices burst out endlessly as if they are still alive.

"Time is the great soul of all things," I wrote, aged about fourteen—the word adolescent didn't really exist yet. "It fills its lungs without ever exhaling." I don't know if I find the formulation as bombastic as my mother definitely would have done if she had been able to read my most intimate writings, but now, almost a century later, I can hear time's constant inhalation more clearly than before, and I am already half dissolved in the air, screaming through its bronchioles, the light-years-long blast of breath that forces its way through caverns of calcium and bone. Perhaps it will be possible, just before I disappear completely, to gain an overview of existence itself as if I have been peeled away from it.

I imagine that I would be able to see life, not just mine and yours, but life as such, down in the depths beneath my feet: churning, meandering. A hundred thousand Grand Canyons intertwined, an expansive tissue of rapids, pools, salt pans and waterfalls, shimmering in an endless night.

Perhaps I would be able to read the patterns unfolding in the fanning torrent, the motifs that develop in it and dissolve in it again, the completeness that it carries with it and the futility of human time that sinks into it. I would then feel as if, just before I vanish into oblivion, it is granted to me for a moment to see things through God's eyes. I would be able to appropriate some of the fatalism through which a rodent fighting against the strangling grip of a snake embodies just as cosmic a tragedy as the fall of Troy—or conversely: the same banality.

A human being should not really think in these dimensions, I know. Life is not a play or painting, to be viewed from outside, but if I am honest I would never have written a word if I actually believed that, and don't you kid yourself that you read for any other reason.

My mother would have lost all patience by now, reading this. "Pathetic," she would giggle with a shake of the head. She would pour her tea in the kitchen and drink it by herself without realizing what a triumph I am granting her.

It doesn't matter.

She's dead.

As she gets up from her chair, her outlines fade in the lamplight and, with her outlines, the room.

"Life is simple," she once said to me. "I don't need any posh words for it. It's doing the washing-up. A person makes plates dirty, washes them clean, wipes them dry, puts them away, takes them out of the cupboard again, makes them dirty, washes them clean, wipes them dry, puts them away, takes them out of the cupboard again, and one fine day the whole pile falls out of your hands."

She fell silent, looked down and drank a mouthful of tea.

I had no answer, at the time.

She was a born poetess.

I T STRIKES ME that Rachida likes scouring or mopping downstairs while I am working upstairs, and a definite sisterly relationship is created between us as she clenches the brush in her fists. I should like to be able to send the pen in my fingers as easily across the paper as she sends her mop across the tiles—the gentle dragging calms me and smoothes my senses.

Except that she washes dirt away and wipes out traces. While I stain the paper with the staggering gait of a drunkard, my ecstasy of ink, she leaves things in their nakedness. She brings the blissful mongoloid smile of the world to the surface, the grinning, gleaming-wet Zen of dumb objects, the names of which she blows off like chaff. And I think: I shall never be able to reduce everything there is to such unrestrained silence in the word, the great night is better than 10,000 months.

"Did you say something, Mrs Helena? Did you call, do you need anything?"

She doesn't whistle in the hall, like the other one, that standing stone, after she has plumped me down on the toilet like a bag of bones in the hope that it will make my bladder empty faster.

Rachida makes tea and fills the thermos. She checks whether my pens need ink and whether the side tables are close enough to the chair. She will soon leave me there until she returns in the afternoon to heat the food.

"We have angels too," she says as she combs my hair and seems to be looking more at my hair than at me. She brushes my sparse locks up without her eye catching the mug with its mummy's grin that laughs at me every morning in the bathroom mirror with my own yellowed teeth. That carcass that, ridiculously, still houses the lust of a girl and, at the sight of the window-cleaners in their cradle at the windows, still sneaks a look at their crotches like a teenager looks at a lolly.

"The same angels as you. Gabriel," she says. "He's your angel too, isn't he?"

She does my nails, looks in the drawer of the dressing table to see what earrings match my blouse. She doesn't find it too much to ask to hang a few carats of innocent dignity around my scraggy neck every day—unlike "her colleague". That bloated cow would probably most like to smother me between her tits.

"Christine," she laughs. "Her name is Christine."

"She's not an angel," I say. "You are. But without wings."

"The boss won't let me. Too many feathers. I hang them up in my cupboard when I have to work, Mrs Helena."

I'm glad that she's laughing, that she takes me from my bed to my chair as if she is leading me onto the dance floor, that I can place my fingers in hers and put my feet in the spot where she has put hers.

She lowers me carefully into my chair.

She asks whether it is close enough to the window.

She lays my feet on the pouf.

She wraps my feet in an extra blanket.

Am I sitting comfortably?

Don't I need an extra cushion behind my hips?

"I've poured the tea in the thermos, Mrs Helena. Would you like the paper first?"

When I shake my head she lays the board on my lap and says that there is enough ink in the pens.

Although she asks whether I'm feeling cold, as she asks she has already knelt down beside me. She rubs my fingers warm until they tingle. I'm glad she understands, understands so much, that she doesn't overwhelm me with favours for which I first have to beg and that her gestures and grimaces do not spell out to me the thousands of connotations of the word parasite. As you get older you automatically calculate in nanograms and micrometres. You weigh friendship like gold dust on tiny scales and the merest grain of sand embodies the grossest humiliation.

She gets up. Looks down at me with satisfaction.

"They and the Spirit ascend to Him, on a Day whose length is 50,000 years.'

"What was that, Mrs Helena?"

"Nothing, child. Something about your angels…"

She always makes sure there is an extra notebook to hand, so that I have to get up as little as possible from my chair before noon. She never sighs when I ask: "Can you fetch me the red exercise book, and put the green one back on the shelf, if you would?" She will never chuckle sarcastically like the other one, that half gorilla, who in the evening grabs the exercise book out of my numb hands with a vicious grimace, flicks the pages through her fingers and shakes her head with a snigger. Then I brace myself for the umpteenth question, the umpteenth sneer—do I really have so many secrets that I have to write them all down before I kick the bucket, and can't she put the ones on the top shelf into boxes? They're gathering dust and you never reread them anyway.

I say to Rachida alone: "When I'm dead, take them with you and distribute them. Make sure the other one doesn't get her hands on them, she'll only take them to the dump, the rodent. When you distribute them: read them or don't read them, and if you don't read them, pass them on. Don't say who I was, that isn't of the slightest importance. I swear by my pen and what the angels dictate to me."

She always seems pleased, childishly pleased, whenever I manage to fill one of the notebooks and she can put it in the cupboard. When I ask her to fetch a few of the old exercise books for me—"Take some from the top shelf, at the back, with the split bindings," I say—she first goes over them with a dry cloth, places them in two measured piles on my board and opens the top one for me.

Then, standing by my chair for a moment, she can sometimes look down at the board and the old exercise book, the yellowed pages, and my very young handwriting, with her hands on the waist of her apron and the duster in her hand, as if glancing into a cradle or a sarcophagus, with the same compassion and tenderness that we reserve for the dead and newborn infants.

"Do you still remember writing all that down, Mrs Helena?" she asks cheerfully, always cheerful. Sometimes it is as if, through my fragile, almost transparent bones, she is addressing the child with the broad-brimmed straw hat and the long ribbons in her collar, skipping over the gaps in the paving stones holding her father's hand—a game I invented myself to dispel the monotony of our walks.

I shake my head.

I never reread myself. Never ever. Never.

I open those exercise books to establish whether I have vanished sufficiently from the lines, faded with the walnut ink bleached by the years, and whether I have gradually become alien enough to find myself unreadable, reduced to score marks that I survey rather than read, as you study a painter's brush strokes.

I follow the cadence of my handwriting and search for the silly lust, congealed in letters, of the girl I must have once been, the child who on the threshold of her adolescence pulled her writing as tight as the thin leather laces with which she tied her bootees—how she forced the flesh of the words into the whalebone of syntax, until her own flesh was full of wheals and she longed to break out! The lust of the flagellant and the libertine is equally insatiable. Lashes and love bites wound and soothe in equal measure. And no one, I say, Rachida, no one can ever escape from the almighty god of grammar.

She goes without shaking her head in disapproval, the angel. She knows when I am addressing her for her own sake and when I am focusing on her impersonal presence, which for me is another word for our soul. I'm glad that she senses when she must leave me alone, and that she lets me sleep when she brings me soup or fresh tea and finds me dozing off. She leaves the pen in my hand but puts the top on loosely to stop the nib drying out. Or she gives the glasses that have slipped out of my hands a polish and lays them on the board with their arms open.

Perhaps she takes the time to have a longer look at my strokes and my scrawl, the calligraphy of my intoxication or my irritation, set down at the time when my daughter was still a babe in arms and demanded all my waking hours, sucked my life dry, my existence—and the haste and the furious pleasure with which in a nocturnal half-hour I could let the ink splash raw

27

from my pen for a moment like fountains of milk that welled up from my nipples the moment the little mite so much as stirred.

"Massage my feet, Rachida," I ask, "Would you? Knead my soles with your thumbs to get my lazy blood flowing again. You have soft hands, soft and adept. You know that I don't want to ask the other one, she always leaves me crippled, in worse agony than I'm already in."

I'm glad at the natural pride she exudes. When she kneels down by the pouf on which my legs are resting, she gives off no air of servility, no subcutaneous arrogance which is usually the sour face of humility. A sovereign intentness flows from her fingers over my shins, my instep and my toes. Sometimes, with my ankles in her hands, she can look up and run her eyes over my calves and thighs, over my pelvis, my belly and breast. She can look me in the eyes with an almost amorous concentration and seems to peel the years away from me. Her look is the look of a woman. We understand each other. Under the eye of the woman every man becomes a little boy with a pop gun. Their love is so childlike.

Sometimes I see her looking at the exercise book resting in my lap, the fig leaf with writing on. For a second an embarrassed smile crosses her face, perhaps because my scribbles remind her involuntarily of pubic hair, the pubic hair that a child would draw, if we were to ask children something like that, just as we ask them:

draw a sun for me,
a house,
a tree,
a soldier, a horse.

From the moment she lays the board on my lap and opens the notebook, the delight of a child who sees the tin of chalks or watercolours being taken out of the cupboard wells up in me. The euphoria and expectation, the same earnest pleasure with which a child, the tip of its tongue between its half-opened lips, draws lines, recreates things, repeats the millennia-old ritual of the hunter summoning up the spirit of his prey on the wall of a cave. The world seems to be paying court to me: write me out, duplicate me. Trace my air strata, my earth strata, my cloaks and my sick memory, and all the gradations between being and non-being that only a human, the most excessive creature that crawled up from my slime, can bring to life.

If she were to wonder why I have never added a volume to the library room next door, when there were still books in there, I should probably reply: one must wait until one is dead before letting go of one's writings. But that would be a lie, or at least an excuse. People who write are sneaky. You claim a space alongside time. A place where you can sit chuckling to yourself, that is what those who write want to hollow out for themselves, a room at the back. So be consistent, I think then, and wait until you're dead.

I have finally got rid of all my books. I realized my childhood dream and gave away the whole library, boxes at a time. I don't know where all those volumes are now. All I've kept are the exercise books. Shakespeare was allowed to stay too, out of a sense of duty. Like St Augustine, because of his nailed-shut doubt, very amusing. And *Yoga for Your Dog* and a few similar titles: titles that my husband brought back from his travels, or that friends have given me as presents because like him they knew that I'm crazy about absurd literature. I love the inexhaustible energy with which someone documents themselves for decades before leaving as a testament a *Concise History of the Corset*. I don't make fun of them. To each his own monsters.

I have also kept the dictionaries. Not to find there, as in a herbarium, the arid pleasure I could experience in dictionaries as a girl, when their columns stretched out before my eyes as if they were gunpowder magazines. From their racks I stole the ammunition for the bursts of buckshot that I let loose on the world. Now I read dictionaries because they've gradually become the only novels I still like.

Daily I absorb a few pages, my way of reading a breviary. I mumble what I read aloud, the rows of words ordered from A to Z that are not able to gloss over their stupid coincidental nature. Word upon word, an eye for a tooth.

I run my finger over the page down the entries. Each word resounds like a cry for help, clawing up from the page like a drowning man's hand; and see how the words, the other words, the ant words, the soldier words, rush to help that dying word, to support it with their lances, throwing rescue ropes towards it, hauling it ashore and forming behind it like a praetorian guard.

Morning roll-call for definition.

Salute the Flag.

Azalea and Azimuth.

The tumult of meaning bursts out from under my fingers.

For years I haven't been able to listen to what people said. I heard them speaking, but I couldn't listen. Everything sounded equally insignificant, charming and light-footed as the notes of songbirds in March on the first warm days. I couldn't bring myself to speak, to chat, not in the restaurants and the cafés where we gathered, my brother, my husband, myself, the others. I submerged myself in the bustle. I let the surf of the hubbub wash over me. I looked around, took in the chandeliers, the fug of tobacco, the velour draught curtains, the palms in brass pots, the nodding ladies' hats, the waiters with their aprons and the routine way they arranged cutlery on the table or cleared plates, carved roast meat, uncorked bottles, the choreography of the habitual cycles. And I thought: they're like migrating birds. Landing after the great crossing, the survivors shake the dust out of their feathers and twitter melodies of relief.

When I read Proust for the first time after the war, it made me almost sick to my stomach. I didn't hear time, great dead time roaring through his sentences—his Loire sentences, his Mississippi sentences, his grammatical River Congos and syntactic Nile deltas, pregnant with sediment.

I heard ambulances wailing,
the wheels of hospital beds scooting over uneven floor tiles,
the hurried steps of stretcher-bearers,
and tinkling scalpels and surgical clamps,
and the bunches of keys on the sisters' belts,
and the hiss of sterilizers,
the calling and long-drawn-out groaning in the largest field
hospital in literature,
where the great healer covers bones with periosteal membrane,
injects cavities with pulsing blood-red marrow,
and forces cartilage between joints,

and attaches muscles to tendons,
and covers them with arteries and main arteries,
and folds up intestines in the hole in an abdomen,
and places the liver on top,
and moulds fat on it,
and connecting tissue, layers of skin;
dermis,
epidermis,
epithelium
—just put the lashes in the eyelid, sister,
with the tweezers.

For a long time I couldn't put a sensible word on paper, furious as I was, a great sulking child that pressed its lips together and with a flushed face full of reproach gaped at the world in the hope of making an idiotic impression. Until I realized that writing is the only way of answering the world back with silence. Does each act of speaking then imply deep contempt?

Don't look so worried, Rachida. I really do still have all my marbles. Speak French to me again. I like your French, it acquires ochre tints when you talk, whereas my mother's sounded ceramic, not dull and not full.

I can deal better and better with sometimes hearing her voice unexpectedly and suddenly, in a flash, seeing an image of her, as she was, at about thirty-five. The moment of stasis on Sundays when she was completely made up to go strolling in the park and before she left the house, with her regal quantities of fur; the feathers in her hat and her parasol paused for a second in the hall and looked at my father to check that everything was in order.

I believe that I am only now capable of seeing the splendour of it all, the shimmering of the morning light on the marble in the hall, the awesomely fine textures of all the material with which the woman who was my mother clothes, decorates, arms herself.

The expectancy on her face seems to extend farther than the prospect of her weekly excursion, as if she suddenly knows she is free from my sarcasm and irritation, because for a long time I considered her a pitiful marvel of the petit-bourgeois fear of life, which was only distinguished from a fossil by the fact that it occasionally moved—but now, now, now…

When she suddenly turns up here and presses her cheeks, hidden behind the grey-white veil of one of her summer hats, against the cheeks of Tatante, my father's younger sister, that is, and stretches out her arms, with her fingers in gloves of wide-meshed crochet work, as we said goodbye, that summer, when we left for our annual vacation with our relations in northern France…

If I suddenly remember her now, in the sepia light that the panes of the glass roof, which have become dulled by soot and dust, strew onto the platform, where the engine spews clouds of steam and hissing sounds from its joints, and the porters load the skips and cases that pursued us like a stream of associations whenever we made the journey, with my brother and me somewhere in between, reduced to luggage that must not be left behind…

Am I capturing her in these syllables, or are the words, which are never simply ours, making a place free in the great throng of things, a well-circumscribed empty space, in which she can here and now take up residence?

WHERE ELSE COULD SHE BE? None of the places where I spent my childhood still exists. I needn't imagine that I can hear the crumbly earth crunching under the soles of my shoes again, on one of the country roads around the house where she was born, with on both sides the bright yellow stubble or newly mown barley under a blue sky from which memory has sifted all impurities, or that I can hear the drumming of the hail on the battered glass of the station concourse, when my brother Edgard and I returned to our town after years away—I can hear it whenever I want. Some travellers dived for cover when the hailstorm struck, but my brother took my hand in his and said, with unusual lyricism by his standards: "These are the wings of Nike."

We went to see her side of the family every summer. I didn't have a particularly weak constitution as a child, indeed I was reasonably robust, like my brother, but we lived in town, under the belching smoke of industry. It could do no harm, she felt, to build up our strength for a few months in the healthy air of her native region just over the border with France, where in the summer above the horizon in the west there hung the typical azure of sky over sea. I could look at it for ages, at the window of my room on the top floor of the house, which the local people had dubbed the Crooked Château.

It hung between two forms of living, between the utilitarian and the ostentatious, as if it had at some time got stuck in a difficult metamorphosis from farmstead to country house. But the eccentric combination of the living quarters, in their half-faded grandeur of pilasters and fluting and heavy pediments above the windows, with the much older sections of more sober stables and barns that surrounded them, marked off a spacious inner courtyard, partly planted with ash and beech, partly paved with hard bluestone, on which on August afternoons the sun could blaze down so fiercely that the heat came close to ecstasy.

"Child, for goodness' sake go and sit in the shade," I hear her call out, while in the cool under the trees she bends over the tub and with one of the maids puts the wash through the wringer.

I don't listen. I am a crazy recluse in Sinai. I imagine I can hear the stones humming; their voice resonates as a deep buzzing at the bottom of the word aeons, which my father taught me. Every year he joins us in the hottest weeks of August, when our town is virtually deserted and his shops can do without his supervision.

According to him the slabs of stone, with their dark sheen that absorbs all heat, are nothing less than polished slivers of the bed of a long-vanished sea. He shows me the traces of molluscs in their surface. The calcified elegance of ammonites and sponges, the branches of coral loom bright white against the blue, like the dark on a photographic negative.

I am filled with pity for those creatures. At that time I follow an intuitive animism, of which my mother has her own opinion, which she doesn't exactly keep to herself. I regard everything as animate, even the fossils of those uninhabited skeletons, congealed in the depths of their stone ocean. In those years I also hope that one night my mother's people's house will continue its stalled transformation and will afford me the pleasure of waking up one morning in a real palace. At the same time I have enough of my mother's earthy nature in me to find the true reason for the ambiguous appearance of her birthplace at least as exciting. One of my ancestors, a farmer with money, had once cherished plans that turned out to extend far beyond his purse. He had wanted to build a sumptuous country house, scrape the smell of earth and dung from under his nails and start living the life of a grand seigneur.

My mother and her brothers still had a very cool attitude to his memory, which surprised me. My ancestor had been dead for almost 150 years, and, moreover, had been considerate enough to give up the ghost before all the money had been squandered on expensive stone and craftsmen. Yet I was never able to view his likeness, painted without much talent, anywhere except on the wall in the corridor between the dining room and the kitchen in our summer residence, in the tall, narrow servants' passage, his place of exile. The portrait caught the steam from the ovens. The changing temperatures of the fires, stoked up in the mornings and dying down in the course of the day, warped the frame and with the frame the canvas. Varnish had been struck blind; the palette had faded, so that the man literally had a green laugh beneath his *craquelé* moustache. He regarded all who passed by in front of his eyes, with tureens of hot soup, dishes of roast meat, bowls of boiled vegetables and me too, empty-handed and curious, with a lofty stoicism that even then I thought ridiculous. He looked like statesman in the wings of power, in full regalia, tailcoat or gala costume, without suspecting a foreground role was no longer to be his. I found it easy to pity in those days.

What struck me about the world back then, but perhaps I should say: what strikes me about it only now is its unprecedented particularity, its details, its multiplicity of forms. I'm astonished by the little lead pellets in the linen cupboards that kept the ribbons of dresses or skirts or blouses free of creases through their weight, and by the door handles, solid brass in the best rooms but elsewhere, in the kitchens and in all places intended for those serving, good old iron—even doors seem to know their place.

Perhaps I used to be more observant, I don't know, but I'm amazed by the fact that, now I close my eyes and wander through those vanished rooms, there were such things as button-backed boxes, just big enough to accommodate the velvety vulnerability of a peach, picked at the right moment, without bruising, and to deliver it unscathed via an unbelievably fine mesh of postal services and rail connections, if necessary within twenty-four hours, at the tradesman's entrance of the residence of a nephew or niece in Paris. Or the fact that there was a cool room in the cellar, where water flowed down the whole length of the white-tiled walls, apart from the doorway, into a marble basin, channelled from a spring near the courtyard, which at the basin end came out of a zinc pipe and at the other end disappeared into a drain, together with the heat it had absorbed en route. And on the wide edges of the basin stood earthenware jugs for the milk, with high necks in which the cream could float to the top. And the cream was skimmed off with special scoops and kept in other, smaller, rounder jugs. And there were small baskets in which strawberries and other berries stayed fresh longer, and only up by the ceiling were there two narrow windows, sufficient to admit a bluish light. It reflected glacially on the smooth surface of the white stone cool block in the centre, on which butter was rolled into shape with spatulas and porridge, cakes or soft cheese were protected from going off too quickly.

In the kitchen there was sugar in hard cones on the surface of the long work table, held in a contraption with a wheel attached that you had to turn, whereupon a tool scraped sugar loose and it was caught in a dish. And there were mortars for coarse salt or peppercorns, and scores, hundreds, thousands of scoops and scrapers and hooks and clamps and forks and tongs and studs and screws... With an extensive range of instrumentation, from explosives to tweezers as fine as women's hair, the world could be mined, melted, distilled, reforged, and with each way in which it was attacked, it revealed different facets of itself. Today you have to consult the physicists, or the astronomers with their arcane instruments, in order still to be able to experience the world as elemental; today's world—a favourite saying of my mother's—comes to us completely streamlined, while in my youth there were not yet any peaches grown which were able to travel round the world unscathed, even without padded boxes, because they never really ripen.

The house was like a termites' nest, managed by workers whose queen had long since wasted away in her bridal chamber, but around whose absence a daily life still developed. A stubborn, possibly millennia-old matriarchy ruled over the seasons. In my early childhood this coincided with the stony contours of Moumou, my mother's mother's mother, over 100 when she finally died when I was about eight. I thought she was old enough, almost prehistoric, to bear the whole of humanity. The vast stretch of her existence took my breath away.

During the long autumn of her life the home in which she had borne her offspring contained her like a reliquary shrine. Deep in the heart of the house she lay for most of the day on a thick, eternally rustling mattress in an alcove right next to a chimney breast. When the shutters of her sleeping compartment were closed and she lay behind them snorting in her eternal slumber, I imagined that the alcove hid a basin in which a mysterious marine mammal was being kept alive. I imagined that every so often Moumou had expelled a hunk of slime and blood from her gigantic body which her older daughters had caught and rubbed clean with linen cloths, and in that way, as they rubbed, modelled into the more or less recognizable shape of a human being. At least that was what I saw happen in the stall, when a cow had given birth, and with her tongue piled the lump of membranes and blood into a calf.

On Sunday two of Moumou's granddaughters put her into a dark-blue or black dress of a cut that had once, long before the Franco-Prussian War, been fashionable, manoeuvred her with some difficulty into a wheelchair with a woven seat and pushed the whole huge contraption into the large drawing room, where every so often I, the youngest, had to greet the matriarch, the oldest of all.

She was virtually deaf. Over one eye, no more than a chink in the geometrical pattern of wrinkles round her eye sockets, lay an alarming blue-grey membrane. The other eye was more like a point of light somewhere far off in the darkness of her skull. She carried the smell of wet cellar stones with her, the clamminess of crumbling walls.

Because she could hear almost nothing and could see less and less out of that single smouldering eye, I had to put my hands in her lap, after which she grasped my wrists with her hands, felt my palms at length, turned my hands over and rubbed my knuckles repeatedly with her scabby thumbs. Meanwhile the heavy heels of her shoes pressed harder and harder onto the wood of the wheelchair's footrest, which began to creak ominously.

It was as if she was enjoying my youth. Cracks and splits appeared in her ancient Ice Age body. Fault lines seemed to grate against each other. Masses of earth shifted and threw up constantly changing mountain ridges in the heavy cotton of her dress. A copper necklace with a medallion showing Napoleon III *en profil* meandered from somewhere under her chin down though those newly formed valleys and came to rest on her navy-blue cummerbund. She bent her head forward and with her one eye seemed to be more grazing the light from my surface than examining me.

Finally, in the ravines of flesh on her cheeks, a mouth slowly opened, pink and completely toothless. Membranes of slime sprang open. From her throat something bubbled up that was midway between a laugh and a death rattle. One of her hands let go of me, tapped the fingers of one of her daughters, who was leaning listlessly with her arm on the back of the chair, waiting for the audience to end. From her sleeve, as if by magic, she produced some paper money and pushed it into Moumou's hand.

Moumou lowered her hand again, with the other turned over my right hand, pressed the note, folded four or five times, into my palm and closed my fingers over it, as if she were entrusting me with her whole fortune.

In her one deep-brown iris I now read the same sadness, that apparently all-comprehending melancholy, which one day struck me to the core when my father sat me on his arm at a cage in the zoo. From a cliff of grey skin, grooved like a relief map, that glides past us apparently endlessly, an eye suddenly looks at me, for minutes on end, it seems, until it closes in a half-moon of lashes.

I hear my father say: "That is an elephant."
But it wasn't.
It was the Countenance of God.

"HELENA, CHILD," my mother would moan if she could hear me. "Where is this leading to? You're shooting off in all directions. There's no line in what you're saying. I can't make head or tail of it, I've lost the thread." Some things she couldn't understand. Even if she'd lived to be 150, she didn't want to, and there's not much point in having her nod in agreement or making her angry here.

She constantly wanted to know why I said something in one way and not in another, why I didn't use normal words or sentences, or didn't simply get straight to the point. It was a habit she presumed to adopt when she not only was my mother but for a while wanted to play tutor, a role which gradually dissolved in that of her motherhood. I was never able to explain to her that you sometimes achieve much more by deliberately talking beside the point than by speaking with a precision that in any case will never be anything but illusory.

She was in the habit of giving me extra lessons during the holidays using the books in the house where she was born, but I had read them all, even the ones she thought unsuitable for me. For a change, to maintain my grammar, she would make me write letters, never to be sent, to relations deeper in France. I thought the whole business was unnatural, but not the imaginative side of things, I liked that. My mother was too sober to give me subjects for essays; she never liked novels or poetry, so she opted for the letter form, which I in turn found dreary. Eventually I started making up relations and I enjoyed it so much that I also wrote to real relations about incidents that had never taken place.

Writing for me has always been something paternal. At home it was my father who had me write letters, who commented on the legibility of my handwriting and laughed and chuckled at the jokes I made. He had a fine sense of the gradations of irony and for the moments when humour can tip over into something else, into sarcasm or devastating sadness, for example. That is why I cannot possibly imagine that a woman ever invented writing. Up to now no one has been able to talk me out of that stubborn prejudice.

Women talk, ceaselessly, and they always talk to themselves, including my mother, despite her pride in her unshakeable common sense. Day in, day out, like a music box whose cogs are worn out, she rattled off short commands, strictures or questions, which invariably carried an undertone of reproach or accusation. She went on pursuing me until her death, a shadow that kept tugging my sleeve or tapping me on the shoulder, and I only stopped getting annoyed when I realized that it was herself first and foremost whom she kept under her thumb—a remnant, not to say an enduring trauma, from the war years, when she was left to her own devices for almost all decisions—but by then she was no longer alive. It is terrible that I can only turn to welcome her ghost into the realm of the fallible, and with that same gesture grant myself absolution for the fact that I am a human being, now that she has been in her grave for years.

I can still picture the sarcastic frown when she asked for my "homework" and started reading. And my own scandalized reaction, not only because she was nosing in my "letters", how-ever imaginary, and obviously didn't think much of them, but mainly because she was entering a domain that in my eyes was not hers. I couldn't stand the fact that with her well-intentioned attempts at education she was essentially appropriating my father, to whom I had to write letters during the war, even though they would never reach him. She wormed her way into the shell of his absence. She who impressed on me that the dead must be silent, gave her own husband the character of someone deceased when she savoured my "little trifles", as she called them.

For her letters were collecting basins for communications, objective reports. Feelings were noted briefly in passing, like the state of the weather, births and deaths. Her expressions of condolence sounded formal, her congratulations on engage-ments and christenings artificial.

For me letters, including this one, have always been a playing field where anything could happen and where I did not simply reveal myself to another person; writing forces me to delay and shows me myself as more or less a stranger. My father under-stood that, but my mother had little patience for subtleties like double meanings, winks or a bon mot.

Nor did she understand that a story as it develops strives for its own specific gravity. It unwinds and allows the person speaking it or writing it down to determine its fate only to a very small extent. Words, images, sentences congeal, and around that glowing core a gravitational field is created that attracts other fragments of images and sentences from mental space, sucks them in and absorbs them into the whirlpools of the imagina-tion. Brainwaves and associations are constantly bombarding the swelling word planet. Some stories brush past the still-liquid surface, drawing at most a light trail in the sky, but most things come and go unseen, and are pulverized silently. There is so much that will never be forgotten, because no one will ever have known that it existed.

"Then it's of no importance, child. If we don't know what we don't know, it doesn't exist!"

She almost snaps it. Where on earth does her voice still keep coming from? The voice, unexpectedly clear and articulated, unmistakably hers, that dry alto, that light vibrato, that I so often hear just before I go to sleep and that seldom says anything but my name: "Helena…" Now questioning, occasionally plaintive, but mostly brisk: "Helena!"

In the past I would have tried furiously to release myself from such twilight situations, I would have shaken my head, to and fro on the pillow, to wrench myself free from the paralysis of the waking dream. Now I keep quiet, and she also calms down.

"The scissors," she whispers. "Give me the ribbon."

And sometimes she is silent, but I can hear her shuffling round in search of a strip of felt, a nail, a length of rope, a length of barbed wire. Wherever she is, things must be as untraceable or imperfect as they are here, on the waking side of dreams.

I think that it wasn't just because of their evasive tone that she could be so scornful of my letters. I think she felt excluded and became jealous without fully realizing it. Perhaps she began at long last to suspect that my words were addressed to someone else, someone who could understand everything, got every quip, was able to place every ambiguity: an invisible third party, apart from her and the cousins, uncle or aunt, imaginary or otherwise—the true addressee. If she suspected something of the kind, she was right.

I write to a man. Whatever I write, to whomever it is addressed, I write to him. I don't want it ever to stop, to have to write "Goodbye", "Adieu", "All the best", "See you soon". His body stretches out in the writing itself. He lowers his limbs into the stream of my thoughts. That unceasing, maddening conversation of myself with myself, the almost endless splitting of voices into voices into voices into voices, comes to rest only when he seals my lips and stills the flood in me.

I could seethe with fury when my mother read those letters, and I was only able to make it clear to her by myself committing the unforgivable. One day she asked me to write a letter to an aunt by marriage in Brussels. In French, as almost all my efforts were for that matter. My mother felt there were all kinds of things wrong with my conjugations.

I wrote a letter. But I wrote it to her. I crawled into my father's skin. They had written each other love letters when they first went out, I knew that. Every child reads its parents' love letters if it gets the chance, it's a law of nature. Neither of them excelled at amorous outpourings. He regularly mentioned "*la plus Grande Joie*", capital letters included, which she could give him and he her. She informed him by return of post that the "*Joie*" could wait a little longer. Honour was a matter of life and death for a woman.

I wrote her a letter as my father. I evoked his voice and tried to make it resonate in the sentences, his jokes when he was in a good mood, the teasing and wet talk with which he was able to disarm her. I let the "*Grande Joie*" passages appear dimly

46

between the lines in a less abstract form than they themselves
had used when they were going out.

When she collected the work that evening, she did exactly the
same as I had done while writing it: she blushed. The house
was blacked out. In the room a paraffin lamp was burning
on its lowest flame, but there was light enough to see that she
went bright red and did not dare raise her eyes from the paper,
because then she would have had to look at me.

I leant forward a little across the table, towards her, with
the lamp between us. A second later I received a slap on my
cheek. It sounded like the crack of a whip; outside the dog
started barking.

She only ever hit me once in her life, and it was then. The
lamp wobbled, but didn't fall.

My mother looked me straight in the eyes. She was trembling.
The print of her palm was still glowing on my cheek. She
crumpled the letter in her fist. She did not take her eyes off me
and stuck her fist into the pocket of her apron.

I could see she was fighting back her tears. I knew she would
send me upstairs, that she wanted to cry undisturbed, and it
wouldn't be over me.

S OMETIMES I WONDER whether all my memories deserve
their name, whether their clarity and directness do not make
them rather phantom pains of the soul—just as an amputee
can have cramp in the toes of his foot that has long since been
removed or someone who has gone deaf is visited by flawless
melodies from his childhood rather than actually summoning
them up. The world is shrinking, inevitably. On the other hand
the echo chambers of memory seem to expand and divide like
living cells. The mind remains restless.

Be that as it may, when you see her come in now, when you see
her sit on a sofa with her hands in her lap and her knees tucked
modestly together, then you too are entering a memory, which
I am definitely bringing to life and have perhaps meanwhile
endlessly reforged and reworked.

I have taken my place next to her, standing, on the other
side of the armrest of the sofa. I am still young and am wearing a dress with a sailor collar. When I put my hand round
the armrest it is quite possible that she and I are posing. If the
scene is intended for us and close family, my mother can easily
also put a hand on mine, a touch of intimacy that you will
look for in vain in the more official portraits in our reception
room at home.

As I grow older, gradually too lanky still to be able to place
an arm on the armrest in an elegant attitude, I will be positioned
half behind her, possibly with my fingers on the woodwork of the

48

back, right next to her head, as if the roles are gradually being reversed and it is I who am protecting her. But the composition would mainly express the respect of a daughter for her mother, who is allowed to sit: she assumes the dominant position.

Now that I am talking about this and distilling the scene from a multiplicity of separate memories rather than calling a well-defined event to mind, I can suddenly see myself looking down at her neck as I stand behind the back of the sofa on which she has sat down. I have always known that the birthmark in the nape of her neck, under her earlobe, close to the hairline at the back of her head, was there, but I only seem to see it properly now: not clearly outlined, more a point where her southern complexion is concentrated. Above it her locks of hair anchored to her skull by a wide-toothed tortoiseshell comb, whose grip not one hair escapes—and all of it so clear and close up. I have to restrain myself from putting my hands over her eyes to surprise her, in the hope that she will turn round and I will be able to see her face, as sharply as the back of her head. Not the face with the veil of habit over it, the greatest common denominator of all my mothers from all my memories, but her quintessence.

I myself could still wear my hair loose, or in thick plaits, but not for much longer. The phases of life used to have fewer intermediate seasons. There was less no man's land between childhood and adulthood. I won't have any more dresses with sailor collars hanging in my wardrobe. As I approach twenty, my dress will increasingly resemble my mother's, in her weekday outfit, with a long ankle-length skirt, and over it a blouse buttoned up to the neck. Soon I will have to wear my hair up too, and from then on for ever. A woman who has been promised or married puts her hair up. Loose hair, loose morals.

You can't simply imagine my father next to me, that's not right. Unless I'm an only child, but that isn't the case. Mothers have their portraits taken with their daughters, growing sons surround their father. Only in a family portrait do fathers and daughters come together. Then I'm allowed to share the sofa with my mother, since I am now not only her daughter, we are both first and foremost the woman, the weaker sex. The thought can still make me grind my teeth, especially because of the naturalness with which she assumed her role. I fought with her more than with my father, who was far too soft to be a patriarch. But perhaps all fathers are soft, and easier to kill than mothers.

Probably he will be standing with one hand on the armrest and the other on the back of the sofa, bending over my mother and me: a gesture that suggests love and devotion, but also clearly shows his place in the whole. He is the paterfamilias, the cornerstone of the family, and my brother Edgard, a few years older than me—he is wearing a suit that seems to be a replica of his father's—would be positioned on my side of the sofa next to me or behind me, but more formal than my father, in his role as son and man.

When I see such portraits again later, I read mostly the lie in them. Not ours—my parents love each other and we love them. We need less hypocrisy than other people to keep the idyll intact and we have no more taboos than the taboos of the age. The real lie is the world itself, by which I mean: the maps with the aid of which we were supposed to get our bearings in those years, and which were supposed to steer us through life, turn out in hindsight to have be more fantasy than guide.

We are well-to-do bourgeois, belonging to an extensive caste within which an extremely subtle hierarchy requires constant repositioning with regard to the others. In that period I can never estimate properly where precisely we are located in that whole system of unspoken laws and commandments. Some of the girls in my class are allowed to accompany me to and from school, I can sit at the same desk with them, our mothers can converse cordially, but it would not be fitting for them to come into our house. Conversely there are girlfriends who can come and play at our house, which does not mean at all that I can just drop in to see them at home, and if I *am* invited some ordinance or other requires that I take my leave well before supper and not too long after coffee.

There are also people who are allowed "inside" at home, that is, upstairs, in our living room; while others must content themselves with the antechamber in the front hall, its stiffly grand armchairs and chairs, and the cool air—only if it is really cold outside is there a fire. That room makes a haughty impression even on me when I happen to enter it.

Twice a month my mother has Emilie, our maid, arrange the chairs in a circle and light the lamps on the side tables, to receive her friends from the sewing group. When she gives me my own sewing box when I am about eleven, with an air as if it is a gold chest from Ali Baba's cave, I am expected from then on to take part in that enervating, fiddly activity. A half-hour at most to start with, it's impossible to keep me still any longer, but the sessions are systematically extended, and you can see me sitting there, messing around with embroidery frames and needles, swaying my legs until my mother says something and I crackle with rage inside.

"*O plongeur à jamais sous sa cloche! Toute une mer de verre éternellement chaude…*" I recite to myself, to while away the time and my impatience. "*Toute une vie immobile aux lents pendules verts!*" And I glance at my mother, dressed for the occasion with careful informality, since although her friends all belong to her circle of intimates, it still requires a whole ritual before a woman looks informal—at least if I remember everything well, if memory has not added extra colour to my mother's official portrait, as she has seated herself there in the Louis Philippe chair, a cascade of linen and lace, in a dressing gown of lined satin with piping and five or six long undersleeves that fan open from the elbow, so that her hands appear from them like the mobile stamens of an exotic flower, and over it a stole of Irish lace, and in the cold seasons a fur boa.

When after her death I am emptying her rooms with my daughter and we are piling up corsets and garters that have been out of fashion for decades, the countless scarves and veils, thin as snakeskin that has shed time itself, in boxes in that old front room, ready for the rag-and-bone man, I have the feeling that I am clearing up the moulds of a monumental female statue, or the bones and ribs of some prehistoric animal.

"We can start our own museum," I said. "Musée royal d'Histoire naturelle de ma Mère." My daughter found that disrespectful.

I never wore my hair up. I resolutely banished from my wardrobe clothes expressing the expectation that I had to become a maquette of my mother, and embraced the fashion of the inter-war years, with its scandalously bared ankles and calves, its low waists, its frivolous accessories like diadems and long necklaces and hip ribbons, alongside which my mother in her still largely nineteenth-century outfits looked as if she was in armour, a stranded cruiser, as formidable as it was impotent. She in turn considered my clothes "hopelessly frivolous".

"Our Helena has the craziness of my father's side in her blood," I heard her say more than once while she was embroidering with her friends. She was proud of her French origins, her Latin blood, which in my view explained her caprices, although the fact that she was French had more to do with the vagaries of history than with any merit of hers. I listened with a mixture of awe and mockery to the Cartesian clarity of her native language, as it had been brought to refinement and discipline by generations of court poets and philosophers, while in her view the French that we learnt to speak was full of glitches and was at most a language for harlequins and poets with a high opinion of themselves—a sneer at me.

At that time I play the role of capricious daughter with abandon, but inwardly I also long for her reprimands. For the telegraphic succinctness of her sentences when she loses her patience: "What are you on about, I can't understand a thing. Finish your sentences and try to breathe." Her rebukes cause shame in me that is nothing but a blushing veil over the guilty satisfaction when I succeed in irritating her.

I have always shown an inclination for breathlessness, for an ecstasy that cancels out the world, time and finally consciousness itself, and instinctively I have always sought out words or bodies

that could stem my boundless yearning, could set my passion
on the ground and bring me to a halt. How I would have liked
to pronounce an infinitely long sentence that incorporated in
itself everything that was, the way a lady of the court from the
periwig period, in whose locks an armada of pearls capsizes,
lifts her countless petticoats as she mounts the steps of the opera
house—or the ladder to the scaffold.

My mother and her companions prided themselves on being
a respectable sewing group, and potential new members were
first invited on a trial basis. If they turned out to be too loose-
tongued, all too fond of gossip, their stay did not extend beyond
that one occasion, which intensely disappointed me: at that time
gossip was the only instruction about life that reached my ears.

When I got older I had the feeling of being an insect that
voluntarily encapsulates itself in the silken threads in which a
spider wraps its prey, the feeling that I was tying myself tighter
and tighter to the habits of being a woman, had to cross a
Sahara of yarn and thread, with that sandalwood sewing box
as luggage, a doll's house version of my womb, decorated with
thimbles and follicles and ovaries. Around me arms went down
and up again when my mother's friends pushed the needle
through the material and pulled the thread tight. We were like
flightless birds dropping their beaks into the water of an oasis
and then stretching our long necks to swallow.

The word that is regularly on the tip of my tongue at that
time is eunuch. Not just the word itself and its piquant connotations, but particularly because I have read that eunuchs keep
their severed testicles in a jug in order to be buried as a complete
man, more or less as my mother and I lugged our sewing things

around with us. I'm certain that she, if I had spoken the word testicles out loud, would have had to pick half her friends off the carpet, if she herself had not fainted from a combination of horror and over-tightened corsage. Certain terms belonged only in dictionaries and encyclopaedias, wrapped in a safe neutrality and the hospital smell of carbolic. They weren't intended to be allowed to fly around indoors like tame parakeets.

"*Va-t'en*," she usually says after a while, when my impatience starts to make her restless. "Go on." And I run upstairs, through the rooms with their velour wall-covering, their rugs, their table covers, curtain cords, antimacassars and doilies and pillowslips and footrests and fireguards and lampshades, their palm motifs and fern leaves, that welter of textures and surfaces that gives off the sultriness of a rainforest, fermentation, mould, wet earth.

Or I go farther down, into the basement kitchen, where Emilie resides. She scrubs the floors there every day. She splashes a spring tide of caustic soda over the tiles and scours the saucepans clean with a sponge of steel wool, which produces a sound that strikes my ear as perfectly circular, the singing of the steel on tin and the impact of the cleaver in the next day's roast—the music that accompanies my weekly penance.

W HAT CLARITY AND HONESTY prevail there. Walls don't hide their stones. Wood is rough from brushing and generous scoops of soda, like Emilie herself, to whom I ascribe a secret wild life, with men and drink, and fights over her rustic earthenware charms. She has her room right at the top of the house, by the roof-tree, more a built-in cupboard with airs than a real room. How strange that at the two extremes of the house, which she occupies, the world is turned on its head—that the basement kitchen, where the storage cupboards and the crockery trays are, lets in a sea of light from high windows, while the attic, closest to the firmament, keeps its membrane of tiles closed and preserves a grey darkness, in a corner of which, as the only point of light, Emilie's room cowers.

Every few weeks she hangs out our linen to dry over the whole length of the attic. Her room is then hidden in a labyrinth of motionless ghostly apparitions, a Platonic world of sheets without a wrinkle, alternating with vests pegged to the line by their sleeves, so that they display the dumb, aggrieved air of those hanged, after the last convulsion. That silent execution is repeated there again and again, a form of inquisition for all the textiles that must be so close to the skin of our heretical flesh.

Emilie doesn't seem to fit into those surroundings. Her surface, full of grooves and calloused hills bearing witness to that display of strange symmetries, comparable with the profile of the tops of dunes in the desert, seems more fluid, more organic than the ethereal perfection of the sheets which she hangs up and later, with arms spread wide apart, as if she were a figure in a Baroque deposition from the Cross, slides into her baskets. Women are beings who bear, be it washing or merchandise, be it the next generation or the memory of the dead. Emilie herself seems to be almost the symbol of that: broad, jug-shaped, battered, an ancient cracked amphora; she who cuts meat and wrings water from shirts.

Every few months the attic next to her quarters remains empty, and all the white wash goes to the bleacher's. My mother provides a separate sum of money for the carriers whom Emilie drums up to lug the whole load out of the house and later to bring it back cleaned. Usually they are women from the neighbourhood where Emilie grew up and where she mostly spends her weekly day off. My mother insists that the army comes no farther into the home than the wash house near the back kitchen, where Emilie has put out the baskets ready.

While she is away I sometimes enter her room, not to rummage around, because there is very little to nose about in. She can scarcely write, she seldom reads books. I absorb the nakedness of the scanty things in the interior. The bed with the metal rails. The cupboard enclosing a sparse wardrobe: two or so aprons, the pinafores she had to put on when there were guests for dinner, the accompanying caps, some underwear of epic proportions, two pairs of shoes, the lightest for indoors, the heaviest, sturdy lace-up boots, for outside. And then a coat and skirt and a couple of blouses: the uniform of ordinariness that she dons on her day off, when the other one, that of service, constricts her.

The mirror above the water jug has areas which have gone dull, as if Emilie's face, on which dark smudges regularly appear and disappear, according to a rhythm that seems to me as mysterious as the cycle of sunspots, has infected the mirror glass, and perhaps even the nature of the light itself, with her affliction.

Sometimes I put my head close to the glass, about as close as Emilie does when she washes in the mornings and evenings, in order to appropriate all her impurities and imagine I lead a life like hers, however unknown it remains to me, apart from those few traces and scars.

No one suspects the stirrings of an ecstatic soul in that moulded body, but on her day off, "my Tuesday" Emilie calls it herself, she usually comes home late, mostly a while after sunset. From her hesitant tread on the stairs, during the longest climb that anyone has to undertake in the house, my mother deduces that Emilie is going as silently as possible to her crow's nest in order not to wake any of us, and she praises Emilie's tact. The first quality in a servant consists in the ability not to stand out, if not a gruesome talent for invisibility. But I have seen more than once in Emilie's eyes the haziness, the nirvana you are served for a few centimes in glasses not an inch high, in the pubs that lay hidden in the nooks and crannies of the town, the side alleys that descended from the main streets to the poor who lived by the river. More than once heavy showers turned to wild streams in those dark clefts. For days afterwards the water stood in puddles and children who seemed kneaded from mud floated sloops of twigs or straw on it.

Whenever during a walk we have to pass one of those alleys because making a detour is not possible, my father invariably quickens his pace. He takes me by the hand, pulls me along and I laugh. It doesn't occur to me that a grown man like him can know fear, the element that dominates childhood and loses both its brilliance and its darkness as one grows up—an awakening that in my eyes has always seemed more a long-drawn-out process of falling asleep.

One anaesthetizes oneself against the lucidity that brings fear with it as one grows up. The unbearable sharpness of vision that it opens in us admits of only three responses: flight into blind panic, lethargy, or confronting the situation as it is in order to act decisively.

My father is too calm by nature to panic. He is the cell wall that surrounds my mother, my brother and me in order to protect us from the dangers of the outside world.

"We've got to hurry a bit, my girl," he says. "It's not healthy for you here, with that stinking water down there."

I try to take as big steps as he over the paving stones, but I can't. I stroll behind him, scanning his steps with the syncopated dance of my heels and soles. Only later does it strike me how much the route of those walks meanders, how small the area of the town covered by our promenades is before they encounter unmarked limits, so that in retrospect our excursions seem to me to resemble the hopeless pacing to and fro of a predator behind bars at the zoo or the circus.

I miss the bustle of the streets in those days. The swarming of the masses, the hats, the caps, the umbrellas, the thronging about among the horse trams, the coaches, the carts. The festive chaos in the time before the car enforces its segregation between pedestrians and bicycles on the street can impose itself on me with such sharpness that I wonder: did I really see all this? Have I stored all those scenes, all those still lifes, unwittingly inside me? The delight of unleashing them is too strong for my constitution, too unadulterated.

I remember the pleasure that took hold of me during family New Year parties, because God, or Time, or whatever, was kind enough to make us a gift of a whole new year, still for a little while as pristine and quivering like the pudding on the silver salver that Emilie brought to the table for dessert.

Our days were dome-shaped, exhibition palaces in steel and glass. Beneath their translucent womb wall were the resplendent palm gardens of our lifestyle, heated with coal and gas.

"What a brilliant stroke of inspiration Belgium is!" chuckles my father during the banquet. The wine frees up the mild irony with which he is always able to disarm me.

He raises his glass. "To Belgium! Our mountains are not too high, and our rivers not too deep. Not too big, not too small. Belgium is completely accessible and navigable."

A country like a Liège waffle, I think now. Crispy outside, but with a heart of white-hot dough. The morality of the Father, king and law forced its rigid system on the town, which divided satiety in unequal portions among the countless throng who hungered and thirsted after pleasure, and what they did not get they would sooner or later steal. That's how it has always been, and so it shall be for all time—history is another word for hunger, and hunger does not speak but gnaws.

If I was to believe the nuns at the school where my mother sent me when I turned eleven, the Almighty Himself had created Belgium, a second Genesis in a minor key. Just to bring Belgium into being He had sent a succession of disputes and revolutions raging through the old Europe like earthquakes, and had made other countries clash until cracks appeared and somewhere a splinter shot out, which was knocked into shape until Belgium was there. Back in the days when the Romans made camp here, and long before that, when humanity was messing about with flint, He, Whose work the nuns regarded as a heavenly form of needlework, had refined the idea of "Belgium" further and further. Old atlases preserve the outlines of his first patterns. He had drawn chalk lines, stuck in pins, changed His mind and begun again, and once more and again till gradually His Very Own Nation took shape and everything was finally where it obviously had to be: between the accursed heretics in the north and the despicable revolutionaries in the south. God's own garden, His second Eden, in which a new Adam this time had, thank God, given everything nice French names and soon filled the air with the hammering of his energy and industry. For we Belgians are hard workers, exulted the nuns and praised the Lord.

But when we went to the sea annually on the train at the end of spring, like everyone who could afford the luxury of a few days off, the country looked so small, so diminutive, that the thundering of the locomotive and the carriages seemed to continue right up to the borders, as if we were nothing more than a nation of cardboard, a painted background for a group portrait or the backdrop for an operetta.

For all the frail ladies' toes that preciously tested the coolness of the waves from the steps of the bathing carriages in Blankenberge, De Haan or Ostend, elsewhere children's fingers were dipping matchwood into steaming cauldrons of liquid sulphur, girls' hands carded cotton, threaded yarn onto spools or chain cylinders, from siphon to shuttle, and twined and twisted, and beat jute and plucked felt, or sewed the gloves that my mother and I put on to stroll along the promenade. It was a world I saw only later, when my brother was instructed to take me out for a breath of air, although it was under my nose all the time, in the corners of the town that my father avoided on our walks.

If there was a pub at the bottom of the alleyways on the steep slopes by the river, which my father always walked quickly past, one of the pubs in which Emilie got up to God knows what on her days off, there was often noise from down below: laughter, screaming, violent disputes, the surf of a volcanic euphoria which could turn into its opposite at any moment. Papers, which my father hid in vain from my brother and me, reported that in those parts of town eruptions spread to adjacent properties, and perhaps without the intervention of the gendarmes would have reached our better neighbourhoods.

On one occasion I see, during the annual Whitsun fair, in the big square in front of the abbey, children not much older than me, loudly encouraged by the adults around them, throwing mud and horse manure at the front of the collegiate church where a service is going on.

My mother pulls me briskly away from the scene. She seldom has a good word to say about priests, but religious matters are among the things in life that a person, as she usually says, can better "leave well alone".

As she pulls me after her through the crowds of visitors to the fair to the other side of the square, the roundabouts and swings suddenly seem more than ghostly machines that unleash nothing but pleasure. Their mechanisms appear, if not finely enough tuned or insufficiently calibrated, able to put natural laws out of action and release unprecedented energies. Festivals and fairs suddenly strike me as pregnant with a hidden power that provoke a disaster that my parents only ever admit into their conversation in the most covert terms.

"*Encore des grèves*," mutters my father one day at breakfast, with the paper in front of his nose. And although his face is his hidden by the opened pages, I detect from the way my mother raises an eyebrow that they are exchanging a token of understanding, as intimate as a bedroom secret, but clearly less frivolous.

"*C'est une menace*," echoes my mother.

For the greater part of my childhood I call Emilie and Co. "*les grèves*", just as you once had the Huns, or the Vandals, and Emilie herself I dub "*La Menace*". It sounds mysterious and Oriental, like Herodias or Scheherazade. My mother speaks the word sufficiently under her breath to strengthen the suspicion that it is a term that belongs to the outer suburbs of language, but precisely because of that it acquires for me the charge of a magic formula, itching my tongue when I see Emilie at work in the house.

Perhaps I once—now I suddenly see her face in front of me again, the weathered yet smooth face of a woman who is both young and old at the same time—perhaps I once actually addressed her by that *nom de guerre*.

She half-turns towards me by the table downstairs, where she is using the mincer. At once fleetingly and closely she surveys me with a look that hesitates between astonishment and private amusement. Only now do I read in her bright-green irises, above which a lock of hair that has come loose always bobs while she is at work, the pride that my unintended indiscretion must have awakened in her.

More a cat than a maid, there is no sign in her of the abject servility with which the servants of family and friends reduce themselves to being part of the furniture. She doesn't read, at least not books. She dusts them with a caution tending to suspicion, as if a curse were etched into their bindings. But later I discover that she reads our old papers from beginning to end before she wraps the potato peelings in them.

Undoubtedly she is just as literate, if not a virtuoso, in vocabulary that written characters consider far beneath their dignity. Where else does the jollity come from with which she returns from the bleacher's with her sisters in calamity, with our white linen and that of neighbouring families folded in the baskets—undoubtedly spread out, held up to the light, examined by scores of fingers for the ethereal cuneiform script of nocturnal vices, fear of death, forbidden embraces, of solitary sins and lonely drunken bouts, which had left its traces in those flexible clay tablets?

The pleasure of her and the other girls sends a threat of uproar through our rooms, our world of muteness, of secrecy out of habit. Conversations, even disputes seldom disturb the order of things more seriously than the sound of the brush strokes with which someone clears up a fallen vase. Our parties are wrapped round with table linen of the finest sort, and feminine silver, and the satin bands of etiquette, to keep the primeval forces that are hidden deep in partying, the suppressed memories of ritual slaughter or human sacrifices, under a lid. Our melodies are bourgeois tunes, at most saucy, and even then you almost need two eardrums to be able to register their ambiguities.

In contrast, what a heathen tumult resonates in Emilie's breast when, after her nocturnal escapades, still with a hint of alcohol on her breath, she launches into frank songs at the draining board and without looking up senses my presence. She knows my ears are pricked up and that I am wobbling in my shoes from sublime horror, when her filthy words get through to me.

Without really seeing me she suddenly brings her fist right in front of my face.

I can examine the hair on her finger joints, half eaten away by caustic soda or bleach, down to its roots. Stiff, dark-blonde hair, almost man's hair.

She holds her fist against the tip of my nose.

A soft, continuous grunting churns through her ribcage.

Something inside her is seething through cavities.

For a moment I'm frightened she will start growling like a cat, open her hand and sink her claws in my face. But she just pushes her fist still closer against my nose and grunts: "I says to her, I says, Miss Picture Postcard, stay away from him, he's mine. And if you're deaf, sweetie, I'll draw a cauliflower or two on that little mug of yours."

I N HER WORLD money is "brass". "A man must have brass and balls," is one of her sayings. For her my father can't be a real man. Even though he certainly has more brass than she has ever seen in one place, he probably lacks a lot of the second, while my brother, to judge by the way she can sometimes sit and ogle him when he drinks milk at her kitchen table after school, presumably does have enough virility on board, but is still too young for a fortune of his own.

"Balls and brass," it gives me a niggling pleasure to repeat the words under my breath as I sit waiting on the couch in the middle of the hall lined with counters in the bank in the Place d'Armes, during my father's visits. Our walks regularly lead there, supposedly by chance; often they are nothing but a long detour to reach the branch where he has accounts.

Everything that revolves around "brass" bathes in the same atmosphere of euphemism and embarrassment that hangs around bathrooms, bedrooms and brothels. We call money "*des moyens*", and you have enough or not. When Emilie talks about brass, her speech takes on an indecent flavour, as if she is unexpectedly pulling down your underpants.

She seems to take pleasure in intriguing my brother and me with her coarse vocabulary. Perhaps she does so to mark her territory, like some savages stick the shrunken heads of their enemies on stakes at the edge of their village, but possibly she also sees us as temporary companions in misfortune, creatures who like her are only noticed when they misbehave.

When, waiting on the couch in the hall with the counters, I repeat her words like that, I taste something like revenge on my tongue. Balls and brass. Everything exudes the silence of cathedrals or hospitals, and coolness, and bathes in the immaterial sheen of travertine. Through the dome that crowns the hall filtered light falls on the motionless palm pots among the couches on which ladies, as motionless, as vegetative as I am, can sit while their husbands or male relations pass their transactions to the clerks on the other side of the balustrade: gentlemen with the self-conscious politeness of lackeys, who speak to each other and the customers in whispers and when they count out sums wear white gloves to muffle even the rustling of the notes.

This is the temple of euphemisms, the antipode to the subterranean caverns where Emilie, I suspect, celebrates her pagan cults.

"Balls and brass." I don't know how old I am, it must be shortly before the war, in the vague time just after my first menstruation, that I find myself on one of those benches again one afternoon and am looking at my father, who is making as if to leave. I see that he takes his gloves out of the pockets of his topcoat, but some coins come out with the gloves. Under the cupola the sound of copper and nickel careering across the floor resounds like a curse.

One of the clerks comes out from behind the balustrade like lightning, kneels, quietens the spinning coins with the palm of his hand, as if treading on flying ants, picks them up and hands them to my father, who is visibly upset. I also see the minuscule but oh-so-sharp mockery on the face of the clerk as he slides the money into my father's hand.

For years I wanted to re-experience the scene, to rewrite the scene by going up to my father, throwing my arms round his neck and giving him a kiss on his cheek, instead of appropriating that spiteful condescension and in my adolescent way relishing the humiliation he inflicted on my father. A real gentleman doesn't keep loose change in his pockets.

The incident lasted scarcely half a minute, but for years after I made the naked ring of coins boom through my head like the ringing of the alarm bell.

My father and his fear, of the people "beneath" us, who bought plates, cord, washtubs, matches and household utensils at prices that were almost as cheap as those of the co-operatives which caused him such worries. Under his respect for the upper classes above ours a truth lay hidden that a handful of falling coins could instantly reveal: that he would never be seen as amounting to anything, the eternal grocer; he may be heir to and the conscientious owner of a chain of businesses, but he would always remain a grocer.

Perhaps I visit Emilie in her basement so often in those years to do penance. To allow myself to be lashed by her indiscretions and provocations: I, the flagellant in the family.

"If you're quiet you can stay, but be quiet, mouth shut," she hisses. She knows the fat would be in the fire if my mother finds me there in the kitchen too often.

I sit down on the chair where in the mornings a supplier usually waits for a dram and maybe a little more, a grab under her skirts and the accompanying slap or unexpected French kiss, and watch her bring the dish from the pantry, pull off the cloth over it, lay the piece of meat on the chopping block, fetch the knife from the hook under the shelf by the wall, and wait.

I think I have come to hear the blade first slice through the soft muscle tissue, the white and red, the limp pink stone. And she also knows that I am waiting for her to divide the pieces with the heavy cleaver.

She raises the weapon slowly and holds it in the air for a while, until she can tell that in my imagination my head is on the block, closer to her apron.

When she finally brings the cleaver down so that the bone cracks under the iron as if it is my own neck vertebrae, I have long since squeezed my eyes tight shut.

I N A CERTAIN SENSE the milieu in which I grew up adopted the sense of duty of the highest classes, the sense of honour from the nobility, but without the hypocrisy that made it viable. And we had transformed the enforced grubbing and hard labour of the workers "beneath us", out of whose midst we had nevertheless once climbed, into an idea of application and industry, but without the explosions that temporarily destroyed all morality and duty.

Women constituted the coat of arms of all that, the becalmed figurehead, and I cursed it. Working-class women like Emilie enjoyed more freedom of movement, the freedom of the insignificant, than we, precious young ladies of the bourgeoisie, doomed to an existence as a human artistic bouquet: colourful, elegant and dust-free under a glass cover so as not to spoil our maidenly tint.

My way of escaping the vacuum consisted of reading and writing. Others lost themselves in their children or married an older rich man, in the hope of a premature widowhood and accompanying independence.

Some, those who had no other safety valve, competed for a starring role in the varied theatrical programme of hysteria, with its paralyses and limbs full of cramp, its monumental fainting fits and the deliriums which you can find in old psychological manuals, and which you can equally well see as a concise introduction to the dramaturgy of the muzzled femininity of my young days—a Sistine Chapel of bourgeois pathos. The slightly more acceptable variant consisted of chronic stomach ailments, migraine-related twilight situations and other maladies that required periods of isolation in partly or wholly darkened rooms, punctuated by cleansing rites with alternating hot and cold baths and compresses, powders, infusions and tinctures.

Even my mother could periodically abandon herself to these with a pleasure she herself did not recognize as such. Her periods assumed the character of litanies, full of self-pity and vengefulness. The calamity usually announced itself with hypersensitivity to children's voices and the tap of cutlery on plates. When she snapped at me or my brother that well-brought-up children never touch the porcelain of the dinner service with their knife or fork, everyone in the house knew what was what. In the kitchen Emilie shrugged her shoulders even higher than before, fearful of the fury that might descend on her. My father let out a resigned sigh. Edgard hit his head with his hand as if he had forgotten an important appointment and I tried to breathe as little as possible.

For the next few days it was as if my mother's body was sprouting countless fine tentacles. A network of ethereal threads stretched out around her and linked every nook and cranny in the house with her nervous system. The slightest movement was transmitted over that invisible system. Vibrations produced vibrations. Even turning a page in one of my picture books, though they were cut from reasonably stiff cardboard, penetrated to the boudoir next to the dining room, where my mother, supported by a geological formation of pillows, lay on the chaise longue, vibrating with anger.

"Child, use the carpet when you go upstairs. The car-pet! Has no one any respect for my eardrums here? Please, Edgard, do your mother a favour and don't trot through the house like a pack of dragoons. Put an old tea towel in the bottom of the washing-up basin, Emilie, I've asked you a hundred times…" And so on.

Gradually her tirades faded into muted, unarticulated lamentations. Her words seemed to crumble, throwing off their crust of consonants and as it were revealing their melted insides. Her hypersensitivity to sound had usually gone by then. The tentacles disengaged from things, slapping back onto her body like extended elastic and recreating it in an imploding universe of pain.

Emilie lugged up even more blankets and pillows, and with the slow body language of a tortoise shoved side tables over to the chaise longue, set out bottles, tubes, flacons, a basin of water, soap and white linen cloths. Meanwhile she had closed the blinds on the whole floor, banked up the fire in the antechamber below and had plonked us down like exiles in the armchairs.

"If the *patron* agrees, I can serve him and the little ones food down here for the time being," she whispered, and without waiting for an answer slunk off upstairs, into the twilight world.

Now and then muted sounds penetrated through to us, a vague groaning followed by the tripping of Emilie's padded slippers, "my cat's paws" she called them, over the parquet floor.

This situation did not usually last long. When I was small my father was in the habit of sending me out on reconnaissance after a day or two. He pushed me in through a chink when the door was ajar. In the dark I could only make out my mother

72

with difficulty, but I could hear her breath. Only when I moved closer could I distinguish her head, largely buried in soft pillows at the foot of a mountain range of blankets that swelled and shrank to the rhythm of her breath. If she turned to me and sleepily stretched out an arm towards me, and didn't turn away abruptly, submerging completely in the pillowslip, my father would know she was on the mend.

Twenty-four hours later she would arise from her linen cocoon. Emilie would pull up the blinds and wind up the clocks, my mother would smother me with kisses at breakfast, run her fingers teasingly through Edgard's blond locks and kiss my father on the forehead, the picture of good humour.

I am sure that her suffering was real. My God, if there is anything I have despised about the fact of being a woman, it's the monthly madhouse of my glands. But I wonder whether she did not partly transform her discomfort into a gentle but nonetheless throttling holding-hostage of my father, my brother, me and Emilie, who as the goblin-like servant of a malevolent queen interceded between the upper and lower world in our house, which closed round us like an oyster.

As soon as everything had calmed down our rooms breathed out audibly, and I did too, behind glass, on the veranda, in the completely walled-in back garden, where otherwise I roamed impatiently along the path, back and forth, back and forth, in the hope that I could hypnotically anaesthetize my yearning for room to breathe, for horizon.

And when I heard the schoolchildren passing behind the fence, exuberant at their few hours of freedom after lessons before they were expected back home, when I heard them swimming in the mild warmth of late spring days, I almost burst with anger. The slamming of the front door, after my brother had thrown off his satchel, had drunk milk in the kitchen and joined his pals outside, sounded to me like an affront. The fun they had, under the window of the room where in the evenings, when the light had lost its force, I was able to take some sun under my mother's watchful eye, aroused pure resentment in me.

I heard them egging each other on, exchanged playful blows. I eavesdropped on the galloping of their heels on the pavement when they set off to one of the pubs on the edge of town, on the banks of the river: establishments where I could only go when accompanied by my father, an uncle, sometimes my brother, and preferably on a Sunday, when the bourgeois aired their bridal bouquets, ordered beer and brawn with mustard and secretly eyed the waitresses.

I was sick with jealousy when Edgard came back from those outings with a Bacchanalian grin on his lips, the grin that forged a conspiratorial link between him and Emilie, and melted my mother's heart to such an extent that she cooed at his wettest jokes like any schoolgirl. If anything could make me even more furious, it was the slavishness of my own sex, the passivity with which they nestled in their shackles and let the reins be tightened and then from their wasp waists poured venom over any woman who did want to break out.

My mother excelled at this. She became the sullen idol I spat upon. The congealed version of a goddess with two forms, of which Emilie embodied the boiling dimension, the fury and ecstasy of womanhood which, when it comes down to it, respects no morality, negates all principles and casts us back into the glow of the melting pot.

These were the years under the sign of the Magna Mater, because the time called adolescence remains the most female season in a human life. Our qualities haven't yet caked solidly around us, and always, I am certain, a core in us remains white-hot and boiling. Its impulses influence the fluctuations of the magnetic field that I call our being, or our soul, or whatever—since words are only words, congealed screams.

In my schooldays, at the venerable institute of the Cistercian Sisters of the Holy Word, my sympathy, although I should rather say fascination, invariably focused on the largely invisible nuns in their godly termites' mound, which was divided by a high wall from the classrooms and covered playground. The young ladies who gave us instruction, young bourgeoises for whom marriage heralded the end of their career, seemed to me much more sterile than those black Fates, who in self-elected virginity glided over the immaculately polished tiles of their corridors with the rustle of canvas around their calves—the wing beats of the Holy Ghost, whom they worshipped in their chapel at dead of night, until in the first light of morning they prostrated themselves before the altar like scorched moths.

My mother thought it important to send me to a religious school. The belief in a supreme being was for her at best a form of edifying poetry, very useful in bringing up children, while for me the true God was the God behind the tabernacles, the totally silent scream between the lines of the Living Word, which made galaxies collide and drove chicks from their egg.

"Stop talking nonsense, child," she would snap at me if she were here with us. "There's nothing on high."

She regularly took little offerings to the nuns; sums of money, food, in May flowers from our garden, for the statue of the Virgin. Then she would converse for a while out of politeness with the sister in charge of guests in the parlour of the convent, sitting on one of the chairs that exuded the smell of furniture wax and were reflected a hundredfold by the copper of the flowerpot-holder and the old kitchen utensils on display. She treated the nuns with the respectful incomprehension she also reserved for doctors, whose knowledge she appreciated, but without the will to share in it. She seemed to find the finesses of the sacred as unappetizing as a view of the opened wall of an abdomen with an inflamed appendix throbbing in it.

If I look at the nuns through her eyes, at the portion of the cloister that I could see from my desk in the class, and the ghosts that shuffled past the pointed-arch windows every day at the same times, on their way to the chapel, I don't see a convent but a machine, a generator whose imponderable mechanism converted hymns, litanies and acclamations into a psychic gravity designed to keep morals and habits in their place.

I have always disliked the fearfulness attaching to every rite, although I know: a ritual without useless exactitude precisely loses its purpose. Behind this lurked the fear of the Egyptians, whose priests begged the sun god all night long to rise again from the kingdom of the dead, or the frightened cunning of the Incas and their attempts to anchor the heavenly disc to the sun stone, like a sheep on a chain, or like a child tries to prevent his mother leaving him by clinging to her skirts.

I don't know exactly how old I was when I suddenly began to suspect that the rituals were meant to keep in check a huge fear of the Word itself, God's Own Name, which there in that chapel had to coincide reassuringly with itself. The circular days of perpetual adoration, the perpetuum mobile of songs and invocations, yes, even the style of the holy in itself, suddenly seemed to be incantations meant to avoid the godhead disintegrating, or, as the sun will one day do, exploding and unleashing a storm of meanings gone adrift.

Wouldn't that be a spectacle? And how would it feel to dissolve in that explosion, and never, never again be able to be completely expressed?

II

WHEN I CAN'T get to sleep, I like looking outside. I ask Rachida before she goes not to close the curtain over the window next to my bed. I want to see the teams of cleaners who work in the middle of the night in the offices on the other side of the water: the olive-coloured worker bees—veiled girls, young men with raven-black hair in light-blue smocks. I like following those kids as they go from floor to floor and make draughtsboard patterns of light and dark slide across the front of the building. In honeycombs of light they dust, scrub floors, empty waste-paper baskets, soap window glass and rub it dry, and I receive the impersonal blessing of their work as a sacrament. At such moments I have the feeling that I am calm enough to be able to survey the splendour of the earth as it is: not beautiful or ugly, but living and dying, pulsating in all its plants and animals.

I like the few hours of desolation at the crack of dawn, the emptiness and the first birds, which for a moment don't have to share the silence with anyone, before the cars drive under the crowns of the trees into the multi-storey car park with glowing brake lights. I like listening to the rumble of the first trains, which at this early hour penetrates far into the centre of town, until the hubbub of life getting under way drowns it out: the buses, trams, cyclists, the footsteps of clusters of schoolchildren, in whose satchels pens or pencils are rattling to the cadence of their tread on the pavement—the glorious everydayness of the world and its banal, but oh-so-vital peace.

*

Then I wait till the bell goes downstairs, the signal Rachida gives me to let me know she's in the house. It may be the other one. I can tell from the ring what awaits me. The other one doesn't so much ring as send a shrill reproach upstairs. Then I pretend to be asleep, squeeze a half-hour's freedom from the night, pull the blankets in a cocoon round my bones and sulk, and realize I'm like my mother, when she was young, when every month her tissues rang the hormonal alarm bell. I grant her those little resurrections now more than I used to.

If it takes a while before I hear someone coming upstairs, then I'm sure it's Rachida who will wake me. Although she knows full well that I've been awake for ages and don't really need to be woken.

I don't want her to find me asleep. I want to say good morning to her. One day she'll knock and there'll be no reply. I'm far too old for an illness that drags on, so know what's in store for me. Cerebral haemorrhage. Heart attack. She always laughs when I say it, but I know why it takes a while before she comes upstairs. First she takes her coat off and puts her apron on, but when she comes in in a moment, you must pay attention to her coiffure. There won't be a hair out of place. She takes time to brush her long black hair. In front of the mirror in the hall she takes her hair in one hand and brushes it firmly and then arranges it over her shoulders again with the back of her hand, first over one, then over the other—that earthy, oh-so-earthy gesture. That's how I imagine it at least: I've never seen her do it, and I haven't been downstairs for ages, but I know she wants to look nice, in case I should be dead in bed or in the chair already with the beginnings of rigor mortis, with the curtains drawn, because I always ask her to draw them in the afternoon.

Unlike in the past, I dislike the pedestrian light between twelve and four. Grey and twilight suit me better these days, or the sheen of the still-unblemished morning.

I like seeing how she is preoccupied with her work, the sacred calm that emanates from her concentration when she reveals the room and me to the day. While I breakfast in bed, she takes a dress or a number of skirts and blouses out of the wardrobe, always about three so that I can choose, and when I have made my choice she looks in the drawers and boxes on the dressing table for the earrings and necklace that go with them, because "being old, Mrs Helena," she says, "is not a disease with us".

The suppleness of her fingers especially can delight me. As one gets older the days increasingly assume the character of light-footed barbarities, peevish conspiracies against the liturgy of habit, in which the body becomes more and more hopelessly entangled. Her dexterity is like a consecration. The way she picks the earrings out of the velvet of their boxes, fishes the necklace out of the box and runs it over the palm of her hand to smooth out any kinks or knots—and I see myself again, on afternoons that are long ago now, going into my mother's dressing room and, in the line of light that the half-open top curtains cast over the dressing table, pulling open the drawer of the chest in which she keeps her jewels, and the way that light at the bottom of that drawer, in one of the boxes, the lid of which has shifted slightly, makes a necklace slumbering there glitter with the treacherous splendour of a poisonous snake.

*

I find it a shame that I can't see her at work when she is preparing lunch in the kitchen, how she peels onions, elicits baroque curly peel from potatoes, cuts carrots, chops meat, just as Emilie, in her brightly lit quarters in the basement, used to carry out her own sacrifices, or the maids in the house in France around the steaming oven set in motion a ballet of spoons and skimmers and guards, which unleashed its own music—and I wonder whether, who knows, she briefly interrupts her work without thinking in order to wipe her hands on her apron, a vision which invariably filled me with a strange ecstasy.

As time goes on I miss such ostensibly insignificant details of those who are no longer there. The thousands of tokens of the camaraderie or armed truce we enter into daily with life increasingly fill me with emotion. Usually I only notice them when they have died away for ever and leave me with the feeling that a whole language has been struck dumb, the complete vocabulary with which a person closes a book or arranges a dinner service like no one before or after them; or the way my husband used to slip out of the sheets beside me and run to the bathroom in the chill of the morning, pee standing up and produce a powerful stream because he knew it gave me childish pleasure, and then come back in in his boyish naked-ness, with—forgive the word, Rachida—his prick at half mast between his thighs, and finally eased his bum into his trousers and with one hand swept the change on the bedside table into his other hand.

I didn't venerate those things enough. I didn't anoint them enough. I betrayed the mysticism of their everyday ordinari-ness. I just hope it isn't one of the thoughts that I speak out loud by mistake, which has been happening to me more and more often recently.

She didn't hear anything. First she took away the tray with the remains of my breakfast and subjected me tactfully to the ritual of defecation and cleaning, then put me on the chair next to the bed and now she is buttoning my blouse. As she does so, she bends slightly forward, so that were are almost looking each other in the eye, but she focuses on her fingers, which squeeze the small, mother-of-pearl-covered buttons into the buttonholes.

"And when I beheld, lo, the sinews and the flesh came upon them, and the skin covered them above: but there was no breath in them."

"What was that, Mrs Helena?"

"Nothing, child."

She has almost finished. "Is that not a sight to behold?"

She smiles without looking up.

Her fingers rustle under my collar, against my throat.

"Those who can behold everything go mad, Mrs Helena."

The day my brother died I knew as soon as she knocked, and actually even before. She had only just started working for me. I had heard the telephone ring downstairs. Almost no one called any more. She had answered, it took a long time. She had taken off her apron. She was wearing that long, dark-brown blouse I had seen her in often and underneath her black trousers. Instead of the wooden-soled slippers she usually wore at work, she had put on respectable footwear, mules. Her veil, which she usually wore round her neck like a wide shawl, hung loose over her hair with its dead-straight central parting.

She knocked, came in, closed the door behind her and stayed some distance away from the bed: "Your brother Mr Edgard, Mrs Helena…"

I didn't let her finish. "So the bastard's gone."

I saw her go pale.

"Yes, ma'am…"

A month or two previously he came to visit for the last time. As usual he climbed the stairs in full regalia, or rather he hoisted himself up a step at a time by the banister, with all the accoutrements befitting a gentleman of his class, with the weight of his years in his made-to-measure but by now fairly baggy suit, and especially that still-elegant but perfectly useless walking stick under his arm.

The ascent took more time each week. After the death of my husband I offered to share a house with him on various occasions. What was the point of us each occupying a huge place, and in his case such a way out of town, in that admittedly extremely convenient property surrounded by a large garden, where the windows admitted charming light reflected by the river water, and where on the carpets and Kelims in the stairwell, the library, the drawing rooms a discretion shod in the softest leather constantly crept across the floors behind my back when I was still able to visit him?

He needed a quarter of an hour to get his breath back, and sat in his chair gasping and clearing his throat, the walking stick against the arm. The other stick, the one he actually used, an aluminium shaft with a rubber cap on the bottom, rested between his legs.

86

Rachida brought the coffee, thank God the nice set, on the tray with the silver. Not the plastic mugs that the other, that golem, digs out of the kitchen cupboard to give me the feeling that I'm a child who spills everything.

"Is Mr Edgard well?" she had asked, carefree as always while she put the cups on the drawing-room table, the jug of cream and the sugar.

"I'm like the donkeys, child. Their legs wear out first too, it seems."

He had poured a dash of cream in his coffee. As he stirred it, he said: "It's about time there was an end to it, if you ask me."

Only when I felt Rachida taking my glasses off my nose to dry the lenses and I, after she had put my glasses back on, saw my brother looking into his cup in embarrassment, did it dawn on me that I must have called out and cried.

My hands were trembling. I saw Rachida's helplessness, she was looking furiously for a single light-hearted sentence to break the embarrassed silence, and it went right through my heart.

Finally she went away.

My brother waited till she had left the room, got up and came over to me. As usual he tried to put his fingers under my chin so that I would look up, but I turned away and stared outside while he cursed my stubbornness.

"I don't know, Hélène," he sighed, "what *matière* you're made of inside…"

Matière, I thought, how frivolous. But I said: "Concrete."

A few weeks later came the news that he had broken a hip and was in the hospital with a prosthesis. Later, that he was to move into a boarding house. I wondered who had arranged that for him.

A courier delivered a package. Inside were a set of keys and a note with the pre-printed heading *house of evening pleasures*—how deep can you fall, I thought.

"I'm sorry, my little gazelle, but I don't think I'll be returning to my house," he wrote. "Keep the spare keys, you never know whether you'll need them one day…"

I saw the question burning on Rachida's tongue, whether I shouldn't visit him. I sensed her disappointment, but I very much appreciated the fact that she remained silent.

My brother always cultivated a form of impermanence, a quality that made all contexts slide off him. He shrouded himself in a sniggering secrecy that reminded me just too much of a cult, and his death did not really put an end to his impermanence. It simply became absolute. I mourn for him by polishing up his mysteries.

I never knew which of the young men who regularly hung about in his house, even when he was well into old age, slept with him. Who were lovers and who were not, as far as that distinction could be made. As time went on they looked younger and younger, though they remained constantly between their mid-twenties and about thirty-five, but he himself naturally got older. They were more like symbols than people of flesh and blood. Radiant emblems of youthfulness, snooty young eels in their smart clothes, their collars starched so razor-sharp that they constituted a danger to their carotid artery, which I could see beating under their tender skin when they were introduced to me.

Nervous and polite to the point of hysteria, meticulously coiffured and manicured, at family gatherings or dinners they put their feet under the table and were silent, longing all too visibly for invisibility, having been first announced "as a friend of Edgard's"—pronounced with all too audible quotation marks.

I wondered which of them he could stand to have with him at night, whom he admitted to his sleep and whether during their slumber they let their fingers wander to the scar on the sleeping trunk half under, half next to theirs, instinctively in search of the vein, the fracture, the line of morbid growth which ran from his hip, via his abdomen and his ribcage, to below his right shoulder, thank God the right side of his body. It looked like a careless line of welding or an aerial photo of a mountain chain. I thought it would feel scabby, dry and crumbly, but when he once allowed me to touch it, it gave way, warm and rubbery under my fingertips. I was frightened of hurting him, but he said: "Doesn't matter, can't feel a thing there."

Except on stormy days, the sultry days, the days when summer seemed about to tip over into autumn. Then he had the bath filled with cold water and stretched out in it because the cold numbed the phantom pain that shot through that long vein. I wonder if his "friends" kept him company, dried his back, helped him into his dressing gown afterwards. They seemed more like tasty morsels, titbits that his tongue longed for when he was satiated with coarser fare.

There must have been others, of whom I caught no more than a glimpse. A more or less regular supply of men who were just too far "beneath" us on the ladder to let them loose at parties without turning the aura of secrecy that always surrounded him into a public scandal. Men who didn't wear hats, but caps, and suits that more or less screamed that they were reserved for Sundays or special occasions, intended to last for years without wearing out.

I think he liked the difference, the distance, the interval, that never quite bridgeable gap between their world and his, that he sought them out for the scarce moments of complete brotherliness, more raw and pure than his more presentable boyfriends.

Whatever the case, he never wanted to move house and never suggested that I come and live with him.

"My little gazelle," he laughed. "You have your books, I have my bad boys."

He must have immersed himself in their lives and bodies, just as I could become completely absorbed by what my mother called "my reading matter", a term I found derogatory enough, and even more when she used it. He had her mouth too, that wonderful, voluptuous mouth, with which she did not so much pronounce words as bid them a melancholy farewell. Her majestic French clothed itself with her lips like a boa. Whenever I think of my brother I hear her talking again, and vice versa, when I call my mother's speech to mind, I am reminded of my brother—of his own berry mouth, the mouth of a catamite.

She found him less difficult to deal with because of course she recognized less of herself in him. But he was also a man. From a young age he enjoyed freedoms I could only dream about, but my mother always loved him more than me. I was never jealous about it. I got to know only too well the latent resentment that can exist between mothers and daughters. You have to be a woman to see through another woman. And if that other woman happens to be your own daughter the contempt proves chilliest of all, since you are looking into yourself. For my mother even innocence was a trick, and I'm not a jot better. I myself hated my daughter because she existed and was who she was, and now she is dead I hate her because she's dead. So I accuse even chance of being an accomplice, because I call children who die before their parents greedy. I was furious when my daughter died, with hatred and misery.

I always thought that I was the only woman in Edgard's life, at least the only woman with whom he shared an intimacy which perhaps went further than that between a wife and her husband, because she respected secrets and had little need for mutual confessions, and because the body did not stand between us as a gigantic kink in the cable. We did not immerse our demons in the holy-water fonts of language; we understood each other without words. That was the fantasy where I housed our understanding.

When one day he confided to me that he *had* known women, at least one, I felt almost deceived and I still don't know why he suddenly told me.

"And did I know her?"

He nodded.

I started running through my friends, reeled off the names of cousins, second cousins and aunts, and even great-aunts, whom I didn't think I could possibly suspect of such frivolities.

"You're too much among the roses and carnations, my little gazelle. You're forgetting in a manner of speaking the bunch of wild flowers…"

I must have stared at him uncomprehendingly, because he continued. "Do I have to draw you a picture, Hélène?"

When it dawned on me, I went deep red. "Bastard," I stammered.

"She was the boss. She gave the sign, Sis. If she came home and didn't pull my bedroom door shut as she passed, on her way to her cubby hole upstairs, I knew she was"— he took my hand in his—"*pour parler diplomatiquement*, she was '*disponible*'."

"I wonder what Mama would have done, if she'd known."

"Papa knew. Or at least something. One day he gave me a talking-to about it, down in the front room. You know that kind of conversation. A man is a man and will always remain so. That there are 'certain solutions', but you had to be careful because not all those 'remedies' were meticulous about hygiene. And there were alternatives, more discreet, *comme on dit* a bit closer to home, a lot cheaper and with less of a risk of '*certaines misères*'... So he knew."

"She must have known too, Edgard. She was always a restless sleeper."

He shrugged his shoulders. "Perhaps, perhaps not."

I was stunned. My father, the man who called me his little girl, his positive little princess, the apple of his eye, his heart-stealer, and my father who gave his son advice to take good care what sexual washtub he dunked his sensitive organ into in order to unload his excess spunk, so as not, let's call a spade a spade, to catch—take a deep breath, Rachida—the clap or the pox...

I disliked the way he enjoyed telling me about his escapades. I could see that from the light-footed tread with which he left my house afterwards, and the way, as he walked through the front garden to the street, that he cheerfully laid his walking stick on his shoulder like a sword or a rifle.

No, he didn't need to draw a picture. I did that for myself, with an uncomfortable feeling of guilt because I dared imagine it, a hand still clutches my throat when I recall the scene. I don't know if it's jealousy, and, if it is, at which of the two of them it is directed: Emilie, naked on her bed, her hair undoubtedly in thick cascades of lava flows on her pillow, a fleshy, maternal image, a drunk, steaming, woman-shaped stain; or my brother, fifteen or sixteen years old, half man, half child, squeezing his way between her thighs, letting his arse be grasped by her fists and fastening on her nipples.

I try to suppress the image. I can't bear its incestuous reticence, the more or less obscene idyll that my imagination makes of it: she putting him to her breast like a son and he shooting his come into her like a lover, and then arising from her tissues unmanned: a worm, an emptied father, melted Icarus, who had penetrated too close to the primordial formlessness of the female.

He liked showing off his body, to me too, in his room, after swimming or rowing, while he apparently casually admired himself in the mirror but equally relished my own, not even hidden adoration.

Women don't have a body, Rachida child. We are walking yolk sacs that, as if by a miracle, push male bodies out of our tissues, imbued with an almost mathematical clarity, a Euclidean perfection, satiated in every fibre with directness and sharp concentration—while I, I am the sea, and you too and all women. Sandbanks on which sons and lovers are shipwrecked. Strips of mud of the kind that a man can only release himself from by leaving one of his boots behind.

My brother on the other hand was my demigod, fortuitously produced by, I felt to their own consternation, an accidentally passionate copulation of a rich French farmer's daughter and a quite wealthy Flemish dealer in copperware, basic kitchen utensils, matches and handmade nails.

He had straw-blond hair when he was young, in thick, almost chiselled curls. He had eyes of a blue you would have thought impossible, and blond lashes, and from about the age of fifteen the endearing beginnings of a moustache, a milk-white nimbus on his upper lip.

I saw how my mother silently idolized him. She could look at him as he ate, played a bored tune on the piano or sat reading, with a satisfaction not entirely devoid of sensuality. I saw how she concluded with satisfaction that he had a good character, that a balanced young man seemed to be slowly emerging from his puppy fat, of more than average intelligence, and socially with enough suppleness to ensure him an interesting bride sooner or later—an expectation she never relinquished and which over the years went stale in her breast and became a resigned disappointment.

When he was a young man, the plus fours and sweaters with their deep V-necks, the sporting style that came across from England after the war, seemed to have been waiting for his limbs. We were no longer swathed in the dark clothes of those who had brought us up, suiting their sombre and cluttered interiors, with their rigid timetables and clockwork habits. We wore white, childish white. We were mad about light-footed patterns in pastel shades on light materials, the christening clothes of a new age. Their loose cut seemed perfectly suited to trips in the car, which freed us from the rectilinear railway and allowed us to follow meandering routes through a land that was licking its wounds.

"It sounds dreadful," I said to him one day. "But actually the war is the best thing that ever happened to me."

We were sitting upstairs in this room by the window. Our chairs were more or less opposite each other, in the bay window. My daughter, whose godfather he was, was playing at our feet with her blocks, and as usual it annoyed me that she never built towers with them, but, as an omen of the cobalt-blue hatred she would later arouse in me, arranged them with the same coloured side upward in boring squares on the parquet floor.

He leant over slightly and brought his lips close to my ear. "Do you know what, my little gazelle?" he whispered. "Me too."

WHEN HE HAD to take me out for a walk, he was generally a lot less fastidious in his choice of routes than my father. Our walks took us through more neighbourhoods and districts than usual: areas where in street after street one parade of introverted gables followed another. Our town was a spongy tissue of alleys and passages, little squares, shady steps under footbridges over which monks must have once glided from one quadrangle to another, or bridges under which dawdled the water of the two rivers, which did not so much converge as fall asleep in each other's arms in our town. You could easily wander its passageways for half a day, crossing the world every square kilometre, and lose all sense of direction. Most of those quarters were linked by a few streets to the rest of the town, which seemed to have been washed in loose fragments on the islets between the countless branches of the river.

We liked to leave our route to chance. I think my brother also liked imagining himself detached from all context as we walked through the streets, over the cobbles, gleaming with precipitation, under roof lines that were lost in the clouds, while we listened to the cadence of our heels on the stones, turned into an alley at random here, retraced our steps there to take a different route. Often we were the only living souls who seemed to venture outside.

Sometimes a gothic gateway detached itself from the fog, an arch crowned by cornucopias in clay or flamboyant stones. Elsewhere, squeezed in between two houses, the remains of a buttress suggested the existence, once, of a chapel or a church, the house of worship of an ancient guild or monastic order, swept away by the Iconoclastic Fury or the Revolution, or simply by a fallen candelabra. Although we never pointed out to each other what struck us, I knew that my brother looked at those fragments as I did; and I also think, looking back, that not only for me but also for him they were much more than purely arbitrary wanderings, but were definitions of space—our own space.

In the shadow of the huge chimneys that towered above the factory buildings round the new harbour, we could imagine ourselves travellers through a forest of prehistoric trees, or, according to our whim, suddenly surrounded by a Forum Romanum that had set down its rows of columns amid our northern step gables and saddle roofs. In the courtyards at the foot of those high, cavernous structures there was always more life to be detected, summer or winter, wet or dry, than in the better districts near the heart of town. The closer you came to the squares and parks of the centre, the more reserved and aware of their façades the buildings became—while on the threshold of those hovels on the outskirts of town, resting more against each other than on their foundations, there were always children under the nodding rooflines and gouty walls playing with a top or bobbin, or crouched together whispering like guinea pigs in an open doorway, from where the smell of boiling potatoes or buttermilk floated into the street.

Through those areas, where my father would never have ventured with me, even when they were quiet and deserted, a restlessness also roamed that I can only describe as tentacular: the rustle of antennae, jaw segments or legs that you could listen to on calm days around large anthills in pine woods.

Here a kind of humanity survived that "our kind" regarded as a more or less amorphous mass, useful as a worker-ant colony, feared as a potential cause of pandemonium: the army of insects that had far too many children and fortunately buried most of them almost immediately afterwards. In the mornings swallowed up by the factory gates at the crack of dawn, and there, behind those walls, beneath the chimneys and their crowns of smoke, they knotted thread to thread, crept between the equally insect-like rattling spinning machines and looms, and in the evenings got drunk, fought out disputes and settled feuds. But in the dark it still provided our fathers and brothers and sons with their share of tarts, and in daylight it supplied our households with linen maids, kitchen maids and laundry maids, and maids of all work—at least if they could be extricated early from the those alleyways, preferably as children, before the dirt had penetrated their soul, or before socialists and other rabble had filled them with too much knowledge and hunger, especially hunger.

My wrists are getting stiff. Rachida, child, bring me some fresh tea and rub my hands warm. You must know those districts better than I do. In my later years I asked my daughter to take me on trips through town in the car. My legs were already too bad even to walk to the tram stop.

I remember the children playing on the pavement, as lively and rowdy as when I was actually a child myself. They squatted on the kerbs, intoxicated by a total sadness, as only children can abandon themselves to a melancholy which cannot, yet, be measured out in the liqueur glasses of our words.

From the doorways and open windows on mild days smoky kitchen smells still drifted out, not of potatoes or milk, but spicier, more piquant aromas. Spicy and piquant as the conversations that drifted out into the street with the smells—women's voices, hand-clapping, everything was as full of life as it used to be, nylon summer jackets, and shopping bags that swayed above the pavement slabs next to bare ankles. In the pubs the men still hung around the bar, although less beer was served, and I remember a chubby chap coming waddling out of one of those pubs, with the most beatific smile on his coarse face that I had seen for ages, and opening his arms wide, looking up at the sun, and saying with a laugh, "Türkiye. Türkiye, madam. In Türkiye always so warm."

"But Mrs Helena. I'm Moroccan," she laughs in alarm, Rachida, and I reassure her: "I know, child, I know…"

When we walked past under the fortress-like walls of those factories, we could hear the machines out in the street. The hissing of valves letting off steam, sirens that marked an end or a beginning. The roar of engines. The tapping, the clanking, the universal rattling. But the town was so fragmented that scarcely a couple of bends farther on a sober gatehouse hid a different microcosm. Perhaps frenetic bustle prevailed there, but a lot quieter and more minuscule: the buzzing of God's worker bees. How unreal to suddenly walk there under the treetops without a breath of wind, dripping in the lifting fog, and to hear deep snorting and grass being pulled out of firm ground, and jaws that chewed it all up and to see the shoulders of cows' bodies resting under a deciduous tree; ruminating, ruminating, with a touch of nirvana in their pupils—and then to hear the clocks in the houses around the meadow striking the hour.

Elsewhere too there was the sound of carillons. Despite iconoclastic furies and other disasters there were enough monasteries and abbeys along the waterways of our town to shake out sackfuls of bell-ringing over the roofs at set times. It was reminiscent of the ethereal aerial combat of songbirds at dawn, the daily dividing-up of the firmament. And it was quite possible that the bells above the churches and convents were also doing battle, not with each other, but with the shrill whistle of the locomotives or the wailing factory siren, a music that threatened to disrupt the precious circular melodies of the divine.

I could try out all my speculations quite freely on Edgard. I believe he took pleasure in listening to me, amused by my increasing breathlessness—unlike my mother. Whenever during the gatherings of her sewing group I gave myself over aloud to my reflections, she usually said firstly that she couldn't make head or tail of the nonsense I was coming out with, which of course pleased me, and secondly that I wasn't allowed to philosophize until I was better at embroidery. According to her it was the same thing. In both cases there was a beautiful pattern and I simply made a mess.

For my mother everything revolved around substance. While substance, Rachida my girl, get this clear, is the least interesting thing about a person, an impure ore like any other; and nothing astonished me so much as the industry of the blast furnaces and the production lines for the assembly of the new man in the decades after the war.

Everything to do with what was holy was cyclical in those days. A symbolic representation of the unchanging quite simply has to bite its own tail if it is to evoke eternity. Even my brother and I unconsciously adjusted our pace when we walked through the narrow streets of that *béguinage*, arm in arm past the houses with the names of saints on their doors. In that closed universe even simple walking took on the character of worship.

The female inhabitants of this mysterious enclave rarely showed themselves even within the shelter of their walls. Yet there were places where high windows let in an abundance of light, and there you could sometimes see them at work, at first sight as still as the statues of the saints with which they seemed to surround themselves everywhere. With their heads in white linen wimples, so fine that they almost resembled pieces of milk-white mist, they bent over the pincushions on their laps, faces smoothed by deep concentration, and appeared to regard with detached amazement the work of their own hands, which, as still as the rest of their figures remained, juggled with bobbins of yarn, moved pins brightly and went on juggling.

Slowly their work gave birth to something best compared to what a spider would produce as a web, if it were suddenly seized by artistic pretensions: a gossamer-thin tissue that expressed, not only in every thread but most of all where those threads were absent, the essence of mysticism, and as such represented one of the greatest realizations of the artistic genius of humankind.

*

Nowhere, except perhaps in poetry and very occasionally in music, have I experienced a more intimate interweaving of something with nothing than in the lacework that there in the *béguinages* spilt from the ladies' pincushions and descended in milk-white waterfalls to the woven baskets at their feet, flowed over the edge and fanned out across the floorboards, so that, in particular on days of very thick fog, those rooms, where only the gentle ticking of the bobbins could be heard, seemed to me nothing less than the secret maternity wards of our national mist.

Compared with this scholastic finesse of needle and thread, the sewing work of my mother and her friends represented little more than clumsy popular devotion, but more especially it seemed to me only logical that Belgium was not a country of embroidery or knitwear, but of lace. In a place where the art of lacking was practised so exuberantly and ubiquitously, something like Belgium was bound to be born sooner or later: a nation that was constantly playing on the fringes of its own emptiness, just as all of us, driven by our soul, our most intimate vacuum, have continually to knit ourselves together.

That was more or less the conclusion of our historians. They filled bulky volumes with explanations for the creation of our fatherland, wedged between north and south, east and west: a region whose specific feature was mainly the absence of specific features, where different spheres of influence operated as capriciously as the high- and low-pressure areas in their hopeless struggle in the sky above our heads. Those learned gentlemen usually came to the conclusion that if Belgium had not been invented, someone would have had to discover it.

*

"Helena, child, my little gazelle," laughed my brother after a while. "Your mental gymnastics always make me thirsty. Shall we have a drink somewhere?"

We usually went to the cafés around one of the stations, never to the establishments which of course he only frequented when the night gave the streets a salutary anonymity. It did us good to feel our tiredness, the pain in our legs from the long walk, and we sank contentedly onto one of the terraces to be able to sit and absorb the life around the station square.

We liked the fragmentary nature of our home town, because we wanted to be fragmentary ourselves, free of the corsets into which the older generation wanted to force us, and I wonder why I should glue the pieces together here. In the museums, where Edgard and I sometimes sheltered from an unexpected cloudburst, the mouth or wing of a seraph on a shard of a stained-glass window from the Middle Ages evoked its figure more tangibly than if the angel had arisen full-length in front of us, high in the transept of the cathedral, where a stone or cannon shot had shattered it.

Why should it be different with people, or with the words that I see clinging together here with some disgust? It is as if I have never been able to shake off my mother's admonition that I was hopeless at needlework. A firm tissue laces itself as if automatically to the pincushion of this page. I see my thoughts take the form of sentence constructions that accommodate an enervating abundance of furniture, curtaining and supporting cushions like the stuffed interiors in which I grew up. Even the voices of my father, my mother, my brother and myself start speaking again as we thought we should speak to each other: with an eloquence that betrayed how closely we listened to ourselves.

Maintenir was the key concept of our class. We didn't have conversations in those days, cultured people maintained them. We didn't give dinner parties, we maintained a table. We did not enjoy reading, we maintained our knowledge of literature. We didn't have friendships, but formed affectionate attachments, maintained the best relations, strengthened connections; we maintained, we maintained and we told ourselves that this was in no way a duty, or a mission, or even a choice. It was quite simply a fact that with the deaf and dumb inexorability of gravity worked equally on all things at once.

And from all that *maintenir* the whole edifice of civilization rose up almost as a matter of course, as natural and unconsidered as the wax that honey bees secrete, and of which their honeycombs are made. Although without the diligence of our own class, we thought, this fine-meshed labyrinth of wrought iron and plate glass, all that architectural know-how, would naturally never have got off the ground. We regarded ourselves without any hesitation as the salutary middle way. Without us the world could only go under in the anarchistic tumult of the mass below us, or evaporate in the drawl of nobility and old money in the stratosphere above—we kept things in balance.

"So God, if I've got it straight," laughed my brother, when I talked to him about my personal theodicy over a glass of mint water, "has actually created the ideal thermostat in the bourgeois."

I laughed heartily with him.

*

However butterfly-light and refined that vanished world considered itself, it had a weight. It weighed on me and on everyone. Everywhere, whether we want to or not, we always carry a whole globe on our shoulders. And, just as in my childhood I regularly visited our basement kitchen to find a less artificial dimension of life in Emilie, our maid, not least in her rough dialect, which, I felt, sounded "more real" than our language, so almost everyone longed, secretly or not, for a form of release from the sophisticated lacework that we at the same time "maintained".

There was a hidden thirst for some form or other of ritual laxative: a collective cleansing that would greatly benefit the metabolism of our civilization. We obviously had to remind ourselves at regular intervals that, all things considered, we remained apes with clothes on, who in a circus of our own making jumped through hoops and threatened to forget that we were basically swinging on creepers and eating bananas. That would greatly improve our health, though admittedly we lost sight of the fact that a person, besides being too sick, can sometimes turn out healthier than is good for him.

Be that as it may, I liked the evening hours, especially in early summer, when the blue turning to purple moved in from east to west behind the increasingly elongated sunset, and in the cafés and restaurants around the station the lights were turned on, while it was not yet completely dark outside—the moment when the pigeons go to sleep and the bats wake up. The city became an area of transition, a twilight zone on the unstable boundary between day and night. The bow was a little less taut, the yoke lifted from the shoulders.

*

"And soon the minister will put his nightcap on," I said to my brother as we both sipped our supposedly well-earned refreshment. "And the market-stall lady, and the bishop and the greengrocer. And then the curtain will fall, and the rest is silence."

My brother was silent, but under his nose his milky moustache went to and fro in a lively way on his top lip, an expression of my father's which he must have noticed and which he may have been deliberately imitating. He liked to make an impression of worldly wisdom on me. When I said something, I saw him thinking and running through a large number of possible answers in his head—for or against, usually against.

He brought his glass to his lips, drank a mouthful and looked out over the square in front of the station, where the last street trader was loading his wares onto a handcart, and sniggered without looking at me. "Dear girl, dear girl," he chortled. "Either your eyes are full of shit, or you don't get out enough. When it gets dark is when the show starts."

He knew more parts of town, more layers and hemispheres than I and perhaps my mother. He was probably less familiar with the establishments that seldom advertised themselves as such on the outside, but behind their closed fronts hid a world of abundant plush, subdued red lighting, intimate boudoirs and painted girls, than with the meat market, which at once more and less visibly took place around the kiosk in the town park, in the vicinity of certain urinals or in certain cafés where an unwritten code of behaviour, facial expressions and phrases gave a double meaning to everything said or not said.

Later, after the war, he would point it out to me as we walked arm in arm through the park. What to look out for. What the signals were. Ways of hanging about. All too furtive glances. Where you sat down, on what bench and how.

I don't know if he told me everything. Perhaps he sometimes pulled my leg, so that in almost every gesture, every detail of clothing I suspected a fascinating iconography of male lust.

"The advantage of the war," he said to me one day, "is that there's always enough meat to be had nowadays." We had sat down on the bench near one of the smaller ponds in the park. He still found it difficult to walk. For the time being long walks were out.

The "meat" in question had gathered on the other side of the pond, on the shadier benches under the trees. It was getting on for evening, a twilit evening in late spring, hesitating between winter and summer. Soon it would become too cool to sit still.

Much battered flesh. Armless or legless. On crutches or, like my brother, forced to use a walking stick, whether or not permanently. Some of them looked very young. With the only hand he had left, a chap who I think was my age, in his early twenties, a flare of straw-blond hair in the blue shadow, was rolling tobacco in a cigarette paper that he pressed tight with a lively interplay of his fingers, brought to his mouth, moistened, pressed again and—it was almost like juggling—rolled over his thigh for a moment with his palm, and put to his lips again. Then, again with fingers like a busy spider, he dug a match out of a box in his coat pocket. Only when he lifted his leg and scraped the match over the sole of his shoe to light it, did I see from the folds in his other trouser leg that he had a wooden leg. He brought the flame to his cigarette, sucked it into the tobacco, and leant back while he simultaneously exhaled a first cloud of smoke and extinguished the match by waving his fingers.

"Poor devil…" I said.

"He's one of the lucky ones," was the reaction of my brother, who like me had sat and observed the whole scene.

I thought that by the less fortunate he meant the dead. But he shook his head and said. "That's something else. Dead is dead. They have wounds. They can blame their misfortune, strange enough perhaps, on the arm or leg they are missing. Or on their scars, like"—he smiled faintly—"this old horse here next to you."

He shifted position. Planted his walking stick deeper in the gravel and leant on it with both hands, presumably to take the weight off his trunk a little. He gave a subdued groan. "Never thought pain could be a blessing, my little gazelle. The others, who supposedly have nothing wrong with them, they're real poor devils. They never get the bombs out of their body."

It got chilly. He wanted to get up. The blond chap on the other side of the pond had smoked his cigarette and ground out the glowing end under his one shoe sole.

As I helped my brother up, I saw them exchange a glance.

The chap sent him a smile, broad and long enough to call ambiguous. I was gradually beginning to crack the code.

"You can have a prize if you want," I said.

"Always," grinned my brother, and offered me his arm.

III

WAR WAS IN THE DAYS when my body swelled up and ripe was one of the words that I stored in what I imagined as a biscuit barrel in my head: a play memory that housed the last remnants of my children's verses, alongside the words that mainly fascinated me since they permanently resisted the demon of my curiosity. Repeat any word for long enough and sooner or later it will unwrap itself from all its connotations, and stand before us, threatening in its naked mystery, but "war" had that quality automatically. It appeared to me now too light, then too weak. Although the sound suggested something gigantic, it seemed at the same time as light as a feather: in itself immense, but too lacking in density of composition to attract a clear meaning. Or on the other hand it appeared a word of infinite weight, a sound-shaped black hole that sucked in all thoughts in order to swallow them up as definitions of its unquenchable self.

In that first year the war seemed something wonderful, the heartbeat of a great event that sounded in all things. I could feel the roar of the gun barrels vibrate through my midriff like pressure waves, and saw the clouds of dust hanging over the fields when I peered out of the attic windows in the summer house in France, towards the land of Artois—my beloved Artois, with its rolling fields of grain, spread out between the wooded banks like ever larger sheets, the more dazzling as the stalks ripened, and the roads that meandered half buried through the fields. You could trace their line in the landscape from the hedges bordering them and the trees towering over them. You could tell from the clouds of dust where the soldiers who were heading for the front were.

When I was allowed by my uncle, my mother's older brother, to use the telescope, which stood up in the attic under a tarpaulin, I could see in those clouds of dust, in places where the roads came up to the same height as the fields, lances reflecting the sunlight, rifle barrels as fine as needles gleaming above a mass of figures marching over the cobbles, or the bustling horses' hooves of the cavalry, and that dust they dragged behind them like a threadbare veil.

Sometimes the horses were pulling heavy artillery, which from the undergrowth fired short bursts of light at me and left green spots on my retina.

"Look closely," said my uncle. "There goes history," and with a sigh he added: "For the umpteenth time."

He was holding the tarpaulin in both hands, ready to drape it quickly back over the telescope. It was a slightly suspicious instrument in times when everyone was suddenly seeing spies everywhere, but I looked through it at length and excitedly, at the hamlets with their ramparts of trees, above which the spire of the church scarcely rose, at the drinking pools for livestock and the duck ponds, and the roofs of the surrounding farms behind fringes of elder and ash, and again I sought out the great river of men, horses, cannon and rifles, the caravan of dust above the deep green and yellow of summer—and it was as if the war consisted in the first place of a mysterious substance, a kind of spice that mingled with the light and made everything more intense, because I remember I said to my uncle, without looking up from the lens, that what I was seeing was so beautiful.

And he smiled, with the tarpaulin in his hands, an embarrassed smile full of regret that glowed in his beard. "Splendid," he nodded. "Splendid, but a shame."

One day I drove with my mother by coach through the fields to the nearby town. She had business to do, purchases to make, but she also wanted to be away for a day or two from the house, which for nearly a year now had of necessity been our home. It must have been late May, perhaps early June. Between the soldiers' shirts hanging out to dry in the branches of the elder at the side of the road, unripe berries were beginning to swell the almost faded flower clusters. When after a bend the coach unexpectedly drove under that canopy of branches and drying shirts, I saw the amused mockery in my mother's eyes. We rolled under the drying washing as if we were a medieval royal couple making their *joyeuse entrée* into a town and being welcomed by the banners of the patricians.

From everywhere in the surrounding fields and fences plumes of smoke rose up, from fires above which hung bubbling kettles. Everywhere soldiers were lying outside their tents lazing about or polishing their boots, or helping each other shave. I don't know what is most poignant when I think back to those scenes: the indifference of the summer, the light-heartedness of the soldiers as they cooked, did their washing, lazed about, or the flirtatious atmosphere, with all those men with bare torsos while they waited for their shirts to dry, or is it the confrontation with my own naivety?

I was intoxicated by the sight of all those bodies, and by the bustle that the presence of the armies caused in the farmland, the delightful unreality of a countryside that was suddenly flooded with the din of a metropolis. In the villages the schoolchildren flocked around the soldiers, who had pitched their tents in the orchards or bleaching fields. They peered into the kettles above the fires, tried to wangle sweets out of the soldiers or goggled at the rifles that were being polished, the greased saddle equipment that gleamed in the sun.

Soldiers at the side of the road got up when they saw our coach approaching and started cheering us as a joke. I waved back and giggled. My mother shook her head with a grin. I seldom saw her playful, but the frivolity of the situation seemed to inspire even her.

"Hélène, child," she nagged. "If you wave, at least do it with a bit of dignity. Like this…" She waved stiffly with her gloved fingers, in the manner of a princess regent in a victor's coach—and I burst out laughing.

If this was history, which according to my uncle I must study well, then history was a delight. I could smell the leather of the boots, the shoe polish, the grease and the scent of those bodies, pale, young, tender. And again I see those good-natured faces, the eyelids that narrow, the sparks of pleasure that glow in them while the lads cheer us, and the hair under their arms when they raise an arm to wave. But I also sensed in my mother that same touch of regret that I felt with my uncle when I stared through the telescope at the blood vessels of the war, which day and night pushed those bodies towards the meat-grinder, to an idiotic death in the trenches or the foxhole.

On arrival we had coffee in the establishment where we were staying, in a side street close to the market square on one of the slopes of the hill on which the town was built. At the window the jovial bustle of a seaside resort in high season lapped past, true, flooded by mainly British tourists, all in the same grey uniforms.

We were almost the only civilians in the restaurant, and we must have looked strangely precious among all that khaki, with our dainty hats, our puffed sleeves and cuffs, the brooch my mother had put on the lapel of her cream-coloured overcoat and not least our gloves, mine in satin, hers in crochet, which gave a certain rococo twist even to the simple gesture of bringing a cup of coffee to your lips.

We attracted attention. Around us, at the other tables, officers—I presume, since I've never had a clear idea of military ranks and hierarchies—were casting furtive glances at the two of us, sideways, as they drank their glass or cup, or looking up supposedly by chance when they cut their cakes.

My mother shook it off. Straightened her shoulders. Looked around. I could see that she wanted to wallow in the illusion of a more or less normal state of affairs—everyday life with its familiar routines, even though almost all the waiters who were manoeuvring their way between the kitchen and the tables with trays full of crockery and cutlery or portions of tart were older men, older than the majority of the uniformed customers, beneath whose whiskers they arranged silver jugs of cream on the tablecloth, poured tea, juggled with carafes or piled empty plates on their forearms as if performing a circus turn. Their helpful manner, perhaps no more obtrusive or artificial than usual, acquired a mocking edge, though those young men scarcely seemed to notice them.

I saw my mother enjoying herself. I saw how she relished the sight of the maid who, in front of the cupboard for the cutlery and the napkins, was polishing knives and forks with a downy cloth and laying the napkins in piles. The child was probably not much older than me, though a head shorter, slimmer and blonder, with a flannel cap on her hair so big that it resembled a washed-up jellyfish that had accidentally been stranded on her crown. She seemed frightened of the tall matron who, in a corner of the restaurant, close to the door, resided behind a tall lectern and whose task was for some reason to prevent hungry customers from looking for a table on their own initiative, a task which had grown into a true passion. With an imposing choker rising from her voluminous bosom, and in one hand the pen, which regularly made mysterious notes in a register on the lectern, the other pointing a guest to a table, she combined excellently and seamlessly the functions of gatekeeper and cornerstone: half a caryatid, because of that hairdo that towered to just beneath the low ceiling, as though she had to support the whole building, and half a Theban sphinx, only prepared to admit within her ramparts those who gave the right answers to her riddles.

I saw how my mother was enjoying herself, and I was too, but actually not properly until now, long after the whole decorum of the bourgeoisie has wasted away in the props store of time. The most important rituals are those whose symbolism we know has definitely faded. The whole tissue of signs, the map of our soul if you like, in which they were embedded, has worn away around them, but we ascribe to them, literally against our better judgement, a short-lived significance—just as I can only fundamentally believe in God when I feel that the world, down to my own cells and bones, exudes His death: death in the afternoon, when Rachida blesses the floors and cupboards down below, and the caustic soda in her buckets deconsecrates my house until everything lies there white and naked, filled with nothing but its own emptiness.

"Don't sit there gawping, child. You'll attract lightning," whispers my mother, above the cup of coffee which she keeps in front of her mouth for an unnatural length of time so as to be able to have a good look round. And when I stare at her indignantly, I see she is sitting giggling, in a rare fit of self-mockery.

It might be one of the countless incidents that you forget, one of those hundreds of thousands of moments that glide through us without leaving a trace, or one of those scarce moments that on the contrary you remember all your life without really knowing why: memories that have the intensity of revelations, but without a clear message, except for the consolation of their triviality.

However, I remember that afternoon so vividly because my mother had scarcely uttered her playful reprimand when the panes in the window frames around us started to tremble. On all the tables teaspoons vibrated in cups and saucers to the rhythm of a swelling rumble that seemed to spread not only through the air, but also through the ground, through the table legs, the legs of our chairs, through our legs, up to our midriffs. Meanwhile an unearthly din mounted. Somewhere huge shutters seemed to be tumbling off their hinges, steel gates to be slamming shut with a massive clang, followed by clattering, like a hailstorm releasing all its stones at once.

My mother and I looked at each other, half astonished, half bewildered. Around us life came to a complete standstill very briefly, it can't have been more than eight seconds or so. Forks with pieces of cake on them froze halfway between table and mouth. A coffee jug hung in the air from the motionless hand of a waitress beneath the tinkling candelabra. The matron at her lectern raised her eyes to heaven, to the creaking ceiling, as if she suddenly doubted whether her monolithically constructed coiffure could cope with the weight of the rattling cosmos. By the crockery cupboard the maid stood looking at the shelves, on which plates were trembling, carafes were trembling, milk jugs were trembling, while in the drawers spoons and forks spread a gentle panic. Doggedly she fastened her gaze on the silver and porcelain, perhaps in the hope that by staring intensely she could keep everything in its place, if the crockery were to dance towards the fatal edge of the shelf.

As soon as the shaking ebbed away and the din had moved over us, into the valley, across the immense plain to the coast, and the panes in the window were the last to come to rest, suddenly the hubbub broke loose again as if at a sign. The waiters manoeuvred between the tables and the maid was once more folding napkins, with the same mechanical sleepiness as before, reintegrated into the hypnosis of normality.

Perhaps it was because of the juddering, which was still ringing in my ears and in my midriff, but as I sat looking round me, at the good-natured banter that went on lapping round us, as though there had never been that interval, I had an uncontrollable laughing fit. I tried to keep myself in check, but the tension built up in my midriff and before I realized it I burst into a laugh that took me so totally by surprise that I got cramp in my abdominal muscles. I heard myself, to my horror, not so much guffawing as cackling hysterically.

At the tables next to ours heads turned. The matron, I just saw, before my sight grew dim with tears, was staring at me as if she would have liked to turn me into a pillar of salt on the spot, and I heard the decided click with which my mother put her cup down—one of the gestures in which she could concentrate her universal disapproval. But before she could say anything the whole episode began again from the beginning. The panes started ticking softly and a few seconds later that long-drawn-out salvo boomed through the whole room, where life again froze.

I saw my mother put her fingertips on the edge of the table, as if to calm the clattering. A second spasm of laughter went up through my intestines, and I heard myself drowning out the noise with my cackling.

I pulled my head into my shoulders, in my coffee the vibrations appeared as circles, but however hard I tried, a new cramp wrested my jaws open, and I myself no longer knew if it was laughing that I was doing, or screeching. It was more like a labour pain that wrenched my mouth open and spewed out something that could be both a cry of fear and a laugh, though I felt neither elated nor fearful.

My mother was pale, she was obviously not happy. And then I saw her look up, and I felt a hand on my shoulder. Someone must have got up from one of the tables next to ours.

"It's all right, mademoiselle. It's just the gun, the big gun in Diksmuide. D'you understand? The gun. We're safe here, perfectly safe…"

The din died away again.

He pushed a handkerchief towards me. Khaki.

"Thank you, sir."

I accepted the handkerchief, dried my eyes with it and was about to return it to the stranger, but he waved away my gesture. He was twenty-five at most, as big a child as I was, now I look back on it.

When I translated what he had said for my mother—"the cannon, the cannon of Diksmuide, Maman, he says there's no danger"—he switched effortlessly into a French in which only a slight accent gave him away as British.

"Excuse me," he said. "Force of habit." He straightened his back to shake hands formally with my mother and me. "Matthew. Mathew Herbert."

"Marianne Demont. And this is my daughter Hélène. She's a serious young lady, Monsieur Heirbeir, but today she seems to find everything *très amusant.*" She was still upset, like me.

"It's all right," he smiled. "They're aiming for Dunkirk, mademoiselle. They're trying to hit the harbour." He looked up for a moment and glanced through the window behind our back, in the direction where the town must be. "People will be having their tea in the cellar today, I fear."

I could see that my mother wanted to ask him something, but at that moment the panes started vibrating again. The matron grabbed the side of her lectern, almost without thinking. The maid quickly stretched out to push a stack of plates deeper onto the shelf. The waiters sought the proximity of the walls.

"It's all right..." he repeated, as he came and sat on the chair next to me, and when the ticking of the windows changed to clattering and everything juddered again, he laid his hand on mine, a gesture that did not escape my mother, and gazed into my eyes.

I looked at the raven-black curls on his forehead, the slightly pursed lips, pronounced cheekbones, and his deep-brown, almost anthracite-coloured eyes, which focused steadily on mine.

"It's all right," I read on his lips, since the din drowned out his words. And for the third time I heard the iron wings coming down over us, and felt the shivers from the bottom creeping into me, moving from the floorboards into the walls, from the walls into the ceiling, and from the ceiling into the candelabra over our table. And it was as if I too came to a halt. I felt his fingertips pressing so hard on mine that they had white blotches when he withdrew his hand.

"It's all right," his lips repeated.

H E CAME TO COLLECT US that evening, a little after dark, after asking us before he took his leave if we would like to accompany him on a little excursion to the roof of the old casino at the top of the hill. "We do it frequently, madame, for special guests. It breaks the routine a bit and I can smuggle you in."

We were to wait in the drawing room of our boarding house, since civilians were not allowed in the street unaccompanied after sunset. My mother was suspicious, even though he had told her that his intentions were completely honourable. When after eleven a party of ten people, five of whom were civilians, gathered in the square in front of our boarding house, she was reassured.

"As you can see, Madame Demont," he said, "I have two arms in good health, and two legs. And..." he winked at me, "while my legs are carrying me upward, my arms are available for you and your daughter, to give support, of course, should the walk prove too strenuous. At times it is on the steep side..." He spoke with a hint of his native tongue in his words, and the slight emphasis on all syllables of someone in whose mouth a foreign language does not undergo the wear and tear of daily conversations. He was also shy and tried to hide it.

"You need as many words as my daughter to explain something," laughed my mother. "And you're forgetting that I'm from this area. I must have climbed that mountain a hundred times before you were born."

She pulled her gloves on jauntily and as she descended to the pavement past him she added breezily: "*Allons-y, mon enfant.*"

"That's all right, ma'am," he retorted, clearly charmed.

The party got moving. We walked ahead of my mother, next to each other, and giggled conspiratorially at the conversation that developed between her and one of the soldiers, who had decided to keep her company. He treated her to such platitudes about the "wonderful evening" and the "splendid view" that lay in store for us, without considering that my mother spoke scarcely a word of English.

"I can't understand a word you're saying, *jeune homme,*" she replied stoically in French. "But I'm sure we agree."

The evening could indeed be described as more or less *wonderful.* The full moon hung above the rooftops and gave the contours of the blacked-out houses the look of massive objects, all equally colourless, bathed in tints of grey and white like us, who seemed to be walking not through a real world, but a world of used-up light that must once have been reflected from things and was now travelling, more and more ethereal, through space and time.

We said little. Sometimes I felt he was looking at me and sometimes I looked at him—the moonlight made his face pale and his eyes even darker. When our eyes happened to meet, we exchanged a shy smile, and we listened to the sound of the footsteps on the cobbles.

Now that the slope was getting steeper and we gradually began to climb above the roofs, the conversations petered out. Only somewhere at the front did an imposing lady, an American who by the sound of it was reporting for some magazine or other, go on indefatigably expanding on the other towns close to the front, which she and a taciturn thin man, who seemed to stand in the same relationship to her as a flagpole to the flag, had obviously previously called at. She regularly voiced exclamations such as "Thrilling, dear captain!" or "Ghastly!"—eruptions at which the two of us giggled every time, more to feed our own silent understanding than out of pleasure.

I liked him. I liked his serious fun, or his funny seriousness. Later, when he told me about his life, I seemed to know everything already, as if his story had been able to transport itself to my mind, perhaps via my fingers, that afternoon, and was waiting there until he stuck words on it.

Undoubtedly my mother would have said now that I need a lot of words to make clear what is obvious: "You're in love, child. A blind man could tell you that." But what does that word mean? Once, twice or three times in your life you meet a person who rearranges your molecules in a trice, someone who manifests themselves as the question to answers piled up in you from long before you yourself could think, and whose existence you had never before suspected. And the only choice you're given is to answer the question or ignore it.

"Are you getting tired, patriot?" asked my mother sarcastically. "You are getting under my feet a lot. If you need my arm, just call…"

He laughed. "I'm fine, madame."

The houses gave way to trees, coolness and the enclosed smell of the forest floor. The front of the casino gleamed between the treetops, almost bright white in the moonlight.

"Almost there, off we go…" said the soldier walking next to my mother.

I had often been there in my childhood. Sun-drenched Sunday mornings with parades by the brass band on the small promenade in front of the terrace, and afterwards lemon sorbet or lemonade. My father liked it here. The spot, I think, stood as a symbol of his marriage, his love of my mother, whom he was fond of calling jokingly "*La Belle Flamande*", just to hear her protest—she thought herself as French as Camembert.

"*Vive le Roi Soleil,*" she would cry because, had Louis XIV been a little less hungry for land and wealth, she would indeed have been a beautiful Flemish woman. Our families were located more or less within the borders of the old County of Flanders, invisible, many times redrawn by history, that eloquent expression of chance, where Latin and Germanic mingled promiscuously. Without the Peace of Nijmegen they might have remained compatriots, and my mother would have had to appeal to different mythologies to distinguish her from us. But I was as fond of the spot as she was, because my double origin lay at my feet there and that hill marked the watershed in my soul—the externalization of my own creation myth.

On the south side the land seemed to descend to the Mediterranean. The sun, I imagined, already had in it something of the bright light of Provence, cicadas, cypresses and the myth of Van Gogh, who sought the essence of colour, beyond pigments, and whom I discovered only much later. Above the landscape that extended to the north of the hilltop the sky had an Arctic clarity, and, in the autumn, when the sunlight fell lower on the earth, the melancholy of summers close to the pole, where the nights dawdle in a sunset that spans the whole horizon.

When we were small my father would take my brother and me on his arm, help us onto the balustrade on the edge of the plateau and show us the old Roman highways that left the town like the arms of a star and cut through the landscape of the south in straight lines. On the other side, which he called "our side", he pointed out the towns of the north. On clear days you could see them like brown-yellow dots in the plain below us, shimmering in the hot summer air: right in the distance Nieuwpoort, under the blue-white haze of the coastline. A little farther down, Diksmuide. Farther south-east the towers of Ypres. Below that Veurne and, closer, Poperinge.

That night the plain was bathed in the alabaster moonlight. Fog banks hung like vaults above places where ponds or streams wound round woods and spires with dew. There was an unearthly peace, the almost continuous thunder of the war was absent—we again knew what silence was.

We were taken to the entrance to the casino. Someone asked us to be quiet: "The boys are well asleep."

A door opened, that of the gaming room which I vaguely remembered from earlier years. There was a smell of sleeping bodies. The high windows cast oblique shafts of moonlight onto the floors, retrieved from the darkness the folded patterns of blankets, a sleeve, a hand, a head. On all sides soldiers were lying sleeping, alone or having crawled together. From their footwear, which lay against the gaming tables on which their rucksacks were resting, the smell of earth, summer earth, of tent canvas, oiled steel and grass rose up to the ceiling with its frivolous plasterwork, which hung surreally above the sleeping figures.

*

"Careful, mademoiselle…" He took me by the arm when I almost stumbled over a pair of boots. As we went on, one of the sleeping soldiers sat up and whispered loudly: "Blimey, George. There's a fucking fairy hovering about…" I was suddenly very glad that my mother didn't understand English.

"Shut up, John. Get some sleep, willya," grunted someone else.

"If you say so, sweetheart." And the figure lay down again, huddling up against the other, because it was noticeably cooler up there than below in the alleys of the town, where the house fronts retained the heat of the day.

A second door opened and gave onto another room, where still more soldiers were sleeping, but less lit by the moon, which did not shine in directly here, but played in the tops of the trees. I heard the party climbing a staircase in front of us, a long set of steps, to the roof, it turned out, after we'd had to wait for a moment before the sentry allowed us to go farther.

When we arrived at the top the strapping American had already taken up a position by the parapet, where she was look-ing at the dark roofs below us. Exclamations like "Unimaginably peaceful!" shot through the night and each time the man next to her, who obviously never left her side, mumbled something affirmative from under his white moustache, though without much enthusiasm.

My mother had her companion lead her over to the other side of the roof terrace and we followed her. Before our eyes the northern plain stretched out under the haze of fog that was drifting inland, and shrank villages and towns which in one place we could locate in that blanket of mist and in another not. Areas of woodland and rows of trees created the impression that we were looking down at a model, with the cosy attention to detail one finds in them.

"Almost picturesque, Walter dear, wouldn't you say?" blared the American woman behind us, and we giggled, and I thought of what my uncle had said. It was splendid. Splendid, but a shame.

My mother put a handkerchief to her nose and said to the soldier next to her that it was surprisingly cool up here.

"Quite so," he replied, without having a clue what she was talking about. I knew she was thinking of my father, and my brother.

Then, in the far north towards the coast, more or less in the spot where my father had pointed out to us as children that Nieuwpoort should be, a red glow suddenly flared out of the mist. The fog banks reflected the flickering, which went out almost immediately.

Then bright white points of light shot hither and thither, though roughly in a crooked line from north-west to south-east, up to the zenith, and descended slowly as they extinguished, before suddenly dying out again—and again, now closer to us, then more towards the coast.

My mother kept holding the handkerchief under her nose, and I heard her sigh: "*Mon Dieu, mon Dieu…*"

"Flares," someone said. "They're firing flares over the lines."

No one spoke. Even the burly American woman had fallen silent and was standing close to the railing, staring at the spectacle through her lorgnette.

The silence became still more oppressive. There was no salvo or cannon shot to be heard, there was only that glow of lines of light, crooked needles above the landscape, and here and there the short-lived flash of what must be explosions, but without a boom or echo, and we looked at them as if at a natural phenomenon, as if down below on the plain the earth's crust were tearing open and two pieces of land were grinding into each other or trying to separate.

At a certain moment almost the whole line was suddenly ablaze. Red and green flashes flared up from the coast to inland, new bullets drew tentacles of light through the night.

Someone behind us muttered, "Poor buggers," realized there were ladies present and collected himself. "Poor chaps…" It seemed more intended to marshal what we knew with our intelligence against the fairy-tale beauty of those polyps of light, to remove us from the enchantment.

"*Mon Dieu, mon Dieu*," repeated my mother.

We waited, he and I, while the others descended the steps. The sentry relaxed and, indifferent to the light show that was in full swing down below, lit up a cigarette, inhaled and blew out a cloud of smoke.

My mother was already on her way downstairs, too upset to keep an eye on me.

"What's wrong with madame?" he asked.

"My brother's at the front, monsieur. Somewhere there perhaps. The last thing we heard was that he had to go to Le Havre. We don't get much post. My brother isn't a letter-writer…"

He nodded. "Le Havre?"

"We're Belgian, monsieur. And we can't go home, to my father…"

"Sorry to hear that," he said, as he closed the door behind us and the sentry bolted it on the other side.

I shrugged. "You get used to everything, monsieur."

The rest of the party was stumbling downstairs some way below us. It was dark in the stairwell, after the moonlit night on the terrace.

He noticed that I was moving uncertainly down the steps. Occasionally our hands touched. I giggled and he giggled back, and I was glad it was dark as I felt foolish.

Somewhere on a landing he took me by the arm, I thought in order to guide me downstairs, but he pushed me unexpectedly against the wall. It went too fast for me to protest, or even to be surprised. I could feel the buttons of his uniform pushing against my ribcage through my overcoat and his own ribcage swelling and contracting to the rhythm of his breathing while he put his head next to mine and rubbed my cheek with his, and his breath blew warm in my ear.

I had put one hand on his back in astonishment, while he kept the other wedged against the wall, with his palm over mine. The only other man to whom I had been so physically close until then was my father, when I was a child, during the afternoons at the seaside, when he wanted to protect me from the waves or a biting wind, but my father had cherished me. His body had never hungered or sought for anything,

There was something childlike about him. I moved my hand from his back to the nape of his neck and stroked the back of his head.

He was trying not to kiss.

Just standing there.

Stroking my cheek with his.

I smelt his smell, which condensed on the wall behind us and in the hair on my neck.

Then he let go of me and went downstairs. "I'm sorry," he whispered, and it sounded as if he had a frog in his throat.

I heard him stop on the landing. The rest of the party must have reached the ground floor by now as the stumbling faded away.

"*I'm sorry,*" he stammered again when I had caught up with him. "So sorry. I didn't mean to, Miss, I mean madame... mademoiselle."

I sought his hand in the dark. "It's all right," I said.

W E HAD LEFT the summer before on 28 June, early in the morning, in splendid weather, the beginning of a Sunday like a generous almsgiving. In accordance with the annual custom my mother, together with Emilie, had filled all kinds of cabin trunks and suitcases weeks in advance. A stream of luggage had gone on ahead and the day after our arrival a second stream would follow us, besides what we took with us on the day itself. My mother was not someone who went on trips, she moved as it were with atmosphere and all. Once the first stream of cases was delivered, the maids in my uncle's house, who after the death of the matriarch were in charge of business matters, would unpack our clothes, put our sheets on the beds and store our table linen in the chests of drawers in the guest quarters, so that as soon as we ourselves arrived she could move into a world governed by her familiar natural laws.

She had looked breathtaking that morning. She had been in a good humour for weeks. In the months before our departure her menstruation pains had subsided from rancorous symphonies to string quartets full of rainy melancholy. It was no longer unknown territory to me. Just over a year previously I myself had started bleeding, very late according to her, but nevertheless in synch with budding nature and the mid-Lent fair. I still attribute it to the roundabouts. Their centrifugal forces unleashed my chemistry, opened the polonaise of the molecules. My mother had reacted with a strange tenderness. She immediately put me to bed for three days. Perhaps she secretly hoped that I would join her monthly revolt, but did not turn into a monument of irritability, until later after the birth of my daughter.

I myself had thought the business at times stupid and at other times a melancholy premonition of death. I leaked periodically like a draughty sow. I felt mushy, overripe, a sack of rust-coloured blood which was torn somewhere. My body was no longer a body, it had become a carcass. I cried easily. I was suddenly a sentimental booby, and I was annoyed with myself.

Emilie came to my room every morning to fill the water jug. "From now on, mamzel," she said the first time, "you'll have to put up with that misery every four weeks." She called it "ministrations". I think it was a bastardized form of "menstruation". She had spoken the word in a tone that betrayed complicity. We were now clearly sisters.

My mother too had come and sat two or three times a day on the edge of my bed, taken my book out of my hands to be able to stroke my cheeks unimpeded and look me in the eye with a beatific pity that I had never suspected in her and distrusted, since in my view it contained an implicit form of triumph, as if she were rubbing it in: "You see. You too. Look at you there, with all your castles in the air. Look at woman, shackled to her treacherous body." But of course she had said something completely different: "The fresh air will do you good, my child."

She had called the approaching holiday "our last summer". My brother had left school at Easter. After the hot months he would start work in my father's warehouses, to gain experience and, my parents hoped, to acquire a taste for bourgeois life before he had to do his military service. As far as I was concerned, she felt that I had spent long enough under the skirts of the nuns to be able to behave like a well-brought-up young lady, knew sufficient foreign languages to say my piece everywhere, and though my French conjugations and sewing left something to be desired, my periods had made it clear that I had entered irreversibly the phase of life in which, as she put it with some aplomb, "a woman becomes a woman".

She was crazy about circular reasoning, trains of thought that by way of conclusion wound up at their starting point. The tension there has always been between us was based on a fundamental difference in the way our souls were constructed. Ideas for my mother were a kind of lid, her medium was tautology, while the engine of my own mind is driven by the hydraulics of paradox, in which thought, how shall I say, can release its excess pressure—more or less as a steam machine is equipped with valves with which it can discharge to prevent it being destroyed by its own power. And when I think back to our departure, it would be nonsense to try to convince you or myself that, hidden behind the easy-going bustle of that glorious morning, I suspected the crash of the whole machinery that kept our world in existence, the fatal forces that were piling up, so that the whole system of communicating balances was imperceptibly at the point of exploding. I would be doing violence to the truth and above all be seeing the outbreak of the misery that was to hold us hostage for four years as a natural given: some physiological phenomenon or other, like a sneezing fit or a fart, unique to the organism of time or history, and it was not. It was a stupidity such as only our species can commit.

*

The town lay under a dome of azure, and in my memory smells of soap and caustic soda. The evening before our *joyeuse sortie*, Emilie had quickly washed the hall, so that when the front door opened the sunlight seemed to slip on the gleaming floor tiles. We had had breakfast and I had waited downstairs until my mother descended the staircase in full regalia, followed by Emilie lugging a set of bags, and bringing up the rear my brother, with a pile of hurriedly grabbed books in his arms, because just before we left he invariably had an attack of hunger for print and felt he should make use of the summer months to brush up his reading.

The coach was brought round to the front of the house. Tatante, my father's sister, had walked through the front garden, the tails of her long, wide summer coat waving behind her, and in the hall had said hello to my mother, who had meanwhile crowned her own proliferation of ribbons and gloves with a formidable sunhat, even more imposing than her sister-in-law's. The kisses with which they had welcomed each other hung in limbo somewhere under the broad brims of their hats. It reminded me of the greeting of the Holy Virgin by her cousin Elizabeth, as you can see in late-medieval or early-Renaissance paintings: two tall female figures bending towards each other, but at the same time keeping their heads some distance apart—so as not to crease their haloes.

My father had stood looking on, with that eternal half smile on his lips, and my brother had provided a little apotheosis by dropping all his books at the bottom of the stairs and unexpectedly letting loose a violent oath, which under other circumstances would have made my mother sway like a standing lamp that had been nudged by a brush handle, but she had turned round, looked at the books on the floor, and then at my brother and giggled sarcastically: "A good start, *mon ami*. It's sealed with God's name!"

"Behave yourselves, children," my father had exhorted us, while he had lifted up my own summer hat to give me a kiss on the forehead. "Don't give Maman any grey hairs. She has more than enough already..."

"Brute..." my mother had growled.

He had bent down to avoid her hat and kissed her behind her ear.

"We're off," she had finally said. She had given her sister-in-law her arm and had gone downstairs with her to the front garden, and we, my brother and I, had followed at an appropriate distance: her train-bearers, her exotic dwarves.

I could say that I remember that morning so well because this farewell, no more dramatic or trivial than in all the summers since my earliest childhood, would happen to prove our farewell to the world as we had known or imagined it up to now, and that the subsequent events serve as the acid that etched the scene of our departure deep into the engraving plates of my memory—or perhaps even the events that were happening elsewhere at that very moment, under the same azure of Europe's last summer: the young lad who slid the bullets into the magazine of his pistol, touched the grenade in his coat pocket and maybe felt his heart pounding in his chest.

The truth is that I have never been very good at goodbyes, a greatly underestimated art. When I was still just a tot I showed, on family visits, a tendency to hide when the time came to return home. I was not driven by curiosity to be able to spy or eavesdrop on my relations to find out what they would say about us the moment we left the house. Nor did I hide because I liked those visits exceedingly. The houses of my relations, certainly on my father's side, were invariably temples of boredom, or better: they contained so little mystery that boredom immediately lost its radioactivity and in a trice halved to dull dreariness.

Real boredom, you see, has something saturated about it—a crimson darkness, a full emptiness. It is the small valley of the shadow of death in our breast, through which we must wade to achieve resurrection. I have never read from any other reason than boredom, the limbo before paradise, and perhaps my urge as a child to consider myself impossible to find was connected with this. For I wanted not just to know, I wanted to see with my own eyes how things would look without me. I wanted to be able to view the world in the light of my absence, and I believe that I wept and stamped my feet so angrily when my parents finally pulled me out of my hiding place, because even then I realized the impossibility of that desire. And yet all my life I have gone on longing for that non-realizable *salto mortale* of the mind—that ineffable homesickness for an abode in my own absence.

I know what my mother would accuse me of now: "It always takes you hours to send someone on their way." She said it often, when she asked for my homework or asked me to add something in my own hand to the letters she wrote to relations in France. "Do get to the point…"

My father on the threshold, under the sloping glass roof in the open doorway. Between the railings of the banisters around the steps that lead to her cellar domain, half hidden behind the hydrangea: Emilie's face. Before she withdraws into her quarters, she stands ready to wave as soon as the coach leaves. Above is the blue, the deep blue that sharply outlines roofs, treetops and chimneys; I still wonder how my father would have dubbed it if it had occurred to him to play one of our favourite games: assigning a name to the morning sky according to a jointly invented and extremely arbitrary classification, and again in the afternoon and sometimes in the evening too. We had already had skies of Saxon porcelain, and the dullness of crêpe de Chine, and buttermilk skies and zinc heavens covered in plaster. Perhaps that morning, after having peered out of the window for a while with his eyes theatrically half closed, he would have called it a *bleu européen*, and turned to me with raised eyebrows, as if consulting an eminent colleague.

He was to follow on at the end of July to holiday with us, until from September onward the town gradually awakened from its summer sleep. In this we were following the habit of the well-to-do. Everyone, by which I mean those who populated my world, fled the town in summer and sought accommodation in the countryside. The country, which for the rest of the year I won't say we saw as backward, but certainly as archaic, underwent a transformation in our heads as the summer months approached and became a place where life was still uncomplicated. The air was pure, the milk fresh, time twirled on its own axis.

I too was not wholly free of that enchantment. I was already longing for the imperial months of July and August. In my imagination a year took the form of a wheel or a clock face, and if you picture the twelve months of the year as the hours on that clock face, then there were two moments in the year when time in my experience moved slower: the dark months in the depths of winter, and the majestically stationary days in high summer. Every hour had its own character for me in those days, its own intensity of light, constantly changing depths of shadow and colour patterns, and no summer was ever more generous with contrasts than the summer of 1914.

On the platform my mother and Tatante had embraced again at length. This time real kisses were exchanged, since my mother had already taken her hat off in order shortly to be able to enter, without too much manoeuvring, the compartment reserved for us.

If I could go back, if the gods were to allow me to re-experience something of that day, I would content myself, and not out of nostalgia but purely for my amusement, with just the sounds of that morning—the slamming of the doors of the carriages, the porters who shouted to each other in our broad local dialect as they unloaded the luggage from the handcart and passed it to the men in the luggage car, the hissing of the locomotive which was already under steam, and now and then blew clouds of white mist from its wheels over the platform, and in the background the ever-present heartbeat of the living town, the music of which at that time did not yet consist of the roar of engines, but of the flamenco-like rhythms of horses' hooves on cobbles.

My mother had already boarded the train. Tatante put her hands on my shoulders and gave me three kisses. Edgard, who the whole time had been nonchalantly standing, reading the papers he had quickly bought, got on behind my back. He now thought himself too old, almost eighteen, still to let himself be cuddled like a schoolboy.

"See you in September," said Tatante. "Enjoy. What a summer." It was a quarter past ten.

The stationmaster gave the signal for all passengers to board. The last doors were slammed shut. The driver sounded the steam whistle and with a slight judder the train started moving.

Tatante stayed on the platform, waving. I found my way to the aisle, because I knew that as soon as we were leaving the station my mother would let down the sunblind in our compartment, and I wanted to look out, feel the town sliding off me and experience the sudden transition from built-up areas to open country.

The haymaking season had begun. Between the fences the meadows lay sweltering in all gradations of green: dark and shiny where the grass had not yet been touched by the scythe, fading to yellow and white where the mown stalks lay drying in the sun. Everywhere, as far as the eye could see, farm labourers and girls wearing caps or shawls against the heat were turning corn, putting it into stooks, or filling the hay wagons, which as their load piled up looked more and more like Chinese galleons. It had to be done quickly. Although it was Sunday morning, there was thunder in the air. The dew must evaporate from the stalks before the rain came.

I won't deny that the sight delighted me, but the countryside has always been more to me than a charming set, although that day it was doing its level best to look like a set, complete with the wings of wooded banks and distant fields sliding slowly past the windows. When I was still a child my mother's older brother had shown me, during the evening walks he went on with me around our summer house, that everything that surrounded me there existed in the first place for its usefulness, and the beauty that I worshipped in them was rather a by-product of use, a nice extra, yes, but unintentional. No tree or bush, but it would be uprooted sooner or later to provide wood for beams or tools, or twigs for weaving the multiplicity of baskets in which eggs, vegetables, fruit and poultry were taken to market. Even the hedges that divided up the landscape into pleasant rooms served first and foremost to keep pests off the fields and to protect the crops from the heaviest buffeting of the sea breeze, not to please me or my father, who in the countryside sought mainly the proof of the accuracy of the paintings he liked—which naturally pandered to his tastes. The canvases of young painters, on the other hand, who in the years just before the war began increasingly to knead their peasants and fishwives in paint, who made the paint into a dark clay in which they modelled figures, he called crude and rough, as I gaped at them open-mouthed. For me they precisely showed the soul of the land, the impersonal clay of which we are all made. Breathlessly I observed the work of time on those canvases. Over the years I saw their areas of colour crumble away as slowly as a landscape, thunderclouds become even more thundery and the ploughing or contemplating figures weather under those skies into animate lumps of matter.

Of course I was jealous, and I still am. Jealous of the paint-ers, of their vocabulary of colour. Jealous that I can't grind language fine in a mortar and make it fluid or thick as I see fit by mixing it with oil, or create a new colour by adding some powder from one word to some powder from another word. Jealous, too, because there is no language with which you can first apply a base, which continues to glow though the tissue of colour that you apply on top. Jealous because I would like a language that carries no meaning, but above all intensity, a meaning that transcends meaning, and which you must not so much read as survey, with the literacy of the eye, the erudition of the retina. I would not house those words and stories in a notebook, but in a kind of album: a sketchbook in which as you turn the pages you come across a miniature, then a genre piece, pages full of studies; fantasies in grisaille, marine skies in watercolour, so ethereal that the texture of the paper contributes—and then again sheets full of shadow, rooms at night, darkened rooms on the edge of abstraction, where a doorknob pierces the darkness with a pinhead of light, as realistic as the glitter of the watch chain that struck me in the darkness of one of the compartments, when I turned round in the aisle after my mother had sighed, "Helena, come and sit with us. You'll look so much you'll go cross-eyed."

If she had been able to read the preceding lines, she would undoubtedly have taken off in annoyance the small pair of reading glasses she needed in her later years and grasped them impatiently in her fist as she said to me in pique: "Do cut a few Gordian knots, and put some full stops here and there. A sentence isn't a sausage."

The rocking of the carriage and the music of the wheels on the tracks had put everyone in a sleepy trance, that mixture of waiting and expectation, impermanence and tempered impatience that goes with travel.

I sat down. My mother was reading the book she took with her every year, some *Guide pittoresque des chemins de fer*, containing all the sights we passed en route. Obviously she didn't mind not being able to see any of it, behind the lowered sunscreen.

My brother had dozed off. I took the papers off his lap without waking him.

"Is there anything in them?" asked my mother.

I shook my head. "Not much. Just love scandals."

"Oh, well…" She giggled and shrugged her shoulders. "If there's anything worthwhile, read it out to me."

There wasn't much. The boredom of the summer seeped through the columns. Adverts for boarding houses on the coast. The calendar of brass-band concerts in the park and the names of artistes of the umpteenth class who would be performing at the casino, with medleys and popular operettas. A short announcement that His Majesty had left for Switzerland for a few days. A letter in which a boastful gentleman, who was organizing a sports festival at the seaside, praised the soul-strengthening effect of "gymnastic clubs" on what he called "our young generations", which immediately prepared them for the burden of working life and the discipline of the barracks. "In particular," I pronounced the words with some sarcasm, because they sounded so official, "in particular the moral aspect of gymnastics must be stressed, since anyone who puts steel in his muscles will almost automatically be proof against the temptation of late-night bars and drinking dens, where so many young men can have only unhealthy ideas, caused"—I cleared my throat—"by a siren call of immoral and anti-government principles…"

"Bravo!" concurred my mother.

"Where is that festival?" asked my brother, sitting up languidly and rubbing his eyes.

"Ostend…"

"God, then we're going entirely the wrong way again…"

It became hot. Behind the sunscreen the noon light blazed and the dry air in our compartment smelt more and more strongly of the woodwork and the velvet of the seats. My mother had sunk back a little and had closed her eyes. I rested my head against the side of the carriage, so that I could see the landscape gliding past between the sunblind and the window. Sometimes the train slowed and came to a halt at a main station, to take on fuel and water. Then there was a swarm of children's heads thronging beneath the window, blond quiffs, pigtails, fingers tapping the bottom of the window glass—until the stationmaster chased away the young devils simply with the severity of his uniform.

Sunday in the country. Peasants in their Easter best, waiting on the platform under the lean-to. White starched shirts, black suits, caps. Behind the station usually a square, dazzling in the noonday sun, a small garden, crowded cafés, gleaming roofs and, invariably rising above them, a spire. During the week you could have heard the shuffle and hollow ring of clogs on the paving stones, certainly early in the morning, when the farmers' wives went off to sell their wares at the markets, and you would also have seen the young men going to work in town. If they had wanted to, they could easily have travelled almost right through the country in a day, and nevertheless be back in their own beds the same evening. The railways in my fatherland, which had branch lines going even to the most remote hamlets, guaranteed everyone optimum mobility, with the paradoxical aim of keeping everyone as far as possible in their place. That's how it seemed that Sunday. Everything had its place, everything its time.

I looked at my mother, dozing on the seat, the index finger of her right hand between the pages of the book in her lap. In her later years she would become the kind of expanding matron who to her last breath squeezed her shape into the old harness. At the last, when she was ill, hollow-eyed and grey because of the cancer eating away her insides, it was as if she had no bones any more, but was only kept upright by the fencing of her underwear, from which her body, whenever I undid those hooks and buttons, seeped out almost like mush.

"Is she asleep?" asked my brother.

"I think so..."

He got up and carefully pulled open the door of our compartment.

"Full bladder," he whispered. "Got to take young Jim for a walk."

"I heard you," growled my mother, without opening her eyes, but her eyebrows expressed enough disapproval.

Only late in the afternoon, when we were eating something in the station buffet of the place where we were waiting for a connection, did we notice that the commotion in the square might be about more than Sunday exuberance. On and around the terraces of the cafés people were conversing animatedly.

"I'll go and see what's going on," said my brother, getting up from our table.

"Probably much ado about nothing," said my mother soothingly.

He was gone quite a while.

"It seems the Crown Prince has been murdered," he said when he came back.

"Ours?" my mother responded in disbelief.

"The Austrian one. In Serbia. He and his wife. Some lunatic shot them down."

He sat down again, folded his napkin in his lap and took a bite of his roll. "There'll be another storm in the east."

"There are always storms," said my mother light-heartedly. "*Quand même*, it remains tragic. Poor souls. No one deserves that."

I did my best to find it tragic, but I couldn't manage to retrieve the human being from the few photographs and prints from the paper. They showed a tall fellow with fairly puffy cheeks, a full moustache and a clearly delineated paunch around the navel. I thought he was a dopey-looking sort, certainly in dress uniform, with a helmet on his head crowned by a dead chicken. He had according to the press no mistresses, or other habits that required discretion, or the accompanying loose-tongued behaviour.

"*Enfin*, we'll read about it in the paper tomorrow," concluded my mother, and I sensed in her words an undertone of eagerness that she usually showed when she read out the society section from the dailies, as if she were regularly invited to tea at every royal court. She called herself a full-blooded republican. "But if you've got kings anyway," she was fond of saying, with her predilection for circular arguments, "you've got them."

In her eyes our own queen, whom she sometimes sneeringly called that Wittelsbach field mouse, did not behave regally enough at all, but my father would then usually add: "They're all odd birds in that aviary. People don't grow up normally in a palace." Only the Austrian Crown Prince, whom he had once seen on the promenade at Blankenberge, did he find a perfectly ordinary chap. "Absolutely no airs and graces. He greeted me as naturally as anyone of my own class."

I tried to imagine them, the archduke and his wife, just arrived in death's realm, side by side, each in an open coffin, hands folded, eyes shut, the horror of the fatal moment perhaps congealed in their flesh that had grown cold, but my brother disturbed my daydreaming.

"Excellent piece of roast beef," he sighed, imitating my father. He had finished his roll and laid his napkin next to his plate. "And apart from that, there are plenty of Habsburgs, there in Vienna. It's not the first horse they've had to replace."

WE ARRIVED LATE in the evening. A servant of my uncle's was waiting for us with a coach and there was another carriage for our luggage. As soon as she got out, the same transformation had taken place in my mother as happened every year. Her usual surly air had gone. I saw a lively woman who chatted cheerfully with the stationmaster, gave the porters a generous tip and actually spoke to the servants in the familiar "*tu*" form, in a French that sounded a lot less precious than at home, where it seemed constantly imbued with an undoubtedly didactic precision. Now, suddenly, the terse, clipped diction of her native region broke through in her sentences.

Even when the servant, after we had got in, handed her a basket containing a jug of wine and three tin beakers, she did not refuse the offer in an aloof tone but passed the basket to my brother. "Come on, *mon ami*. Pour us a drink…"

The servant pulled on the reins, and the coach began moving. The grinding of the wheels over the cobbles echoed with a hollow sound against the walls of the houses in the streets, where downstairs, behind the window, glass lamps were being lit, and upstairs open windows let in cool air and oxygen. In the market the chairs for that afternoon's concert stood folded in rows against the walls of the kiosk and on the terrace of the local brasserie the last customers were emptying their glasses while behind their backs, in the illuminated restaurant, the landlord was wiping the chairs and putting them on the tables.

*

The evening was turning blue. It was not long before we had left the houses behind and the coach was taking us through the fields beyond the fringe of woodland that surrounded the town. There the smell of summer hit my nose, the specific odour of sand and grass and corn. The landscape rolled gently and in the shallow valleys the mist was creeping up behind the alders lining ditches and streams.

I took deep breaths and saw my mother observing me contentedly. She seemed to be revelling in the unanimity she presumed between us, delighted as she was herself to be able to return to the spots where she must have spent so many happy hours during her childhood. Perhaps she returned every year out of nostalgia, and although I took over the ritual from her for as long as the house in France existed—I accompanied it, like her, to its deathbed—it was never nostalgia for a bygone age that drove me there, or the longing to house the past in more durable accommodation than transient flesh or eroding stones. It demands an equally intense labour of the imagination to live in the present, as it does to evoke the past or probe the contours of the future. We make room, we create space. No one can appropriate time without accommodating it in an architecture of hope, or at least in the pavilions of fantasy, in order to provide it with rhythm and proportions, since everything is music. The beauty of the landscape that surrounded me that evening might, according to my uncle, be unintentional, secondary, but it filled me with great contentment—and if I could talk to him now, I would say that what stretched out all around me was indeed not purely natural beauty, but was beauty. Nothing was untouched by human hands, from the land itself, where the first inhabitants of these regions had picked up the roughest stones to make the soil workable, to the church towers, and all of that formed a vast, horizontal cathedral, on which men had laboured for centuries and which remained for ever unfinished.

"Aren't you getting cold, child?" asked my mother. She got out a blanket and laid it across my and her knees. "We're almost there."

"I'll keep warm, don't worry about me," said my brother, with feigned anger that he had to make do without a blanket. He refilled his beaker, and my mother did her best to look piqued, but she was too good-humoured to be convincing.

Meanwhile the road was climbing the familiar, gently undulating slope. The fields and the blooming verge, full of singing crickets, gave way to trees under which it was already dark. Farther along, where the wood thinned out again, we had our first glimpse, blue-grey in the twilight, of the wall with the gate and, just below the eaves, the small arched windows of the stables which during the day let a small amount of light in, so that it always seemed like night-time there. When I was very small nothing could fill me with such sublime fear as the eternal darkness in there, where you regularly heard chains clank, and something that breathed or snorted and stamped with heavy feet on the brick floor. And there was always that moment of breathless astonishment, of expectation and terror, when the grooms entered the stables and a little later came out leading horses by the reins—creatures that seemed not so much horses as locomotives of muscles and manes, and strangely sensitive skin which was constantly shot through with nervous twitches. They were huge, mechanical animals, Trojan horses, whose nostrils issued steam on cold mornings. Beside them the horse that pulled our coach seemed a frail ballerina. The animal began to snort and picked up speed now the destination was near. The servant whistled, behind the wall dogs started barking. The gate opened for us.

We had scarcely come to a halt in the inner courtyard when screaming children surged round the coach, and laughed or peered at us with shy grins, while the oldest, slightly more reserved, looked on in the background and nodded to us. They were the children of the many servants and maids who lived in smaller farmhouses all over the estate of my mother's family and also worked in the stables and barns around the house where we were to stay for the next few weeks. My relations had long since stopped working the land themselves, except sporadically, during the harvest when they were always short of labour; but basically my uncle, who had watched our arrival from a distance, was mainly a businessman.

After he had made his way through the pack of children and first helped my mother alight, I saw, as they greeted each other with two kisses, that her eye lingered for an instant on the luxuriant hairdo on his head, his beautiful grey and white mane, always a little dishevelled, which invariably seemed to remind her that there was something untamed, something wild in him.

"Marianne…" he said between the first and second kiss, and she responded with "Théo…", with an intimacy that needed no further syllables and, certainly from her side, the resignation with which we can love members of our family deeply without liking everything about them.

I myself was very fond of him, and precisely because of his indifference to all kinds of conventions, which my mother attributed to a touch of bad blood on her father's side, a few drops of which, she feared, had found their way into my veins.

"I see my little fortifying something for the journey was well received, *Petit,*" he laughed, when he saw my brother getting off the coach in a fairly unstable manner.

"Splendid wine…" hiccupped Edgard. "Really!"

They shook hands, my uncle squeezed my brother's shoulder and took his chin paternally between his thumb and forefinger. "I'm very pleased. Someone who takes the trouble to do my cellar the honour which is its due…"

They let go of each other, and I knew he would say my name now and for the umpteenth year in a row would exclaim that I just went on growing and that this summer he would definitely have to top me like a poplar, "because you know, dear niece, poplars start wobbling when young".

One by one the servants came to greet us, hat in hand, shirtsleeves rolled up to the elbows, slightly bent over the respectful distance maintained by their handshake, as if we were a delegation of diplomats, finally arrived at a foreign court—and it looked like that, too, within the enclave that protected the high walls of the stables and barns, the vegetable garden, the chicken enclosure, the orchard and the berry garden from the rest of the world: a microcosm with its own customs, most clearly embodied in the figures of my uncle's wife and her older, unmarried sister, whom my brother, with my father's irony, always, except when she was around, called "the inseparable shadow". Now too, now they come out of the house, and look in turn at their lined slippers so as not to slip on the bluestone steps leading up to the front door; they both seem, in their light kimonos, with hair worn up and cheeks powdered all too extravagantly, to radiate a dim light. I hear the soft tinkle of the gold dangling from their ears, and as always it astonishes me, now we greet each other, how soft their skin, which has already lost much of its youthful springiness, feels beneath my lips—almost like the filling of a chocolate marshmallow, despite the thick layer of make-up which from afar gives their faces a cool, almost jade-like glow.

As a child I was intrigued by the isolated existence they lead within the walls of the house where my mother was born. The part of the residence occupied by them and my uncle is a suite of spacious rooms, divided from each other by wide double doors. The parquet on the floors nips in the bud with a dastardly creaking any attempt to sneak around in secret, so that I can never spy on them as if I'm not there while, in their intimate boudoir between the dining room and the drawing room, they let the large pages of the fashion magazines rustle through their fingers while exchanging little cries of glee. Everything is as subdued and padded as they are. In their ponderous dressing gowns, vaguely inspired by what they see in the fashion magazines, but apart from that largely modelled according to their eccentric tastes, they are very like giant silkworms, enclosed in a cocoon of extravagant textiles, without ever bothering to grow into butterflies.

Their boredom is of the superior kind. They spend the greater part of the day fixing each other's clothing and coiffure, followed by a whole disrobing ritual when they prepare to retire in the evening, so that besides silkworms, they are also reminiscent of some tropical plant which spends all its energy on a flowering which is not only as rich as it is short-lived, but is also particularly punctual—on a certain day and a certain number of full moons after the equinox, and only during the brief period when the sun is directly above the earth, or some such thing, since my aunt and her sister were actually not occupied with changing their clothes and fixing their hair in the afternoons.

The kimonos they were wearing that evening as they tripped towards us in their slippers had the kind of frills that my mother rather disapprovingly called "undressed dress", and to make matters worse the two sisters hailed from Tourcoing—the very way my mother pronounced that place name betrayed the fact that it would have been better if fate had had you born elsewhere. "Tourcoing!" she could sometimes conclude, as if the word itself were sufficient condemnation.

After the sisters had joined us at table under the beech tree, where my uncle had prepared a small evening meal, they pressed cloths smelling of lemon verbena oil to their delicate ankles, to keep off the mosquitoes that buzzed high above our heads in the last warmth.

My uncle was meanwhile discussing "that incident" and whether it would have consequences.

"A lot of fuss is what we're going to have," exclaimed my brother, who had not denied himself the umpteenth glass of wine.

"Doubtless," replied my uncle. "But where? As long as they're at each other's throats in the east, to be honest, I'm not going to lose any sleep."

"If you have any fuss, comrade, it'll be with me," interrupted my mother. "That's your last glass. Understood?"

"*Oui, mon capitaine!*" cried Edgard, making a clumsy salute.

"Leave him be," soothed my uncle, and to my mother: "If you'd like to go to bed, dear, your room is ready. I'll keep an eye on them…"

"That's very reassuring…" she replied, and no one could fail to hear the sarcasm in her voice, but nevertheless she got up, tugged my brother's blond quiff by way of a good night kiss, whispered, "Brigand…", gave me and my uncle a pat on the shoulder and withdrew into the house.

A little later the light of a paraffin lamp flickered at one of the upstairs windows. Only downstairs was there electricity, but not even there in every room, only in those where the sisters and my uncle spent a lot of time.

"Cigar, Edgard?…" he asked conspiratorially.

"Oh, why not?" replied my brother nonchalantly, stretching in his chair.

My uncle retrieved a small cigar-holder from his inside pocket, snapped it open and offered it gallantly first to my brother then to me.

I declined. I always found his fixed intention, carried out each year with varying success, to teach us a few of the vices that add spice to life, as he put it, sufficient unto itself. The sins one doesn't taste keep their aroma longest.

The sisters took one too, which they shared after they had lit it. "Nothing better against the mosquitoes, isn't that so, Josine?" cooed my aunt.

"Absolutely, Yolande," echoed her sister.

We were silent. Around me three orange points of light glowed whenever the sisters, my uncle and my brother puffed on their

155

cigars. I enjoyed their pleasure and listened to the sounds of the night. A cow coughing somewhere beyond the stables. The first call of the owl. The high-pitched, ethereal squeak of the bats which sailed round the tops of the beeches and the crunch when an insect was ground up in their jaws. Only above the roofline at the far end of the inner courtyard was there a band of fading light.

"We'll have to wait and see what tomorrow brings," said my uncle at last. His voice suddenly sounded deeper, because of the tobacco.

He exhaled. "Wait and see…" he said again, more softly this time.

I looked on as they finished their cigars and saw how their faces glowed briefly as they sucked oxygen into the tobacco, and how afterwards darkness took possession of us all.

L ESS THAN SIX MONTHS later at least one in three of all the servants who greeted us on the evening of our arrival would be dead. I could list their names, erect on paper my private monument with the inscription "*Mort pour la Patrie*", but memorials are leaden euphemisms: sacrificial dishes or garlands of flowers that we place on altars to drown out the stupefaction in all those bodies. I have always made it a point of honour to read the lists of names on each of those monuments, even the tiniest villages I visited, and invariably their orderliness left me with a wry aftertaste. They stood there, chiselled row on row in bluestone, an alphabetical litany, like the words in a dictionary, but without the slightest explanation, except for their year of birth, and the date of their death, which broke off their oh-so-young etymologies.

There should be mausoleums and extensive cemeteries for the torn-off limbs, the amputated arms or legs, the missing organs. Headstones should be carved under which rest, for example, the hands and feet of Sylvain Gaillac, youngest son of Mr and Mrs Gaillac, who right next to the town hall in my mother's home village ran a wine and liqueur business and who dismissed with typically French nonchalance the fact that their good-looking youngest son was in favour with the girls at the fairs—till he came back without hands or feet. A suckling pig or sacrificial lamb ready for the spit, that's what he looked like, a man-sized infant whom Maman and Papa had to push round in a wheelchair at fairs where not even a milkmaid would give him a second look. He, Sylvain Gaillac, single-handedly responsible for several deflowerings in the undergrowth behind the roundabouts, late at night during the midsummer ball, now had to be fed three times a day as one feeds an orphaned thrush chick, spoonful by spoonful, mouthful by mouthful, and for the rest of his days couldn't even wipe his own arse. There should be a burial chapel commemorating without inflated heroics the right arm of our groom Adelin Rivière, very popular because of the only talent he was able to develop before the front decimated him: his sensitivity during the freeing of a calf from the inside of a cow that threatened to die in calving, the clairvoyancy of his hands, as if, as my uncle said so often, that fellow could feel with his hands how the calf was twisted in her abdomen, and how to release it unharmed. And where is the grave for the left hand of his cousin Hubertin, who had no special merits and was only missed on a farm where manpower was always useful when that hand wasn't there any more—and that was how the war gave countless men back: withholding an arbitrary percentage of flesh. It should have its own cemeteries, rows of tombs for arms, legs, feet, fingers, toes, or a wall for urns with, under small stone covers, for example the testicles of Olivier Douilhet, waiting to be reunited with the rest of Olivier Douilhet, who, it was whispered, took a feeble pride in the fact that some ladies were curious about his absent sex and sporadically rewarded a few by dropping his trousers and showing the fold between his thighs, and how he could make water with it like a woman. Olivier Douilhet grew old, since eunuchs are long-lived, and all through his long life he counted himself luckier than his mate Claude Outremont, for whom the same grenades that unmanned Olivier had spared his balls but had mashed up his cock—there should be memorials for anonymous lumps of flesh, missing in action: bits of rump, thigh muscle, bum and prick, and ossuaries for the splinters of bone of men like François Hautekier, who was a son of the smith, ready to succeed his elderly father above the glowing coals and the anvil, but in whose hip the doctors artificially created a gaping hole so that they could easily cut away fragments of bone with forceps, when gangrene attacked the bone and the microbes reduced it to black mush.

In those cemeteries for fractions of bodies I wouldn't erect a cross, or a statue of a grieving soldier leaning on a sword with head bowed. In a column or a wall I would insert in glass niches the eyeballs of everyone who has lost an eyeball, including at least four eyeballs from local lads, so that the past would continue to gape at us without a fringe of eyelashes ever closing over those icy stares—a grotesque, obscene memorial, certainly, but one which also commemorates, just not eloquently or in hushed reverence, but mockingly or cynically, silently shrieking.

I understand why my brother said later that those who were wounded were usually the lucky ones. I understand that their wounds—the cavities that may or may not have closed, the membrane of skin where jawbones had been shot away, the missing knuckles, the eye socket in which soft new flesh replaced the vanished pupil—left a mark in those young bodies, even if in the form of an absence, which had, as it were, hewn out a tabernacle in which they could house their disaster, just as in the medieval reliquary shrines the toenails of martyrs or splinters from the Cross were stored and on certain occasions shown to the faithful. Their misfortune, to use my mother's love of tautology for once, was their misfortune.

But what is one to do with the others, the apparently unharmed? What mausoleum, for example, would be suitable for young Etienne Leboeuf, who took part in—perhaps I should say sat out, the way we sit out a storm that overtakes us in the open—almost every campaign behind that scar of trenches and barbed wire between the coast of my fatherland and the Swiss border without getting so much as a scratch, and changed his soldier's tunic for the same grey peasant's smock that he had taken off in the summer of 1914 like so many, millions, to obey the order of the generals, the ministers and the posters on the market square, where that word was suddenly there, unattainable and virginal, not yet pierced by definitions or my own breathless memories: "*Guerre…*"

Etienne Leboeuf, twenty-four, with his brown curls and his blue eyes and a blunt, touching, turned-up nose above his eternally scabby lips; Etienne Leboeuf, whose small, compact frame was indeed slightly reminiscent of a bull calf, and in whose eyes something of the passivity of calves shone; Etienne Leboeuf, who never spoke a word about the war and was not very talkative anyway—I imagine him in the trench with the stubborn passivity of a bull calf sheltering under a tree during a storm. Not realizing the risk it is running, it stands there rubbing against the trunk, apparently unmoved by even the most powerful lightning or the most violent thunderclaps; it blinks, shakes its head, waves its tail and flaps its ears to keep the rain off. I think of what my brother, equally tight-lipped, told me very occasionally, about the most silent death you could witness

in the trenches, when the forager with his tins of provisions for
the men in a forward post nearby slipped off one of the duck-
boards and found himself in the sucking mud of a crater full
of quicksand—the silent conflict of someone who knows that if
he dares call out he will attract the attention of the enemy and
endanger not only himself but especially his mates, and at the
same time feels himself sinking, and every swing of his trunk
or arms in order to free himself gives the mud the opportunity
to suck him down even deeper. "All we could do was listen,"
said my brother, "grinding our teeth, crying, cursing under our
breath, I experienced it at least three times or so, once so close I
could hear the lad breathe, the doggedness with which at the last
he grabbed the mess tins and the soup tins in his vain attempts
to gain a hold—I can still hear the tin of the lids and handles
tapping as he pulled our food basket towards him, the breath
in his nose, more hectic and violent as the situation became
more acute and he tried to scoop away the mush, but with
every gesture simply hastened his end. My little gazelle," said
my brother, "I actually prayed then, dammit—and the restless
breathing, the cough and the retching at the first gulp of mud
in the throat, and the last, almost disappointed sigh before the
brown goo reached his lips and nostrils, and the pool closed
over him. I don't know how many met their end through stupid
accidents and not even through the bombs."

Etienne Leboeuf never drowned in the mud, rather the reverse: it
is his small, compact body, the body of a bull calf, which sucked
up the mud into itself. I imagine him in the trench during a
howitzer attack, passively silent, pressed against the wall of his
hiding place, under the rattling corrugated iron which makes

only a thin division between his squat figure and the hell above
his head. Etienne Leboeuf must have seen pagodas of clods of
earth, the short-lived Maya temples of earth and old corpses,
tree trunks and roof tiles and foundations and cadavers that rose
up where the projectiles landed and exploded with a force that
no one could imagine, not even Etienne Leboeuf himself, who,
passive as a calf during a storm, sat out the tempest, crouched
in his hollow in the ground, and did not move, just squeezed
his eyes against the seething earth or the splodges of intestine
of the man—the only incident Etienne Leboeuf ever talked
about—whom he literally saw blown to pieces next to him.

Etienne Leboeuf counted himself lucky when my uncle took
him on as a hand on the farm after the war, excited as we were
about anyone who still had all his organs, and he was grateful
to my uncle that, unlike lots of other farmers, he didn't worry
when he sometimes took off during threshing or when one of
the horses was being shod with chilly hammer blows—sometimes, during the food break, outside at the long table during the
harvest, Etienne Leboeuf would drop his knife or spoon onto
his plate and run to the barn, during churning or the beating of
the threshing machine in which the stalks were ground up. He
left everything behind and disappeared for a few hours. Who
will point the finger at the girls, the young widows, the others,
all those women, who eventually found out where he hid and
strolled furtively across the farmyard to the hayloft, climbed
the ladder and only had to see the blanket of dry grass under
which the lad had hidden shivering under the juddering that
seized his limbs, the tremors with which the war, his war, offered
itself in vain to his memory, wanted to rid itself of his tissue

and blood vessels to be finally born in language—the flesh that weeps and trembles before the word, but the word that cannot deal with that quaking fear.

Who will speak ill of the women who stripped Etienne Leboeuf from the hay like a newborn infant from its membranes, and took his head in their hands, close to their sultry bosoms, and cradled him, and stroked his forehead, and kissed his turned-up nose, and at the same time ran a hand over his belly and unbuttoned his fly to knead his sex until it was purple and throbbed in their palms, and pulled up their skirts and sat astride him in order to rock the deaf-and-dumb wound in his body to sleep in themselves—Etienne Leboeuf, who fed on sex like an infant on its mother's milk. Who knows how many times his life was saved by copulating, in the barn, behind the fence or in a stall where a girl perhaps found him hiccupping with fear under the limbs of a cow, half slumped on the milking stool, fingers frozen round the udder? It happened to me more than once that I quietly retraced my steps because in the dark, under the low beams among the cattle, I heard stammering, groaning, the whispering voice of the woman who pulled his trousers down over his buttocks there against the feeding trough and with her hand took him inside her—and who knows in how many spots, hidden or not, furtive or not, the same thing happened? Countless times probably, the crucifixes or holy water fonts merrily bouncing along on their nails in the wooden attic wall with the pounding head end of the bed beneath, on which one body found protection in another body, the dance of two terrified monkeys.

*

163

My brother said later: the brothels are doing even better business than during the war—the whore was the last refuge for the man without a leg or hands, or the dribbling Cyclops who was once the best-looking man in the street. Who will deny him the consolation of knowing himself squeezed by warm, wet flesh, and dare to find it ridiculous that the poor man grasps the all in all far more divine trembling before his glands empty, and seizes the short moment of oblivion, as gratefully as Socrates his cup of hemlock? I know what I'm talking about, in that respect I have not fought without glory—there should be monuments for them, for the countless men like Etienne Leboeuf and their consolers, Etienne Leboeuf who, as it happens, later married one of his mistresses and in his fear fertilized her no less than nine times. I still see him coming out of church on Sunday in the village where his family lived, his wife on his arm and surrounded by his family: girls who look like their mother and sons with the same squat body, in their eyes the same innocent calf's melancholy as their father, around whom they throng to wheedle a few cents for sweets—and Etienne Leboeuf himself, who at that moment sees me standing under the lime trees in the church square and greets me shyly from behind his bastion of children: still just as taciturn, but calmer, because safe.

It should be a warm, pulsating monument for him and his motherly mistresses, and all those they represent: a memorial that honours the ecstasy and the slightly laughable banality of our copulations; and anyone who threatens to find this suggestion obscene should ask himself which one he chooses of the two reactions to which that stupid war led, for which the bed and the war cemetery can happily serve as symbols. When that deluge of ammunition and mud and rubble finally ebbed, it left shipwrecked people behind for whom the world had collapsed and who had understood the message: that it's better to seek salvation by crawling away from history, either in calm happiness, or in the wombs of the masses, the sweet anaesthesia of the collective. That is the land I saw being revealed after the blood and destruction, and fortunately this time God was wise enough not to stretch a rainbow over the new earth.

Obscene is the word that I reserve for the view of a market square where, after the bang of the fatal impact has died way and the worst of the groaning has fallen silent, the sparrows are copulating again on the shoulders of the statue, and in its fixed place in the sun, on the window sill of a bourgeois house, above the smudges of blood on the pavement, the cat licks its coat clean as if nothing has happened. Obscene the rows of soldiers' helmets that I see on a dyke in the first few months after peace breaks out. My husband helps me through the omnipresent mud. He warns me to put my feet where he has first put his and not to deviate from the slippery path of planks, under which I can hear the sodden earth sighing at each step. He carries his camera on his shoulders and looks to see where he can place the tripod. The water that flows past under the dyke has the same grey vocabulary as the landscape through which it is seeking a path: ochre-coloured, dull green, dull brown under a cloudless, obscenely brilliant sky—it doesn't seem like water, but like gastric juices, fermenting under the lead weight of the sky in earth shot bare. Nowhere does a roof line or row of trees disturb or punctuate the horizon. Everything that could delight me about that countryside has gone: the long, long processions of poplars, the trunks and tops bending obliquely with the wind like a procession of the blind leading the blind, and the shy villages that huddle around the church towers like piglets searching for their mothers' nipples.

The helmets lie in rows on the slope of a dyke; I don't even know if they are Belgian helmets or German. I think that we are near Diksmuide, the place from where the salvoes boomed through the coastal plain the day I met my husband, under iron angels' wings and the clattering and my hysterical laughter. The fronts were right next to each other, divided only by the river, at most about thirty metres. I point out the helmets. They remind me of turtles that have crawled ashore to dig a hole in that earth that you can't really call formless, rather disgustingly pregnant with every conceivable form, and lay their eggs—as if, as if I definitely say, the earth, monstrous placenta, is kneading new life forms, unimaginable hybrid creatures from the mud and the bodies it has sucked in, to populate its bare, obscenely bare surface. Perhaps he can photograph them, because I still believe that you can't suggest anything better in pictures than in a picture from which the main thing is missing—but what is the main thing? He has to photograph the war, but how can you capture the nervation in an upheaval that not only travels through the ground, but through millions who have been left without sons, fathers, brothers, fiancés and husbands?

Years later, years and years later, in the time when my husband and I were the only ones to return each summer, we are looking out over one of the meadows on the slopes of the observation mounds near the border. The earth has healed, is green again, planted with young trees, cattle are grazing again, but a local farmer says that the earth is still full. "If all who are lying were to stand up, it would move, the ground," he says, "like a bedspread on a bed full of playing children."

During the annual trips that I take after my husband's death, to that same house, long since sold and standing empty, I dig for something like regret or pity deep down in myself. But all I find in my cavities is a vague kind of resentment, an ore that cannot be transformed into another mineral, innocent sadness, melancholy if you will, which I can use, and make my child pay for my inability. With an emphasis she cannot escape from, I ask her again and again if she will take me there. Since her father's death I can no longer bring myself to drive.

We seldom speak while we are en route. She holds the steering wheel in her hands, stiffly upright, the kind of driver that can never relax, and I sit next to her, map on my lap, although we both know we're going to get lost. It might be the familiar ritual that colours intimate friendships, constantly supposedly not knowing the way and then the other person says: I recognize that junction, that chapel before those two lime trees, we must go left here according to me. But we remain tight-lipped and I never look at the map.

As soon as we approach the border area I rely on the silhouette of the hills. At their feet the roads dawdle, fork and become increasingly narrow, capillaries in the landscape, as if to smuggle us unseen to the other side. No cloud of dust betrays our route.

Sometimes a guffaw escapes me, equally dismayed and sarcastic, and I see that my child is too stubborn to ask what there is to laugh about. I can see it from the desperate grip of her hands on the steering wheel. I can feel it by the brusqueness with which she accelerates or decelerates or changes gear, and I think: here we are then, a mother and her daughter, the only fruit of my loins that I have ever pushed out of my pelvis, while the grinding, millstone silence of fathers and sons crushes us to dust—two women side by side, two pictograms of resentment.

The map on my lap is no more than a fig leaf, the cloth in which we break our bitter bread. I want to get lost and my daughter knows it. She brakes too abruptly and takes the bends too fast, to make me sick, but I don't turn a hair. Every relationship composes its own soundtrack. If the drumming of hail is ours, so be it.

I wait and say nothing because I know that she'll get fed up with it sooner or later, and will park the car somewhere in the greenery, get out, put her transistor on the bonnet, spread the blanket on the grass, unload the picnic hamper and position herself with a book in her folding chair, as if she is actually enjoying the excursion. I will sit down on the blanket, take a generous helping of cold chicken and, to spice up her horror a little more, prattle about the soil on which her strapped heels are reluctantly resting: my beloved land, dredged up from sea water and crumbling away, as my father always told us, keeps sinking back into the waves, and is pushed up again, like a laundry maid dips the linen into the suds, and pulls it out again, wrings it out and submerges it again, scores, hundreds of times in the terrifying time that doesn't remember our own stories even as an itch—and then I think, again and again: everything is one big cemetery. What do you think, my child, is the world incredibly ancient or on the contrary very young? What do you think of yourself when you see those smudges of chalky soil through the topsoil, there and there and there? Of a cadaver like mine, shrinking skin, gradually bared bones? Or is the world finally, finally getting its first teeth again, milk teeth, piercing through smooth gums? Tell me, what do you think? Fold open the map with which you like everyone else designate, invoke, deform or combat the obtuse bedrock of existence. And I still don't know why I take out my bitterness on her, and where that sour sadness comes from, or why I am so bitter in a time of peace and was so peaceful when I saw the war passing, in the blazing summer, between the wine-red brick houses, the hedges and willows, so close and far away.

ANOTHER OBSCENE DEATH was that of Amélie Bonnard, struck down as if from nowhere, little Amélie, the youngest child of Marie and Alberic Bonnard, always in her winter coat, like that sun-drenched early evening at the end of August when she ceased to exist—perhaps she kept that coat on all the time because they were not very well off at home, or perhaps she just liked that item of clothing, despite the thick woollen material and huge great buttons, much too warm for a summer's day, and she liked strolling round in it coquettishly, with those precious dainty steps, which always struck me when I saw her going to the baker's or to school, as if she had no muscles, but her skin hid a mechanism of springs—perhaps she had put her coat on when the girls who lived nearby came to ask if she could come out to play, in the meadow behind the church, the old cemetery near the brook, in the lee of the thorn hedge, because she felt like a pretty, pert little madam. You know what girls are like, irresistibly attracted to braids and ribbons and pins and chains and their mother's secret box of rouge, which on the sly they smear, as a still unpractised womanhood, too lavishly on their cheeks.

She made herself up clumsily and girlishly that afternoon, little Amélie Bonnard. Since her father works on the railway and her Maman does odd jobs at the butcher's and the *boulangerie*, where she rinses the remains of dough out of kettles or cleans the chopping block, there is nobody to keep an eye on Amélie—how would you be yourself if you are home at a stolen hour and the wall clock strikes boredom and the arms of the copper candelabra above the table in the dining room serve as a trapeze for the acrobatics of the equally bored flies? Who would be able to control themselves, who wouldn't display Maman's treasures on that table, under the bored flies, flick open the hand mirror and open the box of rouge, pure gold dust in your eyes, incense and myrrh, and smear the powder generously, all too generously over your face, until you look like a porcelain doll and you think you're ravishing?

And when the girls from the area and some other mites from the village, teenagers with thick knees and socks round their ankles, come and tap on the window, giggling: "Are you coming, Amélie, to play hide-and-seek round the church and drop the handkerchief by the brook?", who wouldn't be tempted to put on Maman's best earrings, to be able to trip madame-like after the bigger girls and feel the luxurious weight of those huge great sapphires, you imagine, which pull your ear lobes down to your shoulders at every step you take? She must have felt regal and rich and quite a girl, Amélie Bonnard, and perhaps she didn't notice anything when she ran after her friends across the grass and suppressed the urge to catch them up quickly because she definitely didn't want to lose her mother's earrings as she hopped over the tussocks—perhaps she was so absorbed that she didn't even feel pain when the piece of shrapnel hit her in the neck and the girls on the other side of the field dispersed in panic.

My mother and I were on our way to the village, "down", as we were wont to say, because the village centre was on the plain, at the foot of the slope in which the house where my mother was born lay hidden, relatively safe, naturally protected by the slope which behind the house continued upward to the Lost Wood, as my brother and I called the section of woodland that stretched from behind the house to the top of the hill. We had taken the narrow path that descended from the outermost orchard to a side street of the market square, for since almost all our horses had been requisitioned we had to rely mainly on our own two feet for getting about. It is strange to experience something for four years that would later be called a world war, while the war for us reduced the world to a village and the farm where we were staying.

My mother was curt that afternoon. She felt I should also make myself useful in some way in times like these and to her taste I was doing so with too little enthusiasm. A few weeks before she had entrusted to me, under her supervision, the care of the chickens in the *basse-cour*: cleaning out their runs, giving them fresh water, feeding them, collecting the eggs and counting the chicks. I told her that I thought chickens were stupid creatures, almost as stupid as turkeys. She retorted that chickens were not reared for conversation: "You've far too many posh sentiments, dear child," she had concluded, in a tone that suggested good nature but had been audibly marinated in vitriol for several days. She was wearing a straw hat and held it on her head with one hand as she ticked me off. The hedge on either side of the narrow, uneven path sometimes came up to our ears and the twigs threatened to pull the hat off her crown. I myself wasn't wearing any headgear. Summer had passed its climax; blackberries were ripening in the hedge. It was the time of the spiders, and they were already hanging like treacherous stars in their silk necklaces, rocking back and forth on the branches in a lazy breeze.

After a while we had fallen silent. My mother's irritation had ebbed away. When we were on holiday her angry turns were generally more fleeting than during the rest of the year, and in all those years that we were separated from my father, her periods never assumed the dimensions they did when we were at home, as if her whole being at that time was imbued with the deep concentration which also seized her the afternoon that Amélie Bonnard died, while we descended along the path and she watched where she put her feet, so as not to stumble and to avoid her skirt getting caught in the hedge.

Below us the village lay glowing in the afternoon. The roofs reflected the sunlight, which was already beginning to take on an evening hue, and just outside the built-up area the clouds cast patches of shadow on the meadows and the ruminating cattle, which themselves seemed scattered like rusty brown patches in the grassland under the azure. Beyond the village, in the west, above the coastline which on some days I could see even without a telescope, above the invisible sea, the sky was deeper in colour—a blue like a guttural sound.

I can understand why my daughter, later, during the next war, on that Sunday morning when we are standing together at the window in the drawing room below, waiting for lunch, and are looking out, to where spring on heat is blowing an abstract painting of chestnut blossom down the street—I understand why she says: "I thought it would rain any day…" As if war is just as much a meteorological phenomenon and the heavens supply our tragedies with fitting decors—but it is a deathly still afternoon at the end of the summer of 1915. In the hedge alongside the path the first crickets are starting to chirp, among the lowest twigs behind the nettles and the grass sounds the call of the shrew, ready to hunt beetles or worms.

First we had heard whistling and we both looked up, and stretched above the top of the hedge, but saw nothing. Then a bang followed, and another: short, hard, dry. Instinctively we dived for cover behind the hedge, and when we looked up again there rose from beyond the roofs of the houses round the church at the edge of the village two fountains of rubble and smoke, I can't describe them any differently, two claws that for a few seconds climbed above the roof line and then subsided.

As the impact reverberated there was other noise: fragments landing on roofs, breaking glass, barking dogs, voices calling to each other, not in panic, more excited. My mother and I hurried down, attracted by the commotion and without stopping to think if we might be running a risk. We reached the first back gardens, where the path forced its way between two houses, to the square around the *mairie*—and I remember that I suddenly found it all so ridiculous, Madame Ducarne's vegetables in their straight beds behind the hedge, the last runner beans and the young winter leeks and the bolted radishes with their flowers, an armada of butterflies sailing around them, next to Madame Ducarne's ever-open back door; on the lid of the rainwater drain under the window of her kitchen the wooden bucket and the eternal hoe.

*

Between the houses: the boiling square, women walking past with their aprons, stained from their daily activities, still on. Men point to something in the sky—the place where the impact blew away a chimney and smashed it on the cobbles below, as it turns out when my mother and I arrive breathless in the square, just in time to see the girls. The oldest are carrying the youngest, the youngest are crying, the oldest are putting a brave face on it and calling out: "Amélie. Amélie Bonnard fell and she's lying there…There!" Arms are outstretched, fingers point in the direction of the church, a few side streets farther on, in the square with the lime trees. The women walk in that direction, my mother and I in the rear. The girls follow, calm the fear of the little ones, and dry their tears.

Above the back of the church there hangs a cloud of dust, ethereal dull red, yellow ochre, grey-white. "In the field there," cry the girls. "She's lying in the field." Only when we walk past the church onto the lawn do we see the hole that has been knocked in the wall, and the lopsided crosses on the tombs, and the smoke rising from the nave of the church—one of the bombs must have fallen right next to the choir, on the narrow gravel path that divided the back of the chapel from the first row of graves. I heard later that Monsieur Bossuges, who had been buried about three weeks before, Monsieur Bossuges, a gentleman of private means, self-appointed dignitary, who had had a tomb built while he was alive in which the accumulation of cherubs and other feathered creatures supported the assumption that he expected a certain esteem in the hereafter also—Monsieur Bossuges, it was said, was hurled out of the hole that one of the bombs had made in his pathetic one-man mausoleum and was found in his best suit, without footwear, hanging right across the tomb of Mademoiselle Bernier, former schoolmistress, as if he had tried to clamber over a stone fence to lie beside her, which in my uncle's opinion wasn't even that improbable. Monsieur Bossuges and Mademoiselle Bernier lived very close together and when they were alive, all kinds of things were whispered about them which, my mother felt, would have been a lot less interesting if people had simply said them out loud. "In any case, dear sister," my uncle commented, by way of conclusion, "who on earth has himself buried with his glasses in his inside pocket?" What truth there was to all this I never knew, my uncle was not averse to exaggeration, and when we bury Amélie Bonnard a few days later, the *mairie* has had all the rubble cleared and the craters have been filled with it. The glazed tips of the wings of Monsieur Bossuges's angels gleam like children's teeth in the sand.

Because of the rouge it looks as if Amélie Bonnard is not dead at all. Because of the rouge and the earrings, and thick winter coat over her summer dress, she looks like a child very accurately playing dead. It takes a while to find her, flat on her back, an unsightly bundle of blue-grey serge amid the copper-coloured grass of the falling evening. She must have turned round at the last, wanting to retrace her steps, because she is lying with her feet in the direction of the gate in the hedge and the dusty country road, arms next to her trunk, a last convulsion still in her fingers under the thick sleeves of her coat. The eyes, vacant, stare at the clear sky without seeing the clogs and socks, the grazed knees, the skirts of the women, or the face of my mother, who kneels down by her and superfluously, since everyone knows that

Amélie is dead, puts the back of her hand against the child's cheeks, the powdered cheeks, and then turns her hand over, and strokes Amélie's forehead to close her eyes, and then with the chin in the hollow of her palm pushes it against Amélie's upper jaw. "Someone should tell Marie," she says without looking up, and when she gets up again I see she is close to tears—but it isn't necessary to call Marie, more people are approaching down the country road. Above the voices and the footsteps Madame Bonnard calls, "Amélie, Amélie! Where are you?" as she walks towards us and wipes her hands on her apron, covered in smears of fat from her work at the butcher's, and pushes her way through the people, the men who keep an embarrassed distance, the children whom she pulls brusquely aside until she is standing next to my mother and in turn sinks to her knees by her daughter, blushing from the rouge, the earrings glistening in the grass—"Silly child…" she hisses in a voice that is breaking.

She looks unharmed, Amélie Bonnard, an expensive powdered doll left behind by a spoilt rich person's child, but when her mother lifts her head up she withdraws her hand in horror, red with blood, because the back of Amélie's skull is left behind in the grass and her own fingers sink into the soft mass of the brain—and she does not so much utter a cry, Marie Bonnard, as a groan that seems to issue more from her tissue and bones than from her chest, as if all the tendons and joints were howling in their sockets. My mother puts a hand to her mouth and turns her head away. "Send them away," she finally mumbles. "*Les enfants*. Send then away, Hélène. Take them with you to the market square."

*

177

Only when we rinsed her clean in our cellar, where it was cool, as we waited for Monsieur Véclin, carpenter and undertaker for the occasion to make her coffin, was the colour of death exposed in Amélie's body, and my mother and I, who washed the child while her own mother vacantly stroked the bloody locks, we gulped and both bit our bottom lips. My mother had lent her shawl, so that Monsieur Véclin could bind Amélie's head before he took the body away, and then it emerged that the mortuary had also been destroyed, and Monsieur Véclin admitted that because of what he called "the situation" he did not have sufficient planks at home, so that it might be quite some time before there was a coffin—"And you understand, Madame Demont, with this heat…"—then she had summoned me again: "Run home quickly, Hélène, ask uncle to send the dog cart, and bring a blanket with you."

And so little Amélie Bonnard arrived at our house towards evening, under a blanket on the dog cart, followed by a procession of women and children. My mother supported Madame Bonnard, I walked ahead, next to the elderly servant who handled the dog. No one spoke. Behind me was the sound of suppressed sobs. The wheels of the cart crunched on the gravel, the dog panted. In our yard Madame Bonnard took her daughter off the cart and carried her into the house in her arms. We showed her the way, down the steps, into the cellar area, the vaulted passage under the house, with countless side rooms, one of them the cool room, with the flowing water and the big cold stone in the middle, on which Amélie Bonnard was set down.

*

My mother sent all the others away, instructed the maid to bring jugs of water, towels and washbasins and soap. We undid the straps of Amélie's shoes. Madame Bonnard took the earrings off her child and put them in the pocket of the apron she still had on. She could not take her eyes off her daughter's face, which in her hands blushed so unnaturally in death. "We've informed Abbé Foulard," said my mother. Marie Bonnard nodded, but did not look up. "He's on his way." We unbuttoned Amélie's coat, and the stiff material did not easily give. My mother said: "Take her socks off" and then turned to the maid, Madeleine, who was waiting by the door and looking on. "Fetch bandages, from the boudoir upstairs."

We pulled her arms from the sleeves, I took Amélie's shoes off her heels, rolled the socks over the ankles and insteps of her cold feet. Madame Bonnard kissed her daughter on the nose, helped move the body upright and let it rest against her hips when we took off Amélie's dress and vest, taking the material off carefully, over the head that waggled, as if the child were still alive, in a deep sleep or seized by a high fever—but death was already painting her body with its contrary palette, from within it was draining the colour from her tissues. Blood was settling in the arteries, the little blood that had not leaked away into the grass, in the minutes after she had been hit. Amélie's pale limbs, the clumsy arms, the round tummy, the touching crease of the child's sex between her thighs, the fingernails already going blue, made the contrast with the powdered face even more absurd, not to say, I keep repeating the word, obscene. My mother first covered Amélie's thighs with a towel and with a wet sponge rubbed the rouge from the cheeks. "Lather her, Hélène," she ordered me. "Take a basin and lather her."

I washed Amélie's ankles and calves, behind her knees. My movements were continued in the lame muscles of the lifeless body, which bobbed up and down at every stroke of the flannel over the skin. I lathered her wrists, the folds between her fingers, the elbows, the narrow chapels of her armpits, where the hairs would never grow that could drive a man wild with lust—and I thought, as stupid as it may seem, of the week before, when my mother had forced me to help her slaughter four chickens for the Sunday meal: how she had first pointed out the victims to me, among them unfortunately the creature I had out of boredom christened Madame de Staël because it was a chicken that radiated a certain nobility, although according to my mother she had simply stopped laying for good and was only noble enough for the bouillon: "You mustn't give them names, child, that just makes it difficult. A chicken is a chicken."

She had thrust the creature into my hands and snapped at me: "Don't let go or there'll be trouble." Through the coat of feathers I had felt the warmth of that living being in my palms, the vibrating, restlessly beating flesh that, when my mother ordered me to lay the creature on the chopping block, did not even resist, but sank into a kind of hypnotic sleep, the pale eyelids closed over the reptilian chilliness of the pupils, and only when my mother—shockingly resolute in my eyes, a different figure suddenly emerged from inside her, a woman who showed the same routine hardness with which Emilie in her kitchen at home ruled over life and death—only when my mother with a resolute blow of the heavy cleaver separated the head from the body did the creature seem to come to life in its death throes: the legs that scraped along my forearm, the trembling, the dying jerks, the spasms that pushed life out of the arteries and cells with every gulp of warm blood, until the claws finally relaxed, the muscular spasms subsided and my mother, with sleeves rolled up, hands on hips and the bloodstained cleaver in her fist, announced with satisfaction: "*Bon*, that one's gone."

I don't know what dumbfounded me most: the death that I had felt happen, or my mother's transfiguration, from a lady who at home would have called herself *mondaine* without the least scruple if that had not testified to excessive vanity, to a being that just as coolly bit through umbilical cords and major arteries, and carefully prepared that child for her last journey. "Put out her clothes ready, Marie," she said tactfully when we had almost finished drying Amélie. Madame Bonnard nodded and turned to the square box and the holdall on one of the tables in the cellar. She had fetched from home the Communion clothes that Amélie would have worn in church the following year, the clothes her mother herself had worn, for her own Communion. "She was so looking forward to it," whispered Madame Bonnard as she took the top off the box, folded open the delicate tissue paper and did not turn round as she spoke, as if she knew that my mother was taking the opportunity carefully to undo the shawl around Amélie's head, as if she were taking a fragile present from its packaging.

It was starting to get dark. "Give us some light, Madeleine," said my mother to the maid, who was still standing against the door and, in the light of the candlestick she was holding in one hand, looked more than usually like a crudely carved wooden statue, weathered as she was, with forearms that seemed disproportionately long; and now she was standing there with her arms crossed, those long forearms and rough hands, in one of them the candlestick with the hissing flame. She might have been a genie called forth from a magic lamp, who silently fulfils other people's wishes.

Madeleine came closer and held the candlestick above Amélie's body while my mother undid the shawl further, pulling it slowly free of the locks of hair and the congealed blood. Madame Bonnard spread her daughter's clothes out on the table, the Communion dress, the white stockings, the white mules, the mother-of-pearl rosary and the shiny gloves, and more clearly than before used her back as a shield between her and my mother—I could see from her whole attitude that she was doing her best to think of something else. Of anything, but not of her child behind her back, of the bloody shawl that was lying openly on the slab, or the water in the basin that was going redder and redder whenever she dipped the cotton cloth with which she was washing the head in it and wrung it out. We were silent, the candle flame hissed, the water sloshed in the basin.

"Help me a moment, Hélène." I went over to her. My mother gripped my hand, with her other hand lifted up Amélie's head and slid my hand underneath. The head was cold, cold as the stone on which it had been resting. On my fingers I could feel the loose piece of Amélie's skull give way under the pressure of my palm, and it was as if the lifelessness, the deadness, death itself, its chilly nothingness, its festival of freezing, its greedy congealing, transferred itself to my fingers from that head, which was obviously no longer the head of Amélie Bonnard who two or three hours before had been hopping through the grass, but the head of a dead person, which lay in my hand like the curve of a cracked jug.

I shivered. My mother said later: "That was fear, my child. You're as frightened of death as anyone else. Don't fool yourself." But at the moment itself she had said nothing. She had simply stopped her work. With the roll of bandage in her hands that she had wound around Amélie's head from her neck, she had looked up at me. A few strands had come loose from her hair, which she wore up in a bun; they were hanging in front of her eyes, which fixed me for a couple of seconds—a look that could always do more than a thousand slaps or reproaches and needed no syllables to make itself understood: "Don't dream of having a fainting fit or even being sick." I looked away. She pulled the bandage further round Amélie's head. "We've got to hurry," she said quietly. She meant that the body was starting to go stiff. Amélie's head seemed to be screwed to her neck, her lips pressed together more firmly than before, narrowed to a red-blue strip on that under-the-breath body. All the dead mumble.

There was a knock. Madeleine put down the candle and went to the door, which she opened a fraction. "Véclin," she growled. She had a vocabulary of basalt, and language that resounded from her weathered wooden body like the rattle of stones in a tin. "Tell him to wait," said my mother. "We're not finished yet. Send him upstairs. My brother can give him something to drink." Madeleine mumbled something and pushed the door shut again. My mother turned round, put her hands on Madame Bonnard's shoulders. "We've finished, Marie. We can dress her. Come on, turn round. You can stay here tonight, I'll have them get a room ready."

Obscene is the word that I repeat. Obscene the sight of Amélie Bonnard, at noon still a child who probably put her hair behind her ears in front of the mirror before smearing her mother's rouge on her face, by evening a dead child-woman in a wedding dress. Her shoes seemed not to fit, to be too loose around her heels, the gloves too precious, the rosary too pathetic, the veil that we had drawn over her head and the bandage too ethereal in the light of the candle. We stood at her feet. My mother took off the apron that she had worn the whole time, straightened her shoulders and gave a sigh that was like a suppressed sob. There was another knock at the door. Véclin. My mother indicated with her eyes that it would be best for us to go now. Monsieur Véclin came in, cap in hand, servilely nodding greetings; next to my mother he suddenly seemed to shrink. We left him with Madame Bonnard.

I walked ahead of my mother and the maid Madeleine, towards the steps at the end of the cellar passageway. I heard my mother say: "Keep an eye on things, Madeleine. If he dares charge for so much as one plank of ours, I'll knock his brains out with his own hammer."

T HE EVENING FELL, the day dawned. Madame Bonnard kept vigil in the cellar with her dead daughter. Sometimes people came to pay their respects, but as the morning wore on it became quiet. My mother bent over the tub with the maid, Madeleine, and washed the blood out of little Amélie's clothes, the child had wet herself as she died.

"Do go and sit in the shade," she called to me. "It's far too hot, Hélène. You'll be getting heatstroke next."

Noon was approaching. The sun heated the inner courtyard and forged it into the sacrificial dish for the cult of its stasis at the zenith.

Only animals could look the afternoon straight in the eye, blind to what it had melted, deaf to the deathly quiet tumult of things that the middle of the day unleashed and that in my ears sounded louder than the roar of cannon on the horizon, that increasingly was only heard when it subsided. The afternoon exposed the world's nakedness; it showed its arse, the obscene—the word continues to haunt me—grimace of its blunt indifference. It tapped in the joins in the stones, it rustled on lizards' feet over the vines of the ivy against the side of the house behind my back.

Doves cooed, claimed silence for themselves, the din seemed to fall silent. In the cellar Amélie Bonnard, who hour after hour merged more with her own dead self, drew the darkness towards her and dissolved in the amniotic fluid of the great nothingness, however white she was in her robe, however palely she might lie there under her veil of lace blossoms.

"When death comes," I say to Rachida, "I'll stretch out my arms to him and he will find me as you left me, with hair brushed and a necklace on."

"He'll want to dance with you, Mrs Helena," she laughs.

It is she who takes me from the chair to the bed, lifts me up for a second with her arms under my armpits to let me rest on the mattress, and takes my legs by the ankles and lays them on the sheet, and then plumps up the pillows and arranges them behind my hips and back—and finally closes the curtains. I don't like the afternoons any more, not like I used to.

"Have a good nap," she whispers, and goes downstairs into the kitchen. Perhaps she rests on a chair in the back garden, and lowers the long, wide trousers to show the sun her knees and lights up a cigarette—the small sins she allows herself in silence, beneath the leaden grin of the devil of the afternoon.

In hidden spots, on the side of the house, somewhat camouflaged, I tried to absorb the heat and stay so quiet that the lizards, which always shot away into the wide gaps between the bluestone paving slabs, would overcome their fear and crawl out of their crevices, first sticking their emerald heads above the shadow of their accommodation and then, in the twinkling of an eye, re-emerging in a flash from their hiding places and coming to a halt before my eyes on the boiling stone.

The indifference of those tiny reptiles could make me jealous. Their divine inertia was like an elixir whose occult formulas

I just couldn't crack in my own fibre. I was only a postulant, there was too much rodent left in me, too much mouse-grey industriousness for me to be able to embrace the strict doctrine of motionlessness—and if I lower myself in my former shape, there on the bluestone in that afternoon, then I find in the motionlessness I was trying to achieve the core around which, in the years since, has grown the bittersweet flesh of the being that I was to become despite myself: a creature with a soul without warmth that wants to sleep without budging on a hot stone in the long afternoon of history, unaffected by horrors or glories. I wanted to shake off tissue that had worn out, slough off layers of dead skin, shed my skin in sentences so as never to have to resign myself to a definitive form—hungry for the ability of those lizards, which could leave their tail behind in the mouth of a predator. So don't think that this thrashing lump of language on your tongue betrays anything at all of the true beast.

In a side shed Monsieur Véclin was finishing Amélie's coffin. The hammer blows that resounded from the workshop across the inner courtyard had something apprehensive about them, as if the silent presence of the maid Madeleine, who had taken my mother's hint to keep an eye on things quite literally and went to look every few minutes, made such an impression that he was very restrained in handling his tools.

Only Madeleine could "stand" when she stood. She can stand still like the sun over the walls of Jericho. "She's 'standing' again," we would say when, passing the window of the dining room or walking across the yard with two buckets of kitchen scraps for the pigs, she suddenly stopped, the buckets in her hands swaying to and fro on their handles. No one could say with such relish as my mother that the maid was "standing" again. It wouldn't surprise me if we had first heard the saying from her mouth, since it was as it were a concentrated tautology, the pinnacle of her mirror definitions. She could say "Madeleine is 'standing' again" with a subtle emphasis that was able to detach the verb from the sentence for a moment, so that it spread the echo of unsuspected meanings. She didn't need metaphors. She could let the words "stand" as mysteriously as Madeleine could "stand".

Now the maid is "standing" in a corner of the work shed, very close to the open doorway and the yard beyond, while she watches as Monsieur Véclin planes the rough planks, her rough hands in the pockets of her apron, and although she doesn't appear to be paying attention to anything in particular, I'm certain that she registers every curl that the carpenter's plane pushes ahead of it over the plank, from which rises the sharp smell of dry wood, the smell of the patience of trees.

Véclin wipes the sweat from his face with the back of his hand.

Madeleine "stands" and watches. Soon she will report everything to my mother.

"A person feels like a big mug of cold coffee with a good spoonful of sugar," mumbles Véclin, and adds hopefully: "…in this heat."

Madeleine wakes from her ceramic inertia, swallows back, behind the vertical wrinkles that form a kind of throat sac between her lower jaw and her collarbone, a mouthful of spittle and from the sound of it very tough mucus, and says: "It's too early. We don't have coffee until later here, after the midday break. Go on working, *copain*. Help us bury the poor child quickly. It'll taste twice as good."

I wait until death dawns in objects, the naked hour when things lose their leaves and all becomes leggy and dumb, not able to clothe themselves with the habits or meanings in which we usually drape them—as if a short moment of symbolic weightlessness occurs in which the world forgets its coherence and God Himself washes his hands of creation so that everything shudders, eye to eye with itself. I wonder: is everything we do or don't do ever anything other than modulated desperation?

At noon everyone withdrew into the twilight of the house, which seemed to rise from the cellar, where the child lay on the cold slab. Up in her room my mother has the maid help her out of her corsets—and I hear her snort in her sleep, here, in the afternoon of this story.

I wanted to sleep and stay awake at the same time, mount guard over things with the pomposity of our waking consciousness, but also to allow myself to sink into slumber, which like a good father knows us better than we want to admit and always remains realistic.

The roar of the guns, in the east, in the north, towards the south, mounted, ebbed away again, regained strength, a dull pounding, like that of giant fists on a table top far away. Sweat crept over my crown, through my hair, and ran down over the corners of my eyes, down along my nostrils. The pigs were baking in their terracotta mud bath, the cats spied on the deathly quiet explosions of the light through the keyholes of their pupils.

Only in Van Gogh did I rediscover those noons. His unstable suns and the sloppy Milky Ways in his black vibrating nights; the unbearable darkness which frightened him so much that he riddled it with stars as bright as the scorching luxuriance of the eternal noon of his madness. He knew the madness of the cats, but could not find their sleep, so the demon devoured him.

Noon is Emilie's time. In her basement kitchen she undoes the apron, sinks down full-length on a chair which has long since given up complaining and whining about her weight, her prehistoric hips, and cools herself by waving her skirts—the sunlight makes the pans above the stove blush in their copper.

Noon is the smell of sea water, my father's face hanging above the horizon of sleep, the bitter smell of iodine and the texture of sand that grates against my forehead in the hollow of his collarbone, between my calves and the long black hairs on his forearms—I feel his heart beating below my forehead, the beat of the artery in his neck. A little longer and the sunlight itself will clatter off all things, the photons will ricochet round like marbles—or my mother, whom I didn't hear wake up, will pull me roughly by the shoulder and say that I am completely crazy, a religious fanatic, and isn't one child enough to worry about, without knowing if he is still alive, if he is still unscathed and healthy.

She was not only my mother, the being who wove me from her own flesh and blood, a fleshy loom of generations. She was also, in an order beyond biology, the mother of identity. She wanted to establish me in the impatience that forces its way between us and the inexhaustibility of the world and the things in it, which as children we explore with the wings of Hermes on our ankles, and obliges us to compromise—impatience that charred in the afternoon, when praying did not help.

I'm sure that she taught me how to slaughter chickens or instructed me to help her wash the body of the little girl to point out to me that a human being cannot dawdle endlessly at the gate of infinity. One day we must turn round and, as it were, step back inside, accept the world in its external form and for convenience's sake assume that all things are themselves: a chicken a chicken, a human being a human being—and as the chicken clucks, so a human being should obviously speak for itself.

I have never been able to become grown-up in this way and I remain astonished at the countless ceasefires that we sign daily, without reacting to the conditions with a curse or even the slightest sob, let alone a mocking laugh. But who am I? The kind of child that in the playground thinks the rules of hopscotch are for other people and convinces herself that her pathetic infringements win her admiration.

In the autumn when everyone became ill, I am helping my mother out of her underwear. While I strip her for her afternoon nap we start arguing—the only time we had a real argument. When I loosen all the hooks and laces from her corsage—the shell of belts and material falls off her, black as the wings of a bat (is it because she can breathe more freely that she bursts loose, breaks out)—I see her breasts lose their volume and spread out over her ribs. Her nipples look at me as if they want to say: forgive her, she is upset—and under the skin a soft emulsion shifts, towards the navel, around the hips (I think how beautiful she is, how bloody beautiful she is, my mother the swamp woman, certainly now she takes the pins out of her hair and her coiffure cascades with almost audible relief over her shoulder blades, a curtain of fine, long hair, a tapestry, chestnut brown stippled with grey).

I've forgotten why she bursts out, what exactly triggers it, why she is more sobbing that shouting, a sad rage that shivers out, through the fat on her hips, her navel, the tired breasts, the encrusted nipples (I think how beautiful you are, and why must you break down one day?). She refuses the nightdress that I hold up for her and try to pull over her head (I see her back in the mirror next to the window, the full moon of her bottom, the strand of hair that fans out above her hips). She stands there, fearful I would say, whining, eyes red, behind her back on the bedside table my father's last letter before the war separated us. She covers her breasts with her arms—what is she trying to say, what is she shouting, what is she hurling at me in lumps, half word, half whining? She turns round, surveys herself in the mirror, pulls her hair over her breasts, Eve rejected, she looks at me with eyes swollen with tears, desperate—her hair seems to be streaming out through the window shutters (or vice versa, it is as if she wants to gather the whole battered world around her, the threadbare quilt of rows of houses, bullet holes, overgrown fields, streets with their damaged teeth of bullet-marked house fronts and the cemeteries and the graves and the dead and everything).

She sticks her forefinger in her mouth, perhaps she's pricked herself again on the pins during that eternal mending—I heard her pulling open seams. With the twin sisters she pulled the sleeves out of old coats, as though they were drawing and quartering a heretic (I could hear from the tugs, the capricious strokes that something was wrong).

She says, I feel hot. I say, it's freezing outside, Maman, it's never been so cold. She lets me pull the nightdress over her head after all; I hear her moaning in the folds: "Why don't I have normal arguments with my daughter?" She pulls the material over her trunk herself, and straightens the ribbons. "About flowers, fashion, theatre. Instead of over…" She looks up again into the mirror, her eyes fill with tears again, her chin trembles, she scrabbles for a word, "…consonants!"

I burst out laughing. She sent me a look like a projectile, went to her bed and pulled the blankets off while leaning on the bed with one arm. I went over to her, bent over to tuck her in, but she gripped both my wrists and gazed directly into my eyes.

I have never heard anyone whisper so sweetly, manage to spew her gall so viciously in my face, well aimed, with the finesse of a cobra: "*T'as sacrifié ta prudence à ce drôle Monsieur Heirbeir, n'est-ce pas, chérie?*"

I turned round, walked towards the door—I thought, she's got a temperature, she too, she's delirious.

She waited until I was almost outside before giving me the fatal blow, in the back. Deliberately in the mixture of French and Flemish she always used when mocking me, she snapped at me: "*Ne me dites pas des blaaskes, mamzel. Je le sens.*" These "blaaskes" or bubbles were my transparent fibs.

I SAW HIM AGAIN a year after the death of the child. One afternoon the door of the church porch swung open and he disturbed my reflections, in the darkness of the aisle to which I often retreated when my mother sent me downstairs, to post letters, run errands or to deliver eggs to the elderly—jobs that I did quickly in order to take some time for myself, and I liked whiling away those few moments of freedom in the church because it was cool and dark in summer, and quiet when there were no services.

Since the impact of the projectiles, workmen had provisionally closed the hole in the high choir with lengths of wood and dull-green tarpaulin and swept the rubble aside, against the wall of the aisle, perhaps to be able to use a sieve to recover plasterwork or other usable ornaments—for later, when everything was over and we woke up from the impermanence that had all of us in its grip.

Someone had put the saints that had been blown down by the blast and whose stone feet still rested on the plinths, at an angle against the wall, next to the improvised high altar in the transept. The first service that Abbé Foulard had held there had been for the child, five days after her death, on the last day of the summer—the wind turned that morning and all through the Mass made a loose corner of the tarpaulin flap languorously, like a lame green wing. As we sat round the coffin, the planks of which my mother counted, the first rain kept gushing over the floor whenever the wind lifted the tarpaulin.

He was carrying three bags on long straps over his shoulders, and under his arm a small wooden valise, and walked past me up the aisle to the high choir, attracted by the light that slid through the gaps in the roofing of tarpaulin and laths over the walls and fell in shafts onto the cleared rubble and the saints' statues.

He stood there for a while, laden as he was, looked around, sought a suitable viewpoint for catching that light, then put down the bags on a couple of chairs, just before the high choir, kept an eye on the play of light, bent over one of the bags, opened the wooden valise, and only when he stood up again, with a folding camera in his hand, did he catch sight of me. I was sitting in the shadow. He did not recognize me to begin with, frowned, then smiled: "Mademoiselle Demont… What a pleasant surprise," and came towards me with his hand outstretched.

After that first meeting and the little incident in the casino at night I wrote him no letters, made no enquires about him, who he was, whether anyone knew him, where he was. If something was to happen the opportunity would present itself. My mother called me hyper-romantic because of that attitude, and perhaps she is right. Love has always made me lame, fatalistic. If it does not have the character equally of fate and of a blessing, it leaves me cold—or rather, it is not love at all.

He took photos for people whom he called with mocking emphasis "my clients". People associated with the papers across the Channel, who were always short of material, preferably obtained from other sources than the official war photographers. He said that they were crazy about ruins of churches and children— "Works miracles, it seems, a good ruin in the dailies."

He had to do it secretly and also more or less anonymously; he had no official access but knew the way. He had connections, he said, at the press bureau where he was the errand boy for some big noise or other: "Thanks to Daddy. Friends in high places…" He seemed to regret it. "Not that he's asked me anything. Wouldn't want to see his little boy blown to smithereens, somewhere in the mud of Flanders or the…" in irritation his fingers drummed on the camera the rhythm in which he spat out the words, "…bloody fucking Dar-da-nelles…"

When I told him about Amélie, and said he should have come a year earlier, he gave a sarcastic guffaw. "No dead kiddies, Miss. No corpses. Such an inconvenience, to have people actually dying in war… unless of course if they manage to do so gracefully. Saw one of those a couple of weeks ago, near Ypres. Doesn't happen that often. Such elegance, the fellow looked like bloody Michelangelo's Adam the way he'd fallen. As naked too, I'm afraid. Another inconvenience. No nudity! If you happen to die in this war, Miss Demont…" He looked straight at me: "Please do keep your frock on…"

"I'll try my best, monsieur."

He took a few photos of the interior, the deserted choir with the hole, the temporary high altar in the transept, but he also wanted a couple of me.

"I wouldn't want to find myself in your newspapers," I protested, all too coquettishly.

He refused to be discouraged. "It's for my personal collection…"

I asked him if he kept all his conquests in albums.

"Sure, piles of them." He winked. "Have stopped counting altogether…"

He took two or three, with the small camera that he would later give me as a present. "You seem quite a pensive person," he grinned as he pressed the shutter, came closer and made as if to shoot again. "A penny for your thoughts, as we say in England."

"I was thinking, Mister Herbert, that if you were an onion, I'd like to peel you."

He paused, waited till I was looking straight into the lens. "Well, I'm relieved you don't see me as a fruitcake." He took another photo. "Though if I were an onion, Miss Demont, I'd make you cry."

We got up. I helped carry a couple of his bags and invited him for coffee. He offered me a ride in the car which he had parked in the church square. While half the village stood gaping he held the door open for me like a good chauffeur, loaded his things and took me home. My mother was glad to see him. She had the coffee table laid outside in the shade of the trees. As she poured I saw how she enjoyed being able to be the worldly-wise bourgeoise again for a moment.

"One advantage of the war, *mon cher monsieur*," she chuckled as she offered him the dish of biscuits, "is that I'm no longer afraid of mice. What a triumph!"

My uncle coughed politely and retorted, stirring his cup, that for that reason alone he hoped fervently for a speedy peace. "If it continues for much longer, no elephant will be safe from my sister…"

We laughed. The aunts joined us. After our arrival they had withdrawn into what they called their "boudoir" to be able to dust themselves more liberally than usual. It wasn't every day, they said, that "*un vrai héros*" came to visit.

He actually blushed when they said this, and when I recall them now, dressed up and all, with the busy elegance of Chinese earthenware, they move me increasingly often. Whereas I used to make fun of the nest of ribbons and make-up and sentimental magazines that they spun around them, I experienced only much later the doggedness with which they preserved that frilly dream world, their own bastion—with as much assiduousness as a beaver its dam. And I believe also that they offered my uncle a charming kind of consolation: his two child women, about whom everyone speculated whether they took turns in his bed—not least my mother, who just hoped that the uncertainty surrounding that would last for a long time. I think that he saw them as pert exotic birds that from their chosen cage flew circuits through the house and sometimes moved him by landing on his finger in order to please him with their chatter. Now, after all that time, they fill me more and more deeply with melancholy. Sometimes I have to fight back my tears when I remember them as they cut the thick materials that my mother quickly ordered when war broke out, cooing and twittering. Why should the rituals with which they tried to arm themselves against the course of events be any more ridiculous than ours?

"Tell us, Colonel," they cooed. "How long do you think it will last, the inconvenience?…"

"Impossible to say, mesdames," he replied. "Everything is stuck, stuck fast. We stare at the military maps and think we have a full overview. But on the ground it is, well…" he shook his head and looked into his coffee.

"Chaos" was perhaps the word that he had wanted to use, or "hell", or another term that he quickly swallowed, probably because he was thinking of my brother, and my mother's concern.

"We're definitely doing our best to console the *poilus*," cried my aunt. "Isn't that right, Yolande?"

"We write letters," nodded Yolande enthusiastically. "We wait and we hope, and we write. That is woman's patriotic duty. Those lads are crazy about us…" They nodded simultaneously. With their plucked and accentuated eyebrows their faces were like two masks.

My uncle stretched his fingers and studied his nails at length. "Another reason, monsieur, why peace must come soon. I hope those poor devils don't conceive the plan of visiting their *marraines*… They'd have the shock of their lives."

The aunts protested.

"I've posted your latest epistle, Yolande, child," my uncle sighed. "A lot can be said of you, but you're not exactly a voluptuous brunette."

My mother raised her right eyebrow, her moral eyebrow, meaningfully, but said nothing. She also wrote. In a much more businesslike fashion than the aunts. Letters about the energy it required to keep hearth and home more or less ticking over. "Her soldiers" replied to her communications faithfully, if fairly briefly, and usually the correspondence was short-lived. Probably her epistles offered too few illusions, and I myself was not allowed to write to soldiers who were total strangers. My task was to keep family deeper in France informed of our day-to-day lives. Corresponding with lonely trench warriors struck my mother as too risky. "It starts with sweet words on paper," she once said archly, "and ends with lots of panting and exclamation marks on the sofa…"

"Peace," sighed my uncle in resignation. "When the money's gone or the people revolt. Or conversely when the people are gone and the money gets restless. A war on credit needs peace sooner or later…"

My husband nodded and mumbled, more to himself than to us: "Lives are cheap these days…"

After coffee we walked through the Lost Wood. My mother had told me to show him round a little. I led him along the winding paths through the tree trunks upward, to the edge of the treeline, from where you could look out eastwards over the landscape.

We did not say much, after the cooing of the aunts. We sometimes looked at each other from the side and smiled shyly when our glances crossed. Of course my mother had taken the opportunity to question him at table: what his father did—a doctor in a London suburb. Whether he had brothers and sisters—he was an only child. His mother?—died early, he grew up with an aunt in the north, because his stepmother didn't like him very much. She was moved, I could see. He was now given some of the love she usually reserved for my brother.

I liked his silences. A lone wolf. Learnt to fend for himself from an early age. Busy surviving, in the lee, the shade, the twilight. When I got engaged to him, my father took me aside and asked me—the cliché blared round our ears—if I loved him.

"I love his tragic quality," I replied.

My father asked if that was enough.

I kept the answer under consideration.

*

When we reached the top we stopped on the verge of grass under the stragglers of the tall trees, next to the field of barley that rolled down at our feet, and looked out over the countryside. Clouds hung almost motionless over the fields and wooded banks, the distant roofs. When there was an east wind we could sometimes hear the thunder of the distant front line at home, weaker than when it blew from the west, which it usually did. On clear days you could see weak plumes of smoke rising all the way on the horizon, and at night there were vague flashes of light, as if the same storm were always hanging over the earth. That afternoon it was peaceful and quiet. The wind sang in the stalks, listlessly stirring the ears.

He came and stood next to me and sought my hand.

I couldn't suppress a laugh. "Perfect setting for a kiss, monsieur?"

"Definitely…"

It wasn't a kiss to wax lyrical about, more a short confirmation, almost businesslike, of the bond between us there had been at our first meeting. He let go of me afterwards and stood with his back to me, with his hands in his pockets looking out over the landscape.

"Looks like England," I said. "But with a French accent…"

He turned round. "A bit like you then…" he smiled, over his shoulder.

H E SHOWED ME the fronts, later that summer. We had waited until my mother had gone with her two sisters-in-law to see relations near Paris for a few days, a trip that was quite difficult to get under way, and I approached my uncle with the excuse that "Monsieur Heirbeir" had invited me to the coast for two days because he had some leave.

"Ah, *une affairette…*" he had exclaimed, as he pushed back his chair and stood up from behind his desk in the library with an excited "*Finalement!*", since his yearly attempt to subject me to a subversive education was obviously finally beginning to bear fruit.

"Two days at the seaside, two days at the seaside," he said, pretending to sulk. "It's a start, I assume. Be careful, *ma fille*, but without taking it too far… I have to say that, as ambassador of Her Maternal Excellency, but the simple libertine in me has his rights too…"

He came to pick me up early in the morning, in an open-topped car; the day was still unpolluted and smelt of grass and dew. He did not drive into the courtyard but waited a little way off to avoid the maid, Madeleine, who might be on the prowl. He had everything with him to make the cover credible: the cameras, the bags, the papers; *permis* for the cameras, for myself, passes for this and that, where necessary illustrated with the photos he had taken of me a few weeks earlier in the church—I only wondered much later, without ever asking him for clarification, whether he had planned everything, whether our re-encounter had been so accidental. Guests were to visit the front zone that day. We never drive in a group, he said, but spread out. "I'm risking my neck, Helen."

I replied that what he was risking would be a trifle beside my mother's wrath if she should ever get to hear of our adventure— she never found out, never believed anything except that I went to the coast with "*ce drôle Monsieur Heirbeir*", and there somewhere in the dunes or in a boarding house of dubious quality threw away my honour, more or less with the blind-eyed consent of her dearly beloved brother, against whom she declared a winter of discontent which lasted all the longer because she perhaps realized that she had lost the battle for my soul for ever.

The shock when, after driving for a while along deserted roads and seeing only peasants on their way to the fields, we suddenly found ourselves in a stream of soldiers, the dust, the smell of sweat and bodies, the silence, the tread of all those soles over the land and the cobbles—a stream of arms and heads, trunks and shoulders that sucked us along into the arterial system of the war, thrust along the uncountable individual blood cells which made their way between the high verges under the branches of undergrowth and trees.

Here and there, at a bottleneck or where the road made a sharp bend, the flood was checked and we could only drive at walking place. Then he manoeuvred the car between the troops, none of whom paid the slightest attention, as if they were totally focused on their destination—or perhaps it was just their limbs that were going mechanically on, their muscles and joints were taking them blindly northwards, and their thoughts were tarrying meanwhile with what was behind them, what they could not let go of. My husband shook his head. "They live in soldier-time," he said. "That's all."

When gaps appeared in the mass we could accelerate briefly, slaloming, and pass smaller troops of soldiers, not too quickly. No one waved or laughed or whistled, not a voice was raised to call out hello or even to swear. Elsewhere the road clogged up again, and the mass became so impenetrable that we drifted almost automatically towards the side of the road, and I then stood up in the car—"Careful, my lovely," he said—and through the dust that was thrown up from the soft sand by all those soles and that drifted in a haze above the figures, caught a first glimpse of the face of the war. It did not show a uniform face, rather a countenance that manifested itself in a thousand facets, a face that was a parasite on all those faces, younger and older, one clearer than the other, which I saw as little more than separate noses, cheeks, eyelids and lips under the grey powder of the roads looming up out of that veil of dust, with which the face of this war made itself up—not to look at me but to look through me with a hollow stare.

Now and again from that sea of nameless faces a look lit up, clear as the shine on a drop of dew in the morning mist—the faint smile of a young man whose mouth, just under the sharply defined shadow of his cap, unexpectedly opened in the most radiant joy imaginable, or the rather worried-looking eye of a somewhat older man: his bushy eyebrow was raised momentarily, his head looked up automatically and he gave a resigned, almost imperceptible nod. Since then I know that a look can have fingers, and a whole hand if necessary. Over the years my memory has contracted around those two gazes that nestled briefly in mine; everything else around becomes vague and hazy, only the eyes don't. They stare at me ever more sharply and compress a whole life into their stare. I had sons and lovers there, and in so many eyes was the daughter of fathers I have never known.

He drummed impatiently on the steering wheel and was about to hoot, but it occurred to him just in time that it was forbidden, and tugged on my coat to make me sit down again, but there was no point. We were half on the verge, half in the undergrowth. When I craned my neck to look over the nearest figures, I saw farther on, through the clouds of dust and the sunlight refracted in them, the contours of the ammunition lorries. They looked like slow mastodons with, between them, on and towed behind other lorries, towards the bed of the shallow valley out of which that stream of weapons and men was making its way, light and heavy artillery—it reminded one of the procession of an ancient people that bore its idols and statues of divinities out of its temples through the country, their fabulous animals, their steel Cyclopses.

"The herds of Mars," I said, and thought it ridiculous myself.

He repeated that it would be better if I sat down, but I couldn't get the idea out of my head that it was all these men who were dragging the chariots of destruction onward, by invisible cords over their shoulders, resigned and silent—all that could be heard was the crunch of footwear. The high road verges seemed to retreat from them, just as the sea had opened for the people of Moses, although they might just as well have been Pharaoh's army, not suspecting that those earth banks could close again at any moment—but then he pulled so hard on my coat tails that I fell abruptly back into the car seat.

He glanced aside, gave me the grin full of reckless courage that needed only half his mouth to win me over to him for ever: "Didn't mean to hurt you, *ma biche*, everything all right?" and put his foot down.

The peace that came over us when we turned into a side road in order to make a shortcut, the charm of the countryside the moment we drove just about 100 metres from that stream of people through rolling fields, grassland above which larks fell out of the sky and lapwings whooped, past houses where old people were selling newly harvested onions on benches against the wall under the grapevine—it was all unreal. Around the washing places on the market squares of the villages children stopped as we passed and gaped at us open-mouthed. With coarse brushes women scrubbed blue-white bleach over the thresholds of their houses. It was like a lucid dream, because almost nowhere did you see young men. The tissue of everyday life had holes in it. Ordinariness was walking around in rags but only we seemed to notice.

And sooner or later we saw from a distance that stream of figures shuffling past again—the same figures or different ones. The war created its own arterial pattern of road maps in the landscape, which coincided with the old ones where it was possible, but where necessary it carved new routes through the earth, with railway lines that branched like capillaries, temporary depots, junctions, assembly points, base camps. The fronts, if I had been able to see them from the air, must have looked like gaping, throbbing wounds, which from everywhere, over old roads and new, sucked in flesh and blood and fodder and explosives. And even when we found ourselves on deserted roads we could deduce from the grey-white dust on the hedges that a column must have passed through shortly before—sometimes it looked like a Christmas scene, a sugary, live postcard of snowy hedgerows, above which the sun was warming a new day.

He asked me if I was hungry yet, and I shook my head. We could see the plain in the distance, where the masses of people became less dense. The front was close by, the troops dispersed, set up temporary camps in meadows and beside country lanes. Again I saw, like the year before, when I had been to town with my mother, men stirring kettles that hung bubbling over campfires, and whole trees transformed into stationary galleons, with drying shirts and trousers on the masts, which the wind caught as if they were sails.

You could smell the odour of the fires, of the fat with which the saddlery was greased, you could hear the scraping of the curry-comb on the flanks of horses, and their snorting. Someone was playing the harmonica. Children were still shooting as swift as sticklebacks past the resting men.

Older boys watched with their hands in their pockets as the soldiers cleaned their rifles, fascinated as boys are by everything that opens on a hinge, clicks, switches and ejaculates. On their faces one could read regret. Their lower lips quivered with impatience because they were still too young to join the armies. The chaos that reigned there had only at first sight a festive air. The melodies were lifeless, the jokes dour. No one waved or lost themselves in teasing. Even the children were no longer curious, but worked the tents routinely, to the point of rudeness, to exchange an egg or a piece of bacon for some money or a jewel. The soldiers waved them away like flies. Above the treetops, the roads and the farmland hung the virtually continuous roar and thunder of the front; the sound was much less dull than at home. There was more texture, not to say architecture in the booming, which created invisible buildings in the heavens, domes, stone bubbles that immediately crumbled.

We left the hill country. Suddenly the frantic activity ceased and the plain was there, past the last board on the verge, repeating in raucous capitals the ban on hooting. The plain and its rows of trees, its slow processions of crowns. Its monk trees, its own parade of trunks. Beneath them clusters of men emerging from the crowds behind us, laden with backpack and blanket, helmet and rifle, on the way to relieve other troops. Somewhere out there, on the plain.

The plain that I no longer recognized, or only half, because it was no longer, or not completely, the plain where we used to come on excursions by coach with my uncle and the aunts, under the parasols of August, to the villages where we drank the idleness of summer from earthenware jugs, the bitter beer.

The villages with their towers, their sun-scorched squares, their ochre spires, which now seemed different villages, different towers; toy villages that had fallen out of the overfull toy box of a giant child while it had been lugging it across fields in boredom where old corn lay snapped over the earth, overgrown with grass tussocks and thistles. Roofs showed their skeletons, seemed to have rejected their tiles. Window shutters hung loose from the window frames in walls riddled with bullet holes. Somewhere there was a bluestone door frame still standing, there was something clownish, stoical about it, keeping up the appearance of a house in a heap of pulverized bricks out of which the beams stuck like bones. The battered houses, the towers from which a huge bird had pecked a piece, lay staring at each other across the wooded banks that had been largely shot to pieces like schoolchildren still panting after a skirmish, collar ripped loose, glasses trampled underfoot, sleeves torn at the seams—everyone was perplexed.

A wall of straw bales slid between us and the landscape, a dull-yellow wall glided past the car in places where the enemy had an unimpeded view and without that barrier would have shot at everything that moved, certainly cars, I learnt later.

I calmed my thoughts a little, looked at him, my husband-to-be, while he kept an eye on the road, the steering wheel loosely in his hand. I liked looking at him. I liked absorbing his profile, the nose and the lips and the chin, the hair that stuck out of his kepi and, behind his ear, shaved short, lay close to his skin. I liked waiting for him to look back, turn his head half towards me and say something, it didn't matter what.

The straw wall gave way to trees, the road cut through a low hill. It was cool and dark, and seemed to be deserted. I don't know how many we had passed before I recognized, in the patchwork of light and shadow patches in the undergrowth, not only tree trunks and bushes. Only when I detected movement out of the corner of my eye did I distinguish their figures in the shades of brown and green that slid past us. They must have pulled back onto the side of the road to let us pass. I had not seen them at first because they almost did not look like people, rather beings in whom transubstantiation from earth into flesh had not yet been completed. Almost-humans hiding under the trees in order to harden off safely in earthen clothing, earthen helmets, earthen cocoons.

Leaning against a tree trunk a boy with earthen fists screwed open a drinking bottle and brought it to his lips—how am I to describe the flash that animated his whole figure. The dark pupils did not look up but sparkled between the caked-together eyelashes, under the modelled eyebrows, from that face when he stopped what he was doing and raised an arm. At the moment he called something—I don't know what, but the audible relief, the simple joy of being alive needed no language—his lips made fine cracks in his earthen mask, which flaked off and exposed the skin of his cheeks. A skin as dark as the night.

I remembered the shameless curiosity with which we had gaped at the "Negroes" when the war began and troops fairly regularly passed through the village and rested in the square in front of the *mairie*—the intimidating splendour of the cavalry with their multicoloured uniforms, their blood-red hooded cloaks and ornamentally harnessed horses, and the look in their eyes, by which every woman felt pierced as a dubious threat to her very ovaries. Even my mother proved not wholly insensitive to them. "It has to be said," she said one day in a throwaway tone, "they're definitely not unattractive, those savages."

I was reminded of the hidden pride of Madame Gaillac after one of those dark chaps had come into her liqueur shop one afternoon and with a resolute gesture had laid twenty-five francs—"twenty-five!" she repeated at every opportunity, appropriate and especially inappropriate—on the counter under his rusty brown palm. The resulting confusion was only cleared up when the North African, with a gesture of the hand about which Madame Gaillac had for the sake of good taste to remain vague, indicated that he was interested not so much in a bottle of chartreuse as in Madame Gaillac herself, who, she said could "of course" not take up his offer—"What was he thinking, that sultan?"—but nevertheless found it very flattering that at her age her virtue was still worth a pretty penny.

The wood thinned out, and in the landscape that stretched out beyond it a stone cloud formation loomed up on the horizon, at first merging bluish in the sky above the rolling landscape, but more and more tangible the closer we came. A grotesque castle in the air seemed to have become so dense that it had plunged down to earth from the sky. Only because since childhood I had looked up at it almost every summer and had eaten ice cream in the shadow of the tower in the market square, did I recognize the contours of the age-old cloth hall. Iron-coloured and dark, the building no longer rose to the sky, but seemed to have begun a slow process of dripping downward. Window openings had expanded into holes, side towers and pointed arches had lost their sharpness. The erosion of dozens of centuries seemed to be concentrated in the sky clouding over above. This must be the capital of a new kingdom that was running wild over the old land, forcing its root system, its threads of mould between the joints of the walls, picking its way down to the foundations and blooming in devastation and, everywhere where it branched out over the old roads, spread its provinces and prefectures of decay.

The noise of the weapons, the salvoes, the shots could only euphemistically be called displacement of air. Walls of tangible sound clattered through the heavens. In the cloudy sky even more ruins seemed to pile up, and then crash down on the earth, set foot on the ground and coincide with the crenellated contours of the houses of the town. The deepest growl made the muscles of my abdomen quiver.

We passed the sentry post that controlled the access road. In the distance two other cars were heading for the suburbs. The sentry waved us through, probably assuming we were part of the column. My husband saluted. The sentry saluted back; it was more of a nonchalant wave. "One of ours. The French are worse. And the gendarmes in the hinterland. Corrupt as anything..."

"Aren't we all?"

He looked at me sideways with a louche gleam in his eye. "Don't tell me what you're thinking of, Miss Demont... Not onions, I hope."

The thunder subsided, the clouds drew great patches of shadow over the town, reducing the profile of the cloth hall to a black, burnt-out cinder which, however, flared up in deep bronze colours whenever the sun shone through the clouds. As we approached the silence seemed to lose its massive quality and to relax. Birds sang, wind whistled through the willow leaves that bordered the road on both sides. But when we reached the first suburbs and the narrow streets enclosed us, the purr of the engine found dozens of sounding boards in the emptiness behind the house fronts by which it was echoed.

There was no logic in the destruction, no system in the alternation of house fronts pounded totally into rubble and others that apart from the empty window frames seemed intact. With other houses the façade had been blown away but the interior had survived. Wherever the shadow of the clouds lifted, the glow of the afternoon sun flooded the surface of wall cupboards, beds and washbasins which had congealed snow-white on tables, licked at wallpaper, and brought a gleam to dusty bell jars, under which saints' images balanced on a chimney piece as if on the edge of a ravine. The clouds seemed to be teasing us, chased their shadows ahead of us over the cobbles, cast the boredom of a summer afternoon over the town, although the smell of plaster, dry wood, dust, the irritating reek of desolation, strongly penetrated my nostrils.

A lorry drove ahead of us for a while, and four soldiers peered out from under the tarpaulin that covered the back and clapped their hands as soon as they caught sight of us. The air was filled with cries like, "Matey, havin' a good time, are ya?" and they started to sing: "My name's Johnny Hall, I've only got one ball…" The melody crumbled in a tide of rowdy laughter.

I rolled my eyes and looked away, at the houses sliding past, in the hope of suggesting the disapproval that they were probably hoping for.

"Don't mind them, Helen. They're lads…" We passed them and they whistled after us.

He pulled up in a street that farther up led into the market place, or what had once been the market place, two summers before, in what was already in my memory a different world, still undamaged by the first labour pains that were to shudder through its surface and its lives, and from the pools and craters, from its trenches and lunar landscapes, belched forth this new world, which could move through time only in spasms and marked its episodes with explosions and collapses.

How often I have sighed, if not prayed: give us back our mealy-mouthed petit-bourgeois world and the porcelain jauntiness of Sunday tea parties and the honky-tonk of our cosy religiosity and our little hypocrisies and big injustices. Give us back the rites of the days of yore, though we know that they do not touch on any reality, as long as they protect us from a free fall into our infinite hunger.

The market was a market only in name. Only in front of the cloth hall, onto a corner of which the street issued, could something like a square be recognized, of course cleared for the passage of troops and materials past the burnt-out vaults of the cathedral and the heaps of rubble of the houses. It could have been the view of weathered rocky masses in a desert, in which for millennia the wind has hewn out volumes that purely accidentally look like vaults or the fronts of buildings. When the sun broke through the cloud cover and accentuated the devastation with blinding light, the view reminded me of prints of the Arctic ocean, in spring, when the ice fields begin to break up and in the waves surreal vessels, floating ruins, crusader castles and melting pyramids drift into each other.

He took one of the bags from the back seat of the car and hung it over his shoulder. He let a second one rest between his ankles on the cobbles while he waited for me to get out. He handed me the strap of the second bag—"It isn't that heavy," he said—and I don't think he said much more that day.

He seemed to be keeping a careful watch on me; he scarcely took his eyes off me for a moment but read my face meticulously, as if he had absorbed the sight of the destruction too often to have many thoughts or feelings about it and was now trying to evoke it again in himself via me.

When we reached the corner of the market there turned out to be another car parked on the other side of the expanse of bomb craters. The passengers were no more than black dots at the foot of the piles of rubble at which they pointed after they had got out. Their voices reached us, ethereal and shrill across the flat expanse of the square—British, going by the intonation, but too far away to be intelligible.

He pulled me by the arm, we retraced our steps and he led me into a narrow side alley, between the high walls of back gardens. The desolation descended upon me like a lead weight. At this hour—it must have been getting on for dinnertime but no church clock divided up the day—the alley should been full of the roasting smell of the ovens. The clatter of pans and crockery should have danced out onto the paving stones from the back kitchens. Our feet would have had to disturb children's chalk drawings. Out of the windows bed sheets should have hung out to air in white tongues—not the threadbare locks of old over-curtains, faded by two years' rain and change of season, which licked at the walls through the holes in the panes of the window frames.

Only our footsteps were audible, the creaking of the leather strap under the weight of his bag and the ticking of the negatives in their case whenever the bag touched his hip to the rhythm of his gait.

A small gate giving onto the alleyway was ajar and he pushed it further open. Behind it lay the garden of a bourgeois house, of modest dimensions. Two narrow earth paths divided a small lawn into squares. In the sunlight that flared up and died away again an old espaliered pear tree extended its rheumatic branches against the wall under the offshoots of two lilacs. The last blooming bunches let their intoxicating perfume linger over the low outbuildings. A narrow work shed, with the handles of garden tools which had slipped lengthways obliquely along the cobweb-covered windows. Next to it an outside toilet, the door painted blue-green. Against the wall of the house a low lean-to and under it a side door that probably gave access to a pantry. In the house itself a small, bright kitchen on one side of the back door. The sun made the cream-coloured faiences on the wall glow soft yellow. Here and there a tile had been knocked out, but for the rest the room looked as good as undamaged, with the bowls and jugs and earthenware serving dishes still stacked in an orderly fashion on the two or three shelves of a butter-yellow cupboard, and on the small table opposite the sink two coffee mugs, a spoon, a cutting board, dusted with plaster that had come loose from the ceiling and lay grainy over the black floor tiles. There had been people here, to judge by the smudges and footprints in the layer of dust.

He pulled the strap of the bag over my shoulder. "C'mon, Sis, I'm starving…" We sat down on the bench under the window on the other side of the back door, the window of a dining room, with the table in the middle, against the wall a low dresser with the doors open. The contents, napkins and tea towels, lay in disorder between the legs of chairs spread around the table.

I give him his bread. He took great bites out of it. I watched the way his jaw muscles worked as his teeth ground up the hunks. He was looking around him, over the garden walls, to the roofline of the adjoining houses, in which there were big holes everywhere. Chimneys had been smashed, roof tiles shattered in heaps in the gutters under the naked roof-beam. He seemed to be studying it intently.

"Looks different every time," he said, between two mouthfuls. "Never a dull moment visiting bloody glorious Ypres…"

I asked him if he came here so often then, and the casualness of my question, as if he had taken me to his local café, sounded so absurd to me that I had to giggle immediately.

"Every Sunday afternoon after Mass, mademoiselle…" He swallowed, blew a sarcastic sigh out of his nose, "weather permitting…", then looked sideways, shot me a grin and said, with exaggerated preciosity: "It does look rather unsettled this morning, doesn't it, Miss Honeysuckle?"

I prodded him in the side and stuck my hand out for a piece of bread. He got a drinking bottle out of the bag, unscrewed it, put it to his mouth, drank big mouthfuls, while his Adam's apple rose and fell behind the khaki collar of his shirt.

"Better make haste now." He got up and brushed the crumbs out of his lap, then looked at the sky. The sun was half hidden by what was left of a church tower and the tall, slender candlesticks of a group of poplars next to it, some of them bare, others with a scanty covering of leaves. With each cloud that moved in front of the sun the glaring afternoon light changed abruptly to grey. Shadows shifted across the back wall of the house and the bullet holes on the top floor.

He put the bags on the bench, opened the largest one and inspected the large wooden camera.

I went towards the back door.

He called after me not to go too far away. "This isn't a safe place, Helen, really."

Usually he avoided addressing me by my first name, keeping mostly to "Sis" or "Mademoiselle", a teasing "Sweetheart", and very occasionally "Darling". I too often hesitated about addressing him as Matthew. I realized how much irony was necessary to make "Monsieur Heirbeir" sound less formal, and made eager use of my mother's awkward pronunciation of English, or addressed him as she did, as "patriot" or "soldier". Our names seemed too definitive, too perfect, almost too apodictic, not to say all too solemn, like an oath or a promise, unsuited to the playful and provisional tone that characterized our relationship in those days, as if we would have appropriated too much of each other. Certainly here, in the heart of a town in ruins, words like house, roof or room carried an unintentionally devastating sarcasm with them. So when he used my first name I knew he was really concerned. I also saw it in his eyes, when I turned round for a second, just before the devils returned to his eyes and he smiled, looking up as he slid a negative plate into the camera: "Besides, I want your portrait... Call it 'Lost Girl from Flanders...' What d'you say?"

The door did not give. Old newspapers, a calendar, loose sheets slid on their underside over the floor tiles. A classic bourgeois house: tall hall with two front rooms leading into it, and the kitchen at the back, opposite the small dining room where the family probably ate their meals every day when there were no visitors.

On the left the stairs to the upper floors, under the stairs the cellar. On the landing where the stairs made a bend a tall, narrow window was open. There wouldn't have been much point in closing it, since there were no panes in the window frames, just as with the top window above the front door. The blue glass lay in slivers on the floor of the hall and seemed to have been subsequently squashed flat under shoe soles—by looters and perhaps by the residents themselves, when they had left the house.

I tried to imagine them. The kind of people that my mother would probably have called "proper", the word with which she usually described petits bourgeois who lived in houses like this: more or less replicas of more spacious gentlemen's houses but smaller in scale. The man of the house probably didn't work with his hands, but somewhere as an assistant or clerk, proper and affluent enough to pay a maid for half-days, who came at the crack of dawn to bank up the stove, made breakfast, visited the market, washed the floors and before she went home in the early afternoon left a couple of cold dishes on the basement shelf, for supper. Perhaps a gardener came every so often to trim the hedges, or the man of the house did it himself, on Sunday afternoon, by way of a hobby, while his wife and family laid the coffee table against the wall in the shade. In the evenings they would stroll on the old town walls. The mother and her daughters, if they were there, under parasols. The father and his sons with straw hats, as they walked chatting under the trees in the gentle evening light, with ducks that swerved above the ramparts and landed among the water lilies.

I had to swallow down a lump in my throat. I would have liked to see this house as it lay dozing on a Sunday evening like that, after hours of full sun, to see the light in the rooms fading and the decorative earthenware on the dresser lose its shine until it hung pale in the twilight—but the front room, the entertaining room, was a mess. Instead of the window on the street side there was a hole. The window, woodwork and all, had been knocked out of the house front and blown inwards, over and onto the table, where between sections of lath and plaster the crystal tears of a chandelier gleamed. Through the hole in the front wall I could see the house fronts on the other side. In the doorways the rubble lay all the way to the street as if the houses had spewed out their interiors, as if an epidemic attacking houses had moved through street after street.

I turned round. The light had faded, outside it looked rainy. Don't ask me if it was because of the wind, which was audibly rising, or the series of bursts of fire that exploded above the roofs with a thunderous sound that seemed to rise somewhere outside the town walls from the depths of the earth, and above the roofs built a dome of pandemonium, under which the town seemed to shrink—and I don't know either whether the gust of wind that somewhere on the upstairs floor slammed a door shut came together with the noise that made everything tremble, the walls, the floors, made the windows at the back judder in their frames and shook plaster from the ceiling in white trails of dust. All I know is that, just as I turned round, the noise above my head turned the sky to iron—everywhere doors closed and window panes shook. In the back kitchen all the crockery fell out of the wall cupboard with a diabolical crash, the slivers jumping up the walls.

I must have screamed with the shock; the next moment I felt an arm round my waist and he pulled me away, of course worried about the ceiling. We both fell against the stairs. I could feel the treads in my back, the carpet cushioned our fall.

"It's all right. Don't worry…" he panted, his breath warm against my collarbone. "It's quite a way off. It's just the noise… They're ours." He seemed to be saying it just as much to himself, just as much to calm himself. He was lying half on top of me.

A second series of salvoes exploded. He made as if to get up, but I pulled him to me, put my lips against the skin beneath his ear, by the corner of his jaw—the banisters trembled, and somewhere a tread creaked.

I took his head in both hands, his lips slid over my nose. I sucked in his tongue, held his head frantically tight, his face so doggedly against mine that his kepi fell off and rolled down beside us.

I wanted to feel his living, breathing, hectically breathing, body, the ribs that in my arms under the thick military material separated when he filled his lungs, his trunk and his hips, the soft belly that pushed into mine to the rhythm, the hectic rhythm of his breath, and his tongue, the fleshiness of his lips. The thundering receded, the shock wave subsided. It became quiet.

I pushed him on his side, lifted his chin with my forefinger. He looked into my eyes; his face seemed different, smoothed out, happy.

He took my hand by the wrist, led my fingers down across his belly and put them in his crotch. I could feel his blood pulsing, the hardness of his sex under his fly frightened me. He could tell from my look and smiled sheepishly.

Then somewhere above us there was a dry bang; something shook on its hinges, followed by a slight ticking that swelled and subsided, till a second bang resounded and it began anew.

We both looked up at the same time.

Against the wall beside the section of stairs that led from the landing to the upstairs rooms, packed as closely together as a nest of bats awakening from their diurnal sleep, a dozen or so small frames, round, oval or square, with faces in them that we did not recognize—gentlemen with moustaches and side-whiskers, ladies' necks above lace collars and toddlers with the perplexed look of owl chicks under their blond quiffs—started, whenever the window frame banged against the wall, swaying to and fro on their nails, and the corners of the frames tapped against the wall.

They came to rest, but reawakened with every gust of wind. Swaying. Dangling. Tapped frantically against the wall for a while. Calmed down.

"They're in panic," I said. "They've almost been eaten away by the rain. They're telegraphing for us to rescue them."

"Bet they are…" He took my hand out of his crotch, put it against his cheek and pushed his tongue into the bottom of my palm.

The window frame banged against the wall, the frames tapped.

"*Ils sont jaloux*," he whispered, with his lips in my hand.

H E FREQUENTLY TOOK ME on trips with him when the war was over and he meticulously documented what I call the congealing, the great levelling, in all respects after the ravages and the euphoria of peace. The smoothing-over of the tormented earth. The cemeteries where the fallen were gradually put in straighter and straighter ranks, disciplined even in death. The wooden crosses which were replaced by polished stone tombs in charming cemeteries beneath the subdued melancholy of weeping-willow leaves or pine needles—it struck me as a wry euphemism, not to say a sad paradox, that in order to keep the memory of the destruction and oceans of blood alive, they mowed the lawns immaculately, constructed solemn temples, carved mourning statues, lit eternal flames. Over the bones and the corpses and the countless shattered lives an arcadia stretched out that was itself constantly struggling against becoming overgrown, a process that would have spread like wildfire if they had not, out of piety, or out of shame, left the ravaged earth in peace and declared the whole area a cemetery.

But I also remember the rage that seized me when, in the early summer of 1919, we were in Alsace, a part of the front zone where we had not been before. En route I had been dozing in the car, lulled to sleep by the mild temperatures and the pristine green of nature renewing itself. When I woke because the car slowed down, at the bottom of the valley that unfolded before us, at some distance from the road between woody clumps and fields, a broad scar of earth churned into hills and gullies stretched as far as the eye could see.

It was not the sight of it that I found chilling, but the swarming of scores, hundreds, of human figures, white and dark dolls that clambered chaotically over the heaps of earth like foraging ants. Young men supported their wives or fiancées as they helped them jump from ridges. Sucking contentedly on their pipes, fathers pointed out old foxholes and barbed wire, tanks stranded in the earth and abandoned artillery, or they stood on top of all those masses of ground with their hands on their hips, looking out over their surroundings.

It was that easy-going atmosphere that filled me with fury. The swarms of summer hats and parasols. The improvised signposts on the verge. The cars and carriages parked in the fields near the edge of the wood which suggested an open-air fair, complete with pedlars not offering refreshments but grenade fragments or polished bullets engraved with place names and landscapes or decorative motifs—the pleasure I mean, which was not even hidden behind horror or bewilderment. The pleasure of bewilderment in itself, the eagerness of horror that I saw there. But my husband said: "I think it's inevitable, Helen."

He got his camera from the case on the back of the car, opened the tripod and planted it in the soft, mild-smelling forest earth on the edge of the valley. "Are we that much better?" He prepared the camera to capture the scene.

Time gives greater complexity to the texture of the facial expressions on those prints. Their readability has become less unambiguous—like my own. Look at those two women standing there arm in arm on one of the countless paths that the stream of disaster tourists has worn between the mounds of earth and the old bomb craters. They seem to be sisters. Perhaps twins, given their almost identical clothing and coquettish hats, and the fact that they are walking arm in arm.

But why is one of them carrying a bunch of flowers in one hand? Not a hastily picked bunch of wild flowers but a carefully arranged bouquet, as the ribbon that binds the stalks leads one to suspect—where did they lay it? In the nearby cemetery perhaps, or on the approximate spot from where a man, a fiancé, a brother or father, whose body had not been found and perhaps never would be, had sent his last letter?

And even now when I see those solid heads of families again who, holding their children by the hand, stroll between the broom and the briars as if they were at the zoo, I find it harder to get worked up than before. I know by now what weird forms desperation can take in a human being, how the pleasure of bewilderment carefully shields us from a fear or despair that might totally destroy us—what a strange emotion fear remains. The most alchemical of emotions, now turning to lead, now to gold. Isn't each pleasure a hasty prayer, Rachida my girl, an invocation?

I'm reminded of my uncle, who every few days dropped by the *mairie* to open the official dispatches. He considered it his duty to inform the families affected of the death of a son or a brother, a father or husband.

So once every so many mornings he went "down". In the adjacent café he first had a coffee and spirits while he went through the papers, before entering the *mairie* in order, as he only ever said out loud at home with us, to "bring in the sad harvest". He had several times sat on the town council and was doing it from a kind of *noblesse oblige*, a task that he took over from the official town crier who would normally convey the message, but who turned out to be drunk more and more often because he couldn't stand it any longer.

My uncle had the envelopes cut open, at each name gave a melancholy sigh, which became more routine each month, and set forth. Eventually everyone knew what it meant when he was seen leaving the *mairie* and crossing the market square. People held their breath. What side road would he take? People soon realized that he arranged the names in his head according to the houses he would have to visit, that he turned his walk into a circular route which began in the market square and ended at our house. There he would lower himself onto the bench under the tree and did not want to be disturbed until lunchtime.

As soon as he took a particular route one side of the village breathed easier with relief—you could hear the relief creeping through the house fronts that he turned his back on. The joints in the walls seemed to expand as if the stones had braced themselves, and you could see the houses by whose door or front garden he stopped almost cringe. Because everyone knew the purpose of his knocking he did not need to say much. When the door opened and from the darkness beyond a fearful questioning look met his, it was mostly sufficient to nod—unless several men in the same family had been called up.

It is the women who take the blows, he was wont to say. Imagine the look on the face of a mother with two or three sons at the front, not exactly a rarity in large farming families in the countryside. The uncertainty behind the certainty that you are

226

knocking at her door to report the death of one of her children. She has seen you coming across the yard. Above the hedge of the front garden with the country flowers, which have been so immaculately hoed and raked, since weeding helps take her mind off the fate of her boys, she has recognized your hat. She has heard the gate creak. She would like her house to be an unassailable fortress, a thick shell. She sees you coming across the yard or up the garden path. She realizes that this time there is no blood on the lintel and side posts of her door, that the angel with the sword has not spared her house this time—all she does not yet know is which of her sons has fallen.

"Who?" is the word burning not so much on her lips as in her eyes, tell me who: our Jean or Arnaud or Rémi? The names shuttle as it were across her retina: which of the beings to whom she has given birth, whom she has felt pull out of her to the spasms of her abdominal muscles, the life that she saw grow up and nurtured, cared for, gave food and drink, beat and kissed, that caused her laughter wrinkles or grey hairs, filled her with pride with its school results or muscular strength, made her double up with anxiety when it had measles, or about its drinking or gambling habits—the top of the class or the sponger or the petty thief who joined up to avoid the cell and shame. Who is it, monsieur? The oldest or the youngest? Or the middle one, the apple of my eye? There were doors where he knocked a first time, and a second time. On the third or fourth occasion there wasn't much more to be said.

What do you do when you have to tell a mother the last of her sons has died, or after her sons her husband too, and she doesn't open up and you go round the back? You see her in her back kitchen with a basin on her lap, peeling potatoes so furiously that she reduces them to curls. She doesn't even look up when you come in. What do you do then? You sit down at her table and say nothing and wait.

"It's the women who take the blows." He repeated it more and more often when he returned from his morbid rounds and shut himself up in his garden. "Always the same old story, we let ourselves be seduced by the high-falutin' words of the high-ups, the sweet mouth of power, but we always forget the arsehole. Don't stare at me so angrily, dear sister. Your daughter is old enough to listen to other things than sweetly lilting quatrains. She's not a child any more. Look at the arsehole, *ma fille*. Who gets to wave the palm branch and who catches the shit? That is the question on which the whole of history turns."

I think of my husband. He says: "It's inevitable, Helen." "Inevitable," he repeats, again and again.

His voice can still make me shudder with desire, that rather drawling accent, his intonation that was always on the point of turning into a soft groan, as if speaking were lashing him with a forbidden, sexual pleasure.

"I'm not a thinker," he said regularly on our trips.

Then he looked through the lens of his camera, and usually added: "I trust me eyes. I think with my eyes."

"And I with my fingers," I would reply.

THE NO MAN'S land he took me to later that day after the ruins was blooming in the summer sunshine with an exuberance that dazzled the eyes like an affront in technicolour. All that flora, which did not blossom but exploded in kilometre-long smudges of the brightest white, the deepest red or purple and shimmered in the sunlight between the pools and the mud. Butterflies rose in dense clouds above the nodding poppies and marguerites, and the wind carried them along: a paper din as if the angels were hastily leafing through the telephone books of fate—in the calm between offensives they kept count of the bullets and the dead. The unrecovered dead, whose bones in their threadbare uniform tunics lay bleaching in the sun. The unexploded projectiles that lay gleaming like the eggs of a prehistoric reptile among the plant growth.

The life that purred and buzzed. The bumble bees that helicoptered in swarms around the calyxes of the flowers seemed, when they rose, to swell into the bodies of the balloons which went on ropes far away above the horizon into the azure. Dragonflies shot between the clouds of butterflies, birds performed caprioles in flight and snapped at prey. Above, aircraft imitated the membrane wings and tentacular behaviour of the insects. Somewhere shots rang out and, above the butterflies, under the aircraft shrapnel, burst open in puffs of grey smoke. The balloons descended, submerged in the glow of the colour below.

It was as if the earth were practising revenge, an unsurpassed exercise. As if to show how nature would act in the days after the last human being, it thrust out flowers on hairy tentacles up out of its mud-brown folds, made them crane for light and the soggy ground and the corpses pulsate through their veins until their buds burst. In the muddy pools and cadavers the maggots swelled and the pupae ripened, in order when the first warmth came to strew illusions of buzzing and humming over the land.

I tried to capture that abundance with one of the cameras that he had brought for me so that I would make a credible impression that day, with the long tailored coat which I had worn on his advice, with my hair in a bun under a black hat, not too wide, and the bag of negative plates over my shoulder.

The atmosphere in the trench to which he had taken me was easy-going, since the earth was dry after a period without rain. I laughed along with the men who were on guard, Frenchmen. I did my best to add a British accent to my words and the men didn't ask any questions. Excited by the variety my arrival brought them, they offered coffee, or the chlorine-flavoured liquid that had to pass for it.

I laughed with them when one of them, a tough chap whose cheeks had an apple glow, came crawling with the jug out of the narrow hole that they mockingly called "*la cuisine*", and inside had obviously quickly rubbed his moustache with rancid fat or butter to impress me. While we made fun of his vanity countless gossamer-thin wings rustled around his figure. A swarm of crib sheets that had burst open landed on his shoulders, his chest, and a swarming of wings, antennae, compound eyes—perhaps the butterflies saw his uniform jacket as a huge blossom. As he put the jug down on the wooden crate that served as drawing room table, they swirled up, sailed above his crown, landed on his trunk and rolled out long, fine tongues, and combed the material of his tunic, the shine of the buttons, as if a bunch of medals came to life on his chest.

The men laughed and motioned to me that I should get a photo of him. They nodded to me, with an imaginary camera in their hands, and I did what they asked—looked at them there, arm in arm in that narrow trench, all good mates, a stump of tobacco between their lips, surrounded by a frozen swirl of white spots. When I announced that I wanted a photo of the plain, they pushed the crate against the wall of the trench, so I could stand on it and my eye was level with the peephole they had made in the top row of sandbags. The splendour of the landscape was scarcely bearable. The camera was too small, the lens too small for the view of that crazily blooming earth. It was as if the soil wanted only to have its mud-brown mug immortalized in the cold seasons, when the vegetation had withdrawn and the seeds were asleep, the larvae were overwintering in the carcasses, and the earth opened its folds to suck up the mines and the bullets and hatch them out—God knows what will stir in its skirts the day the shells break. What grimaces has it still in store for us?

Obscene is the word I repeat. Obscene the trick they played in one of the photos I took of my husband, much later, in the first weeks of the peace, when my mother was lying in bed gravely ill.

I snapped him that afternoon without his knowing it, when we had stopped in the middle of that bare plain between the old fronts, right on the spot where according to the map there should have been a hamlet, but where there was only emptiness, and a stream on a bed of frozen earth and ice. No sketch or photograph can ever capture the silence that prevailed there, ghostly since there was no longer a house front or alley in which our voices and footsteps could echo. Every sound was concrete, self-contained, and, now the concert of cannon barrels had fallen silent, was a scratch on the grey-white canvas of silence. The crunch when my foot shot through the steamed-up spectacles of ice in the puddles. Our voices that seemed to float lost on the steam of our breath in the chilly air.

He wanted a photo of that spot. I had followed a few steps behind him along a path by the stream, which led to a deserted trench. I snapped him from behind, just before he jumped over a ditch that flowed into the stream. It was a photo for my own pleasure, I wanted to catch the irrepressible keenness with which he went to work on his trips. And I could never get enough of his broad shoulders and especially his back, which I so liked holding in both arms, to knead his neck and feel my way down the slope to his buttocks when he lay on top of me and buried his face in my neck.

Only in the improvised darkroom which he had rigged up here at home in the cellar did it become clear what I had really captured that day.

In the red light first his back in that winter coat took shape on the paper. He understood at once the associations that the image evoked in me, our moments of stolen intimacy—but we fell silent when, at the bottom in the undulation of caved-in mud just above the surface of the water, a forearm suddenly appeared, unmistakably, and then a second, the two hands, folded in a lap, and a head, bent and obscured by the helmet. A man, a soldier, whom the mud, obscenely drained of colour, only seemed to want to expose in that photo—a caricature of a dead man who appeared to be waiting agreeably for the tram; hands in his lap, slumped on the bench, as he dozed, overwhelmed by earth and covered with a glaze of ice.

As the liquid ate more and more meaning into the paper we saw, farther away, on the bank of the stream into which the ditch flowed, between a pair of snapped, submerged tree trunks, a trunk standing, a torso, one arm raised; and above that arm, under a helmet, mostly merged with the mush of earth and glistening with ice, the arc of an eyebrow, the bridge of a nose and an eye socket which, darker and darker as the paper continued changing colour, stared at us with an expression of disgust and reproach, so it seemed: how can you allow me to be brought to light so—obscenely is the word?

I wonder whether those bodies were ever recovered. Perhaps the earth swallowed them up, in the days following, when the thaw set in. Perhaps only the freezing cold maintained an impression of their bodies, and when the iced crystals in the soil became liquid again their tissue seeped away around their skeletons that became stuck in the ground as the land dried out and formed a second body around their bones.

Season after season the ploughshare must have spread their remains even farther, dispersed the 200 or so screws and bolts and props of which the human frame consists underground. I wished I could let their fragments run through my hands. That I could, as archaeologists do with the skeletons of monarchs or plague victims from old mass graves, spread them out on a table, with everything in place, from cranium to fibula. And that they would not only let one read the history of their diseases, the osteoporosis, the tuberculosis, the bullet wound or the fatal sword stroke in their vertebrae, but that, as it were, their hiatuses would come to life and lead us to suspect a whole semantic system—as in our words, which I sometimes compare with false teeth, the echo of other words rattles through their syllables, in which other words awaken, and so on, so that whoever pronounces one word, if he listens hard, can hear the teeth of a whole language chattering in it.

"It's inevitable, Helen," repeats my husband, sliding a plate into the camera, and adjusting a lens. "What if I'd been killed, or your brother? If they hadn't been able to evacuate him in time, and he had bled to death there in the mud and his body had never been found? Wouldn't you want to see the spot where he spent his last moments? And if some farmer were to discover his rattling bones, what would you prefer? A nice tomb, or his empty eye sockets staring at you from under the glass of a shrine that commemorates the catastrophe that cost him his life? It's inevitable, love. Inevitable."

I thought of the incident during our second visit to "bloody, glorious Ypres", of which by now scarcely a stone was left standing. When I stood up in the car, I had a view of virtually the whole town: a grey expanse of rubble that lay in the middle of rolling fields like a huge bird dropping. There was no trace to be found of the house where we had sheltered and made love. In the extensive plain of heaps of stone that with the best will in the world could no longer be called ruins, it was impossible to point to within ten metres of where it must have been.

My husband had got out and walked over to the soldiers and workmen who, at the foot of the cloth hall, almost the only structure that retained a certain recognizability, were clearing rubble. He wanted to take a picture of their work. In the shapeless masses of stone, over which, here and there, a buttress of the cathedral, a corner of the old guild houses stuck out, they had made themselves a path and somewhere in the shadow of the tower they were using tackle to remove heavier fragments.

I had followed him at a distance, meanwhile looking round, in my mind rebuilding the market square from my memories. When I got closer a commotion broke out in their ranks, the tackle was set aside. The men bent down and seemed to be pointing at something at the bottom of a wide ditch they had opened up at the foot of the tower.

My husband also leant forward, in order, between the trunks, the legs, the gesticulating arms, to get a view of what had made the men stop work.

I saw him lift up the tripod of the camera, take it with him and go and stand close to the men—when I joined him he hissed at me: "Don't look now, sweetheart. Take a stroll, dear. Be with you in a wink."

I did as he asked, but not without first, when the men stood to the left and right against the wall of the ditch to give him room, peering into the hole that had been uncovered when the tackle had moved a heavy stone and a more or less concave opening had appeared. In it lay four soldiers, by the look of their uniforms British, entwined arm in arm.

They awakened associations in me of hungry chicks in the narrow, round space of their nest. Probably they had crawled from the crypt that became their tomb up a slope of fragments to near this hole. It must have closed before their eyes when the bombardment, which had driven them into the crypt or whatever it was, pulverized the spire and the falling masonry cut off their escape.

Perhaps they had tried to dig out the hole with their bare hands, but in vain—no one could have dislodged the block of stone that lay inert in the tackle by muscle power alone. It looked as if they had gasped for breath, stretched their necks as the fire of the burning town above their heads sucked all the oxygen to itself, through every chink and gap that proved too narrow for them. The skin of their lips had dried to yellow parchment round their teeth.

Probably they had been lying in their catacomb since shortly after the outbreak of war, and they had lain for four years in that cellar while around them people tried as best they could to lead regular lives in the town, which with every barrage had collapsed a little more.

I waited by the car until my husband returned. He said there must be more down there, they had been able to see them vaguely in the darkness, at least fifteen or twenty, maybe even more. He shook his head. "Poor devils…"

"You want it all ways," I said to him when he showed me the prints later. The careful framing. The tackle with the block of stone. The men left and right against the slanting wall of excavated earth, between them the mouth of that subterranean vault, almost slap in the middle. In the darkness of the hole the pale skulls of those soldiers, like a grotesque multiple birth, four foetuses stranded during birth.

"You allow those poor souls a grave, but you snap them in their death agony. For all the world to see. How inevitable's that? You want it both ways, Monsieur Heirbeir."

He pulled the prints out of my fingers with feigned indignation, took my chin in the hollow of his hand and gave me a fleeting kiss.

"And I think, Miss Demont, I'm not half as perfidious as you and your precious little words. You want it all, you greedy monster, in every possible way, you do…"

He pulled me off the sofa, put his arm round my waist and whispered, as we sailed laughing across the parquet floor to the couch in the bay window: "We're two of a kind, madame."

I LIKE PHOTOS more the less there is to see in them, when they leave all avenues open. That one pile he kept in a separate drawer, in large, flat boxes. They must have been outside his work for him too, or maybe the reverse: perhaps they were the hidden heart of it, more and at the same time less populated than the scenes of the living and the dead that he immortalized for press bureaus and newspapers; their all-too-fleeting, noisy ink.

I mean that country road with the deep tyre tracks, an almost abstract pattern that moves in a wide arc to the horizon, where, not quite cut off by the framing, a narrow band of clouds is hanging dripping in five poplars.

I mean the hole from which the body of a missing soldier has been dug up. A corner of the tarpaulin on which the remains are placed. The sole of the boot that was left on the bottom. Farther on, higher up the slope of the hill, a few heaps of sand, the shaft of a spade. Next to each heap of sand is an identical tarpaulin.

I also mean the operating theatre in the hospital. The operating table is empty, the nurses must have just left the theatre to take the instruments to be sterilized. The surgeons have gone for lunch or a rest after what seems a quiet day. Everything is bathed in spotless white light which picks out all the more sharply the smudges of blood on the floor tiles under the operating tables, three in number, and the dirty bandages in the shiny, enamelled buckets next to the tables, just before they were emptied.

In most of these photos you can't see that it's war, or that the war is just over, and yet they seem to suck all wars from all times into themselves. Whether we die in chain mail or in the flash of a bomb full of deadly rays, the vocabulary remains the same: emptiness and traces of blood and dirty bandages. Look at the arsehole. Who catches the shit? Those of whom there is no sign, just taken away, to the recuperation ward, the mortuary, the final grave after the anonymous hole in the ground? Those photos are waiting. Everything has been brought into a permanent state of readiness for our arrival, alive or dead or decimated to a hunk of meat without arms or legs. Every peace is an interval between two wars.

I can remember him taking this one, I was there. One of the early autumns a few years after the armistice, when we went back to my uncle's house annually as a kind of pilgrimage; my husband, my brother, a handful of others, to spend a few days there. From there he and I sometimes made day trips, or went on two-day ones, always to the area of the battlefields.

That day, I remember, we were walking through a wooded section in the hills around Reims. It was the end of August, hot, late in the afternoon. We were walking some distance apart, and at a certain moment I had lost sight of him. I retraced my steps, but he was nowhere to be seen. Only when he called out my name—"By Jove," he cried, "Helen, look at that!"—did I find him again, in a natural basin surrounded by trunks and undergrowth, where it smelt strongly of mould.

A wall of thoroughly weathered wood with a narrow doorway in it portioned off part of the basin. He stood looking inside and beckoned me as he disappeared into the cave. I followed him, but it took some time before my eyes got used to the darkness.

"*Incroyable...*" he muttered, and I heard him feeling the ceiling of the low cave with his hand.

Instead of earth or stone his fingers, to judge by the sound, met metal: the curve of a roof of corrugated iron that had been laid over the basin, then covered with a layer of earth and finally, autumn after autumn, buried under fallen leaves.

It smelt stuffy, smells I could not immediately place. My foot hit something that rolled over the ground—in the darkness I could only make out contours, unnaturally angular.

"Wait here," he said. "Get my gear..." As if he was afraid that while he was away his discovery would vanish for ever into the earth.

We waited outside, nestled on a blanket on the edge of that little valley, and ate our sandwiches. He was waiting for the right light, the right moment. He had calculated that the sun, when it sank further, would shine through a gap in the treetops directly through the doorway inside, and that's what happened. He went in and positioned himself with the camera against the inner wall of the wooden partition.

In the photo it really is as if he was able to trap the shafts of the evening sun while they secretly entered the underground space, furtively lit the four or five bunks against the side wall, above them the shelves with a few bottles and bandage tins, and the chair that seemed to have been hastily pushed away from a small table in the corner, and even a glimpse of the small notebook open on top of it, the handwriting rendered illegible by seeping damp.

You would say it is a snapshot, but I saw the patience with which he waited until the light reached the walls and the vault of corrugated iron at exactly the right angle. He did not stage anything, did not pull the blankets straight so that it made the impression even more strongly that the bunks had just been made up, or arrange the pillows in such a way that the mould marks in the cotton would come out better, or put the basins or the kidney bowl with a clamp, a pair of scissors with a long bent beak in it, on that low wooden box. Everything is as we found it—apart from that one thing, a pebble he thought at first, a piece of stone in which a strip of calcite or another crystal reflected the sun's rays too directly. He threw it to me, and I sat on the blanket waiting until he was finished. It was not much bigger than a spirit glass and there was earth caked round it. When I picked it off with my fingernails, I felt the coolness of metal, a sharp edge, albeit dented. A piece of tin, a cap, I suspected, but gradually an inscription was revealed beneath my fingers. It could only be read after I had rubbed it clean with my moistened handkerchief. It said: "Oleum infirmorum".

Only in words can the earth tremble in reverse, through the static syllables. Only here can the joints and ligaments stir, bones return like restlessly sleeping children under a grass-green quilt. Here the springs of the earth can whine and grind, its mantle becomes a soft placenta-like mattress. It shivers till it has gooseflesh. It draws explosions together in one point and spews out bullets and bombs. Here the house fronts can crawl out of the dust with wobbly knees, street after street, stuff door and window frames back in their gaping mouths like dentures, and have themselves measured up for hairdos of step gables and chimneys. Around their beams the fallen tiles flap in dense swarms to land on the cross laths and close up—I want everything at once.

And here I grip his fingers in mine, squeeze them and say: "Look. Look at us, Matthew Herbert!"

Without letting go of my hand, he turns round his own axis on the mattress, from his back onto his belly. I am standing against the side of the bed, opposite the tall mirror in the large wardrobe. "Look," I repeat—and then the crown of his head brushes the side of my knee while he turns and pulls hard on my hand. His black hair scraping my pores gives way to his cheeks, his lips, the unexpectedly moist glow of his tongue. The skirt of my dress falls over his head, and his other hand glides up along the inside of my thigh, until his fingers encounter his own fluids, which make a chilly trace of tears down to the back of my knee.

And I say again: "Look!" and give him a teasing tap on the head. He giggles, pulls the material of my skirt round his face like a bonnet and surveys us in the mirror: I standing, he lying.

Behind us the half-open door. The wallpaper with the ethereal roses. The holy water vessel hanging askew. A palm branch. A row of clothes brushes on hooks under another, smaller mirror. Other people's intimacy surrounding us.

"Look at us," I say again. "I never want to forget this."

"Better cover me arse then," he giggles, taking his hand from between my thighs. And grabs behind his back for his trousers until the two white half-moons of his bottom disappear behind the khaki.

I stretch my fingers. He lays his fingers back in mine, turns my hand and strokes my nails with his thumb and now he stretches his neck to kiss my wrist, the collar of his unbuttoned shirt falls open and his shoulder is exposed.

He rolls back onto his back, stretches out his free hand and twists a lock of my hair round his finger.

"Look at us," I repeat—the ribbon of my dress loose. My slip around my ankles. The tails of my tailored jacket creased. "*Look at us.*"

He tugs at my arm. His pupils look at me literally upside down, boyishly earnest. A hint of top teeth between his lips: "Helen?"

"What?"

"I have to pee."

He must have found a po in one of the rooms. A minute or so later the sing-song of his water rang out in something that by the sound of it was made of metal. I heard him pull his trousers up and arrange his shirt before buttoning up again.

"All set and ready?" he beamed when he came back.

I had lain down on the bed again, and was on my back, staring at the ceiling, on which the cracks in the plaster showed a world map full of unknown continents.

He picked his belt up off the floor, put in on and sat down on the edge of the bed to put on his lace-up boots. The material of his shirt was pulled firmly round his trunk, so that the bumps of his vertebrae were clearly defined.

I stretched out my arm to him and, as if that gesture contained a magic formula, the sunlight flared strongly behind the net curtains at the foot of the bed, and just above the window sill threw the skeleton of the bare roofs into relief against the clouds.

"We have to go now," he muttered, without turning round. His fingers tied the laces. "Almost four o'clock… We have-to have-to-go…"

While I got ready, rubbed my thighs clean, put my slip back on, I could follow his tread across the floorboards of the other rooms. The sunlight leaked away again, abandoning the room to a sombre grey.

Outside there was the purr of an aircraft, a little later there was the sputter of artillery. The purring grew fainter, but on the other side of the house, the front, the sound of footsteps swelled, and men's voices. On top of that a dull sighing, a nasal-sounding hum.

When I went to see what was going on, the English soldiers whom we had overtaken on the way here were walking past; they didn't notice us. I could only see the top of their headgear, and the chairs with turned legs and velour seats that a few of them were lugging with them in stacks of two.

They were chatting as they walked along. In the middle of their informal procession, four men were pulling a dusty harmonium. Every few steps air puffed through the bellows, so that it sounded as if the instrument was urging them on with grumpy orders.

They disappeared from sight. Farther on, near the corner of the street, the lorry stood waiting for them with engine running. Their fading footsteps were drowned out by the cannon, which seemed to be beginning a new series of salvoes. The small panes in the window of the room gave a soft tinkle of lament, like girls ashamed of their own fear.

"We really must leave," he repeated. As he walked past, he stroked my hip with his hand and I followed him.

We were driving again. "Everything all right, Guv'nor?" he grinned.

I had turned round in the car to see the contours of the town, merging with the air saturated with damp, disappearing behind the gently rolling hills.

I don't know if I felt "all right". I was certainly alive—my body suddenly clearly demarcated in the space around me, well-thumbed by his caresses; his lips in my neck, between my breasts, on my nipples, in my navel. His fingers between my thighs. The fuss with his trouser buttons. The smell of his hair. The pleasure—but wasn't it more of a throbbing pain, a fist that clenched in my belly?—when his head sank between my legs and he had planted his knees, first the left then the right, on my shoulders. The glorious rawness or raw glory of another body. The rawness of his sex, which if I'm honest I'd never imagined so hard, so covered in blood vessels, and so inclined to turn blue, badly informed as I was by puerile paintings of statues full of *pudeur*. I had an attack of the giggles when I saw it dangling so close before my eyes, above the balls in their touching brown case under the cleft in his buttocks, where it was enclosed by rough black hair. When I pulled the skin over the head of his penis everything had shrunk—I had a second fit of giggling. The third overcame me when his hips were nestling between my legs and I felt his sex lose its way in the fold of my thigh, until he squeezed a hand between us. "Just a minor inconvenience, happens all the time..." he had grinned, largely to hide his own embarrassment, I saw, before his eyes glazed over and the pain centred on my pelvis—the shivers and spasms. The smell of his seed, at once salty and sickly sweet. And his breath, rushing in my ear.

"You're staring, love..."—a hint of freckles around his nose, and the deep, glowing, breathtaking black of his eyes.

I had turned round again, and was sitting looking at him as we drove on and the vault of treetops over the road drew a Morse code of light and shadow over the car.

I would have liked to know him as a schoolboy, and as a lad of, say, eighteen, trailing reluctantly to church after the aunt with whom he grew up, a hymn book under his arm. There in the north, where boredom, he said, submerged the days in the emptiness of a Sunday afternoon with showers.

I would have liked to see his room. The long, narrow window that divided the North Sea horizontally into two colours: grey and less grey. Have liked to know his first girlfriends, and also the more serious sweethearts, suitable for dull conversation in aunt's veranda, the Mauds and Margarets about whom he gave little away—a woman wants everything. I wonder: do men mourn differently? Does the rat of grief gnaw a great hole in their insides too? Why do women double up when they mourn, and men seem to fall apart?

*

It was getting on for evening when he brought me back from the trenches, relieved that nothing serious had happened. I was tired, confused, filled with impressions. In my head the broad strips of colour and buzzing in no man's land alternated with sudden, almost tactile impressions of his body. His taut midriff. The birthmark on his belly, just below the ribs. The texture of his nipples. His sex, which shrank after the ecstasy between his thighs—then the bright white of the wooden crosses in that landscape of poppies and mud pools. All those impressions seemed to be leaking out of my head, evaporating out of my eyes and mingling with the outside world.

The sun was already sinking deep in the west and colouring the damp in the air bright orange. Thunderclouds which rose from the horizon, with their deep blue tending to black, provided a sharp contrast and laid over the treetops and trunks along the road, over the convoys of lorries and horses and men which again surrounded us, a dull, silvery glow. There was something unreal about it, reinforced by the constant rumble of the weaponry—I was also much too hot. It was oppressively hot and my stomach was playing up.

In the villages a suggestion of night was already roaming around, in which the headgear of North Africans on horseback brought an unexpected ghostly manifestation of colour, which for a moment enlivened the ubiquitous khaki. The swirling of the capes that they had wrapped round their uniforms conjured the beat of bird wings in the dusk. The cadence of the hoof beats left a long echo.

Above the horizon there now hung a long band of copper-yellow evening light, above which the black clouds had gathered.

The dull-yellow squares of cornfields absorbed the grey of the sky and were beginning to wrap themselves up in night—and everywhere troops were on the move. The marching songs that they whistled or sang with deep voices floated in snatches on the rising wind.

We reached Poperinge just in time, the narrow streets were as good as deserted, and everywhere there were closed shutters and lowered blinds, because there was an evening curfew. We were audibly closer to the front again. The report of the guns sounded fuller, everywhere houses showed traces of destruction, whether or not patched up without enthusiasm.

He manoeuvred the car through empty streets, narrow alleyways. It had rained, water splashed from under the wheels. Somewhere behind one of the house fronts there was the sound of music, laughter, singing, but apart from that the town seemed dead.

We slowed at a wooden gate. He got out, pushed it open and immediately closed it again after we had come to a halt. The coach house where we now were led to a cloister around a rather fussy inner garden with bolting rose bushes, shrubs and a flaking statue of the Virgin Mary.

"Give us a hand, love," he called to me; he was unloading.

I followed him, laden with a couple of bags, through the cloister, to a flight of steps that led to a long corridor with identical doors on one side at a regular distance from each other.

There was an intense smell of life, occupation, the scent of starch and linen; the towels, handkerchiefs, pillowslips, which lay in orderly piles in one of the rooms, the door of which was open—but the hollow echo of our steps in the deserted rooms contradicted me. I had the impression that I was walking through the inside of a clock that had stopped. The floor beneath my feet was worn away under the tread of countless soles. The twilight hung like dark cobwebs in the corners of the vaulting in window alcoves, and seemed to remember the habits that must have swept against calves or ankles here day in, day out.

He said there was a concierge, "*une gardienne*, sort of", who didn't live on the premises. Anyway, there wasn't much for us to be frightened of. He rubbed his thumb against his forefinger and gave me his grin.

And again I wondered how often he'd been here before, and with whom, whether he was following a familiar scenario. He reminded me of a stray cat, something that moved in the shadows, on the fringe, on the edge, as he had, I suspected, since his childhood, first in the difficult household of his father and stepmother, then with his religious aunt "up north", crept agilely around the other person, approachable when it suited him, shy when he found them oppressive—but I wondered what I was to him: someone he saw as his equal, or no more than a naive mouse?

"Hungry, dear?" He had taken off the luggage in a room with a bed under low beams, a bedside table and a tall, narrow wardrobe.

I wasn't hungry. I was exhausted.

He went back downstairs to fetch the cameras from the car.

The room looked out over a series of back gardens. At the dark windows a candle flame occasionally went past and disappeared again. Above the roofline the clouds reflected the flashes of the distant artillery, the echo of which rumbled through the streets in waves.

It was already pretty dark, and I must have fallen asleep on the bed, a fragmentary slumber. In slivers of dreams I saw my fingers gliding over the rough material of his shirt, the buttons creeping out of the buttonholes, and his ribcage, the soft field of his belly coming into view, so concrete and close-up that I started awake.

He stroked my cheeks with the back of his hand and tucked a lock of hair behind my ear. "It's all right, love…" It was completely dark now.

I got up, undressed and crept under the sheets with him. He slid an arm under my neck and put the other round my waist. I laid my back against his chest, and heard him giggle when I felt his sex swelling, followed by a sniggering "Beg your pardon, Corp'ral…"—but I stretched out my arm and pushed his buttocks closer to me.

We lay silently listening to the noise on the horizon. Occasionally the reflection of the artillery bathed the room in greenish light for a few seconds. Once we were woken when a heavy hit somewhere made everything shake. We craned our necks, expectantly, but that one bang was all. The rain swelled into a downpour, and the lapping of the gutters lulled us to sleep.

I MUST HAVE ALWAYS KNOWN, with the sort of awareness that can seize us beyond all knowledge, that I would be the one left behind, would never know him at, say, seventy, would not see him become much older than fifty or sixty and would never recognize in the wrinkles of the old man the chap whom I knew, as soon as I met him, was the one, he alone. I have always known that it would not be granted me to discover whether the old man I saw in him when we were still young, so young, corresponded with reality.

We all carry our ages with us, from the beginning. They sleep deep inside us and whether they reveal themselves or are doomed as unborn children to perish with our tissue, no one knows—but I have always known, and always been waiting for it, with each of his trips thought: I'll never see him again. Whenever he was away, when the phone or the doorbell rang I would always whisper: that's it, my great happiness is over.

Because he was my great happiness, I never deceived anyone as exuberantly as him. In so doing I wanted to take a generous advance against grief. I absorbed the unbearable otherness of other bodies while he was still there, and I let the deathly quiet clashes, the soft despair while talking to strangers who resembled him, although I knew they were strangers and my behaviour was absurd, jolt through me while he was still alive—to be ready, not unprepared, to pay off the outstanding debt in advance.

Still, after all those years, and always unexpected, at the most idiotic times, loss can hit me, through all the floors of this ridiculously old body—waking just before dawn, or, more frequently still, after my afternoon nap, with, on my palms, as if the body has a memory of its own, the memory of his naked young shoulders: their curve that rests in the hollow of my hand when I sit astride his hips and, when he tries to sit up, push him back into the pillow with his upper arms in my palms.

If only I could rub his body back into being, model it with all its textures and volumes from the air itself. The movement of muscles under his pale skin, when he tenses his buttocks, the hollows in his flanks where I can lay my fists, and his look, his jet-black look in those narrow eyes, narrowed by pleasure when we have a pillow fight that morning, and roll over and over on the bed—his neck, his chin, arms, legs, armpit hair, his balls, his arse, his laugh, and his head, which in the amniotic sheets that envelop us rests on my belly, swelling with my breath. And me pushing him away because his stubble tickles, and him jumping giggling out of bed, going over with sheets and all to the little window under the low ceiling, the bedding in one fist around his waist, a bridal gown of linen and embroidery, while with his other arm he leans against the window frame and looks out, in the light of early morning above the little courtyard garden that plays timidly around him, and when with an accomplice's grin he picks one of my pubic hairs out of his teeth, the linen sliding down from his hips over his calves, his trunk, his legs. If only I could read his whole young, supple body and drink in every unevenness, every peculiarity with my eyes and my fingers: the blotches on his shoulder blades, the rough pores on the skin of his arse, the six or seven short black hairs that grow to a point just above the cleft in his buttocks, and the architecture of his ribs when he leans against the window frame with arm outstretched and with his other hand picks my most secret hair from his teeth, and his smile: half shy, half conspiratorial, as he turns his head away from the window and takes me in, naked on the bed—if there must be an eternity, dear God, give me this one.

We ate a hasty breakfast of dry biscuits and cold coffee. The rain had cleared the sky, clouds were still sliding in front of the sun, but they hung less heavily and darkly in the heavens.

Flemish weather, I called it—and he peered at the sky with a frown. He had to be back at his post by late afternoon, so we hadn't much time, but before we left he wanted some photos of the monastery buildings.

We passed the kitchen, where a massive coal-fired oven of heavy cast iron was frozen in a cold winter sleep and immediately communicated its coldness to our palms. In the small chapel saints of polychrome plaster raised palm branches or instruments of torture aloft, and looked down beatifically on a flock of empty pews under a mosaic of yellow and blue patches of light. In a corner room next to the corridor the dry smell of yarn and textiles had already alerted me: lace cushions were in two strict rows opposite each other, so that it looked as if the nuns and young ladies in their care had abruptly stopped work when they had left their accommodation.

An illusion of industrious fingertips still seemed to be flitting above those cushions, and above the pinheads around which rudimentary floral motifs had come to a premature stop. The lame bobbins that hung over the edge seemed as heavy as lead. It was as if silence were playing through all that fine meshwork and kept a thousandfold silence under that one light bulb which, on a cable that was too long under a sober porcelain shade, surveyed a collection of chairs spread carelessly across the floor.

I heard something creak behind my back.

He had found the switch by the door, but the bulb remained dead.

The first cloister was connected to a second: smaller and also much older, as could be seen from the weathered pilasters, which bore a gallery of open pointed arches, around a smaller courtyard of pebbles. Only when we had walked round almost the whole cloister did we see at the far end the hole that the impact of a projectile had made in the ceiling. Frayed bits of lath and plaster-work hung around the hole; the heavier beams had fallen through it and were sticking in a pile of rubble, on which, when the sun broke through the clouds and illuminated the openings with its full glow, the ethereal green of grass clumps reached up to heaven.

"Look at that light," he said. "Simply perfect."

Like his smile.

We ate a last quick snack on the hill, in the same establishment where we had first seen each other. In the restaurant on the other side of the courtyard the matron still resided at her lectern, just as determined to support the firmament with her hairdo, should it be on the point of collapse. She did not seem to recognize me or consider me worth looking at when she greeted him with a cheerful "*Bonjour, mon cher Matthieu.*"

Obviously the house rules had become less strict, since we were allowed to choose our own place in the restaurant, where there were only a handful of customers, all soldiers.

We chose a table at one of the windows that looked out over

the landscape. "Wine, dear?" he asked, with feigned gallantry, as he sat poring over the menu and peered at me over the edge—his inward glee produced fireworks in his pupils.

I did not intend to let myself be floored. "I don't know, da'ling," I retorted. "White if you must, and not too sweet. It tends to disagree with my stomach…"

"Excellent!" He motioned to the waitress.

I could scarcely fail to notice the wink she gave him after she had noted the order and taken the menu out of his hands, nor the body language of understanding that went on over my head when a second young lady came to arrange the appropriate cutlery next to our plates.

"Blanche and Suzanne," he said, when I looked at him in bewilderment. "*Les deux filles de Madame Loorius*… We call them 'The Peaches'…"

"Because of the colour or the taste?" I asked.

He laid his napkin jauntily in his lap. "Well, you know the saying, mademoiselle… *Mieux on connaît ses pêches, plus on aime les bonnes poires de Flandres.*"

"You're making me blush…"

He giggled and looked outside. The windows were open, letting a cool breeze into the restaurant which drove the oppressive heat of the day before out of the beams. Above the plain the rain of the night before was rising in veils of mist, colouring the fields, wooded banks and distant villages with a blue-green haze, and in the distance became thicker and thicker and obscured the horizon. The clouds were almost motionless above the land. The roads, above which the occasional short flicker of light betrayed troop movements, dissolved in the mist. Farther away, towards the coastline, floated the long, stately cigar-shaped balloons.

"Could sit here for ever," he mused, looking up as the food was being served. "A bit like Kent... Fewer fruit trees, however. Though I like the French accent..."

We ate. He looked happy, and I did too, an innocent, pure happiness—in my breast a child threw a handful of poppies into the air. We looked at each other in turn above our plates, and smiled.

"And now, *mon cher Matthieu*?" I asked as light-heartedly as possible when we had finished, imitating the intonation of the matron, who had left her unassailable position, probably to have lunch herself.

He was playing with the tip of his fork on his plate—something that my mother would not have taken as a sign of a good upbringing—and then looked up. "It may be some time before we see each other again," he said. "Got meself detached." He put the fork down. Pulled a face as if his tongue had found something unpleasant between his teeth. "Guiding spoilt, obese Americans. *I've had it...* I can travel with a regiment, off to Belgium as a matter of fact..."

"When?"

"Soon..." He signalled that he wanted to order coffee. "I can move more freely, Helen. Down here, it's rules, regulations, rules... Drives me mad it does... Besides"—he tapped with his fingers on the small hand camera that lay next to him on the table—"must make the best of Mummy's allowance..."

He meant the legacy that his mother had left him at her death. "She married down. Know what that means, 'down'? Beneath her class, not many steps or rungs, but obviously enough to make her anathema to her blood relations, while on her husband's side, well-to-do but modest middle class, she proved too precious in style to win much confidence. It wasn't exactly a huge success, that marriage…"

So after her death his father, a gynaecologist, decided—"She died of excitement, as you can imagine"—that a new house plant was better grown in more familiar compost, and that his son, if he was not at boarding school, could not thrive better than with his mother's family.

Hence your French, I thought as I listened to him. Hence of course also the obscenities with which he liked to lard his sentences, perhaps to test me. He spoke the swear words too emphatically. They did not trip off his tongue the way they did with the chaps from the slums—who found it as difficult in their way to mask their origin. They who belonged "down". He mixed their patois with his words the way he stirred cream into his coffee: in small doses.

I tried not to let him notice that he had thrown me. "Perhaps you'll bump into my brother," I said, in an attempt at light-heartedness. "He's with the engineers now, I think."

"One never knows," he nodded. "It's a small world over there, *mais peut-être un peu surpeuplé…*"

I was silent.

He saw I was finding it difficult to hide my disappointment and put his hand on mine. "Helen, look at me… We'll write. OK? Besides, it isn't as if I'm leaving for New Zealand, is it?"

We didn't say much when he took me home. I wanted to store every second inside me, every movement he made at the wheel, every sideways look, every sigh, each lock of hair, wanted to register every detail.

He pulled up in the little spinney, some distance from the gate to our yard.

"Give us a kiss…"

I could have swallowed his lips.

"See you soon."

"Be careful."

He nodded. Reversed the car. Waved.

I turned round. It was as if my body was connected by invisible threads to the departing car.

It was about four-thirty, that vague period of the day that hesitates between afternoon and evening. I had the feeling I had been away from home not for a day and a half but a year and a half—an impression that was strengthened when I entered the gate and a few paces away the maid crossed the yard, a basket of chicken feed in her arms. Though she noticed me, she scarcely interrupted her mechanical gait and nodded rather coolly. Something unintelligible crackled from her chest.

When I entered the inner courtyard, my uncle got up from the bench under the tree, where he had obviously been sitting waiting, and came up to me with his eyes rolling. My mother, it emerged, for fear of not getting home well before dark, had returned earlier. The argument that must have flared up when she did not find me seemed to be still smouldering in the garden.

"Of course it's all my fault," sighed my uncle. He looked sheepish and took my hands in his. "And I shall make wholehearted penance. But I also think that the journey to Canossa will be long for you too, and hard. And I think your abductor had better keep a low profile for a while."

IV

VI

I T WAS CLEVER, the earth, said my brother in the rare moments when he disclosed anything about his time as a soldier. Clever and jealous. When you're piled together with ten or so others in a hole in the ground and you feel the floor, behind the planks and props of the walls, coming to life with the impact and the ghastly noise, you know how thin existence is. You have the feeling that the earth has been watching you for days and weeks. That it has been estimating your height, envying you your torso, your arms, yours legs. That it has been spying on the way you walk, counting the moments when your concentration flags as you shuffle across the planks with forty kilos of equipment on your shoulders, knowing that the slightest slip can be fatal—it is silent, smoulders and waits. Nothing can make a man feel as fragile as its convulsions when it wakes from its sleep. You can feel its motions through your intestines. The blows reduce everything to shaking and you wonder whether dimensions like life and death have any point in that hole, where the posts and planks do their best to offer something like firmness, bones, a skeleton. You can't do anything but wait until the hell outside abates or the ground encloses you and finally appropriates your forms. You lie and you tremble with the shocks. You're a lump of half-digested flesh in the underbelly of the world, impelled by its own peristalsis. For all you know, you could already be dead, no more than a membrane of skin and hair between the formless matter outside and the yearning formlessness within. You think: I'm just a shell standing in the way of the merger of mush with mush.

Now and then he puffed at the cigar that he always lit up over coffee. Every few minutes he brought it to his mouth, sucked in the smoke, kept it under his palate for a while and exhaled. Meanwhile he spoke, eventually more to himself than to me—a trance-like incantation. He could sometimes interrupt his dreamy monologue when he came back to reality. If you write down what I'm telling you, you'll see, he grinned. You'll want to dig your own foxhole in that massive, formless sea.

It's so clever, the earth. Capable of summoning up its particles to form a mass, operas and symphonies of mud and collapses and landslides, but it imposes itself equally when you wipe your bum and you feel its grains scratching your arsehole. It grinds between your teeth when you eat your soggy bread. When everything is jolting and screaming, and you briefly stroke the face of the chap huddled up against you, on the narrow bunk, to feel life, the texture of his unshaven cheeks—even then its hunger doesn't let go of you, because your fingers are dry with its mud. It has nestled in your tiniest folds. Garrisons, regiments, battalions are hidden in the wrinkles of your fingers and language too tastes of sand, because when you speak it comes away from your lips and works its way inside. We ate soil, we shat soil and we were soil, a bag of bones and skin filled with soil. It was only a question of time before we tore and emptied, and the earth would have its way.

And when your mate shifts position on the bunk next to you and momentarily digs you in the thigh while his feet search for a place next to yours, on the plank under the dirty, mud-saturated blanket that you share with him, he might just as well be dead. As dead as the knee or shoulder, the arm or leg in the swill above the lean-to that protects the entrance to the foxhole and on which you hear the clods and the limbs dancing. You think: how much longer, when will we be dancing as lifelessly along with them, or are we already? If you call that horror, you don't know what horror is. Horror is the earth in itself if you like, which out of the 100 men who slogged after you between the craters along the paths and the narrow planks, swallowed up thirty or forty en route without a cry or a sigh. It adapts the syntax of its hunger. Where necessary as fluidly as water. Elsewhere as tough as dough or thick porridge that never lets go of you. Some guys compared it to an octopus, a many-armed monster, but I'm not sure, I'm not sure—I had respect for it, a form of respect, the way an antelope grazes peacefully near a pride of sleeping lions: apparently unconcerned, in reality alert from snout to tail to the slightest movement that may reveal that the hunt is on. You don't blame it, it's hungry.

I looked at its new undulations and grooves when we crawled out of its hole after the night. At the geography it had fashioned for itself in the last few hours, and which the following night it was able to shake off in boredom. The stubble of the tree trunks. The body that during the most recent tempest it had hurled from its layers and placed on the gentle slope that was not there the previous day: on its belly, arms under the chest, one leg stretched, the other raised, in no way distinguishable from yourself when you crawled out of the trench and splashed through the mud on all fours. The earth that reduced us to creeping creatures, mud-jumpers, that cast us back in time and declared nature's memory to be the playground of its fantasies, grabbed our bones to hang its formless flesh on and delighted in sending us through the sediment of a beach at low tide like a troop of crabs, just before the deluge—wherever you put your hand, if at the whistle of an approaching howitzer shell you plunged your head in its waters, it burped in your face and exuded the stench of the undigested dead in its bowels. History wobbled and listed. A person should not crawl, my little gazelle; do you know enough to write it down now?

There aren't words enough. It sucks words up as greedily as bodies. You can't imagine a language that has not sunk into its folds like a shipwreck. All our words are magic formulas. We remain savages who after a storm shoot at the sky to punish the gods for their anger or dance in circles to beg for rain. The earth grinned and burped in my face; do you know enough now? That's how far we've come, I thought. That's what all that steel is for, and the cannon and the tanks, the iron Tyrannosaurus Rex, and the copper bombs—to rid the earth of the skin disease of life and the last human being. It helped to give it a name, call it an octopus, or clever and jealous. The coats of the rats that crawled over my legs at night and that I vainly tried to chase away had an unearthly softness—do you know enough now? I remember thinking what neat creatures rats were; how did they keep their fur so clean?

In sultry weather his scar played up. Not excruciating pain, he said, more an obstinate itch that bursts out, from my armpit across my chest and the side of my trunk to my right hip. I lie tossing and turning in my sleep, sticky with sweat. I turn from one side to the other, onto my belly, my back. Sooner or later I doze off, usually towards morning, but the pain keeps my sleep

light, it draws nerves through my dreams. And there is always a
moment at which the pain joins up, a long line of itch that feels
as cold as burning to the touch. Then I start scratching with
both hands. I turn onto my back and kick off the sheets. Sweat
is gushing out of my pores. The itch starts to concentrate in
nodules on my chest, as if it is trying to tear something out of
me, as if my skin is no longer anything more than a membrane.
The harder I scratch, the more restlessly I toss and turn, the
more intensely the itch burns in the scar. And sooner or later I
feel my skin giving way under my hands. I am splitting open,
as it were, with an immense feeling of relief, as the itch and
the pain immediately start to subside. Perhaps it is because of
the bedding that I have pulled loose, perhaps, the undersheet
stuck to my back evokes a hallucination, but my skin seems like
a shell which crumbles and gives way to the texture of thick
material, leather, brass buttons, a belt, a clasp—the harder I
toss and turn or scratch, the more I expose my old uniform.

Sometimes I wake in despair, bottomless despair, when the
uniform is my kit from the trenches: the kepi, the long, thick
coat and the leather pouches for ammunition round my waist,
my drinking bottle and the blanket secured over my shoulder
with a strap, and the small shovel for digging a foxhole in the
stinking earth, whose smell takes hold of me again. On other
nights it is my engineer's uniform, as brand new as the day I
was finally allowed to put it on, and was finally transferred, and
I feel as much relief as then, as much euphoria, because I was
finally allowed to escape the hell in the trenches, and the mud,
I think, hasn't got me—that nice dark uniform with the red
braid, and the black collar shields with the helmet of Minerva
on them in gold. I can't describe the elation to you, the calm

265

but complete relief of being able to have a good night's sleep again in a more or less respectable bed and have regular meals, farther away from the front. I didn't know then that it's patient, the earth, that it would wait until I was nearby again. Weird what our dreams do with us, what we do in our dreams, he reflected.

His soldier's uniform always remained part of him, he was never really able to sweat it out of his system for good. By his tread alone I could invariably deduce which of the two dream figures was smouldering in his tissues. If he was in a light-hearted mood one caught a glimpse of the figure of the trainee officer in the engineers and he was imbued with relief at being able to live a more or less normal life, in a branch of the army where one was regularly allowed a freer rein and a person was more than a hunk of disciplined flesh, fodder for the mud that finally got him anyway. I could hear from his cheerful whistling when he came to call, his simple happiness that the world and fate were in an approachable mood. After the war his life had the character of a long holiday. Fortunately he was not so stupid that he thought a person should make an incision in a stone or leave his initials on a bark for the short time he has to plod around here. Nor like me, who could sometimes get so irritated with him because I was basically jealous of him. Of his light-heartedness, his superficiality, his hunger for young, elegant bodies, supple surfaces of people—but was he really so volatile and frivolous?

There were days when that other figure, the shadow side, the soldier in the mud-caked uniform of the infantry, had the upper hand in him, certainly when that scar played up. Then he walked slightly hunched and used his walking stick to lean on laboriously at each step and not just for decoration. He made an emaciated impression and appeared to be putting almost all his weight on that walking stick: bent forward, shoulders hunched, head buried in them—his eyes seemed larger than usual.

It was not so much a cramped position, more a reflex, as if he wanted to wrap his whole body around that line of wild flesh in order to protect it from unexpected contacts, however insensitive it might be apart from those phantom pains. But even on his good days there could be moments, unguarded moments, even if they lasted only a fraction of a second, when his pupils seemed to emit no light, or darkness, rather an intense emptiness, as if the world and its impressions found no life at all behind the blue gates of his irises, and were unable to evoke any spark or impulse.

I recognize it here in the first portrait in which we are all together again, he, my father, my mother and I. For a long time it was in the front room on one of the side tables, perhaps to make it clear to our guests that we had survived everything more or less unscathed. My mother is wearing one of those ponderous dresses in dark bombazine that she favoured after the war. She already looks a lot flabbier and fuller than in my childhood: she is becoming a real matron. The flu of the last year of the war unleashed a hunger in her that she was actually never able to assuage again. Around her mouth there is a more or less permanent doggedness, her lips are compressed into a pen stroke of sobriety.

An utter resignation emanates from her body and infuses the tableau; there is something about us like stuffed animals under glass. Not only my brother, who has begun cultivating his downy moustache into a proper handlebar, so that a white streak of mist curls between his lips and nostrils. Because of his blond hair, combed smooth, and that attempt at a moustache the contrast with his skin, pale and downy, still that of the baby lamb, is all the greater. Only his eyes, those steel-blue eyes, seem old. Older than those of my father and mother, older than mine, which with a gleam of triumph, or is it desperation, glow among the curls of my coiffure, which is cut more or less level with my jaw line.

Looking back, my euphoria seems close to bewilderment. We are perfect mirages, imbued with the frivolous belief that the world would never again rock on its foundations, while it was doing nothing but licking its wounds and gathering strength for the next round. I look like a slut. In the following years frocks became longer again, much to my mother's relief. Europe lowered the skirt length, perhaps in the hope of turning the tide, but tripped over the hem.

It is as though he foresees it all in that photo, beyond every wishful fantasy, every hope—with his eyes full of that emptiness from where he kept descending into the world of everyday, more or less happy with life as it was, so long as it lasted.

After his death a box of his personal effects was delivered to me. There was almost nothing from those years. His wristwatch. His bracelet. Around his neck he must have worn a silver chain with a ring hanging from it, with a name engraved on the inside: A. Duval. It's not impossible that someone somewhere wore a ring with my brother's name on it on his finger or on his chest, who can say?

His handkerchiefs—why hadn't the people in the boarding house given them to the rag-and-bone man together with his clothes? Why were handkerchiefs more intimate than socks or a tie or underpants? A thin pile of postcards with an elastic band round them, addressed to him. Views of Trier, Chicago, Berlin. One of them struck me because the message on the reverse side went further than the expected fatuities about the weather and the best wishes. "Thank you for taking us on board your silver-lined cloud. Eagerly awaiting a second passage. Love, Paul." Postmark Manchester, no surname.

The wallet: passport, banknotes. On a strip of crumpled paper at the bottom, probably long forgotten by himself: a telephone number with no name, somewhere in the depths of the countryside. When I ring a girl answers: "Veronique here…" In the background, with a questioning intonation, a woman's voice: "Who is it?"

"I don't know…" I hear the child whisper. "Sounds just like a Frenchwoman." Two seconds of silence, then the woman's voice, unexpectedly gruff and close: "Yes?"—I hang up.

To Rachida I said: take the keys with you. Round up your father and your brothers and your sisters and your mother. Hire a van and take everything from the house that's portable and not fixed. Give what you can't use away or sell it. Divide the money between you or give it to the poor, I don't mind, but bring me every scrap of paper and every photo you can find there.

A week later she lays a folder of blank letter paper on my bed, it still smells of the drawer in which it has been dying, the last bill for gas and water, a handful of empty envelopes without a sender or a postmark, and a pair of albums containing the same photos as mine: wedding parties, excursions, trips, babies and people celebrating anniversaries—nowhere a trace or sign of the life that must have been lived in the wings of our own, the life that was his, over which mine and that of my parents draped a cloak of silence... Not a glimpse of sweethearts, boyfriends, lovers, anything that referred to what for him must after all have been the essential thing, to the extent that there is an essence in a person, and to the extent that we could ever grasp it.

Perhaps someone else had beaten me to it. It wouldn't surprise me if he didn't carefully orchestrate his own disappearance without trace. He may, just before moving to that boarding house, have wiped the memory of his house clean, or given a confidant the task of doing the job for him. There were only two photos left, not much larger than visiting cards, which I fished out of his wallet where, judging by the folds and the frayed edges, they had been for years. In neither can he himself be recognized, unless one of the helmets in the background of that informal group portrait is his. Or did he take the photo himself? Is one of the men the one he was thinking of when he sometimes told me how pleasant it could be in spite of everything in the hole in the earth, while outside the inferno raged? "We even kissed, on the cheeks," he said, "when the storm abated and we had survived it again, and there was nothing ambiguous about it. We created a god of brotherhood and a small liturgy of tenderness in order to have something that could raise us above the filth and the dead bodies, that was all. Don't imagine any lewd scenes, my little gazelle, we did not want to degenerate entirely into animals."

And yet I wonder why he himself is not in those photos. In both one face stands out above the indifference of the expressions, and I cannot shake off the feeling that he always kept those photos with him purely because of those two strangers. I don't know if he often looked at them, perhaps it was enough to know they were in his wallet. Nor do I know if they survived or not. They may have been killed, and he may have chosen those two from all the men he had seen die, to hang his mourning and melancholy on. I remember him telling me how impossible it was to keep feeling sadness whenever someone you knew had been torn to shreds or had succumbed to his wounds.

Is one of them the A. Duval whose ring he must have always worn on his chest? That handsome young face in one photo perhaps, among the dozen men standing in front of the entrance to their underground shelter at sunset or early in the morning. Second from the left. Arms crossed. It was foggy at the moment when the photo was taken, so I don't know if it really is a fine bracelet, that thread of light round the wrist of his right hand, which lies clenched in the hollow of the left arm. Above it that face: not surly, but not approachable either, rather intrigued, the most intelligent in the photo, the liveliest.

Three other figures dissolve unrecognizably in the thick fog that seems to seep in over the top of the trench—a milky-white mist that always fills me with a slight horror, because it reminds me of poison gas, which is of course nonsense. In that case they would have worn their masks and no one would have been stupid enough to pose languidly for a group portrait during a gas attack. That young chap also looks too determinedly at the unknown person who took the photo, my brother or someone else, he looks at me a lot less open-mindedly than the other face in the first photo, in the second photo—that has clearly been taken early in the morning. At bottom left a corner of a field kitchen, I suspect: a table or rack of branches tied with rope, on it tin bowls, a drinking bottle with a spout, a hunk of bread. Someone has hung a ladle on one of the vertical branches, and it hangs half in front of the chin of that face: the perky face of a young chap. Like the others, not someone who has often posed for a photo. A farmer's son perhaps; there is an earthy soberness in his smile. The other men, five of them, look almost furtively into the lens. They have taken the butts of their cigars out of their mouths and hold them between thumb and forefinger.

Only that one chap, at the far left, looks with a kind of swank, half hidden behind that rack or table. He doesn't seem the type that my brother would have brought with him to family gatherings or private parties at home. He seems rather to fall into the category of rascals: fellows who do not seem constantly surrounded by a cloud of language, in contrast to the well-spoken young men with whom he appeared in public, and with whom every experience first had to pass through the word, as it were—an accusation that my husband sometimes levelled at me, not to hurt me, but to make me be quiet, to seal me with his body.

We all mistrusted words. A combination of suspicion and bewilderment after years of ambiguous communiqués, lying newspapers, swollen propaganda and the inability of those who came back from the fronts to force what they had been through into an appropriate form, a vocabulary that would not distort, belittle, falsify their experiences.

I remember afternoons when I went to visit him with my daughter, his godchild, in his mansion just outside town. Afternoons spent sitting on the balcony on the *bel étage*, looking out over the large back garden, my daughter playing with her dolls at our feet, without exchanging a word, apart from the child language we used with her, the affectionate names and made-up words. Now, so many years later, I have the feeling that we wanted to submerge language in that child, as if in the source of eternal youth. I wonder: were all the disasters that we brought down on our heads ever anything more than a semantic question that got out of hand?

I could still let loose such speculations on him with the same enthusiasm, and he could listen with the same amusement as in our youth, during our walks through the town. Except that the ironic quips with which he pointed out my contradictions were often missing. There could be an undertone of bitterness in his words when he interrupted me and said: "You're like an armchair soldier, my little gazelle. You've seen the battlefields once, in sunny weather, in ideal conditions, as a tourist. That's all." Usually he confined himself to amused chuckling while he poured us a cup of iced tea.

In the background, beyond the high box hedge at the bottom of the garden, on summer afternoons there was generally the measured plop-plop of a tennis game, soles crunching on gravel, exclamations of triumph or defeat from the mouths of young men who sooner or later would fall giggly and exhausted into the cane chair next to us on the balcony, legs across each other's knees, dispensing playful blows—children.

I've long since forgotten their names, if I ever retained them. They seemed to me completely interchangeable. After the death of my husband I could never watch their flirting without feeling my stomach turning. The very thought that my brother could

273

put their bodies to his lips, in passing steal something of them the way he casually plucked a grape from one of the fruit bowls in the house—while the sense of loss seethed in my bones, an ice-cold knife carved runes of mourning into the flesh of my belly, and there was so little in my growing daughter that recalled her father that I made her atone for it all her life.

With the years I have grown more tolerant. I think that he sought that youth and those bodies because their vocabulary could bring him consolation, a better translation as it were of his silences—and even if he was driven by an extremely childish desire, not so much to possess the other as to be the other, so what? Perhaps in each of those bodies he mastered a language I have never learnt, each time he sought a handful of synonyms, a metaphor of flesh and blood in which, however fleetingly, he felt his own being expressed, if not embodied.

I wish that he were still alive, that I could sit with him on the balcony, surrounded by those boys like playful cats on the cushions of his sofa. Then I would observe how he listens to me, with bored pleasure, with or without gleams of sarcasm in his eyes. I would keep an eye on the moustache on his top lip, to see whether the corners of his mouth remain stationary, whether the moustache moves left or right with his pouting lips in a grimace that expresses scepticism. I wonder whether he did not time and time again seek that moment of fear, the gulf of angst, excitement or icy fever that opens up in the first embrace with a stranger—the strangeness and the familiarity of a body that is animated in every fibre by a totally different spirit, houses different stories, different dreams. I try to imagine the twists and turns and intertwinings of the bodies of those rascals round his, the bony frame of that farmer's son in one of those photos, for example. The grip of those arms, the mouth that at first resists, then opens: who gives, who takes, who drinks and allows himself to be drunk—and with each caress, bite, sigh, cry what bewilderment must have tingled through his own limbs? The rapture, the hunger, the thirst that flowed through so many embraces in those years, on both sides of the lines. All those intertwinings, forbidden or not, lewd or not, for payment or not, that makes no difference. The invisible battlefield, I mean, where a reverse war took place—the mixing, the consecration: take, eat; this is my body.

I see him giggling; I'm sinning against my mother's ban on making the dead speak. He sighs: "You've always liked dressing up your concerns in other people's clothes, my little gazelle. For you the world is a blank sheet that you scribble full to your heart's content. But when the wind of history gets up a person can set their sail in the hope of being spared or perhaps taking advantage of chance. He can try walking into the storm or look for a hiding place. Who will eventually be left standing and who will be crushed under the wheels of the Moloch, no one knows, not even our dear Lord. We are mice running in the treadmill of fate and we can either take the pace or not. No sonnet ever changed the course of history. The world is the world."

They were childish, the excursions we undertook after the war, he and I, and my husband, and anyone who wanted to accompany us, during the annual return to my uncle's house, the final destination of our ostensibly carefree trip. We took our time, chose a meandering route and picnicked on the way. When we sat on the blanket and looked out over the hills, with the hamper in the grass, the cutlery, the fine plates, the ice bucket and the pâté, we regarded ourselves as freebooters, but we were aglow with a youth that could be little more than an anachronism. We looked like a medical team enjoying itself on its day off. We were wearing shrouds or doctors' coats, textiles on which the slightest impurity was immediately apparent. We seemed to want to show the spotless aura of our bathrooms, which in those days were less and less sumptuous annexes of the bedroom with its coital connotations, and more whitewashed private chapels intended for the rites of purification, the anointment with soap and lotion, to which we devoted ourselves with the doggedness of those who suffer from fear of infection, who scrub themselves until they bleed.

Anyone who had seen us driving around the border, and deep inland, would have taken us to be town-dwellers who regarded the world of the countryside, centripetal, cyclical, as little more than a rustic decor with which our self-importance contrasted favourably. No one could know that all that inflated light-heartedness was designed to hide the deathly quiet final destination of our journeys from ourselves.

Invariably the car would finally draw up at the familiar, dull-green painted gate, by the high wall in which the small, arch-shaped windows just below the tiles stared sceptically at the outside world, the way farmers half close their eyes when they have little confidence in the nonsense you're talking. The gate would open. Beyond it they would be waiting for us, my uncle and his family, another year older, more bent or greyer, or still more gangling, with still more offspring in their arms, more than enough of them anyway to give us the familiar

Sicilian welcome. Embraces and loud greetings. Pats on the shoulder and teasing.

They would conduct my brother and me and all those accompanying us to the table under the silver poplars, or to the big dining room. From the pantry the maid would not so much walk as stride to the table, with an air as if the soup tureen in her hands was a sacrificial lamb. Over the steaming plates they would question us about news from the north, how my father and mother were doing, and what had happened in the past year in the bends and side alleys of our extensive family network, which had its own maps, tougher than the official ones. They called us swallows because just like swallows we only fell out of the sky after the winter, town-dwellers who avoided the dark months in the countryside. The autumn and winter months that my mother and I had spent there obviously did not count as proof of the opposite. We remained northerners.

What we drank was not soup but relief. On the cutlery chest tarts with chokers of whipped cream and sugar glaze waited. When they were cut everyone knew that my brother and his companions, and often my husband too, would get up from table. With every course of dinner their impatience showed more openly on their faces, so that my uncle eventually had their portion of cake served in the smoking room, where they would withdraw after the meal.

"If the gentlemen wish to devote themselves to the really important things," he said, "they may feel free to help themselves to my cigars. There is also port. And stronger stuff." We wouldn't see them again before it was time for bed. They stayed in that room deep into the night, sometimes till first light. When I went to wish them good night, and cautiously opened the door of the room, just wide enough to let myself in, there was seldom more to be heard than the crackling of the fire that they had lit to drive away the chill of the night.

Sometimes one of them would be sitting in the armchair, elbows on knees and hands folded, leaning forward towards my brother, my husband or one of their friends in the chair opposite them. Between them hung the silence created when two people break off a confidential conversation so as not to involve an outsider. They looked at the toes of their shoes on the carpet and waited. Someone else stood at the window, glass of port in hand, staring out, even though there was little to be seen but one's own reflection against a background of nocturnal black, distorted by the curves in the window glass and the play of the flames in the hearth. Usually I gave my husband a quick kiss, wished my brother and the others good night and closed the door behind me again. My presence seemed to make them aware of an intimacy that had them more in its grip than linked them together.

I could easily walk back into the scene, as it has distilled itself from all the memories over the years. The fug of the cigars that hangs over their heads in dull-blue veils and when I open the door seems to recede in reluctant whirls before the cooler air I bring with me. The silence of those men in the room. The glass of port or cognac in one hand. The arm resting on the mantelpiece. The round table and the oil lamp on a cashmere tablecloth, an old shawl in which someone has made very symmetrical folds. The crockery in the convex glass-fronted cupboard. The cups and jugs with their female-looking handles that are almost like limp wrists, give to the silent togetherness of the men in the room something coquettish, not to say an almost sexual charge—but I am wary of dragging up such images from the quicksand of the mind and clothing them with language, with flesh. I see their figures: my husband, my brother, the friends who sometimes accompany them, sometimes not, congealed into figures of milky-white, hand-blown glass, not gaseous and not solid. I feel like a treasure-hunter who for the first time in millennia looks into a tomb and encounters the alabaster smile of a concubine. And when I ask my husband what they actually talk about, he replies: "Nothing really. Someone sometimes mentions a name and the others nod. Mostly we say nothing."

My brother often said that in his dreams, too, scarcely anything was said. I think, he said, that the mind is lost for words—we always dream what we can package in words. What is word-less wakes us with fear. The body plucks us in time back to the surface of consciousness and then we say we had a nightmare.

I never dream about the dead either, he said. Or about the horror. I dream silence. The silence of the trench. The scraping of my men's equipment against the walls left and right as they follow me, God knows where, through complete darkness. Only the sound of their equipment against the walls, their breath, their footsteps gives texture to the darkness—then there is the bright glare of a flare exposing an endless trench, a winding passage with walls of sandbags and planks—and then the solid night again that swallows us up. It always lasts hours and hours, that journey in my dreams. Finally day breaks and I smell the forest floor, the scent of pine needles. The branches dampen the morning light and the silence acquires a pleasant feel, a sigh that hangs above us whenever the wind plays in the needles.

The trench forks. The sandbags give way to walls of woven branches, tightly woven structures that reach higher and higher. More and more frequently we pass openings in the wall. To right and left there extend still more passages. Meanwhile the walls have become so high that it is as if we are roaming through a subterranean Knossos, a sunken Venice with canals full of mud—but however the dreams begin and however varied their course, sooner or later they all reach the same destination. The trench winds sharply up a hillside. Where the wall becomes lower again a valley extends down below, in which, largely obscured from view by treetops and trunks, a small town stretches out. I see chimneys from which plumes of smoke escape. The sounds of church bells and horses' hooves resound crystal-clear in the freezing cold of a limpid winter morning that seems to me strangely familiar. I know that the destination is approaching in my dream, because I have the dream so often.

I know that over the mesh of branches and twigs in the wall of the trench a second mesh will be laid, of frozen stalactites which close more and more tightly together into walls of ice. The paths between the walls wind farther uphill and turn into ice steps. I can hear the laborious trudging of the men following me. The echo of their soles on the treads draws a long ribbon of sound behind me—and then I am always overcome by sadness, an unnameable feeling of regret, an unnameable grief, an unnameable resignation evoked by the sounds of the town down in the valley, by the smell of burning wood and coal winding up from the chimneys, and the peacefulness that the sounds and smells bring with them—that wave of regret and longing that goes through my trunk, where on earth does it come from, my little gazelle?

The steps become wider, the ice now looks almost polished, like marble. I feel the embarrassment of my men, as it were pushing me in the back, the shame, and we are carrying the stench of the mud with us. The steps lead to a wide, covered terrace which on one side looks out over the landscape and on the other merges with the ridge. Between white columns is a balustrade, behind which elegantly dressed women on deckchairs relax, smoke and drink and talk and laugh. They are making eyes at gentlemen who are standing chatting by the balustrade in groups of four or five and stretch their necks to emphasize their attractiveness. Between them waiters with trays come and go. Maids clear empty glasses or distribute newspapers. There is music, the hum of a string quartet, laughter—I see the hand of a man resting on one of those bare shoulders, his figure bending to plant a kiss on a neck. No one sees us. No one notices us. No one pays any attention to us.

Waves of rumbling rise from the valley, muted and distant—the echo provokes excitement among the company, as among people following some contest or other. Gentlemen look up simultaneously, interrupt their conversations and peer into the distance while casually putting a glass to their lips. Ladies sit up languidly in their chairs, lean bare-armed on the balustrade and also look into the distance—but what they see is only mildly interesting. A languor hangs over the terrace, a blanket of lethargy. At the same time I feel the jealousy of my men behind me, and rage wells up in me. Who is drinking our blood? Who is eating our flesh? Who throws us over the fence like chicken bones gnawed clean? And then there is that sadness again, that gnawing, amber-coloured regret—why do the years bring so much regret, my little gazelle? What loans must we repay, whose losses must we redeem? Who has lived above his station and mortgaged our existence? Usually I wake up in tears.

He stops talking and brings the cigar to his mouth, shrugs his shoulders sheepishly and smiles faintly. All his life he remained an adolescent, a lad who as years went by could stare out at me more and more perplexed from that old body, in which he seemed locked like a passenger on a train which to his horror goes past the expected destination. His cigars, his walking stick, his unwrinkled clothes—the icing on his refined, fickle despair. He brings the cigar to his mouth and, as he takes a last puff, on his top lip his fine blond moustache squeezes round the smoked-up stub—the mouth of my mother, her catamite's mouth grinning at me on the train to De Panne, where we go to visit him in hospital. Between her eyebrows the permanent crease of contempt at my escapade of the summer before has softened a little. When I look up I see her avert her gaze, and on her lips the grin with which she must have been peering at me while I was reading fades. She looks outside, rocking along with the jolting of the wheels on the tracks. Resignation is what I see as her eyes wander over the farmland, the villages with their worm-eaten roofs and walls and cemeteries in which the crosses proliferate like weeds. There is no longer a cemetery to be found that is not bursting at the seams.

It is already getting on for the end of the afternoon. There were so many hold-ups that day. The eternal whining of military transports to which we had to give precedence. The umpteenth check of the transport permits, certificates, permissions which she extracts from her big bag of rough material, each time with a hint of fear that she will be told: the papers are not in order, this or that stamp is missing, this or that official should have put his signature. I see us sitting in the light, growing stale, of that September day, waiting for the carriage to start moving again, for the invisible elastic walls with which the war is dividing the country into compartments to recede so that we can proceed. I see us sitting there in our sturdy clothes of stiff textiles, cut from the materials that we quickly purchased when it had become clear, three years earlier, that we wouldn't be able to return home immediately, and I feel the same regret, the same pity.

She looks at me and I recognize the regret in her smile, which is now mine. Then she takes a deep breath, blows the regret away and creates hope. After almost three years she will see her son again.

FOR MONTHS SHE SAID NOTHING about my adventure. When she was angry she seemed to find words inadequate as vehicles for her anger—too rough, too blunt, or on the contrary far too articulate. She folded open inwards as it were, and from her folds that deathly silent language welled up, which annexed everything around her in its magnetism. Everything radiated contempt and reproach.

At home she counted on my father to translate her voltages into human words, usually at breakfast. He sat wedged between us at table and spoke to me, alternately emollient and admonishing, sometimes bending over to my side, sometimes back to hers: a needle that leapt pitifully to and fro in response to our capricious alternating currents. My brother would make his escape as soon as possible, taking his plate upstairs with him, and as he climbed the stairs we could hear him sighing: "*Oh là là… Oh là là-là là!*"

As long as her eyebrows did not announce new icy waves, my father tried to speak to me in a conciliatory way, and in the opposite case, when her silence crackled with cold, he would always keep half an eye on her during his sermon to see whether her eyes were wandering to the paper next to her plate. Her increasing lack of interest usually heralded the thaw.

Without him she had lost her domestic toolbox. My uncle had proved that he could not serve as a replacement and I myself had also betrayed her. She no longer walked quite upright now things no longer moved in accordance with her thermal energy. To keep on her feet, and to punish herself, she had the maid tighten her corset until it became an eye-level fortress, a breathing suit of armour.

I see her mending clothes, in the winter after my escapade, when she kept me close to her day after day. She allowed me at most an hour, in the library or when I had to look after the chickens, outside her force field. It was bitterly cold; the days crept by beneath a tin sky. All that could be heard was the rumbling of the weapons, distant or close by, depending on the direction of the wind, and the enervating ripping sound when she, by the light of the candle we had to share, tore open the seams of old shirts or trousers. She grasped the material in both fists, pressed her lips together and pulled the seam open, having first loosened the stitching, in a single tug. She would repair or cut up the pieces. Everything can serve a turn sooner or later. I don't know if she herself felt the threat in those words.

Under the table top in the kitchen, next to the oven, in the chest in her room, the drawers bulged with everything that in her view might one day come in handy: bottle-stoppers, strips of greaseproof paper or barbed wire—her amulets. Without my father, equally anxious, she stored up all her resentments in her bastion of whalebone, which gave her the form of a still, in which her frustrations were so concentrated and purified that the words she could direct at me unexpectedly seemed more a discharge than a question or an order.

She straightens her shoulders. Here, in this paper afterlife, she grasps both halves of the back of an old coat in her hands, but the material does not give.

I read the annoyance in her face, which is about more than

the stiffness of the material. The imminence of her saying something hangs in the air, the silence announces it.

"The scissors, Hélène," she snaps at me.

Her glory, which was the glory of that summer, the summer of 1914, which in my memory is compressed into the sun-drenched afternoon of the day after our arrival. In the summer house of silver poplars the maids are laying the long table. The tinkling of the cutlery on the trays seems to come from the light itself. She in her summer dress: that intense, glaring white shot through with a hint of blue in the long grass of June, and above the deckchair in which my brother is sitting reading in the shade—of course he immediately went to sleep—the energy, the almost suicidal passion of the sunlight that plunges into the treetops and explodes among the leaves: a fountain of slivers, light pearls, drops, sparks. I feel it swelling when, upstairs in my uncle's library, I look up from the book that I have laid on the reading table and am staring through the open window.

I hear the wind stirring the curtains, the farmworkers washing their hands outside by the pump for the approaching meal, the snorting when they throw a splash of water in their faces, and the giggling of the kitchen girls below, interrupted by the deep growl of the maid, Madeleine, who keeps a strict order among her chicks, and with her deeply sunken eye sockets and heavily arched eyebrows reminds me of an ancestral statue from Easter Island. And there is that light, the white horses of light when the wind tosses about in the treetops outside the window; the surf, the flood, I feel it pulling through my midriff, picking me up and putting me down again as it ebbs and splashes against wall behind me. And now too, here, I hear my mother's voice, laughing and good-humoured: "Stop all those *chinoiseries*, child, and come to table finally."

What does it matter, now I close the book and run downstairs, startling the mice in the courtyard and chasing the lizards like a blush over the yellow-ochre side wall—what does it matter that of all the people who have gathered round the table I am the only one still alive? The farmhands have laid their caps in their laps and look sheepishly at their still-empty plates while my uncle, according to his annual custom in honour of my mother, makes an overblown speech of welcome to my brother and me. The children impatiently knead chunks of bread into balls. The aunts, dressed up with ribbons and earrings like temple bells, look like grotesque Bodhisattvas, to the right and left of uncle in the middle of the long table. The kitchen maids are waiting with the soup tureen and step increasingly often from one foot to the other, as if needing urgently to pee. The swarming of the leaves, my mother's dazzling figure, the glasses that are raised and the laughter and chatter in the warm noon of the penultimate day of June 1914. In the papers the commotion about the tragic incident has subsided to a narrow column in which the word "war" is used fairly dutifully—"the umpteenth storm in a teacup" is my brother's opinion.

Three summers later, when we visit him, one of the three sisters can remember that she was on duty when they brought him in. "We have to cut most of them out of their uniforms. He was lucky. His wounds are deep but nowhere did the grenade hit an organ and the stomach wall is intact. We saw that when we cut his clothes loose and washed away the black blood and mud.

They were able to bring him here quickly. Three others were dead on arrival. We put them over there in the corner under a blanket while we cleaned the wounded for the operation. One of the others lay here on the floor on the stretcher. He'd lost a forearm and the explosion had torn his feet from his ankles. They were hanging from his lower legs just by the tendons and when he went into a convulsion on the stretcher, his feet dragged across the floorboards as if they were attached to his shins by suspenders—but actually I shouldn't say anything about that and I think you'd better keep quiet about it to your mother. She looks upset enough already."

I think of the sea, the jade-green sea, the surf that was like molten tin when the waves broke and with foam fingers churned up the sand the day my mother and I went to visit him: it was the first time that she set foot on Belgian soil again. The sea and the pale upper bodies of the bathing men, and their uniforms that lay in heaps on the dry part of the beach, below the promenade—dotted lines of khaki and boots in the ochre sand.

The salt air, the rising of the voices when a wave lifted the bathers up: their heads, trunks and arms rose with the water level and sank again when the waves slid underneath them, rose, arched their backs, then toppled and tumbled into the sand.

Farther out to sea, hazy because of the mist above the water: the contours of ships, just close enough to be able to see the sailors walking to and fro on deck and salvoes like light flashes spewing from the barrels of the cannon.

The sound came later, a wave of thunder that found its own surf in the cheers of the soldiers on the promenade. They threw their caps in the air or waved with both arms. It wasn't clear whether they were replying to the salvoes or shouting at the men below, who braced themselves for the waves constantly rolling in, went under and came up again roaring with laughter.

After each cannonade the ships changed position, back, farther out to sea, far from the coastline where the men, at the call of their leader, all left the water together, ran up the beach shivering and snorting, scores of stark-naked men on their way to the clothes that were theirs, their dot in the sand below the promenade.

The soldiers around us started laughing and whistling. Some clapped their hands. On the horizon the ships' cannon were spewing new pinpricks of light, followed by thick curtains of smoke.

"*C'est un spectacle triste, un homme sans ses vêtements, je trouve…*" I hear my mother whisper, as if unaware that she is thinking aloud. "*Ça me semble si* slovenly. *Surtout quand il n'est pas, comme on dit, excité…*" She looks at me, as if seeking confirmation, and I glance up somewhat taken aback, as are a couple of soldiers peering at us over their shoulders and laughing as they give each other a dig with their elbows.

And we must look odd in our coats that are far too heavy for the season. It is the beginning of September 1917, a Wednesday, and a warm late-summer afternoon, but we seem to be dressed for a harsh winter, in those coats of tough, indestructible material which the aunts made for us when it became clear that we would not be able to return home soon. When it occurs to me that the big bag that my mother has placed at her feet also contains a pair of boots as large as frigates, I can't control myself either and have to giggle.

She turns round, grabs the bag by its large handles and asks what there is to laugh about.

"Nothing, Maman. I think we have to go this way…"

"Fancy a drink, Miss?" a voice calls after us, but she pretends she has not heard anything and gives a tug on the bag like a coachman tightening the reins of his horses.

We walked on along the promenade, among the soldiers spread out over the beach to enjoy the evening sun. No one seemed to hear the constant rat-tat-tat of the light artillery in the background, on the plain behind the line of dunes, and the rumbling farther away, the echoes of the cannon, both out at sea and deeper inland. The growl of an aircraft made a few heads look up, but the plane was too far away to be seen, and when a little later crackling erupted and here and there white smoke clouds burst open in the azure, someone shouted: "That'll teach 'em, bloody Boches…" followed by laughter; but apart from that everyone continued as normal, and the sentries in the dunes remained motionless in the silver-green marram grass. She wasn't interested; she wanted to go to the hospital. Again she pulled roughly at the bag.

I can still feel the violence of that gesture pulling through my forearm into my shoulders. All states of mind that were considered too violent or too coarse for a lady—rage, passion, lust for revenge—she accommodated in a deaf-and-dumb language of her own making, a vocabulary of twists and turns and looks. Only later did I begin to grasp the hidden syntax of her gestures and could I read the restlessness in them, the despair, the disappointment I must have evoked in her, after I had, however inevitably, bitten through the last umbilical cord still joining us. I myself only tasted the feeling of desolation that wells up when a descendant goes her own way with my own daughter. I felt humiliated by the ruthless pragmatism of life, which in our youth lionizes us, but one fine day drops us like a toy that has lost its shine. Naturally I reproached my child with all kinds of things, and I regret it now. September is still the time of year when that regret is at its ripest. It has assumed the colours that the early autumn sun imposes on the world at that season, and it hangs like a heavy travel bag between me and the dead. Its elusive weight seals our union.

I could not live without the dead, believe me, Rachida, my girl. I would feel empty if I could not fill their goblets with my funereal gifts: words that I put in their mouths, which I pour as libations over their altars.

How strange that she, who did not believe in a higher realm and practised a mainly dutiful piety, probably so as not to be out of step, ascribed a kind of hereafter to the dead—because if they really are nowhere any more then we no longer need to show any respect to their absence. If we do, God is still in us, a ponderous emptiness that turns round and round in our caverns. He counts the days and waits in boredom for the hand-ful of hymns with which we might evoke Him. It is purely a matter of vocabulary, or as my mother invariably said to me when we squabbled: "For goodness' sake stop turning words on their heads, Hélène. Soon you'll be taking the world off its hinges and the poles will change places…"

I could make her descend from eternity, let her trickle down onto this sheet of paper in order to reprimand me posthumously for my digressions, but I won't. I recall her as we lay together in that bed, in that attic room in the hotel on the promenade in De Panne that served as a hospital. When the shooting stopped the sun had already set and we could no longer go out in the street to find lodgings, so we had been assigned a room in the roof, a room for nurses on night shift, who would only be coming to bed towards morning.

"It's not the Ritz, I know," Miss Schliess had said, the sister who had to take us upstairs, when she saw my mother looking around her in the narrow room with thin wooden planks for walls, and the two small iron beds under the dormer window, with a few knick-knacks on the window sill, a small vase, a few shells, an empty glass. It could have been a servant's room, Emilie's magpie's nest under the rafters at home.

My mother put her bag on one of the beds and whispered: "Thank you, *ma sœur*. My daughter and I are very grateful to you." She had opened the bag, taken out a small handkerchief and dipped it in the basin which stood on a narrow washstand in a corner of the room under a mirror, and sat down on the chair between the two beds with the wet cloth in her hands.

"Perhaps Madam would like a nice cuppa…"

"Would you like some tea, Maman?"

She shook her head, and muttered: "Please go" and pushed her face into the wet handkerchief.

She looked pale, that evening, and was still trembling from the after-effects of the shock. We had scarcely been able to have a brief glimpse of my brother, in one of the long huts that had been built around the old boarding house, before we had to leave him again.

He was asleep when the orderly took us to him. In the bed next to his a man with lots of cream on his hair, which was combed in a strict centre parting, had been observing us.

"*Il a eu de la chance, celui-ci,*" he had said. "*Il dort beaucoup, pauvre type…* It does no harm of course. *Un bon sommeil,* no one has ever been the worse for that."

My mother had nodded and listened intently to my brother's breathing: deep, peaceful, regular. He was more or less unrecognizable because of the thick bandage round his head, which left only a tuft of hair on the crown free. A second covered the whole right side of his face apart from his eye and a third surrounded his neck and right shoulder. Under his pyjama top his trunk was also hidden by gauze and bandage.

She had opened her bag, retrieved a tin of biscuits from it, a couple of apples and a small bottle of wine, and put everything on the bedside table. We hadn't paid attention to the fact that meanwhile the noise of the guns had grown louder and louder. Nurses were walking to and fro between the beds and the rustle of their long blue dresses and white caps and the energetic cadence of their steps on the floorboards made a nervous impression.

Outside there had been whistling, then a bang—the beams and the wooden floors trembled. The sisters did not seem so much nervous because of the shooting as concerned about the patients; and when, quite close to judge by the intensity, there was a second bang, loud, dry, more a vicious hiss than an explosion, one of the patients, a few beds farther on, had started whining and another, on the other side of the long ward, had jumped up from the sheets, meanwhile tugging at the buttons of his pyjama top as if in a trance. A couple of orderlies tried to calm him down and to button up his pyjamas again, while the nurses attempted to calm the other man in bed—he was all arms and legs and shrank into a ball when a new thud sounded.

A few windows, left ajar to let in the cool evening air, flew open, the light bulbs rocked to and fro on their leads above the beds. Somewhere a few stools fell over, a metal basin spun across the floorboards and came to a clattering halt. More and more patients crawled upright in their beds.

My brother went on sleeping. Meanwhile the air was filled with crackling, salvoes rattling through the evening sky like Morse code messages, deeper thuds, a long-drawn-out whistle followed by a new bang, farther away this time. Only when a new impact, close this time, seemed to lift up the whole hut for a moment did he wake up, but then an orderly pulled us away with him. We had to go to the main building, he said.

He had taken us through a labyrinth of corridors to the central hall, downstairs, in the old hotel, where we were supposed to wait till the shooting stopped. Around us male and female nurses walked to and fro, doctors in flapping white coats ran up and down staircases. My mother sat silently beside me, the bag at her feet, her hat on her lap, eyes closed. The artillery continued to fire, the day was fading visibly, and by the time the violence finally seemed to be abating it was already quite dark, too late to find accommodation elsewhere. One of the senior sisters finally beckoned to Miss Schliess and said, not without an undertone of sarcasm: "We have guests this evening. Take them upstairs."

As we followed her up the stairs, I caught a fleeting glimpse of the old guest rooms, since all the doors had been removed. Beds, most empty, were lit up by the distant explosions. It had already struck us when we arrived. Most wards were deserted. Behind open doors and windows broom handles danced in the hands of orderlies. Bedding, languid as dollops of cream, spilt over the edge of big wicker skips. Elsewhere tough women cleaners were beating mattresses.

Miss Schliess said that the British high command was not fond of this hospital, independent as it was, which admitted both civilians and soldiers, friend and foe.

"Thanks to that little queen of yours," she said, "and her husband's penchant for neutrality."

She took us all the way upstairs, under the rafters of the building, the upper storeys of which looked out over the scores of wards that had been put up around it, even close to the big window, down on the promenade, of the restaurant where we had eaten so often in previous summers, with a view of the sand and the waves.

In one of the other attics the figure of a nurse stood in the twilight, peering outside, where the sky was criss-crossed by the beams of searchlights. There were still the sounds of shooting and thundering, and the growl of aircraft, but farther away. The nurse watched and meanwhile buttoned up her apron by sense of touch. Perhaps she would be on night shift soon, like Miss Schliess, who took me to the fifth floor, where an area served as a rest room.

In the windows the day, apart from a faint glow far out to sea, was completely extinguished. Somewhere above the distant waves stipples of light sparkled and immediately disappeared. Above the land the searchlights still slid to and fro between the horizon and the clouds.

Miss Schliess lit a small candle and brought us tea. The faint candlelight made the white cuffs which she had fished from somewhere in her apron stand out against the calm blue of her dress. She had noticed the bewilderment when I saw her lacing those stiff linen bands around her wrists, just before we entered the room. "Dress code," she had replied. "It's a real convent here, mademoiselle… Dress like a nun, behave like a nun."

She poured tea. The pale pot hung like a ghostly manifestation in her hand. "So you're visiting your brother then?" she asked as she sat down opposite me at the narrow table.

"My brother. And someone else. A friend… Though Mum's not to know…" I drank a mouthful. The tea was lukewarm. "It's a secret…"

"Ah, a sweetheart, a soldier sweetheart…" Miss Schliess held her tea mug near her mouth, hiding her lips, but I could hear from her voice that she was moved.

"Can't blame you, dear. Not too badly injured, I hope?"

I shrugged my shoulders. "Light injuries according to his letter." In reality it was more a postcard scribbled all over, for safety's sake put in an envelope and addressed to my uncle. "Haven't seen him yet. Went to see my brother first."

"Nothing serious, probably… There are others. Haven't been so lucky myself, mademoiselle. Lost me darlin' Henry two years ago…" She tried to sound breezy, but I could hear that she was finding it difficult.

She put her tea mug on the table, and clasped it with both hands. "Sometimes I dream that it's a great big body that we have to put back together. One big mess of bowels and limbs. One long table full of arms, legs, eyeballs, lungs…" She hesitated. "Testicles…"

She brought the mug to her lips again. Behind her back, out to sea, a fierce light flared up momentarily, which briefly silhouetted the outline of her wimple, her ear, her neck. A little later a faint thunder reached the beach. "It's ages since I've seen a chap with everything in its right place, mademoiselle… And these hands…" She put the mug back on the table and spread her left and right on the table top. "The places they've been… Ever had to stack someone's liver back in place, Miss?" She looked at her own fingers and shook her head. "Smelt the smell of an open belly? Filled a hole as big as a football in someone's thigh with gauze, kept your sick down despite the stench of wound fever?"

She looked at me, she had pressed her lips together. I saw that her eyes were moist. "Saw a bunch of our boys bathing, this afternoon." She nodded in the direction of the beach. "Couldn't take my eyes off them. Must have stared at them with me mouth wide open, mademoiselle. The others laughed their heads off… Seen a saint, Elsie, dear? Our Lord Jesus walking the waves?" She tried to smile and brought the mug to her lips again. "Wish I had…"

Beneath her hands, which were not so much holding as supporting the tea mug, there was the glow of the white cuffs. They seemed to surround her wrists like haloes, to support her hands like pedestals, but also to separate them from her body, as if they were infected by the knowledge they had acquired, the arms, legs, groins that she had washed, the wounds and cavities she had entered to remove bandages dripping with blood, to pour scorching carbolic acid onto flesh attacked by germs, pushing eyeballs back in their sockets, rearranging intestines under the midriff.

I drank another mouthful of tea. It tasted bitter, more like an infusion of tobacco than of tea. "I'm sorry, Miss. About your loss, I mean." I was aware of how inadequate my words sounded.

"Never mind, love. Anyway..." She got up, produced a small watch from her breast pocket and glanced at it. "Duty calls. And you go back to your mother, mademoiselle."

S HE LAY ON THE BED, the wet cloth on her face gave her the look of a dead person under a shroud. Her arms lay idle by her body, hands on the belly, between the two sides of her coat, which she had unbuttoned but not taken off.

"Is that you Helena?" when I sat on the other bed, which with its creaking augured a sleepless night. "Is that you, Helena?" It must have been the first time in three years that she directed words at me that did not end in an exclamation mark.

"Yes, Maman, it's me."

She said nothing else. Between us, on the floor, stood the dark material of her bag.

I lay down, the bed protested weakly. The mattress seemed to be trying to shake me off it and, through the rags with which it was filled, to push ribs or vertebrae into my back. I looked at my mother, at the wet cloth on her face and the square silhouette of light with which the dormer window framed her head and shoulders whenever the sky outside lit up because of a flare or a searchlight, and I thought of home, of my father.

What was he doing at this moment, unaware that we were in the same country again, separated by a long scar of trenches and barbed wire, of dead people and hospitals and bare earth? I knew that my mother carried with her somewhere in her bag the few letters that had managed to get through to us. The breeziness with which he had written that it would all be over by Christmas, and that, if people wanted to repeat the adventure

299

of 1870, we couldn't be in a better place than with his in-laws. In our lost backwater of the Republic no one would trouble us, he believed. Sometime later my uncle had also handed over the other letter, which my father had sent at the same time: "Should it come to it again, my wife and children could not be better off anywhere than with you, my dear Theo. According to the rumours they will pass through our country this time. I'm not deaf, or blind. I saw the sort of stuff that was being transported by rail when I was in Germany recently."

I had read those words so often that I knew them by heart. I reread them to be able to hear his voice, his calm concern for our welfare. "Be prepared for Edgard to volunteer," he also said in that letter to my uncle. "He won't wait. I know my brood. I don't expect you to put up more resistance than necessary, and my son will have enough to handle with his mother. What would we do, assuming we were still young, dear brother-in-law? Hide away and afterwards brave the scorn, sit out the shame until everyone has had his say, and then be branded a coward for the rest of one's life? Or fight and hope that we survive the whole affair without too much damage? Let Marianne read this letter, should it be necessary. Tell her that I hope the best for her, and hope that our daughter will give her support. If the worst comes to the worst, they cannot do better than wait until this incon- venience has passed over us, with you and Josine and Yolande."

She had slammed doors in the days before my brother left, probably in the middle of the night or at the crack of dawn. She had resisted with all the means at her disposal. When he didn't appear at breakfast that day, for a moment she was no longer my mother, but a gaping breach in the wall of her own severity. My uncle had bashfully pushed that letter towards her, and she had withdrawn to her room for three days. Not until the fourth morning had she reappeared downstairs, pulled tight and laced up from head to toe. "*Bon!*" she had said before sitting down. "We shall take that inconvenience as it comes."

After that we always spoke about "that inconvenience". "It's taking its time, that inconvenience," she would invariably comment when going through the papers, whose reports she tried to decipher like oracles. "We're going forward, we're going backward, we're standing still, but we're still winning, for three years!" But even in the newspaper articles there was growing weariness perceptible between the lines, the tiredness of an increasingly lethargic war, which more and more frequently struck me as little more than a thoroughly spoilt child. It had set out its army of toy soldiers neatly on the floor and then abandoned them, frozen them in their positions, and its only pleasure seemed to be to crush them underfoot in seething swipes.

"Now they're going to turn the world inside out, that's how desperate they are," she had sneered a few months before, when in the early morning of an early summer day the earth suddenly shook, the hens clucked indignantly in their runs, the pigs kicked their troughs in annoyance and the dogs stared in dismay at the ground beneath their feet while the quake continued under them. "That will do a lot of good!" she had exclaimed sarcastically, sticking a needle into a sock, since there would not be much more question of sleeping in the house.

My uncle's outings also became more lethargic, as he took his ill tidings round the village and hamlets more and more slowly, a nemesis yawning with boredom. The funeral services for the fallen were lethargic, with or without a coffin in the church, the sermons of the Abbé were more and more lethargic, the lethargic process of mourning and the sluggish march of the columns, which I saw shuffling past in the telescope in the attic, under the bare trees in the rains of November, or the troops who sometimes made a temporary camp in the barn, their lethargic bartering for eggs, potatoes, ham or bacon—everything creaked with tiredness, in everything there was a hidden painful joint, everything suffered from chilly bones.

Even in that attic room, that evening in September, under the eaves of the old hotel, the artillery sounded lethargic. The salvoes resounded in bored routine, the searchlights slid grumpily through the sky, the flares were like languorous birds with a long tail, too heavy for an elegant flight—and even the bang, the huge bang which, without the roar first swelling, shook the rafters above our heads and blew the glass from the dormer window over us in a rain of slivers, even it had something lame, something gutless about it.

I saw my mother sit up, pull the cloth from her face in alarm, and shake a few slivers from her lap. She was about to say something when a second impact, close by, ear-shattering, made the woodwork of the windows whine and slammed the frames against the side wall.

A drop of blood was running from the corner of her mouth over her chin. She grabbed for the bag, meanwhile pressed the cloth against her lips, and had only just bent down when another bang smashed window glass elsewhere and blew the washbasin in the corner of our room off its base. We dived for cover, each behind the foot of our bed. I saw that she was pressing her cheeks hard against the rails of the bed and was stretching in order to pull the bag, which was still standing between the beds, towards her over the floorboards. Outside planes were growling everywhere, invisible in the sky, among the rat-tat-tat of the anti-aircraft guns. The searchlights had come to life, and were keenly sweeping the sky. Shrapnel clattered over the roof tiles above our heads into the gutters. Below us, in the stairwell, a woman's voice called: "Everyone downstairs! Everyone downstairs!"

"We have to go, Maman. We have to go at once…"

She nodded, pulled the bag towards her across the floor and crawled out ahead of me into the narrow central corridor—the floorboards were strewn with slivers of glass and fragments of knick-knacks that had been hurled from the window sills and wall racks, and everywhere we were surrounded by the noise of aircraft; their bluebottle-like buzzing and the crackling salvoes sounded louder and closer now that not a single pane of glass remained whole.

We crawled to our feet, shuffling on along the central corridor bent double. Above our heads, seemingly grazing the roof beam, a projectile with an ethereal whistle drew a trail of light through the night. A few seconds later a fireball formed, and the front of a burning house stood out like a mask in the dark.

"We must hurry, Maman, It's far too dangerous here." I pulled her with me into the stairwell. Below us, a few floors down, others must be making the descent. I heard voices and the bump of soles on the treads. We had to find our way in the dark. I clasped her hand in mine, she did not let go of the bag with the other, and we must have been about halfway down when with a huge thud the whole building seemed to stretch from roof beam to cellar, groaning in all its screws, bolts, seams and ligaments, and then subsided.

My mother had let out a cry and a cascade of jars, flacons and preserves had tumbled out of her bag over the steps. She wanted to bend down and pick everything up, but I pulled her with me. "We haven't got time. We must get downstairs. We'll pick it up later."

The downstairs corridor was swarming with people: soldiers, civilians, kitchen staff, cleaners and the teeming blue-and-white shapes of the nurses bringing patients from all directions in their bare feet, in pale pyjamas to chairs or sofas. Most, I saw, only had wounds to the arms or upper body, and perhaps precisely because of that were being treated in the old boarding house—if necessary they could take flight downstairs under their own steam. We tried to make our way through the throng, to find a place where we could sit down or at least stand and lean against the wall. Outside the storm seemed to be abating, there were still explosions and rattling, but less intense and farther away, farther inland.

"Edgard," muttered my mother. "Where's Edgard?"

Doors flew open. Wounded patients streamed in. A woman with a screeching child in her arms wrapped in a soiled sling. A woman staunching the flow of blood from a wound on the side of her head with her scarf. A small boy, deathly quiet, with eyes wide open on a stretcher, apparently insensible to the pain which one of his knees, little more than a bloody mass, must have been causing him. An old woman worked her way into the corridor, hair dishevelled, the sleeves of her coat torn to shreds. "Never thought my corset would save me," I heard her say to a man, probably her husband, who with one hand was holding in place a tea towel wrapped round his other hand.

*

My mother seemed not to see any of this. She kept craning her neck, regularly held her handkerchief under her nose, surveying all the bustle. It was Edgard she was looking for. She was becoming more restless by the minute.

A second stretcher was brought in. Between the two stretcher-bearers the white and blue of three nurses, busily trying to keep the wounded man under control. A hand grabbed at their skirts. An arm grasped at thin air between their figures. A foot, the thick sole of a lace-up boot, slid doggedly back and forth over the wood of the stretcher. There was a chest rattle, an exclamation smothered in gurgling. The foot kicked the stretcher, the arms grabbed.

Someone shouted: "For the love of Christ, Elsie, keep 'em down!" A second scream. One of the nurses leapt back with unexpected coquettishness, but could not prevent a splash of blood landing on her apron. She looked up for a moment and I recognized the eyes of Miss Schliess. She saw me, and she saw my mother. As she bent back over the wounded man, she said quickly: "Your brother is safe. They've got their own shelter outside. Tell her. It'll put her mind at rest."

The stretcher-bearer brought the stretcher farther into the corridor. On one of the staircases meanwhile an elderly man appeared, in slippers and pyjamas, with a kepi on his head. His face was stormy. From under his thick moustache a rain of orders descended on everyone's heads in barking French. Order returned. Logic. Gravity. Wounded over there. Others that way. Sheep were separated from goats, pyjamas from overcoats. The wounded were taken farther into the corridor, where the operating theatres were. The turmoil subsided.

I took my mother to an empty spot on a sofa against one of the inside walls. "Just sit down here, Maman." Miss Schliess's announcement had calmed her down somewhat. Outside the storm seemed to be nearing its end. The thuds sounded duller and duller. Now and then a distant bang made the lamps tremble and our abdominal membranes quiver.

My mother sat down, pressing the now empty bag on her lap against her body. A man next to her, a chap in a trilby hat who, resting his hands on his knees, feet apart, was looking around, turned to her and said: "Some weather tonight, isn't it?" The look she gave him immediately froze his smile.

I left her alone, strolled down the corridor, avoiding groups of people. The faces that looked at me looked empty, broken, and weren't anything like the restlessness behind the eyes of the refugees who in the first months of the war had been given shelter for the night in barns and stalls. The first came from my fatherland, the villages and towns of Hainaut, Namur, Luxembourg and, besides carts and small carriages with hastily collected children and household effects, brought stories about looting and murder which my uncle had kept as far as possible from my mother, until the papers had taken them up with mouth-watering eagerness. The drama of Dinant. The fire of Leuven. It seemed so far away. We heard only the creaking of the cartwheels in the sand of the road, the dragging soles, the requests for milk, a raw egg for a child or a pregnant woman, and permission to light fires, to heat up their scanty food. "Only in the yard," my uncle had decreed. "Not in the stables or barns. There are enough houses on fire already."

*

I looked at the faces around me. A few women, huddled next to each other at the foot of one of the walls, made an all too colourful impression. Under their overcoats shone pearls or gold jewellery, their caps only half hid their coquettishly coiffured hair. I don't know if what made them look away was shame, and if it was shame, I hope it wasn't me that provoked it in them.

I thought of the garishness of all too brightly coloured boas, depilated calves, blood-red lips, and the high-pitched cooing chorus of tarts, the bar floozies, the flora of the night and the boudoirs, which rose stronger and louder from all the people cheering on the soldiers, in those first days of August, when stickers had suddenly announced general mobilization everywhere and my mother had cried out in dismay, "War! War!", as if history was in service with us and had been caught in the wine cellar with the bottle at his lips.

She had sent Edgard and me off in the coach, to see if it was still possible to catch a train in the nearest town with a main station. In the square in front of the station building men were hastily donning their uniforms, the blue waistcoat, the shocking-red trousers, and meanwhile kissing crying children, embracing sobbing wives, sweethearts, mothers, sisters. The tarts cooed, threw flowers and I think even underwear at the cannon fodder that marched in closed ranks from the barracks into the square in the unforgivably sweet sun of that August.

I stood upright in the coach. I asked why they were cheering so, the whores. My brother looked up at me, a frown of bemused surprise on his forehead, and nodded in the direction of the departing soldiers. "If that lot don't do their work, my little gazelle, they may soon be opening their legs for the Prussians. But whether they'll get paid for it remains to be seen."

He had watched for a while longer. There were no more trains; war was now rolling over the tracks. "All civilian traffic cancelled," cried a stationmaster through a mass of mobilized men.

"We might as well go back," he had decided. He had clicked his tongue and slapped the reins along the horse's flanks. At home my mother had listened to us with perplexed astonishment. If she had been able she would have sacked history on the spot.

I walked on. At one end of the corridor, on the stairs that led to our attic room, a group of patients were sitting chatting. The sisters had left them there to keep the corridor as far as possible for civilians and the badly wounded. They reminded me of big chicks, in their white pyjamas, with bandages around their heads or hands. I thought: I must not go too close; doubtless my mother wasn't letting me out of her sight for a second. And I was about to turn round when one figure struck me and my heart was in my mouth.

I walked towards the stairs. A few of the others looked up, but he didn't see me, preoccupied as he was with an orange that lay on a napkin on his lap. His left hand was in a bandage and was resting in a sling knotted around his neck. With the elbow of his immobile arm he was trying to keep the fruit in place, while with the thumb of his other hand he was endeavouring to pick the skin open. He seemed to notice nothing of the noise outside, the people in the corridor, the languorous fear, the lethargy.

I came closer. The fruit shot out from under his elbow. I heard him swear under his breath. Under his pyjama bottoms his toes curled against the wood of the stair tread.

He pushed the orange back under one arm, and I was about to speak when the fruit completely escaped him and rolled over his knees down the stairs. It came to a halt against my foot, and I bent down to pick it up.

He saw my hand, raised his eyes at the same time as me and looked me straight in the eyes.

"Miss Demont… Helen… You keep surprising us…" His face brightened, with that childlike, all-embracing laugh of his.

I should have liked to throw my arms round his neck, but I restrained myself. My mother was watching, doubtless. So I said: "So do you, Mister Herbert. Peeling an orange with one hand… That would be an achievement…"

"Dunno Darling…" He conjured his grin onto his lips. "I've achieved lots of things with just one hand in my young life…"

He winked, stuffed the napkin into the palm of his left hand and threw it to me.

I found an empty spot, a few steps below his, and sat down. "Writing clearly isn't one of them…" It sounded more piqued than I intended.

I spread the napkin on my lap, put the orange in it and began peeling it. I hadn't eaten oranges for ages, let alone seen or smelt any; it must have been since the last Christmas before the war. The bitter smell of the oils that were released when I buried my thumbnail in the tough skin, and the sweetness when it gave way and the white membrane and the fruit were exposed, overwhelmed me. I felt tears rolling down my cheeks and tried to hide it by bending more deeply over the fruit, but the smell and the relief of seeing him after all those weeks were too much for me.

"Oh come on, love… It's not an onion, it's an orange!" he laughed. It sounded both flippant and helpless.

I tried to smile, but it was stronger than me and his quip upset me even more.

"Oh God, Helen…" He made as if to come and sit next to me.

I raised my hand. "Don't… Mother's here." I nodded in her direction. "We were visiting my brother actually."

"I see… *La Mère audacieuse*…" He pulled a face. I saw he was watching her. "Did she make that coat herself? She looks like bloody fucking St Paul's she does…"

"My aunts made it…" I mumbled.

The sadness lifted. I took a deep breath, divided the orange into segments and handed him the napkin.

"At least you had the decency to write and tell me you were dying…"

"Minor wounds, I said, Helen. That's all. Didn't want you to worry…" He offered me a segment. I couldn't get angry, I was too relieved at seeing him relatively unscathed.

"What happened?"

"I just slipped…"

I giggled.

"I did…" He had wanted to snap a troop of Canadians, by the side of the road. He had stepped onto the brick edge of a small bridge over a ditch leading to a field. "And I slipped. Ruined me arm, me wooden camera and some of me precious ribs… So here's your war hero for you, Miss Demont. What d'ya say?"

"You deserve a statue in Trafalgar Square."

He laughed, but I detected frustration in his pleasure. Greater honour could be gained with different wounds. "At least it got me a medal. It's in here somewhere…" With his free hand he started feeling the pockets of his pyjamas. "They hand 'em out like biscuits these days." The thing looked fairly paltry, a limp ribbon in blue material, on which a metal coin was visibly ashamed of itself.

It had become oppressively hot. Outside there was thunder. My mother was fanning herself with an old newspaper and doing her best not to glower too blatantly in our direction. The man next to her had fallen asleep. The first thunderclaps drowned out the increasingly faint noise of the guns.

"And next?" I asked.

"Back to London, probably, to recover. Daddy's Mighty Arm pulling me back across the Channel. Visit Auntie Margaret. Have tea and ginger biscuits in the parlour. Sing hymns. Walk on the beach. Eternal boredom…"

"Sounds great. Will you come back?"

"Of course, love. Can't stand Albion any more. Nothing there. It's like living on a ship. Besides…" He flashed his grin again. "I'd like to try a few more Belgian delicacies…"

"I'll keep you to your word, Mister Herbert."

A sentry came into the corridor and shouted, "All clear!" The people got up, straightened their coats and adjusted their hats or caps. The patients around us scrambled to their feet.

"See you in the morning?"

I nodded. "We have to leave after lunch."

I left him and went to my mother.

"Well, well," she said sarcastically. "Isn't that *ce drôle Monsieur Heirbeir*? What a coincidence!"

We went upstairs. The room was wet. The rain was leaking in through the smashed window. We slid the beds away from the window, towards each other. She lay down and pulled the bag under her head as a pillow. I cuddled up to her on the other side. She had kept her coat and her shoes on like me.

I waited for her breathing to become calmer, and waves of sleep to come over her, but after a while the mattress began to shake softly. She was sobbing.

I put an arm round her trunk. Through the thick material of her coat I was met by the whalebones of her corset, as if it were not my mother, a living being that I felt under my palm, but a creature of steel. I knew that she didn't want me to say anything, so I just pressed my arm more firmly against her ribcage.

Outside there was the sound of men's voices. Glass slivers being swept into a heap. The faint thunder.

She had stopped sobbing. Sniffed.

"Try to get some sleep, Maman," I said.

She said nothing, but shifted position.

"You do know, child," she said suddenly, "that I brought you along so that you could see him?"

I wondered how she knew. Had the aunts got wind of it?

"Your uncle won't hide many more secrets from his dear sister," she said, as if she had read my thoughts.

She took a deep breath and I could feel her lungs swell under the laces of her corset. She swallowed. "And I can't see you eating yourself up with worry, Hélène. I'm not a monster."

She turned onto her side, arranged the bag under her ear and the weight of her armoured body drew me along in her wake.

ONE OF THE TORPEDOES had left a deep crater in the sand between the wards, torn the head off one of the sentries, riddled another with shrapnel, and blown tiles off the surrounding roofs, smashed windows and left a bas-relief of scorings and impact holes in the walls; and when that morning we, my husband and I, rolled my brother on his wicker bed on wheels, like a grotesque pram, to the promenade, soldiers and orderlies were still pushing glass slivers ahead of their brooms across the floors of the wards. One of the projectiles hadn't exploded and was lying asleep in the sand, surrounded by barbed wire, flanked by a sentry who occasionally looked at the thing as if he were taking his dog for a walk and waiting impatiently for him to do his business.

It was a mild, sunny morning. My mother, after breakfast and a short chat with Edgard, had gone for a rest, and the nurses said that, if I liked, I could take my brother out. Most patients were taken to the promenade or the dunes in fine weather, to expose their healing wounds to the sun and the disinfectant iodine in the sea air under a thin, protective gauze. They sat on benches against the sides of the walls, looking out over the road to the promenade, some at first sight unscathed, others sometimes no more than a torso on which a head looked round alertly, with so many decorations on their pyjama tops that I wondered what the current exchange rate was: how many grams of metal for how many pounds of lost flesh?

"Poor devils," said my brother, who felt himself rather

hard done by with his Croix Léopold, however prestigious that decoration supposedly was; but nevertheless he had pinned the thing prominently on his breast pocket and now let himself be wheeled around by my husband and me like a reliquary in a procession. I pushed, my husband pulled with his free hand on the front of the wicker crate to guide the wheels more smoothly through the soft sand.

Everyone wanted to enjoy the September sunshine that morning. Ahead of us, far away over the broad, flat expanse of wet sand, under the supervision of a man on horseback, figures were marching to the music of a small brass band, and the sea wind carried snatches of the melody across the beach. Around us nurses were walking along, chatting arm in arm, and a child, a girl of about ten, under whose skirts only one leg stuck out and whose head, with flapping plaits, was like that of a doll with a paralysed neck, wobbled alarmingly to and fro as she limped enthusiastically on two crutches towards the beach, observed some distance away by a slim woman in an elegantly tailored coat, probably the mother.

It was quite simply a peaceful scene, and an equally peaceful, melancholy September morning, and for the umpteenth time during that war I was amazed at how quickly we, having just a few hours before hidden from fate's wings, threw the everyday routine like a tough carpet over the craters and the dead—and I still don't know whether I found that a form of grace, a sign of indomitability, or a kind of self-anaesthetizing, the calm of a sheep that, in the vicinity of a pack of wolves, too close to escape, summons up a glorious fatalism and looks its fate calmly in the eyes.

*

We found a quiet spot, out of the wind, backing onto one of the wards close to the promenade, looking out over the sand, and parked the basket chair against the wooden wall.

"Now, my little gazelle," said Edgar, sitting up. "Your brother would like to test whether his legs can still carry him…" He spread his arms wide, signalling that he expected us to help him out of the basket.

"Is that a good idea, Edgard?" I asked, because I could see that he was weak. His face, half hidden under the gauze, had that white, fragile glow of frosted glass which long-term pain makes show beneath someone's features and which seems to push the eyes deeper into their sockets; and when we had helped him out of the basket chair—it had been an effort, since he could scarcely move his right leg and he had raised it from the blankets with a single swing—it was now obvious that he was having a dizzy spell. He stood getting his breath back, hips leaning against that carriage, and looking around, at the beach, blinked vulnerably with his blond eyelids into the sunlight, and muttered: "Christ, vertical again at last…"

"I think we deserve a souvenir," said my husband. He rummaged in the pocket of his pyjama tops, produced one of his small cameras and threw it to me. They stood next to each other, against the edge of the wicker basket, my husband so enthusiastically that he took my brother by the hip with his free arm and pulled him close, which produced a suppressed cry of pain from Edgard.

"Sorry, mate…"

And that's how I saved them for posterity, one in salmon-red striped pyjamas, the other in grey and white, stuck together in front of the wooden wall, my brother more or less overwhelmed by the tall, thin figure next to him, the angular shoulders, the slender arms, the long, long fingers in the material of his pyjama top, pale and unsteady in contrast to the healthy complexion and that aura of boyish invulnerability which would never leave him, who was to become my other half, would make him immortal while he was alive—and when my husband said: "I could kill for a puff" and I handed him the packet of cigarettes I had bought the day before at the station, and he offered my brother one and then held the burning match between them like a restless moth fluttering in the lantern of his fingers; and when the match, his last one, went out and he held his own cigarette against the glowing tip of that of my brother, who was a good head shorter—he looked like a stork chick being fed from its mother's beak—I took another snap of them, and I saw how my brother absorbed with his eyes that serene face, the closed eyes that concentrated on the cigarette, the hand resting lightly on his shoulder, the two medals that seemed to be trying to outdo each other, one red, the other blue—he etched it on the copper plates of memory, looked lovingly at that mouth, my husband's mouth; the lips that pursed round the cigarette end as they sucked oxygen through the glow, and then suddenly released spurts of white smoke. And I turned round, and I still don't know why my heart swelled in my breast, why the distant sea, the jade-green sea, the white lacework of breaking waves, the constant din of the surf, the empty beach, that vast nothingness, that breath of space, filled me with almost desperate euphoria—why, why? Are my eyes wet, Rachida? Are my glasses misting up? Why? Do you know that line of flotsam on the beach after a storm, have you ever seen that? The long, winding ribbon of pieces of wood sculpted by sea worms and cutting sand, that pure chance, that narrow congregation of bottles, the leg of a doll, the arm of a pair of glasses, the bladderwrack, shell grit, the sea anemones and lengths of rope at the furthest point reached by the waves the night before? As a child I tried to read them, I wanted to break their Morse code, to recognize in all that had been washed up a single sanctifying connection that would breathe life into all that had been drowned. Why can't I free myself from that image, so long ago, that afternoon, also on the beach, the first of the many excursions that we were to make that summer, we thought, without knowing that it would be the last excursion for years? Why do I hear again the calm rushing sound, the seagulls, the ethereal rustling of the pages of the newspaper that my brother is sitting reading in his beach chair? I see only his legs sticking out of that upright wicker basket, his bare feet and his toes that are rooting nonchalantly about in the sand while, at the extremity of his rolled-up sleeves, the wind stirs the paper in his fingers. In the distance I see children in their navy-blue swimming costumes under straw hats with ribbons splashing through the tidal pools, and on the handle of the parasol that she has planted firmly in the sand my mother's palms resting, while, leaning a little forward, she looks out with her slender neck, over the butter-yellow sand, the azure, the sea: content, not to say happy—and it is as if I hear my father's breath, the rush of the air in his lungs, beneath my ear, under the material of his bathing suit rough with salt, my father who, so we still thought, for a little while yet, would be joining us in about ten days. And I can also hear the sigh my mother let out when, that evening, after we had dined on the promenade, eaten ice cream, taken a last walk, she and I arm in arm, my uncle came to collect us in the coach. My uncle, not the coachman, because he had been called up—and my mother had let out that sigh.

I hear her voice; she is saying: "Ah, this is where the sun-worshippers have hidden themselves…" as she comes round the corner of the ward, Miss Schliess, looking deathly tired under the white sail of her wimple, next to her with arms folded.

"I'm going to put you back in your box," says Miss Schliess to my brother. "You must lie down. I don't want to see you bleed again. Do you, monsieur? No? Good. Then let me tuck you in, love…"

My mother motions that I can go. "Take your knight for a tour. He likes that, I think. Can you manage by yourself, patriot?"

"Sure I can, ma'am. Sure I can…"

We walked along the beach, some way from the houses, in the direction of France, past the villas reserved for His Majesty in the silver-green dune grass.

"With any luck they'll kick 'em back out the same way his grandfather came in, *les Boches*," he said and took my arm.

"What do you think about my brother?"

He shrugged his shoulders. "Dunno… Will take some time to get straight… Convalescence, probably. Deeper inland. If they've got a job for him, at some desk or other, they'll keep him and otherwise your mum will be seeing him again very soon. Permanent sick leave or something…"

"And you?"

"I'll be back… Soon as I can. I've only spent one of me nine lives, Miss." He looked at me and smiled. "You haven't got rid of me yet… Back to being the press boy. I've had my share of shells by now…"

We continued in silence, I liked the nearness of his body, his hip that occasionally touched my trunk, as we adjusted our gait to each other, his arm under my palm.

"I still have to thank you for being such a knowledgeable guide, the other day."

"I'm sure the pleasure was mostly mine, Miss."

"Should try it again then…"

"By all means…" His familiar grin reappeared round his mouth. He took a puff on his cigarette, stretched his neck, pursed his lips, blew out the smoke. "I like you, Helen… I really, really do… But I wouldn't want to hurt you in any way… Can't see me lingering on a sofa one day, comfy slippers on me feet, the missus boiling the kettle. Know what I mean, love?"

"We have staff to deal with that, don't we?"

"You know what I mean, Helen."

I knew. Every minute we had been together I had weighed his soul in my hand, tested its density, tried to detect its lightness, its darkness, and however little I knew of him, I liked his specific gravity.

"We'll see. One thing at a time. Perhaps one day we'll discover we've silently made our arrangements, without the slightest annoyance…"

He bent his head, lifted my chin with his index finger. Briefly pressed his lips on mine.

"Arrangements, Miss?"

"You know what I mean."

We turned round and walked back along the beach. In front of us lay the old hotel. The belvedere on the roof, surmounted by a dome. Above the wards at the foot of the building was the windowless side wall, with the lettering "*Grand Hôtel de L'Océan. Prix Modérés.*"

We both looked at it at the same time, and though we said nothing, we knew we had more or less the same thought: that the price we'd had to pay up to now had been pretty reasonable.

W E WENT BACK regularly later, when the pavilions had been demolished, the doors of the guest rooms had been hung back on their hinges and on the tables silver and earthenware replaced the surgical clamps and trepans. We always went at either end of the season, the loose ends of summer when in most establishments the tables and chairs were under canvas, sunk in their winter sleep, or in the last days of spring, while everything was still waiting a week or two for the great awakening. It seemed to suit him and me, and we became creatures of in-between times.

We said: in a hundred years' time the war that was ours will have worn away as completely around the monuments, the photos, the diaries, the letters and the tombs as the bones of the dead in the ground, leaving at most a discoloration in the sand. We didn't yet know that meanwhile the soldiers for the next conflict were sleeping in their cradles and that tomorrow's cut-throats were hanging on their nannies' skirts, playing with blocks or in shabby attic rooms licking their wounds and writing bitter treatises in the lethal ink of resentment. We said: if we could come back in a hundred years, we would no longer recognize the war, its elusiveness, its totality which made countless small lives dance like needles in its magnetic field, would meanwhile have been reduced to a handful of images, numbers with no flesh on their bones, place names and data—can't we ever do anything except sooner or later tell fairy tales burdened by footnotes?

"I don't know if I'd like to live to be 100," said my brother, who sometimes accompanied us to the place where my husband and I had stayed; but I was the only one to experience the fact that you don't even have to grow very old to see the silent erosion spreading, to see the veterans of that time, that ever-thinning row of crutches, artificial legs and wheelchairs, jingling with medals, give a shaky salute around an eternal flame or a cenotaph, while His Majesty, himself wobbly on his feet because of his new plastic hip, lays a wreath of mourning among the names of the dead and missing.

My husband would definitely have put his hand on mine at this point and concluded: "It's inevitable, love. Inevitable." On one of those trips we saw Miss Schliess again, at a table by the big window of the restaurant; against a plaster sky she was feeding spoonfuls of pudding to two babies who, with their copper-coloured hair and freckles, seemed to be the spitting image of the strapping fellow next to her, the type of Englishman that radiated the blushing good humour of a good side of roast beef. Obviously she had put her Henry to bed for good, and I never dared ask her if he had a grave somewhere or was one of the others whose names are engraved on a marble wall.

We need tombs, something tangible that covers the dead person, blocks our entry into Hades, a sacrificial table or a dish of incense in which we can burn the feeling of guilt after we, in the caverns of our mind, have shot the dead, who have already died once, in the back, in order to be able to carry on. How many have spent the rest of their days crying in back rooms, while working in the kitchen, in their sleep, surrounded by dead ones without a cradle because the urns burst at the seams and the *Dies irae* sounded puny in a world which, without help from above, had brought to life with flair the horrific medieval visions of the Day of Judgement? And here I lie, on my back, on the bed, on a slow afternoon, in a distant corner of the globe where for the time being it is sunny, virtually cloudless, the streets cooled by the gentle, refreshing breeze that the weatherman predicted primly this morning, while under my window life goes calmly on somewhere halfway between nine and five—how risky and salutary our capacity for forgetting is. But how many dead people have I myself kept alive for too long and condemned to the twilight? Why are there so many absent people in my dreams? Why do they still not enter the rooms that are waiting for them there?

I hear my mother's dictates echoing through the void. "For goodness' sake, cut some Gordian knots, and put a few full stops here and there. A sentence isn't a sausage. It always takes hours for you to get a story off the ground. If a chicken doesn't lay, in the pot it goes. We can't hang about hanging about." How long do I want to tremble before the last word?

In the late summer before peace she fell ill, the first of many, and one of the lucky ones who survived, but her long sickbed heralded a winter in which in the mornings the tenants of the surrounding farms carried the stiffened corpses of their dead children up the garden path to the gate, where the cart would pick them up because there wasn't enough wood to make coffins, or time for a funeral service. I thought of Amélie Bonnard in her box of hastily planed planks. At least half the teenagers and giggling girls who a couple of summers before had lured her to the meadow next to the church, that afternoon when she lost her life, now lay in at most a sewn-up sheet around her in the stony subsoil.

My brother, who had returned a few months earlier, still stiff and unsteady, fell ill shortly after my mother, and he also just made it. The aunts got it, too weak with the coughing and the fever to clothe themselves in theatrical nightdresses, as they would doubtless have done otherwise. My uncle and I walked bewildered through the house that was in a delirium around us, coughing up its lungs. The maids criss-crossed the corridors with basins and cold compresses, then the maids also fell ill, one by one, and the youngest died. Only Madeleine was unaffected, her basalt organism obviously indigestible for germs. My uncle said: "What play are we in? What is this, dear niece, a tragedy or a hard-hitting farce? I can understand that those little creatures don't fancy me or the housekeeper, they like young flesh. Who can blame them, but you, my child…"

He was worried. For most of the day we withdrew to his library on the top floor, to the bored ticking of the small coal stove, as if he hoped I was high enough there to escape the clutches of the creatures or the miasmas, or whatever it was roaming through the rooms downstairs. And when the rumours about an armistice became more and more persistent, I said: "As soon as I can, I'm going back home."

He didn't hesitate, he didn't protest. "I'll fight it out with your mother," he said. "But how do you propose getting there?"

"I have a chauffeur," I said.

For weeks the world had been bathing in the melancholy of a long Indian summer, the umpteenth copper-coloured day was easing its way out of the dew as we were already on our way,

324

he and I, in one of the cars of his major. Ahead of us the fallen leaves of the elms or planes above our heads stuck in absent-minded yellow footprints to the stones of the road surface. The rising sun gilded the fog; here and there in the hop fields the diagonal stakes combed the timid light.

"Everything all right, love?" he asked—it had become our motto.

"I'm fine, monsieur."

I nestled deep in the thick army greatcoat he had given me, listened to the purring of the engine, sniffed the smell of the fuel that welled up from the insides of the car: chemical, sharp, yet pleasant. Around us: lushness and undulations, and above all silence now that the guns had stopped firing for good. It seemed to be hanging over the earth in streamers, that silence.

I watched how he used the wheel, changed gear, accelerated, and slowed down, adjusting the tempo with the gear shift or the pedal. If every journey is a story, every route a saga, he was a good story-teller. I could have watched him for hours, but the journey was short, so short. In my head our town and my uncle's house had grown farther and farther apart over the years, two continents adrift, separated by an ever-wider ocean. Now it looked as if my fatherland, all those years, apart from a postage-stamp-sized piece of land in the extreme west, having been absorbed by the expansive elusiveness of that deaf-and-dumb word "war", had suddenly been forced back within its familiar narrow boundaries.

Even with the countless checkpoints we would be at our destination well before sunset, because everywhere the gen-darme or sentry, after glancing at the papers my husband handed him, sprang to attention and almost dislocated his arm saluting.

"The major's ordered unhindered movement. Nice chap he is." A wink. "I think he fancies me…"

"Who wouldn't?"

We saw the ruins of Ypres, a miserable, rotten set of teeth in the rolling hills, where the grass was already tending towards the brown of winter. In the plain between the old front lines the summer's plant growth had already largely withdrawn back into the earth, restoring the landscape to its bleak nakedness. We passed woods that were more like fields full of stubble than woods. Emergency wooden bridges took us over rivers and streams full of water which, under the weight of grey sediment, crept forward onto banks that did not seem to consist of earth, but of the mixed-up contents of hundreds of travel chests and suitcases. After a while the first foundations emerged from the ground left and right on the verge, under the mist as it was lifted and illuminated by the sun—a brick spring seemed to burst forth as the road took us farther and farther from the old war zone, houses, streets, whole villages that were hesitantly rebuilding themselves, first erecting empty walls, then trying roof beams, decorating themselves cautiously with rows of tiles, uncertainly, tentatively, there were still occasional gaps, but gradually everything closed up, a haze of net curtains hung at the windows, doors stood open, women were walking down the street in clogs, women in thick woollen shawls were standing peering at the church clock. And I don't know how far we'd come, but the landscape that surrounded us looked unscathed, and we were driving under a canopy of sturdy oaks which let their shed leaves dance over the road; then everywhere in the surrounding land, from the clumsy towers, the slender spires, the belfry windows and bell chambers, the ringing burst forth, the carillons, the bronze sigh of relief.

"It's over," said my husband, without looking up from the steering wheel. "It's over, love."

We were silent. I felt a lump in my throat and looked outside, at the meadows and the wooded banks and the exhausted fields, at the consolation that emanated from the indifferent world.

In the villages where the church tower had been destroyed or the bells had been stolen for their bronze, the priests sent the acolytes out into the street with rattles. In the market squares in the bandstands brass bands and ensembles were playing drunken waltzes for the frantic dancing of the frantic masses. The tricolour was flying everywhere. Children shouted, "*Vive le Roi! Vive la Belgique!*" and banged on the bonnet, tapped on the window, pulled faces, waved and screamed when my husband sounded the horn to tease them. Sometimes we made slow headway, and I was reminded of the resigned columns, the sea of khaki, of all the faces that had shuffled past me, stared at me furtively, winked, smiled, when I had last sat beside my husband in the car, under a sky full of sledgehammers. Peace was like the absence of gravity, as if the figures milling round our car were the same as all those others, two years before, finally freed from the cohesion of discipline: the anonymous ranks, dancing and drifting about in a Brownian motion of the purest ecstasy, swarming as far as the eye could see as, towards evening, we approached my home town and along the roads troops advancing on the capital were still marching past the lines of civilians, at the side of the road. The women who, with one hand on their breast clutching their shawls, were not staring at tower clocks, but at the faces of the soldiers going past, surveying their figures one by one, to the point of desperation, since there were so many—and is he among them? And is he coming home? And is he well? Where is he? Occasionally there was a child hiding in their skirts, looking up shyly at that strange procession.

I asked him to stop on the sandy ridge near the stream next to the windmill where we had often driven as children with my father on Sunday rides in a hired coach. The sails of the mill lay strewn on the grass, except for one, which was raised in a lonely salute under what was by now a heavily overcast sky. From the windows of the miller's house a trace of soot licked up towards the eaves; around the roof beam there were nothing but bare, charred timbers.

I got out. So did he. Went for a pee against a tree. I heard the wind whistling in the tufts of grass, and a late bird tweeted a tripping melody somewhere in the pollarded willows by the side of the stream.

I looked to the east, over rows of poplars that had gone grey, at the familiar profile of my town on the horizon, the old towers, unscathed.

He came and stood behind me, and put his arm round my waist. "What you looking at, love?"

"Home," I said.

The town suddenly rising round us, a profusion of brightly lit windows in the blue darkness, the glow of lanterns on the railings of the emergency bridges over the canals, the gleam of the abandoned artillery, the dull-coloured sandbags; and while we drove through the working-class districts the streets were swarming with people. In the pubs and cafés the party-goers were bursting out of every door and window, spasms of euphoria vibrated to the strains of the Brabançonne through the packed bodies. But at home it was dark. We parked the car under the chestnut trees across the street. No lamp or candle exposed the familiar ceilings of the rooms behind the window glass.

I crossed the front garden, hurried up the steps to the front door and rang the bell. The jangling died away across the floor of the hall and no one came to open up. I tried again.

No one.

"Probably out in town. Celebrating the peace," said my husband. I asked him to wait outside, went down the steps behind the hydrangea to the basement kitchen, Emilie's vault. The door was not locked.

There was a penetrating smell of drink gone flat in her kitchen, around the oven above which not a single pan was still on the hooks. In the fading light a mountain of empty glasses shone, in the washing-up bowls, in the corners, on the chopping block. On the table, next to a candle-holder with a stump of candle in it, next to a plate and fork, a cooking pot containing a vague mush still felt lukewarm. There must definitely be someone around.

I went upstairs. In the hall the lamp fittings had been torn out of the wall, the palms had been stripped of their brass pot-holders, the chandelier had been replaced by a miserable bulb. In the anteroom the chairs were piled on top of each other in a corner and in the middle of the room was my brother's bed in all its glory without a mattress.

I opened the front door. "No one home," I said. "But some-one has been eating."

"Mind if I put me things inside, love?" He returned to the car.

I went back inside. There was no metal to be found anywhere in the house, apart from that one cooking pot and a couple of saucepans. All the expensive cutlery had disappeared. All the tin. Every cook's knife, every ladle. Most of the earthenware, almost all the carpets. The house seemed to have been cleaned out. In the back garden someone, Emilie perhaps, had dug over the small lawn. In the increasing darkness I saw strictly demar-cated vegetable beds, pale, faded potato tops above heaped earth, compact, globular cabbages. In the house I could hear my husband lugging his things about.

"Might go and join the party as well," he said when every-thing was in the antechamber, his cases, his cameras, the bread and the eggs, and the various jars of preserves Madeleine had given us to bring. "What d'you think?"

"We'll wait," I said, in the darkness of the drawing room. "I know some tricks to entertain us, Monsieur Heirbeir."

I pushed him onto the sofa, fell and met his lips and forced him back in the cushions.

We had dozed off when someone was fiddling at the front door lock, whereupon he leapt up, pushed his shirt into his trousers, buttoned his fly while I buttoned my blouse; in the hall there was the echo of coughing, and his familiar tread across the floor. I got up and left the living room in my stocking feet.

I saw him, by the weak light of the window above the front door, putting his bowler hat on the rack, taking his scarf off his shoulders. And when I said softly: "Papa… it's me, Helena…" his hand hung in mid-air above the hook of the hallstand.

We ate an improvised meal of eggs and bottled vegetables, after my husband had got the oven going with the last firewood and I had beaten the eggs. Somewhere in a side cellar my father had unearthed a full bottle of wine.

We clinked glasses.

"*La Paix!*" he cried. He was still moved.

"Here, here," echoed my husband.

"Good heavens, dear child, I've never enjoyed a simple omelette so much."

He looked as if he'd lost weight. Bags under his eyes, a dull gleam in his wrinkles. He coughed a lot. He'd also caught flu.

"I had to go to the hospital. There was nothing else for it. They've been hard years, child, but I don't think I've ever felt lonelier than when I stood there on the threshold of that hospital, shaking with fever, with my pathetic little case, my pyjamas and my shaving kit in front of a nun who wanted to blast me off the paving stones with one look. The wards were full to bursting…"

"And Emilie?" I asked.

He sighed, looked furtively at the mountain of empty bottles behind us. "Let's say that she got on quite well with the Germanic element in the house…"

I looked at him uncomprehendingly.

"The German who was billeted here… He slept in the anteroom. The first one was all right. Wernher. Good family man. Three children. He was also looking forward to when the misery would be over, and to his wife's liver noodles. But the second one... I think it's best if I say nothing. There are respectable ladies in the company."

"Oh, the young lady has been through the war," I said. "She knows what the world's like."

I saw his eyes dart from me to my husband. Surprised. Not unfriendly.

"I had to let her go, Hélène. The whole street was talking about it..."

We never saw her again. Once, in the following weeks, when my father had gone to see my mother, I thought I recognized her smile in a group of women that shot timidly past my husband and me, a glance that noticed me behind the tall, raised collar of a heavy winter coat, under a big hat or cap under which a head looked strangely bald. One of the passers-by broke into curses, hard as nails in our town dialect. The women buried themselves even farther in their coats. A little farther on they just managed to avoid a rain of well-aimed gobs of phlegm.

"The fate of the harlot," said my husband.

I don't know what became of her. We scarcely knew where she came from. The woman who for as long as I could remember had starched our linen, cooked our food, heated our milk, was largely a stranger to me, an insignificant source of muscle power, an anonymous workhorse. There were more bodies than usual fished out of the rivers and waterways of our town in those months, and quite a few of women in heavy coats. I still hope that she wasn't one of them.

My father sipped his glass and wiped his mouth. "So Mum is on the mend? And Edgard?"

"He'll pull through. The doctor said so too. He'll make it..."

"And his leg?"

"It will be some time before he can walk normally…"

"He's alive. That's the main thing. We're poor, we're hungry. But we're alive. I want to see them as soon as possible…"

"The railways are a mess, Dad. It'll be complicated."

On the way home we had passed the station, the embankment had been blown up and some rails were sticking in the air like stiffly curled ribbons. There was a rumour that the enemy had disabled as many locomotives as possible.

"If necessary, I'll go on foot…"

My husband stretched out in his chair—he had been fighting off sleep for some time. "Perhaps something can be arranged," he yawned.

"He's big pals with his major," I said. "The major fancies him…"

My father brought his glass to his mouth. Before he drank I saw for the first time since we'd been reunited the familiar chuckle playing round his lips. "If you ask me, the poor chap will have to go on fancying for a long time. Don't you think, child?"

He left two weeks later and stayed well into January. It was freezing when he left. The night before it had snowed lightly. A biting wind shook tufts of caster sugar from the bare branches of the chestnut trees. He had had a haircut and had his moustache trimmed. We were standing in the dormer window when the driver of the car which was to take him to my mother drew up at the front garden, sounded his horn and waited next to the door of the vehicle.

"Well, well, I'm gradually feeling more important than our prime minister." He took off his glove. Tapped on the window to let the chauffeur know he was coming. Then he looked up at the grey, overcast heavens.

"What do you think, child? Porcelain? Murano glass? Quicklime?"

I stood close to him, raised my head and surveyed the sky for a while. "Water vapour," I said.

Laughing, he pressed the tip of my nose with his index finger. "My daughter has grown up."

He picked up the small suitcase standing next to him on the floor. "Off to the Great Mother. To tell her that the world has changed for good. I hope she'll accept it. You know what she's like. The world will have to be very sure of itself. Are you certain you want to stay here? Will it work, child? Restrain yourself a bit with the visits of your English boyfriend. You know the neighbours…"

"Dad, please!"

He was silent.

Now he laid his napkin next to the empty plate. "I'm off to bed. The master of the house is tired." He looked around sarcastically. "Hovel seems to me a better word… If you're planning to stay, Mister Herbert…"—he spoke the words with an exaggerated British accent; he had clearly got wind of something—"my daughter will build you a nest. Good night."

They shook hands. He gave me a kiss on the forehead. When he had almost left the room, he turned, looked at us in turn and said in a good-natured tone: "And be good. I'm still your father."

I arranged some blankets and pillows on the sofa downstairs. There weren't enough mattresses in the house. When I had finished I saw to my astonishment that my husband simply nestled on the seat and started unbuttoning his shoes.

I pulled him with me. "Idiot…"

"What? It's me bed, isn't it?"

"Only in the morning, honey. You're sleeping with me…"

I pushed him upstairs, past my father's bedroom. I could hear his regular breathing. He was deeply asleep, didn't react at all when my husband stubbed his toe on the foot of the chest of drawers and let out a powerful swear word.

I pushed him into my room, one floor higher, closed the door behind us and peeled his shirt, his trousers, his underpants and socks off him like a fruit skin.

"Christ, Helen, it's freezing up here. Could lose me nuts any minute…"

He caught his breath when I squeezed them in my palm.

It had started to rain, a friendly licking and pattering against the window. We lay listening to the town, where the din of the festivities abated only slowly, occasionally giggling when below us in the street a drunk wandered burbling down the footpath, in a drink-sodden medley of numerous national anthems.

"I'm knackered, ma'am."

I giggled, drank in the sharp smell of his armpits. His head rested on my breast.

"And now?" I asked teasingly.

"Off to Brussels in the morning. Be back in a couple o' days… Rather fancy the idea of setting me gear up in the cellar…"

"And then?"

"Dunno. Stay here. Shan't go back. No way, love. Job with the press perhaps… Suppose that'd be nice. No need to worry,

335

for the time being…" He raised his head, gave me a playful bite in the skin under my chin. "Mummy's allowance, remember? And you, love?"

I was silent. Thought. "Studying," I said. "Reading. Seeing the world. You must show me the world…"

"If you say so, love."

"And I want your child, eventually…"

"Oh God…" He gave a sigh and cuddled up still closer. "Better start with ham and eggs then, in the mornin'…"

I laid my hand on his cheek. Kissed him on the crown of his head. In his hair.

He was soon asleep.

V

"YOU HAVEN'T RESTED AGAIN," Rachida chides me when she pushes open the door of the room to check whether I'm still snoozing, and now she sees that I'm wide awake she contracts her eyebrows into a frown of feigned anger. She can never get angry with me, and she knows that I know, and also that I'm quite capable of exploiting it.

She walks round the bed, meanwhile laughing and wagging her finger: "You're a rascal, Mrs Helena."

"Thank you, child. Always have been."

In passing, on her way to the window, where she opens the blinds, she catches sight of the exercise book at my side. "You should turn the light on if you want to read or write. You'll ruin your eyes otherwise."

She opens the window. The smell of the summer evening. The residual warmth of the day in the stones on the front of the building. The scent of asphalt, grass, the acid aroma of the tame chestnut trees in the street without a breath of wind.

"I'm as blind as a bat anyway, child."

She takes the tray off the bedside table, stops at the edge of my bed and gives a leisurely, theatrical sigh. "Again you've not eaten anything… just half a sandwich this morning and now just some cold soup. You must eat, Mrs Helena."

She walks round the bed again, towards the door. "Eat and sleep. That's what Dr Vanneste says."

*

339

Dr Vanneste. The new one. Fresh from university, still wet behind the ears. God knows what's happened to the old one. Perhaps he collapsed or tripped over his bag on the stairs and broke his neck. One can but hope.

The new one came in, put out his hand and said, undoubtedly because it's in the course on *How to Break the Ice with the Patient*: "Hallo. I'm Yannick Vanneste."

"And I've got migraine," I said.

"I'm doing a practical internship." He put the pressure gauge round my upper arm and pumped the air in so hard that my lower arm almost came out of the elbow socket. "But next year I shall be qualified."

Twenty-six or twenty-seven. Solid, tall. A real hunk, but in his head there was a little boy throwing walnuts. When he pushed the thermometer into my mouth I instinctively sucked down on his fingers with my whole palate and he muttered something like "those little chompers of yours are still in good shape, little lady"—meanwhile checked the blood pressure and said to Rachida that it was on the high side: "Fifteen…" He took the thermometer out of my mouth. "And you've got a wee bit of a temperature…"

Wee bit of a temperature. Little lady. Baby talk: verbal dummies. If I were his age, I'd give him a proper temperature.

"Is she eating enough? Is she sleeping enough?" He asked Rachida. Then bent over the bed and winked: "Let's have a listen."

He slid the stethoscope across my ribcage over the thin material of my nightdress. Those fingers. The intent listening. The supple wrinkles on his forehead, which do not yet make lasting furrows.

"Looks good." He took the stethoscope out of his ears. "Is her liquid intake sufficient?"

I ostentatiously coughed up some phlegm from my windpipe and muttered: "I have been suffering from vaginal dryness for quite some time."

I saw Rachida's jaw muscles tensing, her eyes didn't know where to look. Dr Vanneste went pale.

"You're blushing, doctor."

He blinked, recovered and opened his bag. "I'll prescribe diazine, for the blood pressure. One tablet twice a day… There you are."

Rachida took the prescription and let him out.

"Liquid, liquid… If I were sixty years younger, I'd have shown him what liquid is… What do you say to that, child?"

"You were very very naughty, Mrs Helena," she says, putting the tray down and coming and sitting on the edge of my bed. "I'll boil an egg. I'll pour you a glass of milk and do you a sandwich. And then…" She pats the blankets with the flat of her hand. "Then I shall come and sit with you and I shan't go away until you've finished everything… Otherwise we shall get very angry."

She gets up. Pulls me upright. Arranges the pillow behind my back. "I'll tell a story. While you eat, I'll tell you a story for a change." She pulls the sheet over my legs and smoothes it out. "Is that OK? The story of Said with the Lovely Eyes."

"Who's that? A desert prince who turns old women into salamanders?"

She giggles. "I shall tell his story the way my mother always told it to me. But if you stop eating…" She takes her hands off the sheet and holds them at shoulder height with fingers spread wide... "Then I'll stop talking at once. You'll have to decide for yourself how it ends."

She adjusts my nightdress, straightens the collar with a few strokes of her index finger, then goes over to my chair, folds the blanket up and shakes out the cushions.

The ending. Why always that last dessert? Why that elaborate laying of the table, that juggling with cutlery, that measuring of the distance between the glass and the plate, that elegant folding of napkins, setting out bouquets and polishing candlesticks? I like table tops covered in crumbs and smeared with jam, and the casually folded newspaper which equally casually counts its fatalities and crimes—a chance form for the formless chance of every day.

The words and the voice of my mother, and the silence of the body, and the war, which never let itself be embraced by its name. When I was young I wanted to be able to capture it in one light, call down the consolation of completion upon things and my thoughts. But I couldn't. I thought I was still too green, too impatient, and now I don't want it any more. No more consolation, no rest. Just sleep without sleep.

There comes an age, Rachida child, at which I won't say you hunger for death, but you are ready to await it. To be able to become old enough, so that you can await death with the same casualness with which you wait for the bus at the corner of the street, without excitement or hope—it would be my idea of bliss, if I still worried my head about such things. I'm already in seventh heaven if I can keep all my teeth in my mouth while you watch how I eat.

My finiteness, or what is left of it, can still, albeit seldom, fill me with fear and dismay, but at the same time in the certainty of death there is a dim vision of an impersonal consolation which is not necessarily at right angles to life and may be a close continuation. The certainty of one day no longer having to eat or drink or sleep, or, despite all hormonal dryness and fragile bones, fanning the fire of desire—no longer having to go round in circles or send best wishes to people whose birthday I always forgot anyway, but freed from time to return to the great scheme of things.

"If I were young now, I would go out of town, Rachida my girl. Cycle out of town and swim in one of the old river branches. I would go into the water in my bare feet through the reeds on the bank, to be able to feel the mud like a soft cushion under my soles. And then I would say: it's just dead earth, dead, soulless earth. An old mountain range, a tombstone that has worn away."

I take her hands in mine. Stroke, as my mother's ancient grandmother once did, with my thumb over the backs of her beautiful olive-coloured fingers, so soft and smooth in my calloused claws.

"I can dab them with iodine," she says. "That will make those spots paler."

I thought for far too long that words have nothing more to say, but it is so good that they do not completely fit with things and lead a life of their own. Did I say it aloud? She's smiling, but I can see that she's not really listening. Perhaps she thinks I'm starting to wander. She frees herself from my hands, retrieves the hairbrush from the drawer of the bedside table and runs it through my hair—or what's left of it.

"It's almost music, the cadence of your brush in my hair. I should stick words on it. Listen, pull it slightly slower through my hair and listen: 'The lamp had to burn far too long in the vacuum…' When I used to go walking with my father I always made up sentences that fitted into the rhythm of our footsteps."

She draws the brush with long strokes across my crown, keeps her eyes fixed on me, snorts a laugh. I can see her thinking: she'll come round. But she says: "You're dreaming aloud again, Mrs Helena. That's what happens when you get so little sleep."

"No, child, I'm wide awake. We're apes, we preen each other with words. Listen to what your brush sings: 'Time… to break bread… on the table again.'"

"That's what I like to hear," she smiles. "I'll put plenty of butter on."

When I was young I regarded words as compact, stable units, intriguing stones that I collected so as not to be empty-handed in the face of the world. I made breakwaters from them against the spring tide of light and colour, of smell and sound that could sometimes descend overwhelmingly on me—the world in its brutal splendour, its breathtaking selfhood, which would overpower me and annex me in the tumult of its constant becoming. In other words I was afraid I would die of pleasure.

As time went on I came to see them increasingly as mirrors or lenses, or prisms which dissect the white, undifferentiated glow of the world—as my father was wont to reflect when, at home after a storm, I stood next to him at the window, look-ing at the rainbow over the wet roofs: "And to think that such splendour consists solely of refracted light…" Carnival in hell was what Emilie called such weather, when the sun shone and it rained at the same time.

I regard them as mini solar systems, words, atomic nuclei around which the electrons of meaning charge, like little planets with weak gravitational fields, the ethereal atmospheric layers, and deep down in their geology a messy memory, although unlike this planet they have no core, not even a figurative one. All I try is to order them in such a way that their constellations evoke figures that otherwise would remain unseen and unknown. I have never filled all those exercise books with their signs for any other reason than in the act of writing to squeeze my foot in the door of the definitive, like a pushy door-to-door salesman of magic cleaning products.

"The time is finally ripe, child, to clear the last shelves. Put everything in boxes and take them away. Distribute them, all those written sheets. Do what you want with them, but make sure their fate is uncertain."

"First I'm going to boil your egg, Mrs Helena. We still have time."

"I'd like to be buried in those bookshelves. Wouldn't it be wonderful to pull them off the wall and make a nice coffin of them?"

"For that you'd need to shrink a lot. At least forty centimetres. Now I know why you eat so little."

The books, the dead, my mother's voice in my sleep and the garden without limits; in my head they open more and more grandly that space without location, where a time prevails outside

345

time, and which since childhood I never have stepped out of with more than one leg. The greater part of our mind is an Indian god stretched out in the alert sleep of a cat, dumbstruck, but far from deaf, and if necessary all-seeing. As we get older, Rachida my child, I'm not ranting, as we get older everything we do or don't do, and say or keep silent about, is drowned out ever more loudly by the breath of that alert sleep in us, which we try in vain to tuck in with words, but which also drives our words. We all speak from *horror vacui*.

"Do you want me to take the photo of your mother too, Mrs Helena?" she asks casually, treacherously casually. I know that she's testing me, that she thinks: she won't go through with it. How many times have I resolved finally to clear the decks, and how many times has she hoisted me up on the tough thread of her *joie de vivre*?

My mother. She now hangs in a distant corner of my mind; in the dust clouds and gassy mists that make up memory she is a dark, burnt-out star. Her messages reach me as a radiation that is not light, more an energy with different wavelengths, travelling from a tangible absence. All I can do is demarcate a space in which her dull echo can resonate.

She becomes even less material when she occasionally appears in my dreams, whereas I still associate my father with the material, with words like wall, buttress, rafter—my father, who was basically more maternal than she was, the head of the family, the man who formed the mould from which she derived her severe figure. I have never seen anyone as helpless as she was when he died. Even I never equalled her when I lost my husband in turn, but maybe I did with my daughter—when I received the news that she was dead, I broke into a rage that was perhaps nothing but desperation turned on its head. How strange, the manoeuvrability of our emotions. Pain becomes pleasure. Fear euphoria. Love hatred.

When on my last reluctant walks through town I passed places to which memories were attached, I was no longer seized by the melancholy that I experienced until I was about fifty, the years when youth seemed about to tip over into old age. I recognized the fronts of houses where I had once partied and dined. The bourgeois ostentation of cornices and balustrades in wrought iron had a museum-like feel. Some of those houses had become shops, wine merchants' premises or restaurants, or clothing outlets in whose windows one glimpsed the unmoving elegance of mannequins. Some were still inhabited and had remained more or less unchanged, paintwork a little flakier, stones a little more impregnated with rust, and divided up into student rooms. Sometimes, through an open window, I could see a bit of ceiling, a rosette in stucco, meanwhile stripped of the chandelier under whose arms I had raised glasses, sung, danced, argued, and hushed up forbidden loves. Or I saw a section of a mantelpiece, meanwhile painted in different colours, a corner of a poster in the place where once a tall mirror hung which long ago confronted me with my own reflection like a satirical poem. There was where the pianola must have stood whose melodies we sang, and over there the sofa where I was unfaithful under subdued lighting, or the palm plant in the stairwell, under which I blubbed at my own restlessness and shame, while I bobbed merrily along on the weightlessness of those centrifugal years between the two wars, when I finally escaped from under my mother's wing by marrying—against her will, but without her sulking.

Times had changed. My brother took over my father's business and brought it to new prosperity, and I left my daughter with my parents in order to follow my husband on his travels and study history. History. In my mother's eyes an idiotic but otherwise innocent pastime, a form of flower-arranging for decadent people like me. I didn't stick at it for long, I had a child that wanted breast-feeding, and noticed that knowledge infected my writing, impoverished my thoughts till they became nothing but sociology set to music. History, that prosthesis cobbled together with erudition from scraps of paper, potsherds and bone fragments, on which we limp through the annual accounts as if time were full of signposts. I gave it up. My mother triumphed, for once without a word.

I still judge her and her life too unjustly, the narrow niche that she was able to carve out for herself in time, which without her choice or will was hers, as if the dubious freedoms I was able to appropriate were a personal achievement—as if time is the work of my hands.

How could I not look back with at least mild mockery at the little hussy I now see reflected in my mind's eye: a child that smoked cigarettes in cigarette-holders to make a sophisticated impression and adorned herself with affairs and friendships which all too soon went flat or sooner or later turned to melancholy, mine or theirs. As I found moving around town increasingly difficult, looking more and more often at the ground, frightened of the slightest unevenness in the paving stones of the pavement, I looked increasingly inwards, into my own rooms.

I wish I could keep life in my fingers, so it would show the compactness and brilliance of a diamond. I would turn it over and over, study each of its facets, absorb every play of the light, until it extinguishes in my palm because my fascination has finally been quenched. Melancholy turns out to be no more than a thin, transparent membrane, the umpteenth amnion surrounding a human life until, having become brittle, it tears open or springs loose and we stand a little closer to our original nakedness.

When I had trouble walking, I took the tram to scour the city, got off at certain stops and made short journeys on foot, to the next stop, and later still I could usually persuade my daughter to take trips in the car. She did it devotedly; no one could act as scornfully as she could. As long as we didn't have to spend too long in one room, searching for words that didn't sound too untrue, she was prepared to do anything for me.

It was she who found my husband. While waiting for the taxi that was to take him to the airport he had lain down on the bed for a moment. The taxi came, the driver hooted. No one came down. My daughter ran upstairs and was gone some time. The taxi hooted again. When I went upstairs I found her in the doorway of my bedroom. She was standing speechless watching my husband on the bed, in his light-beige summer jacket, his hat on his chest, feet hanging over the edge of the mattress, next to the valise. When the taxi driver hooted again she went back downstairs. "I'll send him away," she said. "He's not needed any more."

I never saw her cry, and I couldn't either. We sat through the funeral service like stiff dolls, my insides seemed to have turned to zinc, dry rain pipes in which my heart pounded dully. My only thought was: it was just about time. His eyebrows were starting to get bushy, his nose hair too. Down appeared on his ears, he already had a double chin. He wasn't made for old age. What more is there to say?

He stays away from my dreams, like my child. I sometimes imagine that the two of them are enjoying themselves royally somewhere in a part of my head, some convolution of the brain to which they had mislaid the key. I stand at the door and knock in vain—all I hear is an echo of zinc. Only once did I dream of him. He was sitting here in the chair by the bed when I dreamt that I woke up. He had lit a cigarette; I also caught the smell of the nylon of his summer jacket. He inhaled and blew out the smoke.

"You do know, don't you, Helen, my lovely, why I drop by so seldom?" he asked and went on smoking. He looked dejected.

After his death I asked my child to take me every year at the end of the summer to the house where my mother had been born; the others had dropped out, being too old by now, too weak, too dead. She always acceded to my sighs with infectious reluctance and on the way there we were as silent as the grave. Once we had arrived and she had parked the car at the foot of the hill, near the path leading upward, she didn't even need to refuse ostentatiously to go any farther with me. She knew that it was quite enough to get out, light a cigarette leaning against the bonnet and search for a scarf in her eternal handbag, the scarf that betrayed the nun *manquée* in her, like her belly, the belly of a virgin in a panel by Memling, apple-shaped, swelling, as if her skin, her membranes enclosed not a womb but a clenched fist.

I blamed myself for years for having sent her, in a fit of conformism or to please my mother, to the nuns' school from an early age. I saw her change over the years into a bigoted type, against whom my mother, for as long as she lived, would never hear a word said, since for her everything was preferable to a creature like me, who mostly got things wrong in life.

She only survived my mother by a few years; just before her death she got one of the nuns to call me, a colleague of hers, at that girls' boarding school where she had hung on after her schooldays as a teacher of religious studies and practical nincompoop. The nun said I must hurry. In her voice lay the dregs, I imagined, of the repeated reproaches she must have heard from the mouth of my child, but I did not even pay my respects to her body. I didn't even know she was ill.

I'm sorry to be overloading these final pages with corpses; I'll be as brief as possible. She supervised, she taught, she died. She wore suits of tailored insignificance and devoted herself to a cult of virginity that looked very like grass widowhood. The pupils called her the chalk line. For a while the rumour circulated that she was having an affair with the head, a priest. I would have been delighted, but when I asked her cautiously about it, she shot me a grimace of contempt that immediately gave me intestinal cramp. I blamed myself for not removing her from the school in time, not having encouraged her father more

often to pay her a little more attention. Not having told him to
his face that *I* might be happy to be the dovecote at which he
could alight at will in between his adventures, but that the child
hadn't asked for it. But one day, I can't remember when, let
alone whether we were having a fight or not—one day we were
standing staring out of the window and she said, with a calm
that still sends shivers down my spine: "How else can I atone
for the shame of being your daughter, Maman?" She turned
away with a scornful little laugh. I was in pieces. I didn't glue
the pieces together, for years I walked over them ritually in my
bare feet and absorbed the stabbing pain.

The first time I dared to return with her, a few years after the
death of my husband, it was a fiasco. I felt her eyes boring
into my back after I had left her by the car; she maintained a
stupid silence. I had first, with my legs half out of the door,
exchanged my footwear for a pair of boots and then taken the
path to the back gate. When my husband was still alive, the last
owner welcomed me like a princess for a while. "*Eh bien voici*,"
he would cry. "*Not' châtelaine.*" He showed us the silos and the
milking plant, and the new barn or the potato cellar, but his
pride hid a man frightened to death who knew he was deep in
debt and liked a glass too many to anaesthetize him against the
fear. He had my uncle's beard, in which the smoke from around
the hearth eternally lingered. As the years went by, at the long
table in the back kitchen of the annexe where my mother had
heated so many kettles, he poured us increasingly generous shots
of liqueur, while behind his back his mistress of the moment,
as angrily as the previous or following one, scoured pans and
counted the glasses with resignation. We drank and indulged

ourselves in stories which I have repeated far too often to do it again here. Around us you could almost hear the ivy and the grapevine anchoring the shutters to the window frames and the moss covering the slate roof with wet cushions.

The last time I went there with my husband, the gate was closed. We went to the only surviving café in the village to ask what had happened. A few village elders recognized me, the daughter of the lovely Marianne, the Fleming, *comme nous, nous sommes aussi des Flamands, au fond, écoute*—and spoke to me in the language I remembered from my childhood. A language like crude ore, like flint. A Flemish that rose from the chalky soil and became flesh before my eyes.

A factory-owner from Calais had bought the property for a song after the bailiffs had seized everything. He had rented out the surrounding land, and had the house locked up and the contents auctioned off.

"There's nothing there, madame," he informed me when I rang him to ask him if anyone in the village had a key to look after things. "The place is a ruin. Much too dangerous."

When the following year my husband died, going back would have affected me too deeply. My life was one great map strewn with places to avoid, a flight from the curse of memory.

Four or five years went by. The day when I finally put the boots on and set off, I felt my daughter's eyes in my back. I could almost hear her thinking: she's still not over it, poor old dear, still looking for her forgotten paradises.

I had to return without accomplishing my mission. The back gate was overgrown with brambles, elder had woven its branches between the railings, there was no way through. You should have seen the pity, the haughty pity on my child's face when I came back to the car with twigs and thorns in my clothes, a gash in my calf and dead leaves in my hair. She said nothing, she was always like that. Too cowardly to say what she thought, always letting other people do the dirty work, intriguing, and letting other people play through her fingers like bobbins, threading the lacework of her cosy little intrigues and always washing her hands in cups of rancid innocence—how did something like that come from inside me, I wondered. I gave birth not to a child, but to a rusty nail.

A few weeks later I forced her to take me there again; I sent her off to the seaside and she left me behind with great pleasure. In the pockets of my overcoat was a big pair of secateurs. I cut loose the branches around the gate until I could use the handle again, and made my way through the brambles and nettles around the first row of stalls, past the chicken runs and reached the inner courtyard, stumbling over the tufts of grass shooting up between the gaps in the paving stones. They were largely buried under sand and rotted leaves, the subsoil seemed to be sucking them up, as if an invisible titanic effort, an army of worms, were burying the house by gradually pulling it into the ground.

At first I couldn't open the side door, the door on the south front. A lead weight was leaning against the wood on the other side, and only after I had pushed for ages, with my full weight, did it give way and fall with a dull thud on the floor. A shiver of rustling went through the climbing plants across the stones of the house front.

Someone must have put one of the old mattresses, those ponderous pre-war mattresses, against the door, perhaps to discourage intruders or vandals. The monster lay heavily at my feet, leaving just enough room to push the door open thirty centimetres or so, so that I could get in.

Now I look back on it, it is as if old Moumou, the primeval mother, was pushing against the inside of the door to keep me out with the full force of her primordial size, her femininity without frills—as if wanting to say: "Stay away, child. That's enough, we'll manage by ourselves. Decay takes little effort, we can do it alone."

And when I went through into the kitchen and saw the gap in the floor tiles, the wound of sand where the old stove had stood which the rag-and-bone man had obviously ripped out, of course to sell the steel, the desolation almost assumed the bitterness of a reproach. I saw the dust rings in the wall that marked the silhouette of the saucepans as they had once hung from large to small like a scale of copper above the chopping blocks.

And the farther I went, the heavier the atmosphere became, the more hands seemed to press against my trunk and exhort me to retrace my steps—but I wasn't there to gape. I had come to mourn, that house was my burial chapel, the storehouse of all my dead, for whom I could weep only there. I wanted, up in my uncle's library room, to surrender myself to the handful of memories that could transform the sound of zinc inside me into a requiem, take possession again of the longing that seized me in the days when my husband was recovering on the other side of the Channel and my mother guarded me with a restlessness in which I now increasingly detect the signs of the flu that was to confine her to her bed for weeks and release me from her clutches. I wanted to be able to pull that longing over me like a mourning cloak.

Only up there could I escape from her restlessness, flopping on the chair by the table, next to my uncle, who was doing paperwork with mittens on. It was winter, and one of my mother's attempts to keep a grip on things was to skimp on firewood and coal. My uncle blew on his fingers; I meanwhile pretended to be writing letters.

"The irony, child," he whispered into his beard, meanwhile listening to check whether she wasn't coming upstairs again, my mother, for the umpteenth time, supposedly looking for something in the room next to ours, eavesdropping as she rummaged about to the drumming of her heavy heels. She must have been the only spy who hoped that by being conspicuous her presence would not be noticed. "The irony is", said my uncle, "that we're not doing at all badly at present. In the past I had to fatten two pigs to get the price they're now offering for a single ham. We don't really want for anything."

She knew it herself. Behind her whalebone our prosperity precipitated as guilt. She made the aunts prepare food parcels for distribution in the village. I don't know if she sensed any of the resentment that smouldered not even that far under the surface of gratitude, when she paid her charity visits to the poorer families in the area—the paltriness that cries out for revenge of knocking on the door of a woman who has lost half her family with a jar of jam or a piece of pâté.

*

"Are you all right, my child?" asked my uncle. "I don't think the thaw will be here by tomorrow."

We felt allied in our penance. Sometimes he interrupted his paperwork, went over to one of the shelves against the walls, and showed me the cover of one of the books he collected for the saucy prints they contained. They were generally daring farces from the eighteenth century, with titles like *Plaisirs Secrets*, usually sewn into a single volume with the sequel: *Le Regret inutile*. We could giggle at them like teenagers. "She'll come round," he said reassuringly.

I didn't know that a body could long so violently for another body. My man, my companion, my spiritual brother, his flesh that revealed itself as a synonym in mine. I lay my head again on the soft skin of his belly, the membrane of skin that swells and contracts with his breath between his pelvis and ribcage. I hear the gurgling of his intestines beneath my ear, the hidden processes in the factory of the metabolism, as gruesome as it is ingenious, the beat of his heart, accelerating as he breathes in, slowing with each out breath, pumping his blood through his tissues. Even his brain must pulse to that rhythm under the natural helmet of his skull.

The hair that grew outward in an arc on his forearms and legs fascinates me again as powerfully as when I rested my head on his naked chest for the first time and plucked at those black hairs with my fingers. What hunger, what longing, what lust could rage through my limbs!

I think of my father in the hour of his death, forgive me for digging up yet another dead person from the inside pockets of my memory. I'm thinking of the surge of his breathing, as he lay on his back under the sheets, the increasingly long silence between his breaths—and my fear, which welled up in each interval, but, together with the fear, strangely enough, the amazement at the precision, not to say tact, with which the organism that was my father was recalling the life from his farthest arteries and cells, was drawing the warmth out of his feet towards itself, and seemed to be concentrating everything in his head, and just before he died smoothed the last folds out there too. I saw life sliding out of him, his cheeks sunk, it was almost a kind of relief.

My husband, on the other hand, lay on the bed with amused surprise, as if he would never have expected that nothingness could be so friendly, while when we had sex he was always a lover who gave himself over in deep contemplation to *le petit mort*. There are men who climax with a blissful grin, as if an opium bubble is popping in their head, and there are those, like my husband, who in those few seconds of ecstasy seem to dream up a whole treatise, a concise theology of ejaculation. Only when I saw the wrinkles appearing in his forehead and his midriff tensing did the spasms start in me, shimmering as far as the roots of my hair and my nipples. They sent starling swarms of gooseflesh through my pores.

Naturally I never talked about such things to my uncle up in his study. He was no longer alive when my husband died, and he was more the type who liked corny puns. But I did tell him about the sense of loss, the confusion of suddenly having a body that could no longer define itself, and did see him more than once give a melancholy nod. When he read my letters, the letters my mother told me to write, he sometimes said: "You're threatening to become a mystic, my dear niece. Albeit the excommunicated type. But that doesn't matter, they're the best."

After that one time I never returned. I went to the village and waited in the café next to the *mairie* until my daughter, who had actually caught the sun, returned from the coast to pick me up. I still don't know if I trembled with rapture when I left the property under the shade of a hedge that had grown into a substantial row of trees, I savoured the dry smell of the bricks for the last time, and the dull, ochre-coloured sand under my feet, and on the bluestone slabs heard the lizards shooting off as shyly as a name or a date you can't remember—or was I on the contrary shivering with the deepest fear a person can feel: that of their own futility, when the scrolls close and the hymns fall silent and above the candlesticks and flames go out, till we hang blind in time like a glass window behind which no sun any longer glows?

What more is there to say? The house later finished up in the gravel mills of that factory-owner from Calais, ground into sand, and the trees on the farm may already have been cut up for firewood.

I hear Rachida coming upstairs. I recognize the jingling of the cutlery on the tray now she is climbing the stairs. Listen, first she will try to turn the door handle with one hand, without letting go of the tray, but she seldom manages it. She will whisper a few curses and put the tray on the cupboard next to the door.

*

Of course she will have taken endless trouble as usual. The egg perfectly soft-boiled, the top cut off and the yolk sprinkled with fresh pepper. She will have toasted the bread in the oven, poured the lukewarm milk into a jug—the smell hits my nose. She will also have put a flower in a vase, a marigold or orchid that she cadged from the flower stall on her way here this morning. "He goes for my smile," she always says. "The wider my smile, the dearer the flower he pinches off the stem." If now, while she opens the door and disappears back into the hall to get the tray off the cupboard, she hums the 'Snap, Crackle and Pop' jingle, I fear that she's having a frivolous spell today. Listen.

"Look at everything I've made for you, Mrs Helena," she says triumphantly. "And what a lovely rose from the garden. It must make your mouth water when you see this. And you remember what I promised you just now?"

S AID WITH THE LOVELY EYES was my mother's father's father, Mrs Helena. My mother says that he had opal eyes, thin Said with the opal-blue eyes and the mother-of-pearl teeth. In the street or in the market the girls never first made eyes at him and closed their eyes, because everyone wanted him to look at them and swim in his irises. One of those girls drowned in his eyes and became my mother's father's mother—I'm using lots of words, Mrs Helena, because you're eating slowly and my story is very short, but now you must have a bite, and a drop of milk, thank you. Said, Said al-Amrani, never saw his son. He became a soldier and one day had to sail on a ship to Marseilles. People said a war has broken out on the other side of the sea, the Lord of All Things be praised, that's one war less for us. That's what my mother told me when I was little, that's why I use little words to tell the story of Said with the lovely eyes, I've never heard it any other way, because Said has been dead for a very long time, and everything that is dead must be silent—careful, there's a bit of yolk on your chin. Said had to go to Marseilles on the boat because he was a soldier, a soldier, my mother always said, in the Régiment de Marche de Chasseurs Indigènes à Cheval. When I was little she did a dance with her fingertips in my hair when she said Régiment de Marche de Chasseurs Indigènes à Cheval, she repeated it at least ten times an evening. I laid my head in her lap when she took me to bed, and she rocked me to sleep with her stories and the magic wands of her fingers in my hair. Thin Said with

361

the lovely eyes became a soldier because his own father was dead and his bride and his mother, and also his little brother and sisters were hungry. Said wasn't a thief, my mother always said, because anyone who steals to fill an empty stomach is not stealing. Without the empty stomachs of our family, Said would never have become a soldier in the Régiment de Marche de Chasseurs Indigènes à Cheval and he would never have seen Marseilles. In Marseilles there are no high mountains, there is no gleaming fringe of ice on the threshold after the night in Marseilles and the women have gold teeth, Said wrote home, to his family, because we could write, we come from a good family, Mrs Helena. Everyone learnt to read and write in our family, but reading and writing doesn't fill the stomach—you mustn't leave the crusts, I'm very, very strict this evening. If you don't eat them I shall soak them in milk and feed them to you. Said had to go to the north, to the far north, where there were no mountains at all, but where there was ice, all day and night ice that doesn't melt, like with us in the mountains. In the north men creep about fighting in the earth, Said wrote home. My blanket is dirty, it is grey with ice and earth, and all our horses are dead. You think you've almost finished, but I've caught you out because in the pocket of my apron I've got two biscuits, soft chocolate biscuits. One day no more letters came. The mother of the father of my mother's father waited and Said's bride waited, with her fat tummy in which my mother's father was swimming about. They waited a long time, a very long time, but no more letters came, only a message that Said with the lovely eyes was dead. *Le soldat Saïd al-Amrani est tué lors d'une attaque à pied au Front Nord.* That's what it says in that letter, I have it at home. The mother of the father of my mother's father and

Said's bride wanted to know where Said's body was, but there was no body any more, Mrs Helena, I looked it up, he is just a name on a list, that's all. My mother said the earth looked into Said's opal eyes, where are his opal eyes now? First you must drink some more milk, those biscuits are for later. When my father came here long ago, with my mother and my brother, who was already born and is also called Said, my father said: if I find his bones I shall bring them to the surface. I shall wash them and wrap them in a shroud. My father was underground too when I was small. Not to fight, but to work. Digging coal for the stove in winter. If I find Said in the ground I'll bring him home, he always said to my mother, who in turn always told me, I'll have them pray Janaza for him and bury him in a worthy grave. But he never found Said with the lovely eyes, only flowers, deep in the earth, coal flowers black as the night, those are my mother's words. Do you know what the Janaza is? Every evening my father taught me to recite Al-Fatiha by heart—that was his way of telling me stories. I can still do it, with my eyes closed: Bismillāhi r-raḥmāni r-raḥīm… Al-ḥamdu lillāhi rabbi l-'ālamīn… Ar-raḥmāni r-raḥīm… Māliki yawmi d-dīn… Iyyāka na'budu wa iyyāka nasta'īn… Ihdinā ṣ-ṣirāt al-mustaqīm… Ṣirāṭa al-laḏīna an'amta 'alayhim ġayril maġdūbi 'alayhim walā ḍ-ḍāllīn… I said to my father that I didn't understand the words, but he said: later, when you start Arabic, you will understand the words, but you must repeat Al-Fatiha often enough, much more often than now, because only then will the holy words detach themselves from what you think and start to float, like a roof over your head, and if you do it well, if your lack of understanding is good enough, then between the roof of the words and the roof of your head the whole world looks you in the eyes—and that's true, Mrs Helena, and that's why the verse is called "The Mother of the Book". You are that too. When I come here and my mother asks me who I am going to care for, I say I'm going to the mother of the book, and then she immediately knows it's you. You're making a lot of crumbs now. Come on, I'll wipe your mouth. Eat everything up in your own time. I'll wait. Afterwards you must sleep. You've eaten. I have told you the story of Said with the lovely eyes, the short story of his short life. And as my mother used to say when I was small: that's all there is to tell. The animals are asleep and the night owl keeps watch. You must sleep now, she used to say, Rachida my almond blossom must sleep. I'll take the tray with me. I'll leave the curtain next to your bed open, then tonight you can look at the stars and the lighted windows, but if you close your eyes, Mrs Helena, then, as my mother always said, you'll soon be fast asleep.

THE WORLD OF YESTERDAY
STEFAN ZWEIG

'*The World of Yesterday* is one of the greatest memoirs of the twentieth century, as perfect in its evocation of the world Zweig loved, as it is in its portrayal of how that world was destroyed' David Hare

JOURNEY BY MOONLIGHT
ANTAL SZERB

'Just divine... makes you imagine the author has had private access to your own soul' Nicholas Lezard, *Guardian*

BONITA AVENUE
PETER BUWALDA

'One wild ride: a swirling helix of a family saga... a new writer as toe-curling as early Roth, as roomy as Franzen and as caustic as Houellebecq' *Sunday Telegraph*

THE PARROTS
FILIPPO BOLOGNA

'A five-star satire on literary vanity... a wonderful, surprising novel' *Metro*

I WAS JACK MORTIMER
ALEXANDER LERNET-HOLENIA

'Terrific... a truly clever, rather wonderful book that both plays with and defies genre' Eileen Battersby, *Irish Times*

SONG FOR AN APPROACHING STORM
PETER FRÖBERG IDLING

'Beautifully evocative... a must-read novel' *Daily Mail*

THE RABBIT BACK LITERATURE SOCIETY
PASI ILMARI JÄÄSKELÄINEN

'Wonderfully knotty... a very grown-up fantasy masquerading as quirky fable. Unexpected, thrilling and absurd' *Sunday Telegraph*

RED LOVE: THE STORY OF AN EAST GERMAN FAMILY
MAXIM LEO

'Beautiful and supremely touching... an unbearably poignant description of a world that no longer exists' *Sunday Telegraph*

THE BREAK

PIETRO GROSSI

'Small and perfectly formed… reaching its end leaves the reader desirous to start all over again' *Independent*

FROM THE FATHERLAND, WITH LOVE

RYU MURAKAMI

'If Haruki is The Beatles of Japanese literature, Ryu is its Rolling Stones' David Pilling

BUTTERFLIES IN NOVEMBER

AUÐUR AVA ÓLAFSDÓTTIR

'A funny, moving and occasionally bizarre exploration of life's upheavals and reversals' *Financial Times*

BARCELONA SHADOWS

MARC PASTOR

'As gruesome as it is gripping… the writing is extraordinarily vivid… Highly recommended' *Independent*

THE LAST DAYS

LAURENT SEKSIK

'Mesmerising… Seksik's portrait of Zweig's final months is dignified and tender' *Financial Times*

BY BLOOD

ELLEN ULLMAN

'Delicious and intriguing' *Daily Telegraph*

WHILE THE GODS WERE SLEEPING

ERWIN MORTIER

'A monumental, phenomenal book' *De Morgen*

THE BRETHREN

ROBERT MERLE

'A master of the historical novel' *Guardian*

COIN LOCKER BABIES
RYU MURAKAMI

'A fascinating peek into the weirdness of contemporary Japan' Oliver Stone

TALKING TO OURSELVES
ANDRÉS NEUMAN

'This is writing of a quality rarely encountered… when you read Neuman's beautiful novel, you realise a very high bar has been set' *Guardian*

CLOSE TO THE MACHINE
ELLEN ULLMAN

'Astonishing… impossible to put down' *San Francisco Chronicle*

MARCEL
ERWIN MORTIER

'Aspiring novelists will be hard pressed to achieve this quality' *Time Out*

JOURNEY INTO THE PAST
STEFAN ZWEIG

'Lucid, tender, powerful and compelling' *Independent*

POPULAR HITS OF THE SHOWA ERA
RYU MURAKAMI

'One of the funniest and strangest gang wars in recent literature' *Booklist*

LETTER FROM AN UNKNOWN WOMAN AND OTHER STORIES
STEFAN ZWEIG

'Zweig's time of oblivion is over for good… it's good to have him back' Salman Rushdie

ONE NIGHT, MARKOVITCH
AYELET GUNDAR-GOSHEN

'A remarkable first novel, trenchant and full of love, highly impressive in its maturity and wisdom' Eshkol Nevo

MY FELLOW SKIN
ERWIN MORTIER

'A Bildungsroman which is related to much European literature from Proust and Mann onwards… peculiarly unforgettable' AS Byatt, *Guardian*